THE ELYSIUM CONUMDRUM

Terence S. McNamara

Inspiring Publishers
P.O. Box 159, Calwell, ACT Australia 2905
Email: publishaspg@gmail.com
http://www.inspiringpublishers.com

A catalogue record for this book is available from the National Library of Australia

National Library of Australia The Prepublication Data Service

Author: Terence S. McNamara
Title: The Elysium Conumdrum
Genre: Fiction

Paperback ISBN: 978-1-923250-48-2
Hardcover ISBN: 978-1-923250-49-9
ePub2 ISBN: 978-1-923250-62-8

To JM for allowing me the time to write
and AP for the inspiration to do it.

PROLOGUE

For millennia, we have contemplated our own essentiality, believing our minds, the vessel of thoughts, were separate from the physical organs containing them. We created a metaphorical cocoon around our ethereal selves, detaching us from the physical universe, asserting the eternality of our souls and the higher nature of our being. By 2065, we discovered means to make those beliefs real. Then, secure in our understanding of the world, we discarded our long-held fear of the dark night that we had, since our earliest beginnings, shrouded in ritual and mythology. The shadows in our psyche filled with expectation rather than apprehension. The science fiction horror movie became a love story. By that time, it seemed to all those who cared to consider it, the darkest recesses of science had been illuminated, and we were finally at peace with the universe and with the place that we had created for ourselves within it.

Leading up to 2065, there was a change in what it meant to be human. As has always been the case in the history of life on Earth, this metamorphosis originated from just a handful of individuals. This is their story. It was a convergence of events and a unique assembly of characters that forever redefined who we were as a society and what we were on the cusp of becoming as a species. It appeared as if we had looked into the eyes of God and seen ourselves.

Conceived by design, not accident, and garnered by increment, not upheaval, we gradually became the knowledgeable and willing heirs of a new destiny. We breached the final divide, that abyss between death and eternity. We seized control of the very essence of our being, gaining the ability to change and renew it at will. Discarding our physical fear and limitation, time became a vanquished foe, no longer capable of confining or tormenting us. In doing so, we turned our minds to the heavens, with the vast cosmos no longer a barrier, we were free to seize the potential of universal promulgation. We no longer needed to wonder whether there would be life on other planets for it would be us. No matter how long it took to arrive there, the time that we had was now as limitless as the distances that impeded our journey. That journey is a story for another day, but with our breakthrough, who could assert that we wouldn't be the first or the most ancient? No one could refute our claim to supremacy.

Perhaps by engineering our escape from the genetic inevitability of death, we uncovered the stepping stone to the stars. Our boundless soul now mirrored the infinite universe that lay before us and impregnated the now ambiguous past that lay in our wake. We had become the god of our own species, dreaming confidently of ascending to the position of a celestial god.

CHAPTER ONE

In the late autumn of 1936, a produce truck sputters and backfires up a hilly dirt road north from Zossen, forty kilometres south of Berlin. It slows just long enough for a small stowaway to jump unnoticed over the rear of the truck. First his backpack, then the boy, land with a crunch on the gravel roadside. Immediately, he scouts the best route down to the gully below. A chilly northern wind greets him, prompting him to zip up his jacket. The wind carries moisture from freshly ploughed fields visible beyond the wooded gully. The only sounds are the rustling trees and the fading noise of the truck as it rounds a bend at the hilltop, its gears grinding. The wind promises a harsh winter, causing him to tilt his head back to the darkening Sunday evening sky, sniffing the air, convinced he can distinguish its scent from that of New York air. His senses are heightened, an intense awareness long lost, a purity forgotten. He begins to realise he has made it.

Now there's no need to rush, so he allows his internal urgency to ease. As he pauses, the emotions of his journey start to wash over him. Looking down at his six-year-old body, he feels its frailty, which frightens him. It's as if a door has slammed shut behind him, cutting off retreat. Yet, this was the moment he had planned for over the past twenty-five years. He now understands how a visitor from another planet might feel, stranded by fate on Earth. He needs to survive, to explore this strange world brimming with new possibilities. He loses himself for a moment, as if in a dream - a midnight adventure in pyjamas within a fairytale. But this is not a dream, he's actually here, and he's alone.

After scrambling down the steep embankment, he enters the gully clearing. Although he anticipates what he'll find, he braces himself as the sight of the crashed car and its deceased passengers comes into view. The car has veered off the road, rolled down a two-hundred-foot hill, and collided with a large oak tree at the southern edge of an open field, separated from the ploughed fields beyond by a barbed wire fence. He watches the car engine smoulder. The driver and his wife, seated next to him, have been thrown through the windscreen upon impact, bleeding to death on the car hood. The two children in the back, a boy of six and a girl of eight, are also dead, their heads smashed against the vehicle's roof as it rolled down the embankment. Though distressed by the scene, he feels detached from the car's occupants' plight. He knows who they are; he came here to find them.

The family in the car had been returning to the city after visiting the children's paternal grandmother, who resided in the care of an elderly friend in Zossen. It had been a long day for them; the drive from northern Berlin to Zossen was substantial, and they had set off early that morning. Fatigue overtook the father, a rising star in the Nazi Party, as he drove back. Just twenty-nine years old, he held a senior position in the new government, which was demanding and highly stressful, leaving him little time for rest. Today, he found his eternal rest.

The driver's father had died a hero in the Great War, a loss from which his now largely incoherent mother never recovered. The wife, lying lifeless next to him, came from a distinguished family with ties to the Habsburgs. Both her parents had perished when the Lusitania was sunk by a German U-boat at the onset of the Great War, a detail that added to the family's intrigue in the eyes of the Reich. As both the husband and wife were only children, and with the crash claiming all immediate members, this unfortunate family's lineage met a tragic end. This made them the perfect fit for the boy's plan.

He approached the dead boy, whose body lay on the grass, one foot still wedged under the front seat. The door, meant to keep him secure, had been ripped off as the car rolled downhill. Now upright, the car's front end was crushed against a tree, having slid the last twenty feet on the gully's damp grass to its final position, its brakes locked in the driver's desperate, futile effort.

"Seat belts might have helped," he mumbled cynically to himself. After freeing the boy's foot, he picked up the lifeless body by the hands and dragged it through the fence, laying it on the freshly tilled soil of the field. Returning to his bag, he pulled out a small shovel, stolen from the truck. Back at the boy's side, he began to dig. Upon finishing his grim task, he camouflaged the grave within the ploughed earth, ensuring it would remain hidden, and the body buried deep enough to evade the farmer's plough. Feeling a need to say something over the grave, he remained silent. Why should he bother? His only feeling towards the Nazis, and by extension this family, was pure hatred. He delved into his memory, his emotions, for a fitting phrase but found nothing. The only thing enveloping him was the pressing need to move forward.

He stashed the shovel in the nearby underbrush, then sat on the family's picnic blanket, which he had salvaged from the trunk of the car, and laid it on the grass. Fatigue was setting in. From his knapsack, he pulled out a sandwich and a can of orange juice; it had been a long day, and the night promised to be even longer. Under the moonless, pitch-dark sky, he fumbled with his pocket knife, trying to open the can. As he munched on his sandwich, he occasionally froze, clearing the excitement from his mind to carefully contemplate his next steps. He knew the wrecked car would remain undiscovered until the next morning, when a passing motorist would notice the broken bushes by the roadside and the vehicle tracks leading down the embankment. Until then, he decided, he would try to get some sleep.

Franz Gothenburg was in his laboratory on 10th Avenue in New York City. Situated on the top floor of a three-story walk-up he had purchased over fifty years prior in August 1999, the building served as his private lab. Now aged one hundred and thirty-five, and having undergone his second full organ replacement - an operation made relatively risk-free in 2065 through the growth of replacement organs from the patient's own tissue - Franz was a very successful man. He had also availed himself of five skin regeneration treatments, another extremely popular product of AIOGEN's biotechnology.

Although Franz no longer resided in the old brownstone, having moved to a more fitting limestone-clad townhouse on the east side of the park, he continued to use the 10th Avenue property, which was otherwise vacant. The commute from his home to his lab, via automated quadcopter, took less than five minutes. As a major shareholder in AIOGEN, the world's largest bioengineering company, Franz had made his fortune by supplying electronic components for their *Augment Program*, and previously, for smart bombs manufactured for the American military.

Franz had come into possession of a Brain Content Download (BCD) device, stolen from AIOGEN, its use being illegal outside the company. AIOGEN had perfected a process some years prior that allowed the entire content of a human brain to be mapped and copied. This work was a byproduct of their development of Augments: fully-grown biological beings based on the human genome, utilized for military and domestic services.

In order to secure approval to produce these human-like Augments, social pressure forced AIOGEN to replace the biological brains of the Augments with electronic ones, as a safeguard against the Augments ever gaining self-awareness. This electronic augmentation of a fundamentally biological being had led to their name. AIOGEN used a human-like body not only for aesthetics but also because most military equipment and household utilities had been designed to accommodate the human form, considering its size and dexterity. Building on AIOGEN's successful human organ regrowth technology, now a common method in organ transplant and skin regeneration surgery, the company had fully mapped brain function and physiology to understand the nerve linkages needed to replace human brains in the Augments, leading logically to the development of BCD technology.

Franz wasn't supposed to have the BCD, as the usage and possession of such machines were tightly guarded secrets. He was also in unauthorized possession of the more recently developed

BCU, a brain content upload device, which he had procured alongside the BCD. The contents of a BCD could be uploaded into a brain genetically identical to the one from which the content was downloaded. The informational segments captured in the BCD procedure aligned with the microscopic molecular structures within the specific donor brain, with the content only decipherable once re-introduced to the unique brain that had originally contained the information. Any attempt to upload a BCD copied from another individual would result in a disordered jumble in the recipient's brain, rendering them mentally incapacitated. Crucially, Franz knew both devices functioned, as AIOGEN had just the previous week used them to successfully revive their top bioengineer, Dr. Jack Pierce, who had been killed in a car explosion.

Unknown to the wider scientific community, Franz had secretly perfected a process in his lab that could send inanimate objects back in time by folding the time continuum back onto itself around the object. The objects would always remain in the same spatial location from which they were displaced in time, his equipment only altering the time coordinates within which they resided, not their physical position. Franz had discovered long ago that objects could only be sent back in time, not forward; he hypothesized that the timeline needed to be fully laid out before it could be displaced or bent backwards for revisiting.

Time was left in the wake of the expanding universe as it inflated from the Formative Event at its core, with time progressing at different rates in different locations within the universe, but always advancing with the universe's expansion. The Formative Event was now widely believed not to be a Big Bang, but a Leak, as mathematical models often failed when considering the event as an exploding singularity. The prevailing theory posited that our universe was formed when a massive collapsing star in a five-dimensional universe caused our universe to flash into existence, spewing its compressed matter onto the wall of its event horizon as it imploded into a black hole. This occurred on the other side of the boundary between the two universes, with the dying star continuously secreting vast amounts of compressed matter over millennia. The result was a four-dimensional outcome in our universe, expressed from a five-dimensional event.

In our universe, time did not exist prior to the expanding universe's arrival at any given point in its trajectory. It always travelled away from the Formative Event, with the Formative Event marking the beginning of time and the current location of an object within that universe marking its end. Franz had authored several papers on the subject for his alma mater, Harvard University, the most recent being in 2036, but since then, he had made significant strides in applying his theories. His papers had generated considerable interest within the scientific community, but in recent years, there had been no updates regarding his progress in the lab.

A division of Gothenburg's company had once been involved in the astronautics industry, and it was through these endeavours that he had gained expertise in space-time manipulation. Spacecraft designers aimed to compress space up in front of a moving craft, akin to how a rug would bunch up when pushed from one end along a polished floor. This compression created what the *Star Trek* generation called a *warp field,* a concept now fully understood and termed the *Space Compression Horizon* within Gothenburg Industries. The greater the energy applied, the larger the Space Horizon Compression created. This allowed the spacecraft to traverse the "rug" in much less time by traveling through the compressed ripples, without having to surpass the speed of light, a known constant in this universe except within the realm of quantum mechanics. As the spacecraft progressed, it continuously bunched up space before it, leaving uncompressed space in its wake. This decompression behind the craft assisted its forward motion, like a wave pushing objects forward on flat water. However, instead of working towards lateral compression of space-time to facilitate faster spacecraft progression, Gothenburg was aiming to fold the continuum back onto itself, leaving the object in its original spatial position but at different time coordinates. This process required significantly less energy, especially considering the small, non-living objects he was working with. Unbeknownst to his colleagues, he had made considerable progress since publishing his pioneering paper.

Gothenburg had discovered over the years that only non-living entities could survive the time translation due to the energy inevitably imparted to the object during the process. He had experimented with mice and lower organisms like amoebae, but no living entity survived - their biochemistry was too delicate. It seemed to him that the creators of the old *Terminator* movies had almost gotten it right, but reversed: no flesh, only metal could survive the process.

His excitement was particularly palpable this morning as he had just completed an experiment that had sent an object further back in time than ever before. He had opened a section of the ancient walls of his lab that he knew had remained untouched since their construction over a hundred and fifty years ago. In the now open cavity, he had placed a small canister equipped with a timing device designed to remain operative for more than a century. Upon connecting it to his displacement machine, he observed it disappear momentarily, only to reappear in a dishevelled state, covered in dust. He had calibrated his machine to send the object back ninety-nine years, fifty-five days, two hours, fifteen minutes, and forty-five seconds. Upon opening the canister, he found the timing device displaying a reading nearly identical to his target time, accurate to within a few minutes. Overwhelmed with joy, he saw no reason to delay his plans further and proceeded to pack for his journey to Germany.

Gothenburg had lived in a small German town named Sperenburg until the age of eleven when, in 1942, he tragically lost both his parents in the Nazi purges. As a Jew, both of his parents had perished in the camps during the war. He wasn't certain where or when, but he knew they had been taken away, having witnessed the arrest from a hiding spot his parents had prepared for him at their home in Sperenburg. They never returned. With the help of family friends, he had managed to escape Germany. The loss of his parents at such a tender age, and the sense of impotence that the traumatic events had seared into his mind, had indelibly shaped his life. The grief never left him, and these events were his driving force now. He packed his equipment and arranged for a charter flight to the nearest airport to Sperenburg.

Upon arriving in Sperenburg, having rented a car at the airport, he was pleased to see the remnants of the old water mill where he used to play as a child. He remembered a particular day when, after a disagreement with his mother over unfinished chores, he had decided to run away from home - a common impulse for six-year-old boys. He had found refuge in the old mill that day. Huddled in a corner of the mill for the entirety of that late autumn day in 1936, he sat chilled and underdressed for such a grand adventure, intent on teaching his parents a lesson about respect. As night fell and fear set in, he returned home to find his parents seemingly oblivious to his absence - in 1936 Germany, there wasn't much concern about the wanderings of a curious six-year-old.

Franz carried his equipment into the old mill and found the spot where he had hidden one hundred and twenty-nine years earlier. He placed a box he had prepared which contained the BCU device, along with the headset required for the brain content transfer, and the informational contents of his own brain. The package was no larger than a briefcase and, when closed, resembled a leather case. Franz had configured it to only open to his genetically identical hand, regardless of its age. Prior to executing his BCD, Franz had memorised every minute detail he could glean from modern records about the war, the history of Germany during and since that autumn of 1936, and numerous assessments of the causes and aftermath of the war. The case also contained a recorded message voiced by Franz himself, set to play upon the box's arrival, reassuring his six-year-old self that it was safe to open it. The recording played upon the innate curiosity of a six-year-old and included the melody of his favourite childhood music box playing in the background.

He connected the time translation equipment to his case, set the timer, and pressed send. The box vanished and, unlike the vessel in the lab, did not reappear. Franz was comfortable with that outcome, assuming that his younger self had received the box, followed his instructions, used it, and then destroyed it after completing the BCU procedure. Without delay, Franz packed his remaining equipment and headed back to the airport.

The case had indeed hit its mark. The six-year-old Franz saw it even as it appeared not far from where he was hiding. He was startled and frightened by what he saw. Then as a strangely familiar voice and sound came from the box, he became calmer. It beckoned Franz to open it and at the suggestion of the voice he put on the head set and the upload of Franz's BCD was completed within twenty minutes. The boy was left with a headache but he now knew exactly what had happened. He was delighted that he had made the transition. He stood up and felt the energy and the exuberance that only a six-year-old body can contain. It felt to him like he himself had been transported back in time to that spot, now having all the knowledge and experience that can only be accumulated by a one-hundred-and-thirty-five-year-old soul. He destroyed the box using the tools available to him at the mill as per his plan to avoid its detection and burnt the remaining shattered parts in a fire. It was just after eleven on the morning of the car crash.

He immediately left the old mill and stole a ride on one of the many trucks carrying agricultural products into Zossen. He hadn't yet eaten the sandwich or drunk the can of orange juice that he had brought with him for his escape that morning. It was only after he had climbed aboard the truck that he realised that it would have been wonderful to see his parents again after so long and perhaps to say goodbye to them, to warn them. But he couldn't bring himself to get off the truck, knowing that he would not be believed and knowing that his parents would not let him leave again to undertake his objective. It was them after all that he was out to save. He put from his mind both the joy he would feel to see them again and the thought of the misery that would overcome his parents later that very night when he failed to return home.

After struggling for several hours in Zossen to find a truck heading north towards Berlin that Sunday, he had finally made it just on dusk to where the car had left the road. Franz had memorised the circumstances of the accident from a newspaper clipping. The family who had lost their lives that day were ideal for Franz's purposes. He knew that he could do little to change the events that were unfolding in Germany of 1936 as a six-year-old Jewish boy, but as the son of a highly regarded leader in the Reich, an Aryan whose well-connected family was even known to Hitler himself, the possibilities were much more substantial.

Franz awoke early the next morning at the crash site. He disentangled himself from a pile of spare clothing from the car's trunk that he had piled on top of himself for warmth. He had gotten little sleep in the cold night and wretched circumstance. The thought of his now undoubtedly frantic parents searching to find him preoccupied his mind. He opened the family's carry bag in the trunk of the car and placed the clothes and his knapsack inside it. He closed the trunk lid as best that it could be closed and went over to the side of the car and began to smash his face against the hood. After several half-hearted attempts, he eventually bucked up enough courage to do it properly, breaking his nose and causing it to bleed, lacerating his forehead and knocking himself half-conscious to the ground. He struggled back to his feet and took his place on the grass near the back seat of the car where the boy had been sitting on his journey home.

The deceit started to trouble him as he lay there, with the early morning sun bringing out the scent of the damp grass, but he forced it out of his mind. He allowed his senses to take control of his thoughts. He could smell the earth, taste the blood in his mouth, and his mind began to wander. He hadn't killed the boy, he wasn't responsible for what had happened to the family. There was no reason for him to feel guilty. Even so, he found it hard to shake a sense of duplicity as he waited for a passing motorist to discover them.

Thus, Franz became Frederick. A passing motorist came as expected, and the young Frederick was taken to a local hospital for treatment. He was left at the hospital for two days, although his wounds didn't warrant such a lengthy stay. No one could determine what to do with him. Attempts were made to contact his extended family, but none could be found. His grandmother in Zossen was deemed incapable of caring for the child, so his placement remained undecided right up until the day of the funeral for his adopted family in Berlin to which, under the instructions of local authorities, he was transported.

As was fitting for a man of his adopted father's status, Hitler attended the funeral in person. After the cemetery prayers, Hitler approached the boy to offer his personal condolences. Frederick was paralysed with fear as Hitler approached with a slow gait and solemn expression. Frederick experienced a whirlwind of emotions as this man, this devil whom he'd vilified his entire life, knelt down on one knee before him. Unconsciously, Frederick's gaze fixated on the holster on the hip of Hitler's bodyguard standing twenty feet behind him. Frederick had to physically restrain himself from reaching for the gun. Here was the demon in human form, and it began to speak to him with a human voice. Unable to look at his face, Frederick stared down at Hitler's shiny brown boot next to his uniformed knee, now knelt on the wet concrete. Hitler's adjutant stood directly above him, holding an open umbrella that sheltered Hitler and the boy from the drizzling rain. Frederick was so close he could smell the polish on Hitler's leather attire and the musty odour rising from his woollen overcoat, damp with rain. For a fleeting moment, he glanced at Hitler's eyes but could not maintain the gaze.

"Du bist Vater war ein großer Mann, Friedrich," Hitler said, praising the boy's father and taking the boy's hand in his own, giving it a comforting pat. "And your mother's family also is very well regarded. Your father will be missed by the Party." Hitler stood and turned to his adjutant, "Was wird aus dem Jungen geworden?"

"It hasn't been decided, my Führer, he has no living family except for a grandmother too frail to care for him. Er muss zurück in die Klinik," the assistant replied, explaining that the boy was to be sent back to the hospital after the funeral.

Hitler turned back to the boy, who still had his head bowed, neither looking up nor moving. "Bring him with us after the ceremony, use my car. He can stay in the visitor's accommodation until we sort this out. It is not appropriate for him to sit in some country hospital alone at this time. Notify the authorities in Zossen and arrange for a nurse to attend him."

The boy looked out the window of the car as it left the cemetery. A forgotten world passed before his eyes. He could see it was Berlin but it was so different. He couldn't believe that he was there amongst it all. Hitler's official vehicle screamed its way through the traffic with its police escort, the noise heightening the boy's feeling that this was just a dream. It had all come together so quickly just as Franz had imagined it over and over in his mind. Now it was true and he was home again and his focus turned immediately to what he had to do next.

CHAPTER TWO

Helen Jamison cradled a cup of coffee as she waited at Café Saint-Michel, situated opposite the bridge that overlooked the river. From her vantage point, she could see Notre-Dame Cathedral through the window. Her thoughts were drawn to its age and its fully restored beauty. It was early November 2065, five days before Franz Gothenburg would send the BCU device back to his childhood self, and nearly a week after AIOGEN's top researcher, Jack Pierce, had been murdered.

Helen was a tall, athletic woman with a captivating face. She didn't consider herself beautiful, but most people she met held a different opinion. Her unpretentious nature added to her allure. Her experienced eyes, a deep shade of purple, now lacked the certainty of purpose they once held. She was waiting to meet her contact, Françoise Marsolet, a freelance journalist for *The Times* in London. Paris presented a grey November day that matched her mood. As she watched crowds take countless photographs in front of the cathedral, a light rain began to fall. The smell of the newly wet pavement, wafting in through the open café door, drew her further into her thoughts.

"Ms. Jamison?" a heavily accented voice asked, jolting her back to reality. She turned to see a scruffy-looking man standing at her table, cradling his briefcase as if it were a newborn.

"Special Agent Jamison, yes," she responded, making no move to stand. "Sit down, before you attract attention. You have something for me? Does anyone know you're talking to the FBI?"

"I don't think so," Marsolet responded, now looking around anxiously at the faces in the restaurant. "I hope not."

"Of course not," she replied curtly. She instantly regretted her tone, realising she'd inadvertently heightened his apprehension. "Have you passed this information on to anyone else?"

"No, I told my contact at the FBI that I had it. I try to be helpful when I can, and he helps me sometimes."

"Let me see it."

With practiced ease, Marsolet reached into his briefcase, pulled out a large brown envelope, and passed it to Jamison. "Sorry about the papers. These are mainly copies of original, now deciphered, email correspondences. The emails are between a Yemeni arms dealer named Yasser Fahd and a person referred to as 'Jimmy' in the emails."

"Jimmy?"

"Yes, Jimmy. He's actually a member of a group of local jihadists with links to Iran, a guy named Mohammed Ahmed."

"And you know this how?"

"My source is impeccable. I've worked with him for ten years, maybe more. He's reliable. He risked his life to make these copies."

Slightly sceptical, Jamison began to upload the documents onto her notepad while giving them a cursory glance. She immediately forwarded them to her boss. The necessity of this face-to-face meeting eluded her. Some people, many of them journalists, had a flair for the dramatic, she reminded herself.

"There's a reference in there to AIOGEN and an intermediary called Zimmermann," Marsolet felt compelled to point out. "That's the Augment stuff you guys are always looking out for, isn't it? It looks like someone is setting up a sale of stolen intellectual property."

"I'm sure you're right, good work. Thanks. Anything else?"

"No…no. I thought you guys would be keen to see this stuff."

"Look, Monsieur Marsolet," Jamison said, rising to leave, "thanks for all your help, we'll keep your cooperation in mind. And yes, this is very important. Nous apprécions votre collaboration, merci, au revoir." She then turned and walked to the cashier.

Marsolet was left sitting at the table, aimlessly cradling his briefcase and feeling that his clandestine encounter was less theatrically engaging than he had hoped. Jamison didn't have much patience for people like Marsolet, a sentiment rooted in her past experiences with tattletales at school — an attitude rather inconsistent with her chosen profession. She was personally surprised that the U.S. had managed to keep a lid on the Augment technology for so long and thought it was only a matter of time before it crossed borders. Nonetheless, she was happy to follow the lead, as it likely meant a trip stateside. She would remember to feign reluctance when discussing this prospect with her boss.

A knock sounded on the open door of Detective First Class Jason Cleary's office at the One Nine in New York City. He looked up to see a tall, attractive woman dressed in business attire that he surmised must have been inspired by the latest Parisian fashion trends.

"You Cleary?" she asked with a brusque tone.

"Maybe, depends on what he's done."

"Look, I don't have time to mess around," Jamison retorted, flashing her FBI identification at Cleary. "Are you him or not?"

"Sure, what can I do for you, Special Agent?" Cleary quickly closed the file on his desk, ensuring its contents wouldn't be glimpsed by a passing FBI agent, no matter how attractive she might be.

"I'm told that you're investigating a guy named Zimmermann?"

"Yeah, he's involved in a murder case I'm working on."

"Murder?"

"Yeah, this Zimmermann guy made a few calls to the victim leading up to the killing."

"Whose murder?" Jamison had taken a seat, her brow furrowed in thought. "Not that AIOGEN guy?" she queried, rapidly connecting the dots between the potential intellectual property theft and the car-bombing that had killed Jack Pierce at an AIOGEN event at the Metropolitan Museum of Art the week before.

"That's him. But why's it your concern?"

"Boy, have I got some news for you, my newfound friend," Jamison quipped, leaning back in her chair, putting her feet up on the edge of Cleary's desk, hands folded behind her head. She was already envisioning an extended stay in NYC to piece all of this together.

"Perhaps it would be best if you remove your feet from my desk if you indeed wish to be my friend. Let's take this from the top, shall we?" Cleary rose from his chair. "Jason Cleary, Detective First Grade NYPD. How do you do?" He leaned across the desk, extending his hand toward hers. "You know, from this angle, I can see up your dress just a bit."

Abruptly, Jamison stood to avoid any further impropriety and shook his hand. "Helen Jamison, Special Agent Jamison to you. And I'm doing just fine, thanks."

"Well, I'd salute, but I'm not wearing any underwear. You know, you should give a guy a bit of warning. I would've baked."

They both sat down simultaneously, maintaining eye contact like a pair of seasoned predators. This time, Jamison crossed her legs and pulled her skirt down over her knees.

"I think you meant to say 'salute' because you're not in uniform," Jamison corrected Cleary. "It has nothing to do with your underwear — or lack thereof. You might want to jot that down, Detective. Besides, I'm fine with informality and I'm not part of the NYPD." Realising she was rambling, Jamison decided to steer the conversation back on track. "Do you have any suspects for the AIOGEN case?"

"Not really. We looked at a handful of protestors who were outside the event when it happened but came up empty. There are two protestors we've yet to interview, but the others are religious folks. Didn't feel right."

"Because they're religious?"

"Because they don't seem guilty."

"You rely on intuition around here?"

"Something like that, yeah. You guys don't read the vibes over at the Bureau?"

"We read the facts, detective." One-all, she thought, always keeping score with the males in her profession. "I know that there is a lot of angst about what AIOGEN does with its Augment program, so I could see why you would want to look at the protestors. But, I've got a guy in Paris who says that Zimmermann made an illegal intellectual property purchase from someone at AIOGEN. He doesn't know who, but it's all been bought and paid for by some nasty cockroaches with links to somewhere you don't want to know about. Strictly confidential, of course."

"So, you're thinking that this is all cloak and dagger nonsense? Murder is usually a bit more personal than that."

"Not in my circles."

"Got anything to support that view other than an itch in your panties?"

"No," Jamison said with a double-take, checking the position of her hemline. "Don't you think that it's a bit coincidental, you know, Pierce dead and an IP theft in play? What's the old intuition say about that?"

Cleary thought deeply. "It says…I'm hungry. You want some lunch?"

"Sure, why not? Just something light. I'm still on Paris time."

"Light it is…Paris, eh!" Cleary stood, grabbing his brand-new winter coat, which he flung over one arm while pointing Jamison to the door with the other. "You are going to give me what you've got on this Zimmermann guy, right? There were parts of his file on the National Database that I couldn't access. Go figure."

"Only if you promise to put on some underwear. That's an image I didn't need in my head this morning," Jamison said, deflecting the question.

They both headed through the office toward the lifts. Cleary was unconsciously guiding her with his hand on her elbow. As they walked past Cleary's partner's desk, Jim Jacobs asked him to bring back a sandwich. Cleary looked back at him with disdain, and Jacobs gave him a thumbs up and a cheesy grin.

At lunch, both officers were getting along just fine until the discussion returned to the issue at hand.

"So, you married?" Cleary asked, pursing his lips, knowing it was a pretty blunt question and waiting for a smack in the mouth or a terse response.

"Wait a minute, Jack," was the terse response. "I'm here for the business, not the scenic tour."

"Jack's the vic. You can call me Cleary, or Honey…either."

"Well, look, Hun, you shouldn't be taking a girl the wrong way just because you saw a little leg. I'm too busy to worry about guys like you. I might get my feelings hurt."

"Feelings?"

"See what I mean."

"I just thought that you must be at a loose end. You're just in from France, right? What say we make the most of it?"

"You're a romantic at heart, is that it, Cleary? And who said cops weren't fun. Besides, when did I say I was at a loose end? I have friends."

"I'm gonna need names and addresses. Come on… dinner? We can split it."

"Pass." Jamison said, standing and pushing her chair back in under the table. "I'll call you tomorrow. I want to talk to that Zimmermann guy myself, and you may as well be in on it."

"There, you see, we're cooperating," Cleary said. "It's a beginning," he shouted after her.

"Don't get your hopes up," Jamison said under her breath as she walked away.

"Looking for Mr. Frederick Zimmerman," Jacobs said loudly to the female shop attendant as he and Cleary entered Zimmerman's midtown jewellery store. They were keen to get to Zimmerman before the FBI did. He put away the badge that he had just held up to the glass door to facilitate their entry.

"He's out back" she replied somewhat nervously. "I'll go get him."

Zimmermann emerged from the back of the store. A large, overweight, fifty-something white male with balding long hair and horn-rimmed glasses. The store clerk did not return with him.

"Can I help you, gentlemen?"

"Sure, you can, Mr. Zimmermann, is it?" Zimmermann nodded, so Cleary continued. "We want to know why you killed Jack Pierce?" Zimmermann looked flabbergasted. "We know who you are and what you've been up to. It would be better for you if you just tell us what happened!"

Cleary just loved to shake the tree to see what might fall out. They had nothing on this guy other than his record and his unexplained telephone calls to Pierce. Cleary wanted a reaction from Zimmermann rather than an answer.

"How dare you come in here and say such things," Zimmermann said, blustering unconvincingly, then collecting himself, perhaps a little too quickly for Cleary's liking. Cleary noticed that he didn't ask him to repeat the name of the person he just accused him of killing.

"Are you saying you don't have links to arms dealing in Yemen?" Cleary threw that one in for good measure, much like a soldier might throw a second grenade over a wall in case the first one hadn't done enough damage.

"That was…a misunderstanding…years ago, that was all cleared up. Please keep your voice down…my daughter."

"Well, the FBI hasn't forgiven or forgotten. Do you know Jack Pierce, Mr. Zimmermann?"

"No, not…"

"Whoops, wrong answer. I think you had better come with us," Cleary said, feeling vindicated for the dramatics but surprised that it had yielded anything. Jacobs moved towards Zimmermann and pulled out his cuffs.

"No, no, wait," Zimmermann added quickly. "I called him a couple of weeks ago, maybe three weeks ago. I don't really know the guy. I just wanted to…to sell him some jewellery."

Cleary wasn't buying it. He knew about the calls, plural. For him, there was nothing like catching someone in a lie.

At the precinct, Cleary's boss, Lieutenant Burgess, was on the way back to his office as Cleary and Jacobs arrived at their desks with Zimmermann in tow.

"We got the guy on that Pierce thing, boss," Cleary said for Zimmermann's benefit, continuing the cliché B-movie cop impersonation. Zimmermann became noticeably more distressed, his mouth half open in disbelief as to his predicament. The Lieutenant ignored Cleary and continued to walk past the three of them with an indiscernible roll of his eyes. Familiarity with Cleary's antics caused the Lieutenant to say nothing in response but let him go about his work, which more often than not, he completed successfully.

"Just need to ask him a few more questions, that's all, then it's case closed." Cleary liked to say "case closed," it had become a habit. "Mr. Zimmermann, you sit down right there." Zimmermann obliged.

"Can I see you, Cleary?" the Lieutenant turned back and asked as he got to his office door.

"Sure thing, boss. Make our friend uncomfortable, will you, Jacobs? I'll be back in a minute."

"We've got word from the hospital," the Lieutenant continued, closing the door behind Cleary. Now alone in his office, he went on. "They've revived him."

"Revived who?"

"Pierce."

"Boss, I was at the scene. There was nothing left of him to revive."

"They've Replanted him, at least that's what they're calling it." There was silence as they both absorbed what had just been said out loud. Cleary momentarily dumb, mouth open. "They re-grew his entire body and put his last smash in it, and the guy is awake, apparently."

"What, they re-grew the whole fucking thing?'

"Yeah."

"Fuck me. And put his brains back in. They can do that?"

"Apparently."

They stood there looking at each other, but the extent of their combined knowledge of the matter had been exhausted.

"You better get on top of it, Cleary. You got the lead on this."

"On what?"

"This…"

"So, it's not murder?"

"The BIE was involved in authorising the Replant and they are still calling it murder. They sent us written notification already. He was killed, according to them, and it doesn't matter that they have used New Science to revive him. So, no change in the charge, it will still be murder."

Social protocols and ethics had been developed around the new technological realities. Legislation was initially slow to catch up with the spread of the New Science but laws had, in recent years, been fully developed into a comprehensive set of regulations covering all implications of this new world order in medical therapy and Augment production. This diverse set of laws and regulations had become popularly known as New Law, a term used exclusively to refer to all statutes or rewritten sections of old statutes enacted to control the New Science. The body in charge of the creation and dissemination of the New Law regulations was the Bureau of Intellectual Ethics, or the BIE, and it had become the preeminent governmental institution when it came to regulating for the social consequences of the now fast-moving world of bio-engineering.

"That can't be right. The victim is walking around and we've still got a murder to solve?"

"Not walking around yet but that's it. Get over to the hospital and interview the guy. Maybe he's got something."

"That's got to be a first, interviewing the murder victim."

"Do it today, Cleary," the Lieutenant said, sitting down at his desk opening some paperwork, casting a dismissive look towards Cleary.

"Sure," Cleary said, and he went back to the Zimmermann interview still scratching his head. Zimmermann had been given the opportunity to collect himself and was asking for a lawyer.

Cleary pulled Jacobs aside. "Give him to central booking and have them hold him for seventy-two hours on a national security warrant. Let him stew. The FBI wants to talk to him in the morning, anyway. Then I'll meet you out front. We have another interview to do and you are not going to believe who it is."

Jack Pierce awoke in Mount Sinai Hospital seven days after the car bombing that had killed him. Francine, his wife, lifted herself out of her chair and walked slowly to his bed as she saw him awaken.

"Hello, stranger. Just bumming around, are we?" she said nervously.

"What the hell? Francine, what am I doing here?" Jack said in a croaky voice, emerging from what he thought must have been a deep sleep.

"Well, not dying apparently," Francine replied awkwardly.

"Dying? What happened?" Jack said, rubbing his eyes and then his head. With increasing anxiety and some discomfort, he pushed himself upright in the bed, propping himself up on one hand and waving off any assistance from Francine with the other as he swung his legs over the side of the bed.

"Well… there was an explosion," Francine began cautiously, knowing this was going to be a difficult explanation given that she didn't understand it herself.

"There he is," the doctor said gregariously, entering the room with large strides. "How do we feel?"

"What the hell's wrong with me, doc? What explosion?" Jack said, looking back to Francine.

"Look, I think we need you to get some more rest. I don't think we should be going through that at the moment," the doctor said, pushing firmly on Jack's shoulder, gesturing for Jack to lie back down on the bed.

"What explosion?" Jack repeated in a firm voice, remaining upright and looking straight at Francine, expecting an answer.

"There was an explosion… in your car," Francine began again anxiously, "and I was told you were dead," she began to cry and reached for her purse to get a tissue. However, her hand was shaking so much that she couldn't open the bag. "You're not dead, and I don't understand what's going on," she continued with rising hysteria. Jack began to examine himself for signs of trauma. "I'm sorry about our fight, Jack, I really am. That's all I could think about, sitting here watching you."

"Mrs. Pierce," the doctor interrupted again, "I don't think…"

Francine continued insistently, "These people, Jack, these people… my God, they can't explain it to me and I'm not stupid, I want to know what is happening, what is going on?" Francine began to cry and looked at the doctor and then back to Jack as she fumbled with her purse again.

"Mrs. Pierce, please." The doctor signalled for some help from a passing nurse. "Take Mrs. Pierce out to the lounge, will you? Have her calm herself, perhaps with a sedative if she wants," he instructed the nurse, who obligingly put her arm around Francine's shoulders and steered her towards the door.

"Jesus, doc, what happened? I feel fine," Jack said, looking around the room for a mirror, "A little tired maybe, but…"

"Look, Jack, I want you to lie down so I can examine you and then we'll talk, OK?"

"Talk to me," Jack said assertively, refusing to lie on the bed.

"I guess someone had to be the first, Jack. We nearly didn't make it," the doctor began to blabber. "Those bureaucrats at the BIE, Jesus, I don't know who the hell they think they are… first we had to grow the…" He stopped himself, realising that he was becoming incoherent. "What's the last thing you remember?"

Jack paused and thought. "I was at AIOGEN, I was going in to get my smash done, and I wasn't looking forward to it, and I was talking to the operator about whether they had found any drug yet that eased the side effects. And that's it. I guess that's the last thing… now I'm here."

Within AIOGEN, downloading the contents of a human brain had become known as a "brain smash" due to the migraine-like headache it caused the donor and an overwhelming post-download feeling that the skull had been flattened or squashed. The side effects were unpopular and lasted for up to 24 hours, but otherwise, the procedure had been proven to be completely safe and took less than twenty minutes to complete. Confidence in the downloading process was such that all senior AOIGEN personnel were required to put a monthly smash on file as part of the company's intellectual property protection regime.

"Jack, that was over seven weeks ago," the doctor explained. "Your last smash, last month's smash, was corrupted somehow, we had to go back to the one before. There's an investigation underway as to how October's got corrupted." The doctor paused and decided to get to the point. "I guess there is no way to dance around this. In any case, you know more about this stuff than I do." The doctor pulled up one of the chairs, sat down, and continued. "We took the clean smash and we… well, we uploaded it. We uploaded it into a fully replicated, genetically identical, appropriately aged body — your body, Jack, with your genetically identical brain. Into you, Jack, into your head… my God!" The doctor paused, contemplating what he had just said and not fully understanding it himself.

Jack was speechless. The doctor continued, "You're Exon patient zero, Jack. You are the same age you were when the bomb went off — thirty-eight — the BIE wouldn't let us change that. And just as handsome as ever, let me say, but you now only have four percent body fat, so your abs are back, which is a good thing, I suppose. But you are exactly the same person. They let us remove that X2X indicator gene from the replicant, which was always going to get you into trouble at some point in your life… and a couple of other small genetic exposures we found… we eliminated them, too. But basically, to get back to the point, you are exactly what you were before the bombing, and as far as we can tell, your brain activity is identical, normal, brain scans are normal, and your physical condition is excellent."

"Are you telling me," Jack said, coming out of the trance induced by the doctor's meandering explanation and realising the enormity of what he was being told, "that this is a new body? That I was killed, that I died, and now I'm sitting here talking…"

"Settle yourself, Jack, I know it's a lot to absorb, but as far as we can see… look, work with me here," the doctor said, returning to a procedural approach. "What was the most immediate thing you remember prior to the conversation you had with the BCD technician?"

Jack thought for a short while. "I had come down from George's office, we were talking about the roll out of the new genetic protocols for the TPS400 Augment order."

"That's right, sure, and the week before, socially, say the Thursday night, what did you do?" the doctor said reassuringly, patting Jack's knee.

"The dinner party with Russ and his wife at Lu'tece," Jack said, now calmer as everything seemed to be in its place in his head.

"The name of your first cat?"

"Timothy," Jack answered.

"That's right, I think," the doctor said, flipping through the loose-leaf pages of a questionnaire he had attached to a clipboard. He stopped flipping and looked back at Jack. "Jack, we are going to have to do more tests, but we have to believe that this has all been seamless. Everything looks fine both on your physical tests and in your brain scans. You can see for yourself that the only thing missing is your memory since your last smash," the doctor said, somewhat personally reassured. "Do you notice anything different?"

"Compared to what," Jack said curtly. "What the fuck have I got to compare it to other than what you are telling me YOU put in there?" he said, pointing to his head. Jack began to get to his feet. "Are you saying I am physically fine? When can I get out of here? I've got to figure this out."

"Jack, you can't go anywhere," the doctor said, glancing over to the security guard visible through the glass wall of the hospital suite, "at least until the authorities are sure that nothing went wrong during the procedure."

"What am I, infectious or something?"

"No, but you are clearly distressed," the doctor offered with some authority. "Please sit back down."

The certainty and accuracy of the doctor's statement caused Jack to calm himself. He sat back on the bed, realising the futility of any other course of action. He needed to be rational. Francine re-entered the room, somewhat calmer herself.

"Spooky, huh? I'm assuming he told you," she said sheepishly, but with genuine concern. "How do you feel?"

"I'll get back to you on that one if that's okay," Jack responded sarcastically.

"You were considered too valuable for the company to lose, for the country to lose," the doctor continued. "They pushed hard, Jack. Frank pushed hard to get this done for you, I mean. It's only a one-off approval from the BIE until they consider their long-term position on the procedure. Frank sure knows how to get something done. I don't know how many butts he had to kick, but he got what he wanted. He's been told you were regaining consciousness; he's on his way over."

All in all, this event had punctuated an interesting year for Jack, in the Chinese proverbial sense of that expression. As the old maxim entreated, he did live in interesting times, and he was about to be confronted with that aphorism's other two corollaries: he was about to attract the attention of those in authority, and he would, good or bad, find that which he sought. He was about to discover why the Chinese referred to those three apparently innocuous euphemisms as a curse.

Jack's life had followed a direct line of ascent since high school, without misstep or misdirection, imbuing him with a rarely challenged self-assurance. Even though not yet tempered by adversity, his disposition possessed a grace that obscured the severest attributes of his overconfidence. This and his practiced self-deprecation made him liked by most of those with whom he came into contact. For the people who did genuinely like him, the hardly noticeable swagger in his walk was neither loud nor out of place — an eccentricity, perhaps, probably well-deserved given his achievements, certainly not an affectation. He had always been in control of his life and of the people around him. It was a predisposition he actively nurtured, even though of late, he had become confused about his relationship with Francine. He was the only child of doting parents, both of whom were still living, and still married, and he had a drive unexhausted by years of productive and successful endeavour.

Genetic engineering had in recent years become quite the thing to do for the upwardly mobile executive, given that the quick profits had long since disappeared from the now highly competitive software and e-commerce industries. The topography of the scientific world had not changed as much as had the economic realities that once dictated its direction and application. Today, genetic engineering created markets that didn't previously exist, and it was revolutionizing many of the old medical industries.

In the middle of the last century, it had been astrophysics that had occupied the brightest minds in the scientific community. That pursuit had promised so much in the days of the Apollo Program, but the *Star Trek* generation was to end up disappointed. By 2049, Captain Kirk's multi-rebooted persona, the most recent being female, would be attending only the Earth-bound conferences and would not be boldly going anywhere else. The manned space program had proven costly and dangerous and had delivered little to the average household since Teflon and the microwave oven. That modest real reward, despite the years of perilous effort, represented a meagre yield indeed on the huge expenditures that had drained the public purse in the later part of the twentieth century and for the first twenty years of the current one. Sub-orbital space tourism had become popular, and there were endless machinations about an orbiting hotel, but nothing had as yet been forthcoming. The defence industry had benefited greatly from the space program, but the military machine was now knocking on Jack's door rather than looking to the heavens.

Helium-3 mining on Earth's moon was well-established. Helium-3 had become widely used in fusion reactors, and fusion energy provided clean and relatively inexpensive energy for all. Rare on Earth, the extraction of the element from the moon required surface mining only, about the first thirty metres of material. The Helium-3, with no lunar atmosphere to impede its accretion, had been deposited by the sun on the moon's surface for millennia. The demand from the new fusion reactors had created a financial imperative to return to the moon. Equipment, largely automated, had to be adapted for the large amounts of lunar dust created by the mining. The persistent and indefatigable dust was forever hanging due to the low gravity and the lack of any cleansing breeze, largely defeating any consideration of making the moon a tourist destination. The electrostatic particulates spawned by the machinery meant that the suspended lunar sediment made for a bleak landscape in some areas, all but impervious to light. To the naked eye from Earth, the moon had come to look more like a cotton ball than a lifeless, sharply defined, pockmarked planetoid. The viability of the mining was assisted by the discovery of commercial quantities of silver and titanium in the same top layers, along with much sought after yttrium, lanthanum, and samarium. The extraction and sale of which subsidised the three private sector mining ventures underway there since 2042.

After an aborted attempt in the 2029 Mars launch trajectory window, a privately-funded but government-subsidised manned expedition using the remnants of NASA's post-shuttle Falcon Heavy Lift rocket system had, on its second attempt, finally reached Mars in 2031. It had, to the surprise of few, found an empty world and after nearly twenty successful robotic landings, it now offered little for the enlightened mind and nothing to mitigate the risk of any further exposure to human life. No settlement was established nor considered in any future planning because there were more interesting projects that attracted private and public funding.

There was promise for space exploration enthusiasts on the horizon with privately funded work underway on the manipulation of space-time itself, much in the same way that the gravity of a massive planet could, as was proposed by Einstein and was now measurably known, change the shape of the space-time continuum, the very fabric of the universe. The spacecraft designers knew how it all should work, but the amount of energy required for such a task was proving hard to assemble on a usable platform and any worthwhile execution of the theory as it pertained to space travel seemed unlikely in the medium term. As a result, the funding for such projects was receding. New York-based scientist Franz Gothenburg was known to be working with micro-time displacement of nonorganic materials as an extension of these space-time distortion mechanics, which he had used when his company was part of the spacecraft development industry, but there had been no news of his progress. His company, too, had moved onto more profitable undertakings, now supplying equipment accessories for the Augments produced by AIOGEN.

So it came to pass that it was bioengineers who had become the superstars, and it was bioengineering that had brought the planet back from the brink of global environmental disaster. A little less than fifteen years earlier, it had come to prominence with the engineering of a new organism based on blue-green algae that, when propagated into the world's oceans, reversed the downward cycle of global warming. But that was only the beginning, a beginning that subsequently attracted massive investment.

The US community's religious predispositions had meant that the USA had, in the early days of the development of the New Science, yielded ground to others researching in this area. But in the end, the USA had brought to bear its massive industrial and technical resources and with typical American proficiency had won the day assisted in no small part by the brilliant mind of one particular American, Doctor Jack Pierce. The economic and military imperatives had become far too much to resist post the Trump administration, which had laid some of the ground work for what was now regarded as a new industrial revolution. But the newest developments in bioengineering sat uneasily on the souls of the religious segments of American society. Tensions existed and the cracks that had opened had begun to grow into social divides. The New Science was moving quickly and there were some that were dragging their feet behind it instead of marching to the drum beat that resonated so loudly from the new prosperity it had created.

The New Science has transformed many fields, among them the American defence forces. Jack Pierce, as the most senior researcher and departmental head for AIOGEN, was at the heart of this revolution. AIOGEN was the only company globally providing genetically engineered, near-human biological organisms, colloquially known as Augments, to the American military. They also supplied a less aggressive, more civilized variant to a broad network of domestic and international household appliances distributors. However, it was the Exon project that marked AIOGEN's new breakthrough. Named after the nucleic acid sequence of a mature RNA molecule — an exon, in contrast to an intron — this project symbolized the company's core activities.

By 2049, bio-genetics had surpassed its initial goals of organ, skin, and nerve cell regeneration — goals envisioned by early cell replacement advocates like Michael J. Fox and Christopher Reeves, who sought cures for trauma patients and individuals suffering from debilitating nervous system disorders. AIOGEN's early sales growth was largely due to its organ replacement services, which provided tailor-made organ replacements grown from the patient's own genetic material. But it was the development and sale of equipment using bio-electrical interfaces to control organ output and nervous system communication that propelled AIOGEN into a financial league of its own. The idea of pacemakers controlling heart function wasn't new. Significant progress had been made before AIOGEN's research with electronic interfaces within human optic nerves and the leg muscles of paraplegics. Yet these developments were rudimentary compared to what AIOGEN achieved with its range of products using electronic organ and muscle augmentation. They had made it possible for every organ and muscle's function in the animal body to be electronically controlled and monitored by non-organic, human-programmable electronic manipulators.

New methods had been discovered to access and influence nervous system pathways, to regulate and control hormone production within the human body. Organ output and functionality — including that of the human heart, spleen, thyroid, and pancreas — could now be precisely controlled using their equipment. The devices utilised a direct electronic interface between a living organism's nervous system — its bio-electrical pathways — and man-made artificial electronics. AIOGEN created machines or, more specifically, computers that could directly communicate instructions to and receive feedback from living nervous, muscle, and endocrine systems. This made it possible — and even desirable — to augment many biological processes with computerised support, especially those indicating any level of natural impairment.

This work paved the way for remarkable progress in the treatment of heart, other organ, or muscular diseases and was used to reverse the effects of hormonal and other chemical secretion imbalances in patients suffering from many forms of hormone production disorders, including brain function impairments and emotional dislocation. As a result, the reputation and regard for this brave new world of bioengineering grew steadily during the late forties and fifties as AIOGEN introduced each of these new developments. The New Science led to the discarding of old suspicions, and the new procedures and their associated markets were embraced by the global medical community.

However, it was the full-body units, the Augments, which had recently become the primary source of AIOGEN's revenue. The pinnacle of regrown organ replacements was full-body replication. Having mastered the electronic interface with the living nervous system, it became possible to replace the organic brain of a fully grown unit with an electronic one. Society eventually accepted the use of the human genome in growing biologically-based equipment due to this brain substitution and the pressing demands from the military and service industry. Community consensus was reached only after it was unequivocally established that these machines would never develop self-awareness. AIOGEN had effectively usurped robotics from this realm of commercial and military application.

Robotics — the construction of human-like, fully electromechanical equipment for industrial, domestic, or military purposes — had been deemed unviable compared to full-body electronically controlled organic Augmentation. These entities, whether mechanical or biological, needed to function in a world designed for humans, thus necessitating human-like size and attributes. For military purposes, mechanical assistance could be added externally to the biological unit, serving as a shield, tool, or weapon. Robotics had been relegated to accessory development and hobbyist pursuits, with standalone, fully electromechanical human-like robots now residing solely in museums.

However, beyond its military applications, the Exon Project was poised to overhaul the established world of clinical and cosmetic rejuvenation, potentially sidelining the social attention on Augments. At the core of the Exon Project was brain content duplication. In designing and building the electronic brains for the Augments, AIOGEN had gained a complete understanding of the human brain, including its interaction with the body and its methods of storing and utilising information. This knowledge, coupled with AIOGEN's existing organ and body part cloning capabilities, opened up formidable and long-sought-after possibilities. The convergence of these two technologies was beginning to stir significant societal concern. AIOGEN had thrown its full weight behind the Exon Project, which was receiving substantial corporate resources.

By July 2059, Exon had successfully tested and perfected the brain content downloading process. Still, it was the benefits of uploading that had sent shockwaves through the scientific world and society at large. This time, legislators were proactive, and negotiations concerning the use of and restrictions surrounding cloning and Brain Content Duplication (BCD) upload technologies were already underway between the Bureau of Intellectual Ethics and AIOGEN. Religious groups had started to formulate more organised responses to the use of the human genome in organic equipment manufacture and the looming prospect of BCD uploads. In some cases, these responses turned violent. "Brain smashing 'destroys the soul and is against God's law'," they declared. "God's Law, not New Law," was their rallying cry. AIOGEN had become the target for demonstrations, one of which had formed outside the Met on the night of the company's gala, which Jack had attended one week earlier. As Jack had pressed the ignition key to start his BMW after leaving the gala, the car had exploded into a ball of flames, killing him instantly.

CHAPTER THREE

It would be three days before Frederick saw Hitler again. The bandage that had so effectively concealed him at the funeral was no longer on his nose, and the bruising and swelling on his forehead and face had diminished. He was left with only a pair of black eyes and a yet-to-heal broken bridge of his nose. His nurse had dressed him in a Hitler Youth uniform she had specifically ordered for the boy for his meeting with Hitler. As they walked to Hitler's office after being summoned, the nurse held his hand, and the swastika on his free arm swayed in and out of his peripheral vision. He looked down at it, overwhelmed with revulsion and a sense of unease. He felt that this was all wrong; he had made a terrible mistake and should not be here, wearing this uniform symbolising evil. His fixation was abruptly interrupted by the nurse tugging at his hand, leading him through the vaulted doors of Hitler's office in the Chancellery. Hitler was standing at his desk, which was nearly eighty yards away, pointing at some documents and explaining something to the man beside him. The boy couldn't hear what was being said, but he immediately recognised Hitler's guest. They waited at the door to be called over.

"Ah! Da ist er, mein kleiner Soldat," Hitler said warmly, his face brightening with a smile as he saw Frederick in his uniform for the first time. The boy was taken aback, involuntarily pulling free from the nurse's hand and stepping back towards the door, still struggling to adjust to his surroundings and the surreal experience of being spoken to and smiled at by Hitler.

"You are looking much better; thank you, nurse, for bringing him. Are you feeling better, my boy?" Hitler continued, as the boy was nudged on the shoulder and compelled to approach the desk.

"Ja, mein Führer, wir danken Ihnen für die Nachfrage," the boy replied nervously, gathering his composure. Franz, who had spoken perfect German all his life, had no problem doing the same as Frederick. "Herr Speer, it is a privilege to meet you," Frederick said, now more composed and returning to his plan. He reached out his hand deliberately and formally to shake hands with Albert Speer, the Party's official architect, who was on the brink of being appointed as General Building Inspector for the Reich Capital, reporting directly to Hitler. For the moment, Speer was content reporting to Rudolf Hess, second-in-command of the Party, but he viewed Hess as merely a Party mechanic who lacked both the concept and understanding of his vision for the New Berlin. Speer knew, however, that Hitler believed in the power of architecture and its impact on the collective spirit, referring to it as "the word in stone." If that were the case, then Speer was set to become its Chief Orator.

"A pleasure to meet you too," Speer responded, shaking the boy's hand. He looked at Hitler with a half-smile, impressed by the boy's manners and his recognition without introduction. Hitler's smile widened as the two men exchanged surprised glances.

"Are we discussing matters of interest to a small boy?" Frederick asked.

"It depends on how intelligent that boy is," Speer responded, looking to Hitler for guidance on how to handle the boy's unexpected curiosity. Hitler shrugged his shoulders, intrigued by the boy's question and his demeanour. Frederick moved a little closer to the desk to see what was laid out there, his hands submissively behind his back.

"Is it the Paris exhibition designs?"

The following year, Germany was set to participate in an event similar to a World's Fair in Paris, the Exposition Internationale des Arts et Techniques dans la Vie Moderne, attended by most developed nations. Frederick recognised the German Pavilion designs from his research.

"They are beautiful, Herr Speer," he commented. Both Speer and Hitler exchanged bemused glances. "You had better watch out for those accursed Soviets," Frederick continued without pause. "They are directly opposite us, aren't they?" He pointed to the layout without touching the paper, his finger hovering over the position where the drawings showed that the two pavilions indeed faced each other across the promenade leading to the Eiffel Tower. "They always aim to make some insulting point about communism!"

"Your father has educated you well, Frederick. How do you know about such matters?" Hitler asked.

"Politics greatly interest me, my Führer, and I make a study of it."

"You don't need to be concerned about the Soviets, my boy," Speer said reassuringly. "I have seen a preliminary of their designs and they appear quite feeble, I assure you. The Führer was considering withdrawing from the exhibition when we were positioned opposite them, but I convinced him it was a great opportunity for us."

"You should never believe everything you read about the Soviets, Herr Speer, about their assertions or their claims. That would be a mistake, especially for someone as talented and intelligent as yourself."

Frederick was well aware that the Soviets intended to make a political statement with a then-secret change in their pavilion design for the Exhibition. The nurse, thinking the boy had said too much, quickly approached and placed her hands on his shoulders, turning him abruptly towards the door.

"I'll take him to have some lunch, my Führer. Say goodbye, Frederick."

Hitler was left with his mouth half open, considering whether he wanted to hear more from the boy, wholly impressed by his apparent intelligence and insight. Speer shared his sentiment, but neither man said anything, simply standing there as they watched the boy being led off to lunch.

"I am genuinely impressed by your work, Herr Speer," Frederick paused momentarily, having slipped free from Nurse Helga's grasp, and turned back to have the final word. "You serve the Fatherland with great distinction, and I hope to see you again someday." The word "someday" was distorted by the nurse tugging him again by the hand as she ushered him off. Hitler began to applaud as the boy and the nurse moved towards the door. Frederick turned back and smiled at Hitler, solidifying a well-crafted first impression.

"Now, that is what young Germany has become, my friend. It is all in the breeding, you see," Hitler said with great pride and an unrecognised irony.

Long before he sent the BCD package back to himself, Franz had decided that a strategy to kill Hitler was prone to failure. He had come emotionally prepared for violence, but it was not his first choice. It wasn't because he deemed it impossible for a small boy to kill Hitler given the right opportunity, but because it was unlikely to achieve his ultimate aim – the avoidance of the Holocaust. Franz had millions of lives to consider, and the risk of failure and his own death could leave his mission unfulfilled.

Franz understood that Hitler was not a lone actor, a single person whom history would brand as the sole cause of the horrific events of that period. Demonising Hitler, however deserved, was an oversimplification which suited historians wishing to lay blame at the feet of a devil, rather than critically examining the complex events, the Nazi organisational hierarchies, social circumstances of the day, and the complicity of others both in Germany and abroad, including notably, the apathy of other world leaders.

A detailed examination of those times would inevitably expose the contribution of other persons within and outside of Germany. Sadly, the superficial scrutiny of post-war events by English and American historians glossed over the deep-seated social hatred towards Jews and other marginalised groups, and more pointedly, the failure of global leaders to exhibit leadership and challenge these perceptions during those difficult times. The impact of such academic failures continued to plague society post-war.

The recounting of history in terms of devils and angels might satisfy a six-year-old's understanding but has done little to inform policy makers and educate the public about the root causes of such an unthinkable outcome. Churchill, one of those mythical angels, ominously predicted that *those who fail to understand history are destined to repeat it.*

Perhaps the unimaginable horrors of the ensuing war drove the victors to oversimplify its origins, in an attempt to justify their own involvement, by attributing it solely to an evil emperor seeking world domination. This naive analysis has yielded little more than platitudes about bogeymen and has failed to inform productive public policy in the subsequent years.

Franz understood that anti-Semitism was not restricted to Hitler and his inner circle, nor confined to certain parts of Germany. It was a collective malady rampant throughout the country, Europe, and even America. He knew that in 1936, as many American establishments denied entry to Jews as in Germany. He fondly remembered a movie, *A Gentleman's Agreement,* starring Gregory Peck, which delved into this very issue.

Most crucial to his planning was the understanding that whoever would succeed Hitler, if he were killed, would likely harbor the same bigotry. The potential successors included even Heinrich Himmler, the architect of the Holocaust. Regardless of who it would be, Franz was convinced that the outcomes were unlikely to change with Hitler's death. Franz had conceived what he thought was a better plan but remained prepared to act more directly should he fail to achieve his desired result. For now, there was time to explore all options.

The time when the boy would see Hitler again came just two days later when the nurse was asked to bring him back to Hitler's office. Speer was there also, as was one of Hitler's senior assistants. As they entered, the nurse was asked to wait outside. The boy stood at the door alone.

"Nun, hier kommen Frederick," Hitler summoned him over. "We have received word from our people in Moscow that the Soviets have changed the design of their pavilion to include two colossal Soviet figures at the top, seemingly ready to charge across the road to destroy the German pavilion. How did you know to refer to such a thing the other day?"

"I didn't know, my Führer. It is obvious from studying them that they would not miss such an opportunity to make their point."

"So, it was a guess then?"

"An assumption, my Führer. I am sure that Herr Speer can come up with something equally intimidating to reflect back at them."

"I already have, yes. You are quite the intuitive boy indeed," Speer answered, and then turned to Hitler and said, "I think I need to speak to your little friend here before I do any of my planning in the future." Both men laughed. "Have a look at this, Frederick!"

Speer excitedly showed the boy his revised design for the German pavilion, which now included huge Greek columns facing the street, seemingly impregnable to any military challenge from the Soviets. The columns facing the Soviet pavilion were topped by a huge eagle looking down on the Soviets, appearing ready to snatch up any Soviet intruder who dared to cross the road in anger.

The boy laughed. "That should do just fine, Herr Speer. Nothing can get through there. And if they do, our eagle will get them, is that correct?" All three laughed. "This will win us the gold medal for sure, I think."

Frederick knew that in the end, both Germany and the Soviets would win the gold medal for the design of their pavilions that year, the judges being unable or unwilling to split them at the Exhibition, both countries having spent exorbitant sums one to outdo the other.

Hitler came over to the boy and put his hand on his shoulder. "You show great spirit, boy, and do not lack the courage to speak up. You know, I believe in fate, and it is fate that has sent you to me, I am sure. Tell the nurse to bring you to my residence for dinner tonight. I have some other people I would like you to meet. Herr Speer will be there, and you can wrangle with him some more about architecture. Perhaps you could give me some of your other opinions if indeed I have the courage to hear them."

Dinner that evening was a surprisingly simple affair. It was Hitler and Eva Braun, Albert Speer and his wife Margarete, Joseph Goebbels with his wife Magda, who was also a long-term member of the

Party, and the boy and his nurse Helga. Hitler's meal was vegetarian, but he was serving trout in butter sauce for his guests. He planned to show a movie after dinner.

"So, we have a little genius with us tonight?" Goebbels asked, looking at the boy seated next to him as he dissected his fish, wanting to bring the boy he had heard so much about from Albert into the conversation.

"Not at all, Herr Minister," the boy responded, not waiting for anybody to respond on his behalf. "Just a small German boy with an appetite for knowledge."

"Well, I hope also you have an appetite for your fish, Master Frederick," Helga said, trying to keep the precocious young man in his place.

"Albert here tells me you anticipated the move by the Russians in the design of their Paris Pavilion. We could use a good strategist in the Information Department."

"Perhaps after school, Herr Minister," Frederick replied quickly in a serious tone, knowing that Goebbels was being sarcastic. Both comments met with generous amusement around the table.

"You might have put your foot in it there, Joseph," Speer said to Goebbels with a smile. "You might have just acquired another employee."

"I think it's delightful," Magda proffered, "that our youth are growing up with an interest in politics and are so obviously well-educated and from such a fine family… my sympathies to you, young man."

"Your condolences are appreciated, Frau Goebbels," Frederick replied politely.

"Yes," Eva added sympathetically, "it must have been terrible for you to lose your family so suddenly like that, Frederick. If there is anything we can do for you, please let us know."

"We live in troubling times, Fraulein Braun. We must all bear our share of the burden." Frederick was being very serious and privately recalling the loss of his own parents.

With that remark, Hitler put his fork down on his plate with a clang, pointing at Goebbels.

"I think you'll be working for him before too long, Joseph, not the other way around." Everybody laughed loudly, of course.

"Do you have a film for us this evening, Herr Minister?" Frederick asked, deliberately stepping out of the convention of the day requiring that children be spoken to before speaking. Frederick was looking for a more senior place at this particular table than his apparent age would otherwise permit.

"Yes… a new film… from Czechoslovakia," Goebbels replied reluctantly with a quizzical look on his face, not used to being questioned by a six-year-old. Goebbels shot a look of disapproval towards the nurse.

"With Lida Baarova? She is very pretty, don't you think?" the boy responded before the nurse could say or do anything to contain him. Frederick had, with that remark, achieved his goal of getting Goebbels's attention. Goebbels was wooing the young Czech actress and had thought, mistakenly, that he was doing so undetected by any at this table. Frederick, of course, knew all the sordid details.

"Yes… that's the one," Goebbels said as he coughed and wiped down the front of his shirt, cleaning off the spilled food.

"What about 'King Kong'? We should do that some other night," the boy continued, not wishing to overemphasise his remark about the actress or further indicate he might know more than it was possible for him to know. He knew that *King Kong* was Hitler's favourite film.

"The way you are going, young man, there won't be a next time," Speer said, being one of the people at the table who did know about Goebbels's predisposition towards the Czech actress.

"The boy has a point," Hitler interjected, oblivious to the undertones about Goebbels's affair, "and good taste. 'King Kong' is a fine film, although I hate to see animals suffer. We will do it another night, my boy. I am tired of these new era films you keep dragging in here, Joseph."

"How does a little boy like you know about Lida Baarova?" Magda asked, having her own suspicions as to why Goebbels had chosen the film.

"I like to keep up to date, Frau Goebbels. What we feed the masses shouldn't compel us to allow our own tastes to wilt, surely," Frederick said in a nonchalant fashion, taking another forkful of fish into his mouth, knowingly causing all at the table to look at him in bemused disbelief.

"What do you know about feeding the masses?" Goebbels asked Frederick derisively, expressing air through his lips with a *tsk* to punctuate his comment.

"Enough to know that feeding them cake doesn't stop them from wanting baklava, Herr Minister, or playing them German folk songs cannot close their hearts to Tristan."

"Ah! Yes, well said," Hitler announced as he started to clap loudly. "I told you he had courage. You'll need to be quicker than that, Joseph. I think he has you there. Yes, Wagner, good boy."

Hitler was obviously proud of the boy's intelligent response to Goebbels's disparaging question and glad that he had invited him to dinner to provide such amusement. The boy had courage under fire, Hitler thought to himself, and was not easy to intimidate.

"You are a strange boy indeed," Goebbels responded, somewhat taken aback.

"I know and appreciate that it is your job to focus the collective mind, Herr Goebbels, and you are particularly talented in that regard, perhaps even the best in the world." Now for some flattery, Frederick thought. "But one must not forget those amongst us here with the intelligence to know what you are doing, and on whose back the future of the Reich must inevitably be carried."

All at the table were listening intently, including Goebbels, who was now reconsidering his view of the boy.

"You think that I patronise our ruling class?"

"Perhaps," Frederick confirmed, as Goebbels's face went white, "but I suspect you know exactly what you are doing." Goebbels settled. "You most certainly have it right with the media, opera, and film. Your choice for us tonight is enlightened."

"But… but not the arts or literature?" Goebbels added, tritely. "And you would know better of course."

Frederick thought for a moment.

"I understand that you have a job to do in controlling the information flow to the general public via the written word. But book bonfires can only take us so far, Herr Minister, even though any history written by the English and the French we have every right, perhaps even a duty, to discard."

"Well said, my boy," Hitler remarked, still eating.

Frederick continued with that encouragement.

"Berlin has always been the centre of artistic endeavour and progress. For years, the French have had that pretention, but that has not been the reality of it. Berlin has remained the centre of the world of art for at least the last two centuries, despite what the French and English did to us with that despicable Treaty." Frederick was referring to the Treaty of Versailles at the end of the First World War, and everyone in the room knew what he meant and shared his genuinely held view of it, nodding along as the boy spoke. "But you make all the new artists out to be degenerates and in doing so all that you do is chase them away to Paris. Berlin has always been the beacon of artistic enlightenment in a dark world, and must, in my opinion, remain as such. So what if they draw a face without perspective with two eyes looking at you like a squashed fish. Better they pick up a brush than a gun, and better that we nurture them here for us to shape their opinions rather than allow those opinions to be cultivated by some French communist like Pierre Laval or monarchist like Albert Lebrun."

There was silence. The people at the table were bewildered by Frederick's loquaciousness, but they also knew what Hitler thought about progressive art. Hitler was himself a trained artist and a very opinionated one. They waited for Hitler to speak, knowing his sensitivities, and all continued head down to finish their meal, pretending not to notice the silence that had descended on the room.

"You are indeed a smart boy," Hitler said, now not smiling but instead vigorously chewing on his vegetables. "I like you, Frederick, and your politics, but your opinion of modern art is sadly mistaken. I will take it upon myself to educate you. In the meantime, we will continue to run those degenerates, as you so correctly refer to them, out of this city and be the better for it. Eat your fish."

Goebbels was privately more receptive to the boy's views, despite his silence for the rest of the evening. As one of the Reich's most highly educated Ministers, he had always held the Berlin art scene in high regard, and he had often indulged in discussions on this very topic in the many coffee houses scattered throughout the city. These places were the hub for Weimar's avant-garde crowd, who took it upon themselves to keep up with modern trends in visual arts and theatre. Recently, Goebbels had kept his opinions on modern art to himself, aware that expressing them could invoke a rebuke similar to the one the boy had just received. Nevertheless, he thought the boy made a compelling argument. Goebbels understood the power of communication and persuasion, and he knew that contemporary art had a loud voice that resonated around the globe. In less than a week, the boy had made an impression on Hitler's closest advisors, including the Führer himself.

In the weeks and months to come, Frederick continued to confound those who crossed his path, not least the teachers at his Berlin school. Soon, he was being home-schooled, as the structured environment of school seemed unsuitable for him. The truth was, no school was willing to subject its teachers to the humiliation of being outsmarted by the boy's intellect.

Frederick remained under Hitler's patronage, who had grown to enjoy their sporadic conversations. The boy had nurtured this relationship and had gradually started to influence Hitler's perception of him as someone with an uncanny foresight. The Führer was gradually introduced to carefully rehearsed snippets of Frederick's knowledge, which seemed visionary to Hitler but was merely historical fact to the boy. These insights were never of immense importance, always similar to his playful deception with Speer about the Russian Pavilion in Paris. Frederick knew from his history books that Speer would have eventually uncovered the Russians' intentions regarding the Paris Pavilion. However, he had seized the opportunity to elevate his status in front of Hitler and make an impression on Speer.

Later that year, Frederick utilised another similar event to further showcase his prescience. He predicted that Hitler's

Exhibition of Degenerate Art in Munich in 1937, known as *Entartete Kunst*, would have the opposite effect to what Hitler intended. Hitler wanted to portray modern art, particularly late impressionism and abstractionism, in a negative light. Frederick's point, which followed from the perspective he had shared with Goebbels at their first dinner, was that the German people had always held their own opinions about what constituted worthwhile viewing in the realm of contemporary art.

Hitler had scheduled *Entartete Kunst* simultaneously with his personal exhibition, *Grosse deutsche Kunstausstellung*, the *Great German Art Exhibition*, where every art piece was personally selected by the Führer. Hitler's intention was to show the general populace, by comparison, what was great art and what was mere rubbish. As it turned out, and as Frederick had accurately predicted, there were lines out the door at the *Exhibition of Degenerate Art*, with nearly three million well-informed and art-hungry Germans eager to see it, while only a polite few attended the *Grosse deutsche Kunstausstellung*.

Frederick managed to persuade his initially reluctant tutor to take him to *Entartete Kunst*; attending the exhibition was one of his lifelong dreams. Artists such as Noble, Kirchner, Beckmann, Picasso, Matisse, and van Gogh were all featured, some of whom were his personal heroes. Many of the pieces exhibited there would be lost in the impending war and never be seen again. Attending the exhibition marked the first of many indulgences Frederick allowed himself as he navigated the treacherous waters he had plotted for himself.

Frederick chose carefully when to present his views to Hitler, ensuring not to overly offend him. Instead, his insights aimed to gradually reinforce the perception that he could, in many cases, accurately predict future events. Always superstitious, Hitler was beginning to view Frederick's perception and unique intelligence as a potential asset that the Reich could exploit, even though he publicly admitted nothing of the sort. Hitler's esteem for and fondness of Frederick grew with each passing month.

Frederick was now cautiously searching for the right moment to utilise the personal capital he had accumulated with the Führer to execute his plan.

CHAPTER FOUR

Jack Pierce felt apprehensive as the elevator doors opened on the 80th floor of One World Trade Centre, AIOGEN's head office. The company had several floors in the building and had chosen the location as its headquarters after the success of their Augment equipment in Afgan III. Jack had an office there as well as at the main plant in Jersey. He had come to this office this morning primarily because Frank Dugan, the CEO, wanted a meeting with him and Su-Ming Lee, the Head of the Exon Project. Jack was eager to get back to his team in Jersey.

Frank's PA poked his head through the doorway of Jack's office even before Jack had seated himself and said, "One o'clock," then left as quickly as he had appeared. Jack was reminded of the standard prank played on new executives in this office, where someone would ring the extension of the nervous newcomer and all they would hear was "Dugan… get up here!" in a loud, gruff voice, followed by the sound of the phone being disconnected. The newcomer was then left with the dilemma of whether they believed it was actually Frank Dugan and go as commanded to his office, or assume it was a prank and risk not going. Frank Dugan had become heartily sick of nervous management rookies showing up at his door and sheepishly asking whether he had sent for them. What made the joke particularly effective was that Frank's PA could never provide any help to the victim because it was assumed Dugan had personally called them. Having made the journey up to the CEO's office, the newbie then had the pleasure of being welcomed to the company by its chief executive telling them to "Fuck off, you idiot." The prankster was usually impossible to trace but could be implicated if found laughing in the office when the newcomer emerged from the elevator looking gaunt and chastened. This prank was a favourite pastime of George Sanders, the Head of IT at AIOGEN, and a long-time friend of Jack Pierce.

"Jack, need any help?" Jack was startled out of his musings by Carol leaning halfway in the door of his office and halfway out of her blouse.

"No, just finding my feet. Thanks, anyway."

"Maybe lunch?" Carol stepped all the way in.

"Don't think I can today, I expect it to be a hell of a day actually. I haven't got the time."

"Let me know if you need anything, I'm just down the hall. All you need to do is whistle."

She wasn't Lauren Bacall, but she was beautiful. She left, leaving Jack still thinking about what she wasn't wearing. He and Francine hadn't been getting along lately. Looking down at the tent that had formed in his pleated suit pants, he was glad that anatomically he was functional in that area, but he was left wondering whether Frank had, undisclosed, done him an additional favour in that regard as well.

Always punctual, Jack entered Frank's office at 1:00 p.m. on the dot. He was greeted by Frank and Su-Ming Lee.

"Jack, sit down. Getting back into it, I presume?"

"Sure. No problem."

"Su-Ming here wanted to brief you on where we are up to with Exon and get your input, given you're patient zero. Strictly QT, of course."

"The upload is really only step one, Jack," Su-Ming began without pleasantries. "We're happy to get that step out of the way, of course, but there's a long road ahead, a path we can travel from here. And it's a little bit more than even you might have imagined, Jack."

"Exon," Frank explained, "has been focusing of late on precursor epigenetic methodologies," still a little unsure of what Jack remembered.

"Sure. What have we got?" Jack asked, although he thought he already knew.

"I suppose you could say we've achieved something momentous," Su-Ming paused, her smile evident. "We've discovered the holy grail of cosmetic modifications, Jack. We can now manipulate gene expression with utmost precision, turning it on or off at will. Coupled with our proven full-body regeneration protocols and BCU technology, we have the complete package."

"The ultimate facelift, you mean? The BIE is on board?"

"Not yet. That's where you come in. We can now make significant changes to an individual's gene functioning to influence their appearance, abilities, and impairments — using their own unique genetic makeup."

"You mentioned something about advanced epigenetic methodologies?"

"We've far surpassed the 5-hydroxymethylcytosine your team is working with in Jersey. Our method is not a shotgun approach like methylation, Jack. We've developed a precision tool." Su-Ming's enthusiasm was palpable.

"Altering genetic sequences to achieve varying outcomes isn't new, Su-Ming."

"We've got that, but there's much more. We possess the tools, Jack — the cosmetic tools or clinical tools, whichever you prefer — that were previously unimaginable. We now have the precision and predictability of results."

"Regenerating human organs from an individual's DNA has been commonplace for years," Frank interjected to summarise. "They're perfect matches for each individual, eliminating the need for anti-rejection drugs. It's been a tremendous benefit to the medical field and society at large. We owe you a debt of gratitude for perfecting the full body regeneration procedures used with the Augments. Now we can regenerate an entire human, including their brain. We also know the upload process works. Connect the dots. Take any human's unique genetic sequence, regenerate the entire body while altering certain, selected, gene expressions, and perform the Replant — what you end up with surpasses any facelift."

"Jack, we all carry genes that date back hundreds of thousands of years," Su-Ming continued. "We all have them, you know that. Some are dormant, others are active. Our genetic makeup is a compendium of countless sequence mutations — some are a result of natural selection, while others are due to external factors like viruses or cosmic radiation. We can now modify the expression of these sequences as we please."

"I think this will terrify the general public."

"Jack, you more than anyone understand how this can benefit humanity," Su-Ming pressed on. "Consider the potential impact on the treatment of genetic diseases caused by gene deletions or inactivations, like Angelman or Prader-Willi syndrome, Parkinson's, or gene repeat disorders like Huntington's. This is monumental, Jack."

"You're using cosmetic as a cover, but arguing clinical. Which is it, Su-Ming?"

"It's both, of course."

"Look, we don't operate outside the law, nor do we desire or intend to." Frank, ever the political pragmatist, spoke up. "Government oversight of these protocols is more rigorous than ever. That wasn't always the case — once, lawmakers were virtually blind, their guide dogs more aware of ongoing developments than they were. Those were the dark days of our field, marked by a complete disconnect between scientific reality and public policy management. Nowadays, politicians are ahead of the curve, reviewing and guiding rather than stifling progress. While our industry drives a significant economic engine, especially here in America, neither we nor the government would permit anything harmful to reach the public. The BIE is staffed with astute individuals. We just need to present our options to them — let society decide what is or isn't beneficial."

"We have a meeting set up with the BIE on the Tuesday before Thanksgiving," Su-Ming adds. "We want you there, Jack. And we want you to start integrating some of these new procedures into your work at the Augment plant. It will give you an efficiency boost, if nothing else, and what we do with our own product is our business. Some of these processes need proof of concept on the production line. We planned to discuss it with you the night of the function."

"Sure, we're always open to improving our procedures, Frank. But I'm not sure what I can contribute to your meeting with the BIE. I don't want to be a guinea pig at show-and-tell."

"You add credibility, Jack," Frank laughs. "You are the preeminent bioengineer in this country, with all due respect Su-Ming. You're not a guinea pig, but a survivor who is here because the procedure works. You are living proof that all of this is okay. They know how fortunate this community is to have you back. You're a hero, first across the threshold."

"My wife said the same thing the other night, I'm not so sure…"

"Sure, sure, but that's how future generations will see it. And you'll be able to inform the BIE about how these new gene-modification procedures are working out in your lab with the full body regeneration military Augment program."

"I don't know, Frank…"

"Look, we can completely regenerate a terminally ill patient or even someone who's been killed or severely injured, as was your case. But Exon introduces the possibility that you don't have to be the same old plodder you were before you got sick. I'm not saying you were ever a plodder, Jack. I'm speaking about the general populace, you understand. Now, not only can we screen out the genetic impairments like we had permission to do with you, but we can also alter the sum total of what your genetics can provide. We're not talking about screening zygotes as in the Pre-Vet program; we can maximise your personal potential with the genetics that you already have by controlling their expression within an adult human. With this procedure, you can become everything your mother always wanted you to be."

"Frank, I'll come if you want me to, of course. But I'll need a briefing on what you guys expect from me before we attend that meeting."

"Done deal."

The Pre-Vet Program screened zygotes, fertilised embryos, created by couples to illustrate, in booklet form, what each embryo would grow up to be. The booklet presented adult depictions of each zygote, including height, eye, and hair colour, as well as numerous other physical attributes like intelligence and athletic ability. Pre-Vet eliminated genetic disabilities in the screened embryos and reduced the burden on the healthcare system, making it the preferred social and governmental option. As a result, authorised pregnancies came with certain healthcare benefits and educational subsidies, so almost all parents chose to fertilise as many embryos as they could and screen before implantation. Natural pregnancies were not covered by government health insurance. The economic argument in favour of subsidising Pre-Vet was that it would produce a populace free of genetic impairments; a fitter, smarter citizenry is more productive and economically beneficial than one burdened by genetically predisposed, underperforming individuals. Predispositions to obesity, alcoholism, and violence could also be identified and screened out. Besides, the world population was nearing ten billion, and the average IQ had been declining worldwide for many years because underprivileged families were having more children without the means to educate and develop those offspring intellectually. There were, as always, those who believed that natural was the best way, the only way, which by 2065 was distinctly a minority view in America. Those who participated in the Pre-Vet Program found themselves at a significant birth-cost advantage, and their children were on average ahead of natural-birth children competing for academic positions, jobs, and even mates. Selection was limited to the number of zygotes a couple could produce, so the decision was largely left to them as they would have to bear the financial implications of the outcome. Eugenics became fashionable again and was now politically acceptable at the molecular level. All zygotes showing genetic disease-based impairments were legally required to be destroyed because carrying them to full term would be a financial burden on the state, not just the burden that genetic diseases place on the health system, but the displacement of otherwise economically productive parents who would have to care for such offspring.

What Jack had developed at AIOGEN for the American military had made him integral to national security, a fact that influenced the BIE when they authorised his Replant. The Augment soldier was a powerful weapon and, since the Third Afghan War, had become pivotal in the military's deployment strategies in most conflict scenarios. It was known that a squad of Augments could be deployed in any given area and effectively left to their own devices to achieve their assigned objectives. Best of all, they could execute those tasks with minimal collateral damage to the civilian population or infrastructure because they were on foot and because they only did what they were sent to do. Due to their size and capabilities, there was little to stop them from achieving their objectives. They would even clean up after themselves before leaving.

The American development of smart bombs had peaked by 2035. These weapons had reached a stage where they were small enough to turn off a light in a specific house or large enough to destroy an entire neighbourhood. However, smart bombs were very expensive to manufacture, had a single-use deployment protocol, and for all their sophistication, they were still bombs and, therefore, highly impersonal and sometimes embarrassingly imprecise. Most significantly, it had been realised that a war could not be waged from the air alone, and that there were tasks, very specific tasks, that needed to be done on the ground and in some cases, done carefully enough so as not to escalate the conflict.

The Augments were not indestructible — they were living tissue — but they were replaceable. Replacement was also reasonably priced, thanks to the economies of scale achieved by producing smaller domestic models that AIOGEN sold for use as household servants. Better still for the military, the death or injury of an Augment in any conflict left no emotional or social scar. The terror effect of killing the nation's finest young men and women had been eliminated, along with the associated adverse political reactions to such casualties. The military was left free to prosecute any authorised campaign, constrained only by economic considerations and the political will to carry it out. If an Augment was destroyed, it was simply replaced, leaving no grieving widow or widower behind to console, or irate member of Congress to placate.

There were no human ramifications resulting from the destruction of an Augment, except for the enemy. The Augments used by, and designed specifically for, the US military were ruthless and efficient killers programmed to show no remorse or mercy for an armed enemy combatant. If their opponent was armed and hostile, they would be dead sooner rather than later. Like the smart bombs that came before them, there would be no prisoners, but with Augments, there would be no civilian casualties either. The ferocity of this approach amplified the psychological effect of their deployment. The utility of the Augments meant that the source of any hostile shot against any American force could be found, no matter how long it took or what terrain it occupied, day or night. Endlessly, tirelessly, that enemy combatant would be hunted down and killed. There was nowhere for an enemy to hide, and now very few nations willing to harbor them. There was no nation capable of preventing Augments from entering their territory if that was their assigned task. This was now all known and proven, and on the battlefield, the Augment was feared.

This new military and logistical reality had caused a substantial shift in diplomatic thinking surrounding localised conflicts. Borders had become irrelevant and the pursuit of the enemy combatant became unconstrained because collateral damage was now controllable. The prosecution of the conflict became more justifiable because the consequences of that pursuit were more inconsequential, except, of course, for any fugitive enemy. Incursion into any sovereign territory became more acceptable because of the precision with which the Augments acted and the fact that there was no nation capable of stopping a determined squad of Augments from doing whatever they were sent there to do. The USA was very keen to keep this technology to itself.

During the latter part of the Third Afghan War, enemy combatants had used Iran as a safe haven. At the time, there were political sensitivities associated with any ground incursion across the border, and airstrikes were not achieving their objectives but were inflaming tensions with Iran without productive military outcomes. The first substantial deployment of Augments in history took place in south-eastern Iran. A large enclave of hardened extremist fighters had gathered thirty kilometres inside the Iranian border. A squad of twenty-two Augments was dropped into the region amid great social and diplomatic controversy on all sides of the conflict. There was no attempt to hide the fact that they had been deployed — the US Military wanted the world to watch. Two weeks later, the combatants hiding in Iran had been chased through most of southern Iran right to the opposite border. The Augments didn't stop until all enemy combatants had been found and killed. Their effectiveness and ruthlessness surprised even their most ardent advocates. In the process, as it happened, no civilian was killed or seriously injured. Except for a few dubious civilian complaints which were later discarded by an international tribunal, the operation had been what the military regarded as a clean kill. No house was demolished, no infrastructure was destroyed, even the livestock escaped unharmed. Once the Augments had been extracted, it was as if they were never there, except that every last one of the nearly thousand-strong enemies they had been sent to find were dead. The Head of the Joint Chiefs described the operation as "immaculate," a term emblazoned, George Bush-like, on a banner behind her in her press conference to announce the success of the action after the Augments had been extracted. It was a single-word headline looking for the front page of a newspaper, and the world press didn't disappoint. There were large elements of the media who felt at the time that she would eventually have to eat that word and the banner it was written on, inevitably looking foolish they thought. But with a 100% elimination of the enemy combatants by a twenty-two-unit squad of Augments, zero civilian casualties, and the quick closure of the war shortly thereafter, the tagline stuck and no one ended up looking foolish. It had never been determined why the Iranian diplomatic response to the incursion had been so reserved. Some believed that it was because of the complete absence of collateral damage, while more pragmatic observers saw it as a direct result of witnessing the capabilities and effectiveness of the Augments firsthand. There was a natural reluctance, most thought, on behalf of Iran to see the conflict widened "given the circumstances." Whichever it was, the benchmark had been set and the reputation of the Augments had been cast.

The Augments, as a military tool, had become popular within the American Military Forces. They were feared on the battlefield, and in later years, the mere threat of their use was sufficient to "normalise" most situations or subdue potentially rebellious sections of "unassimilated" enemy territory without a shot being fired. Since the large-scale deployment of the Augments to military service, human defence force casualties in conflict situations, excluding accidents, had fallen to almost zero.

The story was similar in law enforcement. Crime rates had fallen in all major U.S. cities that used the police version of the Augment, and with the recent rollout of law enforcement Augments to beat duty in New York, it was widely believed that violent street crime was set to be completely eliminated, provided that sufficient numbers were deployed. The effectiveness of the Augments in a police situation was highly regarded, and they could be relied upon to avoid injuring non-criminal citizens. They were exceedingly polite and were well-liked by the law-abiding populace. However, when they issued instructions with their deep, reverberating voices, everyone in the immediate vicinity, criminal or otherwise, paid attention.

At the One-Nine, Jacobs caught up with Cleary on his way back from a late lunch.

"We've got a lead on that missing protester. And you're not going to believe this, he's got a jacket."

"That's what I'm talking about right there. Good work. Forget this spy cloak and dagger nonsense. Let me see."

"The guy is ex-Special Forces, a Marine no less. His name is Jake Thomason. He's been written up a few times but never arrested."

"Those guys know a thing or two about blowing shit up, don't they?" Cleary handed Jacobs back the file after giving it a cursory glance, and he turned back toward the elevators.

It was late in the day when Cleary and Jacobs pulled up outside the premises where the missing protester worked — a warehouse across the river in Union City.

"What do we know about this guy?" Cleary asked Jacobs before getting out of the now-parked car.

"Not a lot. Honourable discharge. No arrests. Got a picture of him here. Looks tough. Do you think we need backup?"

"Let's give the guy the benefit of the doubt, given his service."

Both men exited the car and headed for the service entrance of the warehouse.

"You got a Thomason working here?" Jacobs called out to the nearest worker.

"Out the back, in the office," the warehouseman pointed to a ramshackle office in the corner of the warehouse, next to a large open shutter door which led to the outdoor hardstand at the back of the premises, which was sparsely populated with shipping containers.

"You Thomason?" Cleary had recognised him from his photo, so he didn't wait for an answer. "I'm Detective Cleary, and this is Detective Jacobs from the One Nine."

Thomason was a large man in his late forties, strongly built but a little overweight, with arms like oversized piano legs. His worn, unshaven face had an expression of a man who had seen everything and feared none of it. He'd fought in a lot of wars, mostly with himself, at night, alone.

"Can I see some ID?"

The officers obliged.

"You were at a demonstration outside the MET on the night of the 26th. We were just wondering what put you there."

"Just a concerned citizen, officer. Is that a problem?"

"Might be. You seem to know the date pretty well. There was a bombing that night. You know anything about that?" Cleary was, as usual, straight to the point, but this time without any bravado.

"I heard it go off. Didn't see anything."

Thomason took off his gloves, put them in his hard hat, and threw both onto a desk that was grey with sediment and covered with the bits and pieces of what looked like a dozen unfinished jobs. He strolled out to the back lot and lit up a cigarette. The officers followed him.

"Nasty habit."

"Well, I can always grow a new pair of lungs if I need 'em, eh! I'm sure those boys down at AIOGEN wouldn't mind."

"Why weren't you carrying ID the night of that demonstration?"

"I was. Oh! You mean that phone ID transmitter nonsense? Don't use one."

"What, you don't use public transport, public utilities?"

"If I can't drive it or walk it, I don't go."

"Is that part of a religion or something?"

"No religion. Just don't like the intrusion."

"What else don't you like?"

"I don't like you much."

Thomason looked into Cleary's eyes, assessing. Cleary didn't flinch. Thomason didn't hold the gaze long, he was the first to look away, no war today; he had gathered what he needed to know. If he wanted a fight, one was available. Cleary had also seen his fair share of conflict and was still standing.

"Do you know a Jack Pierce?"

"Yes, he's the head of Augment technology at AIOGEN."

Cleary looked at Jacobs, somewhat surprised that this man knew who and what Jack Pierce was, and moreover, that he was willing to openly admit it.

"Is he someone you don't like?"

"I don't like any of that stuff they do up there, that Augment nonsense. It put decent Marines out of work. Today's Marine is some pimple-faced midget pushing buttons in a bunker. When I went through, men were men, and Augments were experiments in a test tube."

"You don't like the Marines anymore, either?"

"I love the Corps, let's get that clear. Those things are not Marines. There's no honour in what they do. The men in those bunkers wouldn't have the guts to shoot a man face-to-face. They'd soil themselves."

"Shooting someone is a serious matter, Sergeant, even in war. What about blowing one up?"

"I didn't blow up that AIOGEN guy if that's what you're asking."

"So you know it was Pierce in the car?"

"Everybody knows it was him in the car, detective. He's a celebrity, isn't he? All those people are corrupt. What they do to the sacred human body. They're building things God never intended. And that Pre-Vet stuff. We're going to get a whole human race that looks identical. They are all going to meet the Devil himself, I can tell you that."

"And it's your job to introduce them, right?"

"Get fucked."

"Those are some strong sentiments there, Sergeant. Perhaps you'd like to come down to the station with us and share some more of your insights."

"You guys aren't taking me anywhere. Either arrest me or get lost. I've got work to do."

Thomason threw his cigarette butt on the ground, extinguishing it with his boot, then slowly headed back towards his office.

"That's not nice. You're hurting my feelings," Cleary called after him.

Thomason stopped and turned back to the officers, stretching out his clenched fists as if offering them to be cuffed.

"Make your move, detective. Either get on with it or get lost. But I think you're going to need some backup if you're planning on ruining my evening."

Cleary thought carefully, looking Thomason straight in the eye. He agreed with the Sergeant's assessment: he and Jacobs were probably about twelve men short. He didn't think that some strong beliefs were enough of a case to risk damage to his new winter coat.

"We might take a raincheck this time. But don't leave town or anything, because we are going to need to talk to you again."

Thomason turned to walk away with a dismissive wave, saying, "Well, come heavy because I don't believe in the police state either."

Cleary, with a quizzical look on his face, turned to Jacobs as they were walking back toward the car. "How the heck has this guy never been arrested?"

Jamison had reported back to her boss in Paris about her suspicions of a link between the murder of Jack Pierce and the technology theft. Her boss had agreed that she should stay in NYC to investigate the possible connection between the bombing at AIOGEN,

Zimmermann, and the information that Marsolet had provided. She sat down with fellow agent Jim Briers, whom the local Bureau office had assigned to assist her with the case. They began to review what they had on Zimmermann, Jack Pierce, AIOGEN, and the Yemeni arms dealers.

"This looks interesting," Briers offered.

Briers was a very young-looking twenty-seven-year-old agent with no field experience. He was dressed in a black Armani suit with an open-neck white shirt. Jamison thought to herself that a red tie would go well with that suit; she was old enough to remember a time when men wore ties.

"You see this guy in this photo here," Briers pointed to a face on the photograph he was holding. "That's our Yemeni arms guy. We only know him by his codename: Topaz. And look here, here he is again in this photo, picked up by routine terrorist surveillance in New York. And guess who that is talking to him? We need to start a plug board..."

Briers suddenly dashed out of the room without telling Jamison who it was he saw in the photo. She was left standing there, shaking her head, arms folded. He returned moments later, pushing a mobile whiteboard and began rummaging through his desk for some magnetic buttons, which he intended to use — old school — to stick the photo onto the whiteboard, a task he quickly accomplished.

"You see this guy here," he said, pointing again to the same photo now aptly positioned on his whiteboard.

"Yeees," Jamison responded politely.

"That guy is Imran Kalmati. He is the Head of Pakistani intelligence for North America, working out of their consulate here in NYC. The person sitting next to him is your guy, Zimmermann. The Bureau has suspected this Kalmati of playing both sides and..."

"Give me the short version, will you, kid? Do we read a lot of files in our spare time?"

Briers wasn't quite sure how to take Jamison's gruff attitude, so he truncated his briefing.

"Kalmati's on tape, poking around AIOGEN employees, making noises about big bucks for good info — and so is Zimmermann. My guess is that the three of them are collaborating on an intellectual property deal that involves senior AIOGEN personnel. Is that simple enough?"

"Don't get smart with me, kid. I'm armed. I'm also tired, and I have a personal life, you know. I'm not in town long. Which AIOGEN executives was he talking to?"

"All of them, I think. I have a list here. He got an invite to that function they held the night of the bombing."

"Don't you think that's a bit coincidental?"

"I'm just looking at some of the transcripts from the phone taps. Most of it seems pretty innocuous."

"The fact that he's at the function, I mean, the night of the bombing. Don't you think someone like him might know how to arrange for some fireworks if needed? Can you get me a copy of those tapes?"

"Sure, no problem."

"Good, send them to my notepad tonight. I need to get out of here before I collapse — I'm still on Paris time. And can you find out from the social secretary at AIOGEN who invited Kalmati to the party? Also, send someone to pick up that Zimmerman guy in the morning and let me know what time they are going to have him in here." She leaves, then immediately returns, plodding back in the door of the office. "And call that cop at NYPD, Cleary, at the One Nine, and ask him if he wants to be here for that Zimmermann interview, but don't tell him about Kalmati. I don't want him sticking his nose in Bureau affairs. He thinks the perpetrator is some gangster with a chip on his shoulder about AIOGEN or someone personally linked to Pierce, OK? Let's just let the locals go about their business," she said, again turning toward the door and gesturing with both her hands palm down in a *let's leave well enough alone* motion.

"Sure, no problem, and I'll go home at some point as well, maybe get something to eat, if that's OK?" Briers was talking to himself, Jamison had already left. "Then I'll fly to Paris for croissants and bring some back in the morning for the meeting."

Cleary was staring at a perplexed Briers in interview room 12B at the Bureau's NYC headquarters at 10:00 am the following morning. Zimmermann, whom Cleary had brought with him, and Jamison made up the quorum.

"Give birth overnight, did we, Special Agent Jamison?" Cleary asked. "He's a nice-looking young agent. Who's the father?"

"Put it back in your pants, Cleary." Jamison got up and turned away from Cleary so he wouldn't see her holding back a laugh. She thought that was pretty funny, and knew Briers didn't think so.

"Mr. Zimmermann, can you tell me about your contacts with a Yemeni arms dealer known as Topaz?" Jamison opened the batting, standing.

"I told Officer Cleary here that it was all a misunderstanding."

"That's Detective First Grade Cleary, you jerk," Cleary interjected.

"I'm not talking about the incident a few years ago. I'm talking about a couple of weeks ago," Jamison continued, and Cleary's ears perked up. "It doesn't look to me like a misunderstanding."

Jamison pushed two photographs across the table to Zimmermann, both were of him having lunch with the man the New York Bureau knew as Topaz. Jamison had begun to believe that this Topaz was the arms dealer that Marsolet had fingered in Paris, a man he had named Yasser Fahd. She had sent a copy of the photo over to the Paris Bureau to get a positive ID from Marsolet.

"That looks like a pretty serious conversation," Jamison said, then dropped a copy of a bank statement from Mr. Zimmermann's jewellery business on top of the photographs as she walked past. "And that looks like a pretty serious amount of money, third from the top. We traced it back to a Swiss bank account and, after some trouble, to a Hong Kong bank account in the name of your company, Mr. Zimmermann. Seems like a lot to pay for jewellery and a lot of trouble to hide it?"

"It was a loan, not a sale. That guy arranged a loan for me and he didn't call himself Topaz, Jim something."

"He doesn't look like a Jim to me," Cleary said as he helped himself to the photos and the bank statement, studying both.

Cleary's application to get a copy of Zimmermann's bank records was still in the works at NYPD. "There's nothing going out of here that looks like interest payments, or principal repayments. Can I get me one of those loans?"

"Look, your guys didn't pursue this back then, why are you coming at me now about it?"

Jamison knew that Zimmermann was deliberately let go on the previous occasion to see where he would lead them, which was how they got onto Kalmati. She ignored his question.

"Who do you know at AIOGEN?"

"Nobody particularly." Cleary was about to contradict him and remind him of the phone calls to Pierce, but Jamison intervened before he got the chance.

"We have you calling as many as five of their senior employees around the time of the bombing, including you contacting Jack Pierce two weeks before. Just selling jewellery, were we?"

"Five employees?" Cleary said out loud. "You shithead, you didn't tell us that." Cleary looked at Zimmermann for a response, knowing that he hadn't said anything to him about any other calls when Cleary had asked about the calls to Pierce. "You didn't make those calls from your cell or your office phone because we would have picked those up when we looked at your phone records." Cleary was talking through clenched teeth. "Using a burner, were we? That doesn't look good for you, Mr. Zimmermann. What exactly are you trying to hide here?"

Jamison also decided it was time to push harder.

"Isn't it true, Mr. Zimmermann, that you were following up on leads provided to you by your Yemeni contact? You were recruiting. Isn't that true?"

"No, no."

"Be careful what you say here, Mr. Zimmermann. This is an official interview. They aren't the only photographs we have. And we have some video as well, full colour, surround sound."

"I think I need to speak to my lawyer."

Jamison laughed.

"This isn't the local PD you're talking to here." Jamison's voice became loud and assertive, and she began to point her finger at

Zimmermann. "You've been dealing with a bunch of terrorists in Paris, and we have the emails to prove it. I'll have you six thousand miles away in some country you've never heard of and could never find on a map before you can say 'I'll take the cell on the left, please.'" She put both hands on the table in front of Zimmermann and was now talking straight into his face. "Your lawyer's not going to want to come find you over there and if he does, we'll lock him up, too. Tell me what you know or this is going to get very ugly, very quickly."

"Wait… wait?" Zimmermann began to think that his position was untenable.

"What, what?" Jamison mocked. "Were you recruiting at AIOGEN?"

"…Yes," Zimmermann shrunk back into his seat.

"Who was your main target?"

"Pierce."

"Did you get him?"

"Maybe."

"What do you mean 'maybe'? Don't you mess with me, sir, I'm not one to be messed with."

The men in the room were beginning to feel a little inadequate.

"I mean I don't know. The guy you call Topaz had someone else talking to him, another guy that I hadn't met. Kalmati introduced them."

Jamison ignored the reference to Kalmati. "You had Pierce killed, didn't you, just to motivate the others to be more receptive?"

"No, no… this isn't a war, it's just business. These people get approached all the time. You Americans shouldn't be the only ones with this technology. We don't kill people, we pay them. I wouldn't know the first thing…"

"So you had the Yemeni guy do it."

"No, he has the same approach. The contact is no good to us dead, and if we made an example of one, it would just scare the others off and attract attention. I'm sitting here because someone got killed."

"You bet your ass that's why you're sitting here," Cleary chimed in. "And you arranged it. What were you supposed to do next?"

"They told me to lay off. They told me to put it all on hold. I'm not sure whether it was because of the bombing or because they hooked someone. I don't know."

"Hooked who? Pierce?"

"I don't know. I told you."

Jamison believed him, maybe. She thought Cleary was right; this guy didn't have the vibe of a killer.

"Briers, take this guy down to booking, will you? And make him sign a statement. Get a printout of the record of the interview. Make sure he fills in the gaps."

"Booking, what are you charging me with? I need to call my daughter."

"Take your pick on the charge, sale of state secrets will do. Just get him out of here, will you. Damn jerk." Jamison didn't like snitches or terrorists. "Do you know what would happen if that technology turned up in the Middle East, you prick? It would make suicide bombers look like pretzel vendors." Jamison was venting the residual adrenaline in her system.

Briers pulled Zimmermann to his feet and escorted him out of the room.

"Let him call his daughter," she shouted out the door after Briers had left with the prisoner.

Cleary looked at Jamison, reassessing his opinion of her and gathering himself after the performance.

"What?" Jamison said.

"That was quite something. Do you do a lot of that? In case you were wondering, I was paying attention. There's a ton you're not telling me about this case, and I think you're about to seriously upset me. Who's Topaz and this Kalmati guy? You don't want a turf war on this, Special Agent. I expect a full report on what you've got on Zimmermann and this Topaz character on my notepad by close of business today, or we've got a problem. Clear it with whomever you have to, but decide today or I'm taking this right up the chain and I'll be screaming obstruction."

Jamison was suddenly alone in the interview room, feeling a little chastened. "Damn," she muttered to herself. Usually, she couldn't care less about what the local police thought or did, but she didn't want a breakdown in communication with the NYPD either. Perhaps Cleary was feeling a little bruised, a little insecure, she rationalised. He had already had his go at Zimmermann and came up empty. As she collected her things and her thoughts, she brushed off what Cleary had said and allowed her concern to be replaced by a feeling of self-satisfaction. She had only been in town a day and a half and she had made good progress; one arrest, albeit the obvious one, but probably not the guy who did Pierce. Nonetheless, it was fair to say that she liked this part of her work very much, and right now, she felt she was pretty good at it.

CHAPTER FIVE

The year 1938 had been one of change in Germany. Frederick was now eight. Hitler was *Time Magazine*'s "Man of the Year," having beaten out Gandhi and Roosevelt for that privilege. This was largely because of the economic miracle he had performed in Germany, making the progress made by Roosevelt's "New Deal" look very modest by comparison. In March of that year, Austria had become part of Germany once again in the Anschluss. That same month, Hitler had pledged to protect the German minorities in Czechoslovakia and the Sudetenland from the racial violence against ethnic Germans, which had become chronic in those territories. The Austro-Hungarian Empire had been dismantled at the end of the Great War, and the Habsburg monarchy had collapsed. Czechoslovakia and various other states were made independent from Germany as a result of that breakup, due in part to initiatives by America's Woodrow Wilson, aimed at neutralising Germany's economic and military strength. All these states still contained large and now-isolated German populations. Hitler had come to power saying that the Treaty of Versailles had to be overturned not only because of these territorial losses and the shattered German community of Middle Europe, but also due to the enormous economic burdens on Germany resulting from the payment of financial reparations extorted by the British, French, and Americans. History would later show that the Treaty was so ill-conceived that it did, in hindsight, guarantee further regional conflict.

Hitler had pledged the reunification of the German-speaking territories of Middle Europe, including the reunification of Germany with East Prussia and Danzig, by reacquiring what the Nazis referred to as the Polish Corridor, a section of coastal Poland that separated Germany from these two now separate ethnic German states. In Czechoslovakia, the tensions between the Germans and the local government were temporarily resolved by the signing of the Munich Pact. Ratified by Britain, France, and Germany in September of that same year, it ceded the Sudetenland, then part of Czechoslovakia, back to Germany as a concession to Hitler. It was this document that Neville Chamberlain would end up waving to the assembled press on his return to Britain from the Munich Conference, claiming that he had secured "peace in our time," words that were to haunt him until his death from bowel cancer in late 1940. Hitler saw the Munich Pact as an entirely different piece of paper. For Germany, it was simply the first steps towards undoing what had been imposed on them at the end of the Great War. It was a beginning of repair, not an end to negotiations as Chamberlain had suggested.

Czechoslovakia broke off formal alliances with France and Britain as a result of the Munich Pact, leaving it unprotected by any formal military association with the West and thus paving the way for its reacquisition by Germany using the force of arms. In executing the Munich Pact, France and England lamented the loss of the Czechoslovakian army to the international allegiances assembled to keep Germany in check, some four hundred thousand well-trained but poorly equipped men. The die had been cast. Hitler saw Britain's and France's inaction towards the eventual forcible reunification with Czechoslovakia as tacit approval of his plans for Middle Europe. However, England and France's acquiescence was due to the absence of any alliance with Czechoslovakia at the time of the invasion. That inaction, and the associated lack of clarity regarding the reasoning behind it, sent what Hitler interpreted as a very clear message: that the remainder of his well-articulated program could now proceed without objection.

Hitler perceived these changes as the inevitable return to conditions reminiscent of 1867 when the Habsburg realm, The Central Empire, consisted of Germany plus parts of modern-day Poland, Montenegro, Romania, Serbia, and Ukraine, along with all of the Czech Republic, Slovakia, Slovenia, Croatia, Austria, Hungary, Danzig, East Prussia, and Bosnia-Herzegovina. There was no clear indication from the West at that time as to how far Germany could go in its endeavours to reunite loyal German communities in Europe, but Hitler had made it very clear that he intended to reassemble them all. It would be later asserted that any German attempt to re-acquire territories other than what had been conceded in the Munich Pact - namely, the Sudetenland - would be viewed by England and France as a resurgence of German imperialism that needed to be contained. However, their actions at the time indicated differently, and Germany of the day believed, with good reason, that the West's acquiescence regarding the Czechoslovakian invasion was support for their entire reunification objectives.

Lord Halifax, then Lord President of the Council and fourth in rank among the Great Officers of State in the United Kingdom - only below the Lord High Treasurer but above the Lord Privy Seal, and soon to be Foreign Secretary under Chamberlain - had personally communicated to Hitler during a hunting trip to Germany in November of 1937 that England considered Germany's claims in Czechoslovakia, Poland, Danzig, and East Prussia as legitimate. Most of the British cabinet at the time and many political commentators saw German reunification as inevitable, including King Edward VIII and the American Ambassador to Great Britain, Joseph Kennedy. His son, John F. Kennedy, later concurred when, as President, he assessed Hitler as "one of the greatest men; the old trusted him, the young idolised him. It was the worship of a national hero who had served his country... Within a few years, Adolf Hitler will emerge from the hatred that surrounds him as one of the most significant figures that ever lived." It was only after the dust had settled on a devastated Europe in 1945, with twenty million Europeans lying dead, that Halifax, Chamberlain, and numerous other senior British ministers and high-ranking international counsellor officials, including the now ex-King and Joseph Kennedy, were labelled as appeasers. Once a term used to describe peace-seeking leaders, by 1945, "appeaser" had become a term of derision. British, French, and American historians post-World War Two decided that Hitler did not seek reunification but aimed for total world domination, a strange verdict given that Hitler knew little of any world outside the bounds of the Austro-Hungarian Empire and had never written or spoken about any plans beyond the reunification of Germany. However, after the Allies had expended so much financially in the Second World War, with so many lives lost and so much devastation inflicted, it was decided that a greater sin had to be placed on Hitler's shoulders than his pursuit of German reunification. If Hitler was only acting in the national interest of Germany, how could the Western powers justify their disinterest in a negotiated peace that would have averted such loss of life, leaving in the end all territories they supposedly sought to liberate in the hands of the Soviets, with Europe divided? As it turned out, they eventually discovered the greatest of all excuses lying in the rubble, one not related to Hitler's world domination, but to racist hatred. However, to assert that the Holocaust, while abhorrent, was their reason for refusing at that time to deal with Hitler is of course pure fiction. With the benefit of hindsight, political and diplomatic engagement with Germany was needed prior to matters getting so out of control, as Joseph Kennedy had called for at the time, to both avoid a war and perhaps prevent the events that culminated in the *Holocaust*. Leaving Hitler isolated to act alone and in defiance of the West proved perilous. However, following Churchill's ascension, the English were not in favour of reconciliation with Germany. Like many key decisions made in a democracy, Churchill's position was a product of the system's adversarial nature, with one side of politics denouncing the other in an attempt to differentiate itself in the pursuit of power — Chamberlain the appeaser versus Churchill the warmonger. As it turned out, Churchill was not a visionary; he was simply a politician.

In the 1930s, appeasement was considered a legitimate, even necessary, political strategy after Woodrow Wilson's League of Nations failed to provide collective security. In reality, few appeasers would concede everything for the sake of peace, and few warmongers, except perhaps Churchill, would not compromise to achieve the same objective, with the truth often lying in the middle ground of politics. Nearly one hundred percent of the American population at the time were proud appeasers, including Joseph Kennedy. Today, such individuals would more likely be termed pacifists. Americans had had their fill of European conflicts in the Great War. However, by 1950, appeasement was not viewed in the same positive light, even though the alternative strategy, championed by Churchill, had seen twenty million dead in Europe alone and vast sections of the continent devastated. Much was made by historians about the just punishment meted out to Germany for both the war and the violence against the Jews, but the more pertinent question was why the war and the genocide were not prevented. Even more frustrating was that the stated purpose of the war was to "liberate" Poland and the other states reacquired by Germany in the 1930s, an objective that was never achieved despite the grave cost paid by all Europeans. Half of Europe, including all former German territories and half of Germany itself, lay in ruins under the iron boot of the Soviets, with Stalin, Churchill's ally and friend, continuing to perpetrate mass murder of Jews, kulaks, and political adversaries on a scale never seen before in history, dwarfing the genocide in Germany. By the time of Stalin's death in March of 1953, over ten percent of the population of Soviet-controlled states had been murdered, all with the acquiescence of Churchill and his allies.

By 1938, the relatively uncontested forced repatriation of Czechoslovakia and the reunification with the Sudetenland had placed Hitler on a pedestal with the German people. This, coupled with his highly successful restarting of the German economy, put him in a position where the German populace felt that he could do no wrong, a view that he personally shared. The response to his initiatives led Hitler to conclude that France and England had no appetite for contesting his publicly stated territorial aims or his demonstrated economic management credentials. Within four years of his appointment, Hitler had transformed Germany's economy from one with over sixty percent unemployment to one with single-digit unemployment. By 1938, he had put the country back to work in what can fairly be called the greatest economic miracle ever seen in the post-industrialised world. Much would later be made of Roosevelt's "New Deal," but by comparison,

Hitler's economic management after the Great Depression stands as a truly remarkable feat. Historians often overlook these realities when assessing Hitler, tritely asserting that he had somehow "mesmerised" the German people into following him through his speeches, to the point where the occupying powers post-World War Two outlawed the rebroadcasting of any of Hitler's speeches, fearing they might work his evil magic once again on an apparently susceptible populace. The reality was far simpler — there was no oratory black magic; he had earned their trust by putting them back to work.

Frederick had once again successfully predicted the outcome of the negotiations in Munich. He even suggested to Hitler that he should exploit Chamberlain's heavy smoking habit by insisting that the Munich conference be strictly non-smoking. Hitler, himself being a non-smoker, appreciated the idea. The boy asserted that it would create a higher level of anxiety and therefore urgency in the British delegation, causing them to push for a resolution. Hitler took the suggestion literally, holding the conference at an Austrian palace where the protection of the ancient artefacts required a no-smoking rule. Whether it actually impacted the result in Munich is unlikely, but the outcome was very much to Hitler's liking, and he regarded the boy as a tactical genius.

In September of that same year, Germany erupted into social discord, with Jewish synagogues and commercial establishments being attacked and firebombed during a night that was later called Kristallnacht, or "The Night of the Broken Glass." Thousands of Jewish Germans lost their lives that night or later in internment camps. As Frederick well knew, it was a turning point in Germany's treatment of European Jews and political adversaries. He believed that if he didn't act now, he would lose any chance of influencing future events. Though his task seemed daunting, there was no time for Frederick to waver. It was time to utilise the credibility he had built with the Führer to achieve his objectives.

As had become his habit, Hitler sought the boy out for one of his regular discussions, inviting him to a dinner that included only Hitler, Speer, and Frederick.

"Besides, it will give us the opportunity to rebuild," Speer said, concluding a conversation about the events of Kristallnacht.

"You have been strangely quiet, Frederick," Hitler noted. "It is not like you to refrain from expressing your opinion on such matters."

"Yes, but you will not like what I have to say, my Führer."

"Since when has that stopped you? If you have the courage to say it, then I believe Herr Speer and I can handle hearing it."

"I do not approve of the loss of life, my Führer, especially at the hands of a public mob. I think it undermines what we aspire to be as a nation."

"But they are Jews, my boy, good riddance. And besides, it wasn't just a public mob; our own people were there, instigating matters at my command," Hitler retorted.

"I don't care who they were. Maintaining public order is vital to the National Socialist Agenda, and it must remain so to prevent a loss of public support for the government. Additionally, I think there's a much more important issue at stake."

"And what would that be?" Speer interjected, coldly throwing his napkin onto the table, clearly displeased with Frederick's criticisms.

"It gives comfort to our enemies, Herr Speer, something they can use to justify their opposition to us and strengthen their portrayal of us as barbaric and poorly led." There was a chilly silence, but Frederick dared to continue. "Much, if not all, of what you have accomplished so far, my Führer, has been to rectify the grave injustice done to us at Versailles. You've done as you promised the German people you would, and you've achieved this with minimal violent conflict. Simultaneously, you've revitalised our country's economy and restored our national pride, all within an astonishingly short period of time. The people regard you as their savior, no offense intended to Our Lord. In all areas – the economy, public works, spearheaded by Herr Speer, and the return of lands, even the reunification of Germany – you have uplifted our nation to a higher level of prosperity and dignity."

"Yes, and we must move forward and use that momentum to rid this country, this continent, of a great scourge," Hitler stated.

"And in so doing, we risk losing our own souls and forever condemning this country to be labelled as barbarians."

"I don't like your tone, boy. The elimination of the Jews is central to our party's core beliefs," Hitler retorted, his disapproval mounting. "Our platform is well known and accepted by the people. My God, even Marx proposed it. Churchill himself wrote of the sterilisation of lesser peoples and was an ardent advocate of eugenics."

"Churchill is a hypocrite. His view of life is coloured by what he sees through the bottom of his whiskey glass. He fears German domination of the European economy. They see how much you have accomplished here and how little they have done since the invention of the steam engine. India can only prop up their economy for so long. Churchill needs to dominate you and Europe. It is not you seeking world domination; it's him aiming for European domination. He will say whatever is politically convenient to achieve his schoolboy comic book ending to the German-English conflict, be it military or economic. Roosevelt is his puppet. He seeks to be a Rough Rider like his uncle, something he could never be from his wheelchair."

"You see Churchill for what he is, that's for sure," Hitler interjected.

"Herr Marx was speaking of a war of the social classes, and he foresaw a time when the underclass would need to be killed off to make room for a new communist community, replaced by what Herr Marx asserted would be a better generation," Frederick responded.

"That may be so, and Herr Stalin is doing his best to make that prediction come true," Speer chuckled. "He and Marx viewed Jews as that very underclass, Frederick."

"That is most certainly true, and history will judge them for it, but why do we follow a Marxist platform in the face of such barbarity from Stalin?"

"We are the National Socialists, my boy, and Marxist doctrine forms much of our original platform," Speer responded.

"But do we want to follow those accursed communists into hell itself?" Frederick demanded, striking the table.

"Settle down, Frederick, and lower your voice," Hitler commanded. "How can you say such a thing? It was Marx who asserted the need for a holocaust: 'The classes and races too weak to master the new conditions of life must give way… must perish in a revolutionary holocaust.' Those were his very words. I've had enough of this. I've come to care for you like a son, and this is how you repay me? Resolving the Jewish problem is the highest priority on our domestic agenda."

Frederick continued despite Hitler's admonishment. "Yes, and Marx will have his holocaust at Stalin's hand. There will be more than twenty million people killed by him and his henchmen before he's through, not counting the dead from the military campaigns about to be engaged. He will be reviled forever for what he's doing."

"Twenty million?" Speer asked. "How can you know such a thing?"

"We can use these acts of genocide against Stalin when we seek America's help to fight the Soviets once we have secured our position in Europe."

"America's help! You have lost your mind, Frederick," Speer interjected.

"Bear with me for a moment, please, my Führer," Frederick persisted, feeling it was now or never. "You can achieve all of your objectives, as stated in your political mandate, without staining this country with the blood that, regardless of the events that follow tonight, will never be removed."

"What events? Do you foresee something, boy? Speak if you do." Hitler's superstitions began to take hold.

"May I walk you through what I see as a potential future for our nation? If you're willing to listen, I will be satisfied. Perhaps in the drawing room?"

Hitler agreed to Frederick's presentation, and both men settled in with a drink, Speer with a cognac and Hitler with orange juice. They felt comfortable, thinking this discussion was going to be at least as engaging as one of Goebbels's films and, knowing Frederick, more controversial. Passions on the subject had waned. By relocating the discussion to the drawing room, fervour had been replaced with a desire for intellectual discourse and entertainment. Both men were convinced that the boy was wrong about the Jewish issue, but they both had enough regard for the boy's intellect and his ability to conceptualise the future that they were happy to hear him out.

"Next year, you will sign a pact with the Russians in an attempt to neutralise their interference with your plans in Poland. It's a pact you'll view simply as a delaying tactic for your ultimate intentions against the Soviets, particularly the liberation of Ukraine. The pact will usher in a time of great cooperation between Germany and the Soviets. In that pact, you will agree to divide Poland between you and cede the Baltic States to Russia."

"The boy has read my mind… again," Hitler said, and both men laughed. "A lucky guess, perhaps," he added, clearing his throat. "Right or wrong, Frederick, you must not speak of such things to anyone else. Obviously, you see the logic of bringing the Soviets with us into Poland. It creates a common border with them and provides us with options should they threaten our security. Their participation should neutralise any objections from the British."

"I could have told you this, my Führer, and I'm no master strategist like the boy here," Speer added, and both men laughed. "Something less predictable, Frederick, please, you disappoint."

"By March next year, you will form a pact with Italy, which will become known as the Pact of Steel. Mussolini will, however, prove to be nothing but a burden to you. Even now, he is hated by his people, and you will find he doesn't have the support to give you what he says he can give you."

"You are probably right," Hitler mumbled to himself under his breath. "The man is a pig, but perhaps an essential pig, and I like his politics."

"Your acquisition of the northern part of Poland, and subsequently East Prussia and Danzig, is certain. The Polish armies cannot stop you. The Soviets will join you, and you will divide Poland between you, giving you the border with the Soviets that you covet. It will take you no more than three weeks."

"Of course," Hitler quietly stated, unimpressed as he took a sip of his juice. "Unless they cooperate with my proposals, I shall introduce Poland to the Industrial Age. You are right, but it is an outcome that is also obvious… if that's what I decide to do."

"But the British and the French will not accept your reasons for going into Poland. The British and the French will declare war because they are committed to doing so by the Munich Pact."

"Not so. Ridiculous. They already wrote off Munich when we went into Czechoslovakia. They hate the Soviets more than I do, and they will see that I am simply seeking to regain the Polish Corridor and take the strategic advantage of a shared border. They will want me to keep the Russians under control. No, no, you're wrong here, Frederick. East Prussia and Danzig are our rightful territories. They will see, even the English will see, that we are merely reassembling what was ours in the first place. Besides, it would be futile to declare war. No one has the stomach for a repeat of the Great War."

"They will declare war but will not declare war against the Russians for reasons best known to themselves. The Russians are not part of the Munich Pact, to be sure, but that doesn't matter; it's the protection of Poland to which they are sworn. To that end, they will act against you but not against the Soviets for the very same transgression, the invasion of Poland, and why that is so is beyond my comprehension, indeed beyond the dictates of logic."

"That is not likely, Frederick. I would have thought they would have to act against both of us if they act at all. That is, in part, why they will not act. How could they justify a war against us and not Russia? Or, more pertinently, declaring war on both of us would be lunacy. That is part of my thinking in bringing Russia with us into Poland. I think, in the end, it's me that they will approach to go up against the Soviets, not the other way around."

"You forget Churchill's deep hatred of the German people and his vested political interests in a war with us. He has stated over and over again that Germany is THE great threat to Britain; his political reputation is intrinsically linked to that proposition. In the version of events that I'm giving you, the British and French will declare war against Germany and not Russia, and they will seek Russia's assistance to fight you. The Soviets will annex Estonia, Latvia, and Lithuania in the week after the Polish campaign is completed, and still, the British and the French will not declare war against them, only Germany."

"You must be wrong."

"The English and the French will wait for you to act after they declare war. Nothing will be done for six months."

Hitler and Speer laughed at the boy's prediction with Hitler musing, "That sounds right."

"The French soldiers will call it the silent war and contrast the inaction in jokes and songs with the devastation of the Great War, a repeat of which they deeply fear. During that time, the French will be looking anxiously for a proposal from you. The French would at this point negotiate, but in Britain, Chamberlain's reputation will be destroyed by supporters of Churchill, so no such negotiations will be possible. The Labor Opposition in England will call for a negotiated settlement with Germany as the preferred option to war. It is indeed the logical position for them to take. Churchill will, as he always has, take the position of complete victory against us or self-annihilation and consider no other course of action but war. Just ask the men who served under him in the past, such as the Australians at Gallipoli. Death or glory like the schoolboy novels he covets."

"I faced the Australians at Fromelles," Hitler confirmed. "They were good men, well-trained. They were sent to their slaughter at Gallipoli by that fat drunk in a campaign that any moron could see was fruitless. The idiot left them there at the bottom of those cliffs for nine months, nine months, being picked off by the Turks. The fat idiot couldn't admit he had got it wrong and persisted beyond all sense of logic."

"I rest my case in regard to this scenario then. You can see why he will act as I'm saying."

"You are a smart boy; you have me making your case for you. You knew I fought the Australians in the War. Very smart."

"Churchill's view will prevail regardless of how reckless it is, and he will become Prime Minister in late 1940. Chamberlain will be dead of the bowel cancer that is already running through his body. Churchill's bravado will later be described as heroic, and the political ridicule he has faced in recent years because of his suicidal attitudes towards Germany will be forgotten."

The two men became silent. There were specifics in Frederick's statement that seemed entirely plausible but impossible for the boy to know. The projection sent a chill up the spine of both men.

"Churchill will negotiate," Hitler asserted quietly after pausing to think. "We will beat the French if they persist with a war no one wants, and the English could not stand alone. He will negotiate. It would be pure lunacy to do otherwise. Why waste so many lives over nothing? I would leave them to their little game of castles and lords, and I would leave France to self-rule. I have no interest in either of them other than eliminating their opposition. If we did win a war against them, I would give them back everything they want except their beloved navy and their corrupted empire. I have no interest in anything other than the reunification of Germany."

"They will lose their empire by the late forties regardless of what happens in this coming war. India will succeed, and they will evacuate Palestine because of bombings executed by Jewish terrorists," Frederick confirms.

"Jewish what? The English must already know that it won't be possible for them to play colonialist any longer. But what of this European war you speak of?"

"You will beat the French, as you say," Frederick continues, "within a month of starting action against them, but even when you do defeat them, Churchill will not negotiate. 'Die or go down fighting' is all his whiskey-addled mind knows, regardless of the consequences. He will wager it all, millions of British and European lives and every building standing in London and Berlin on that war, and he will convince enough of the English that he is right to ensure that they continue to resist even if alone."

"No, no. I can envision him wanting to do it, but I can't see the others allowing him. If we have conquered the continent as you say, in such a forceful fashion as you assert, we can place the English in a position where their opposition will become inconsequential. We will bomb them back to the dark ages. We will sink their shipping. Churchill will lose popular support when London is nothing but a pile of bricks."

"All of which is logical, my Führer. Why continue in a war they cannot win? They will, of course, eventually see the light; what sensible leader would subject his people and his country to such devastation. Unless…"

"Unless what?" Speer asked with urgency, moving to the edge of his seat, now enthralled.

"Unless the Americans enter the war with the British while we are preoccupied with the Soviets. It will be too much for us. War on two fronts again. You have said it yourself, my Führer, that this was Germany's mistake in the Great War and that this would be a mistake that you would never repeat."

"Why would the Americans enter later if they don't have the stomach for it in the first place? They have no interest in European politics anymore. The memory of their losses last time they interfered is deeply ingrained in their psyche… as well it should be."

"You are correct in assuming that the mood amongst almost all Americans is that another European war would be a great folly and none of their business. Just ask Ambassador Kennedy. His speeches forewarned of a change in European politics and he counsels against American interference. The first war was costly to them both in human life and financially. Nearly twenty million people lost their lives in that war and one hundred and twenty thousand of them were Americans. Why would they repeat such insanity?"

"Exactly."

"But you know that this is not now, nor will it ever be, the opinion of Roosevelt. You know this to be true. He will continue to seek a reason to enter the war in Europe, even if against popular support. And you, my Führer, will give him that opportunity."

"I would not be so foolish as to do such a thing."

"Japan will attack the Americans at Pearl Harbor on December 7th of 1941."

"Can you give me the exact time, Frederick?" Hitler asked sarcastically, laughing.

"7:00 am, a six-carrier fleet, they will come in with the sun behind them just as dawn breaks."

Hitler sank back into his seat, not expecting such a frank and precise response. "How could you know that? Besides, what do I care about a Pacific war," he said with a dismissive wave of his hand, "and why would the Americans come into a European war just because they have been attacked by Japan?"

"Because you will have already signed a Pact with the Japanese in September of 1940, which will become known as the Tripartite Pact. You will declare war on the Americans consequent to your obligations under that Treaty. Japan will very soon now come looking to you for that agreement and for trading support because the Americans will blockade them supposedly in protest to their territorial ambitions in Asia."

"The Japanese have been acquiring territory in Asia for the last two hundred years. Why would the Americans suddenly act to blockade them now?"

"Because it is the very fact that you signed a Pact with the Japanese that Roosevelt will bring on the fight with them. Even his cousin Teddy, in the Roosevelt Corollary to the Monroe Doctrine, believed that Japanese rule of Korea and the Yellow Sea was valid and appropriate. Despite this, FDR will blockade Japan claiming that they are imperialists pointing to Korea as an example. He will impose the oil embargo knowing that the Japanese will retaliate with force against the blockade, and he will do it for the specific purpose of having you declare war on the Americans because of your alliance with the Japanese."

"It is a possibility," Speer confirms whilst Hitler mused. "The Japanese delegation in Berlin is making noises about some kind of alliance. And you could have known nothing about that, Frederick."

"The whole conflagration after December 11, 1941 when you and Italy declare war on the United States will become known as the Second World War. By 1945, Germany will itself be a pile of bricks and all that you and Herr Speer have built will be rubble, and all that you have done or tried to do for the German people will have been for nothing. The German nation will be split in two, part to the Anglo-American coalition and part to the Soviets, the so-called allies of the English. Our Fatherland will become known as East and West Germany, two separate nations, one of which will be held under the yoke of a communist regime and all the land you have recently and so courageously regained will be lost forever. The world will descend into a fifty-year struggle between the Soviets on the one side and the Americans and West Europeans on the other. Your predictions that it is the communists whom the West should be fighting will echo through that time without recognition as to its author. And here is where we started this conversation. Your extermination of the Jews will give the countries allied against you justification for their aggression, justification after the event, justification for Churchill's no compromise approach despite the fact that they have aligned themselves with the greatest Jew-killer of all time in Stalin. The killing of the Jews will cause the world to see you as the devil incarnate and the horrific costs of that war will be justified because of what you do to the Jews. You will be blamed for this coming war and the sixty million people worldwide who will die fighting it."

"Sixty million people," Speer repeats in disbelief.

"The Americans will devastate entire German and Japanese cities, killing every man, woman, and child. Hiroshima, Nagasaki, Hamburg, and Dresden will be levelled, but no charges of genocide will ever be directed towards them for their acts, only towards you for what you do to the Jews. The horrors of Stalinist totalitarianism will be hidden from the world for decades simply because he helped the English achieve their objectives against Germany. Stalin will be *Time Magazine*'s "Man of the Year" in 1939 and again in 1942. This murderous brute will become Churchill's and Roosevelt's poster boy. Europe will be left divided, and Stalin will crush Eastern Europe under his boot, including its Jewish population, and nothing will be done to stop him. The slaughter of the Jews will be a sin for which, in their eyes, only you deserve to be punished."

"Insanity. It cannot be so," Hitler stood and began to shout and wave his hands dismissively. "It is perversely extreme to suggest it would be so. They act…" Hitler began to splutter, coughing and poking his finger at Frederick. "They act supposedly to save Poland and end up leaving it and half of Europe in the hands of that rabid dog Stalin. The English accuse us of wanting world domination when they have been at war with almost every nation on this Earth, stolen every piece of land they could stick a flag into and banished the land's true owners. THEY are lecturing us about Jews. THEY should wash the blood off their own hands before pointing a finger at us. No nation is stupid enough to support a leader who would pursue such insanity, and so soon after a Great War that apparently proved nothing. No nation, no leader, is insane enough to expend sixty million lives because some drunk in London has got a chip on his shoulder about Germans. They will not befriend Stalin. They cannot be blind to what he is doing to his people."

"They will, it will be so," Frederick also stood to face Hitler and was pointing back at him, yelling. "Churchill will be the hero, and you the rabid dog, not Stalin. They will sing songs about him and Roosevelt, and they will write the history books again, allowing Stalin to hide in the shadows." Hitler's face went bright red. "Sixty million people will be killed, and Germany will be burned to the ground. The blood of six million innocent Jews will be on your hands. All will be lost because of YOU."

Frederick struck Hitler on the chest and began to punch at him repeating, "You, you, you will destroy our country," in his squawky little boy voice now incensed. Speer grabbed both of the boy's arms.

"Halt die Klappe," Hitler slapped the boy across his face. "How dare you."

Frederick stood staring at him, tears in his eyes, having now shaken free of Speer. Unflinching, he momentarily looked around the room to see where Hitler had put his sidearm.

"You test me, boy!" Hitler lowered his hand after a reflex to strike the boy again. He collected himself, troubled, insulted. "I have had enough of this rubbish. Get out, both of you." Speer and Frederick hesitated. "GET OUT!"

Frederick stormed out, now certain he had overstepped his position, thinking that all was lost. Persuasion had failed, and other methods needed to be contemplated.

CHAPTER SIX

Jack arrived at his appointment with the company psychologist at 2:00 p.m. He was more than a little apprehensive but happy to unburden himself about the deep self-doubt that had overtaken him. By nature, he was a positive person and always worked through any problem presented to him in a calm and organised way, but he just couldn't shake off the negativity that had beset him. Today was the day that Franz Gothenburg would send the BCU device back to himself as a child.

"But you were killed, Jack, for God's sake!" was the first response from the psychologist, Dr. Rehnquist, after they had begun their session and Jack had described what he was feeling. The look on Jack's face indicated that this observation had not escaped him. "What? You don't think being blown up in a car park might have some effect on your state of mind?"

"Very funny, Doc, but what if this is not real?"

"Not real?"

"Yeah, they had my mind in a jar and just stuck it back in! What if this is all not real? I understand the physics of it. I work with replicated organic growth and bio-electrical interfaces all the time. Just in my case, it wasn't just a refit plus a tummy tuck, they regrew the whole lot."

"Then what is it? Isn't copying brain synapses just as straightforward now as a facelift? It's complex, but it's known, right?"

"Is it?"

"You would know better than I, Jack."

"This is my brain we're talking about, Doc. This is me we're talking about."

"Jack, you're being emotional about this and understandably so, but the science is solid. They duplicated your body, which is straightforward these days, and copied your brain synapses, combining the two. It's no different than Kirk being beamed down to a planet from the Enterprise — you know, disassembled and reassembled."

"Like that's a real analogy or ever going to be possible."

"You're upsetting me, Jack. I'm a Star Trek fan." They both laughed. "This could just be a bout of depression. It might not have anything to do with your Replant except that the related shock could have brought it on. You're about the right age for that type of problem. Have you noticed these kinds of feelings before?"

"Do you think we have a soul, Doc?" Jack wasn't listening; instead, he asked the question that was truly troubling him.

"What do you mean?"

"You know, a spirit inherently your own, something that resides in you, that is of you, but precedes and outlasts your physical being — a soul."

"The religious scholars have been asking that question for five thousand years. Who am I to tell you that the answer is one thing or another?"

"Because I'm asking you," Jack said impatiently.

"Me. Personally… no. No afterlife. No god. Therefore, I guess no soul in a religious sense. But that is just my opinion. There are many people who believe otherwise."

"Let's just stick with those present, shall we?"

"Well, in that case, as a clinician, I believe that a person's self is constituted by the aggregation of all that the person knows, all their experiences, and all they have been taught, thought up, or dreamt of. These attributes are set within the genetic material with which they have to interact. The human brain is a genetically specific receptacle into which these things are placed by education, experience, and self-awareness. That receptacle comes into this world with certain genetic predispositions, which seemed in the dark days of science to come from nowhere. But we now know exactly where they come from, we can point to which gene it comes from, and how that gene expresses itself. We understand completely the workings of the human genome and what it delivers not only in terms of physical characteristics but also the pre-dispositional impact it has on personality and inclinations.”

“Do we?”

“Jack, these things are known. You carry those same predispositions with you now because you carry the same genetic makeup. I’m not making this stuff up for your benefit. If you stand up, you will not fly up to the ceiling — gravity will keep you on the floor. Try it, and you’ll see that I’m right. These things are known.”

“So you’re saying that given a specific set of genes, then everything, I mean everything, that makes up a person is constituted by the information stored in a bunch of electrical pathways in the brain. There is nothing at the margin. Nothing is hiding in the gaps, nothing that can’t be codified and measured and collected or seen by examination with the appropriate tool. Is that it?”

“You know that’s it, and you know logically that has to be right. Where else would it be? Where else, other than in your physical brain, could it reside? In your heart, where love resides? Great organ, but not capable of storing information. There are no gaps. Come on, Jack, it resides in spirit form… really? You’re our finest bioengineer, a world leader in your field. Would you listen to yourself? The only real question is why do you doubt these facts now?”

“Because I feel that something’s missing. What if they left a piece of my mind in that jar? Or didn’t collect it in the first place?” Jack was agitated and confused and was relieved to say out loud what he had been thinking for the past two weeks. “I think they might have left something behind.”

“Calm down, Jack. Let’s look at this rationally. They have done all the tests, you’ve answered all the questions. You have complete recollection. Nothing is physically wrong with you or with your brain.”

“Did you ever come back from a trip or a holiday, Doc, and you kept thinking you left something back at the hotel but couldn’t think what it was? Yet you just knew it was something important. Well, you take that feeling and multiply it by a thousand and you've got what I'm feeling. And then add to that the fact that there is no way, absolutely no way on this planet, that you could ever go back and get it. If you can picture that, then you're in my headspace."

"Don't you think that this feeling would be a normal reaction to the Replant? I mean, if you were the scientist working on that procedure and you were asked to project possible physiological side effects, don't you think you might guess this one? There is nothing back at the hotel, Jack. You've brought it all with you, they checked all your bags in. That's as far as I can stretch that stupid analogy." They both laughed. There was a pause. "That fear in you is arising because your prior receptacle was destroyed in a ball of flames. You can't go back and get anything because you died. You died, Jack. You must be deeply concerned by the violence perpetrated on you. It is a natural fear. The shock is real. You know that the Replant procedure has comprehensive integrity protocols. Don't you remember that whenever you have had that feeling about leaving something behind on a trip, it was usually just post-departure anxiety, that it usually turned out that you actually didn't leave anything behind? There is a reason that you can't put your finger on what you're feeling or on what you think is missing, Jack, and that is because it doesn't exist."

"How would I know?"

"Jack, please, of course you would know if it wasn't all piecing together in your own head. Your expectations are being met every day. You have the information in your head that enables you to find your way around without guidance, work without supervision, and people are reacting to your actions in a way that meets your expectations. It all fits together. That must tell you something."

"None of that changes the fact that somehow I feel that I'm not really me, that I'm someone or something different."

"Even if that was true, Jack, now listen to me." The doctor was sure to get Jack's attention because Jack seemed to be descending into psychosis. The doctor pulled his chairs closer to Jack. "Even if that was true and nobody in this room or at the plant believes that it is, what could you do about it? Stop for a minute. What path can you now choose apart from being dead in a car park? Pick the outcome you'd prefer. You have always been a logical and pragmatic person. Work the problem. At the best of times, people change from one year to the next, they grow and they change, their circumstances change. Go with the flow. Maybe you've changed, maybe you haven't changed. Either way, it's okay. Play the cards you're dealt, isn't that what you always say?"

"Yes."

"You've got the body you want, you said it yourself. No test that you or the company can come up with says that anything was missed. Get on with it."

"Maybe that's right. What else is there to do? Maybe I'll just change my name to The Phantom or something else equally spooky and move on." Jack was starting to feel a little relieved. What Lindquist was saying made sense. There was no need to dwell on it. The only thing to do was to move forward.

"Look, Phantom, I can give you something for the anxiety and maybe we should talk on a regular basis for a while."

"That sounds good. And thanks. It was good to talk it out."

"As always. Stop worrying. Do you think you need some more time off?"

"No… God, no, I think it would be better if I just got stuck back in."

"That's it. Take this, Jack." The doctor handed him a script. "And set an appointment for, say, next week with Marlene on the way out, will you. Tell her I asked her to clear some time."

"I will. Thanks again, Doc."

Jack and Francine arrived back home around the same time that afternoon. Francine was agitated and still a little drunk from her lunch with Julia, her best friend and confidant. Julia had made her face up to the fact that she had hidden a sexual dalliance from Jack prior to the bombing and that she had been given an unexpected opportunity to make that right by telling him before he found out for a second time, he having uncovered it the night of the gala. Jack was still processing his discussion with the doctor and hadn't noticed her mood. Francine collapsed herself onto one of the lounge chairs. She had made herself a martini.

"Jack, I think we need to talk."

Francine had decided on the way home from lunch that she was going to get in front of this the second time around. She didn't go to the gala with Jack the evening he was killed because they were fighting over a message Jack had found on their service, a message from her boyfriend. That fight was never resolved but she was not going to be put back into a position of being found out. That situation had made her feel cheap and she was at the very least not going to repeat that mistake.

Francine's words sent a cold shiver up Jack's spine. He immediately increased the amount of scotch he had put in his glass and his thoughts went to what he had done to the domestic Augment that morning. How could she know? The words Francine had uttered were magic female words, the words that every man dreads. No possible good could ever follow those words, he thought. In fact, in the history of mankind on this planet, nothing good had ever come from a conversation that started with that invitation. At best, he was going to be chastised for something he had done wrong and there would be no sex for a while. At worst, it meant that he had to sit through some interminable examination of her emotional state and review things that men don't particularly want to examine or feel comfortable discussing. Either way, it was not going to be pleasant and the outcome almost certainly was not going to be good for him. Instinctively, he started with something to lighten the mood and began to prepare his apology.

"You're home early."

"I've been seeing someone."

"Seeing someone?"

"Another man." Francine had bottled things up for so long and now wanted to be brutally honest. Perhaps it wasn't going to be interminable after all.

"Oh." Jack began to withdraw into himself. He put down his scotch and started simply to collect the facts. "Do you love him?"

"I don't know, maybe."

"Are you sleeping with him?"

"Yes."

"Jesus. When were you going to tell ME?" Jack emphasised "me" sharply and loudly. Francine jumped. He picked up his scotch and finished it in one gulp.

"Can we not get all macho about this?"

"Macho? Get fucked, no wait, that is something you have already arranged apparently. Do I know him?"

"No. Jack, I'm sorry. I'm confused. Please sit back down and let's talk about it."

"Are you going to keep seeing him?"

"I don't know, Jack. It started out harmless enough, a bit of flirting, you know…"

"No, I don't know."

Jack walked slowly to the bedroom. He had collected enough information. He pulled a bag down from the top shelf of his closet and placed it on the bed and opened it. Francine followed him into the bedroom.

"Did you hear what I said? I want to talk to you about it." There was no response from Jack. "What, are you just going to leave?"

Jack looked at her as if she had gone mad. One thing was certain; he was not about to follow her agenda.

"Is that all you think of me… of us?" Francine continued. That remark caused Jack to withdraw even further into his own emotions. "What do you want me to say? I said I'm sorry." She grabbed his arm as he walked past her heading to the bathroom to collect some toiletries. "Jack, don't go, please let's sit down. I told you about this before, I mean before the bombing, and we were trying to work things out, Jack." She was lying. She was trying to reconstruct history, a version in which she had been honest. Her confession to Julia at lunch had reminded her of how she had felt the day Jack came across the message from Dan.

Jack didn't know what he felt or what he knew back then. Things began to fall into place for him now. He had thought that it was the bombing and the Replant that had made her more distant. He didn't go into the bathroom to collect his things. The melodramatics were already too much for him. There was something that always happened to a person's dignity in those situations, he thought — the yelling, the self-justification, the lying, all of which he found repulsive and intolerable. He wanted it to stop now. He left the bag on the bed, picked up his coat and car keys, and left the apartment without saying anything further. There was nothing more to say, there was nothing there that he wanted to take.

Jack had spent the last two nights at the club and wasn't fully paying attention to the preparations for a protocol he was about to run with the new TPS400 Augment. The new model required an increase in size and strength in order to carry the new generation pulse weapons ready for deployment in the American military. The 400 had increased bone density compared with the previous military model to match its enlarged muscle mass, so that it wouldn't break its own arms when it used the power that the additional muscle gave them. However, Jack was having some difficulties getting the connective tissue dynamics correct in his design and the muscle ligaments were failing right where they meet the denser bone. They had also upgraded the fight programming, something they had copied from one of the latest role-play video games. They were about to test both when Cleary arrived alone to see Jack.

Cleary had felt a little exposed when he didn't get what he should have gotten out of Zimmermann during his first interview, so he decided to re-interview some of the AIOGEN staff to see what else he might have missed. Jack was the first on his list. Cleary still hadn't received anything further from the FBI about the missing pieces of Zimmermann's file and he was more than a little peeved with Jamison so he hadn't suggested that she come along. He had filed a formal complaint about the lack of cooperation. Jacobs was off running down an old Marine buddy of Thomason's.

"Mr Pierce, thanks for getting me in here. That security is tighter than a fish's arsehole. I wanted to go back over a few things with you, if that's okay?"

"It's Doctor Pierce, but call me Jack, detective. What can I do for you?"

"What was it exactly that you were working on just prior to the bombing?"

"Now, there's a good question. This, I think. We're just about to run a test. Want to take a look?"

Without waiting for a response, Jack led Cleary through a couple of doors and into an open testing area three stories high inside the plant building. The area had a heavily fortified cage running around its perimeter, leaving about four paces between the cage and the thick concrete walls of the room. The caged area was about one-third the size of a football field and was filled at its base with two feet of sand. Just as they arrived, two Augments were ushered into the cage. Neither of them was armed and they weren't wearing any other non-organic armoury or equipment. The cage gate was secured behind them and the two attendants that had brought them left through the same set of double doors opposite to where Cleary and Jack were standing.

"The one with the blue vest is the old series 300 and the red one is the new 400," Jack explained to Cleary. "We're trying to see if the new genetic design and the new programming for the 400, which are confidential, of course, have any discernible benefits in a hand-to-hand situation. Our simulations show that there should be, but you never know until you put them into a skin-only situation."

"They have to be nearly eight feet tall," Cleary said.

"Not quite. Just under two point three metres. Both models stand the same height."

Cleary thought Christmas had arrived. Augments were not allowed to be used for martial arts entertainment purposes, as it was believed that it would demean their status as fighters of crime and protectors of national security. There had been some attempt to use robots for extreme fighting, but that fad had largely come and gone. There was still cage fighting on net-TV but all participants were human. Some of those guys were big and mean, but this, Cleary thought, was going to be a real blast. He had been around police Augments for a long time but the military units were so much bigger and stronger, he observed, never being this close to one in the past.

Both Augments moved to the centre of the cage, awaiting instructions, standing and facing each other. Cleary was drawn forward out of curiosity and he put his figures through the wire of the cage and leaned up against it in anticipation of what he was sure was about to happen.

"I wouldn't do that if I were you, Detective, you might want to step back a bit." Cleary obliged. "Let 'em at it, Bill."

In a blink, the 400 had the older model by the neck with one hand, choking it, driving forward in a run. It grabbed the unbalanced 300 by the mid-section, lifting it into the air as it threw it about thirty feet across the sand onto its back with a shuddering thud. The sound of it landing and the reverberations it sent threw the floor caused Cleary to take another step back.

"That's what I'm talken' about," Cleary exclaimed, the surprised look on his face belying his bravado.

The 300 was back up on its feet without a moment's hesitation and ran back to the 400, covering the distance in what seemed to be a blink. The 300 had the newer model by one arm and had its other hand behind its neck attempting to trip it with its leg to bring it to the ground on its back so it could get on top of it, which it did successfully. The 400 started to strain backwards and then it rolled onto its side, pulling the 300 with it as it tumbled. With its knee strategically placed on the other Augment's stomach, it pushed the 300 with a thrust of its leg, regaining its own feet and pulling the 300 in a jujitsu manoeuvre into the cage fence. The 300 fell back to the cage floor with a thud. Stunned, it struggled to stand.

"Wow," Cleary said almost involuntarily. "That's worth the price of admission, right there."

Seizing the opportunity, the 400 jumped onto the other Augment and was sitting on its chest, pounding the Augment underneath it with thunderous blows to the head. Jack wasn't sure whether to let it proceed and risk irrecoverable damage to the 300, but just as the thought crossed his mind, the 300 managed to roll onto its side and took the other Augment with it to the sand. Both Augments were wrestling for control of the encounter.

"Let's see who wins this hold and then shut it down," Jack instructed his assistant.

The words had barely left Jack's mouth when the 400 ripped the arm of the older model, regaining its position of ascendancy on top of the other. It began to beat the other Augment in the head with its own arm.

"Shut it down," Jack said with some urgency. "Shut it down." The action came to an immediate halt. The 300 was bleeding profusely, and some of the blood had sprayed in Cleary's direction, a drop of it catching his cheek. Both Augments scrambled to their feet, though the 300 wasn't upright for very long.

"Get the repair team in there as quickly as you can. And clean up that mess… please."

Jack looked around at Cleary and saw him wipe the blood from his cheek with the tip of his middle finger and look at it. He was pondering the inhumanity of both the fight and the participants.

"You okay?"

Cleary collected himself. "Fuck me dead, when's round two?"

"They're quite something, aren't they?" Jack said. "The bathroom is through there if you want to clean up."

"I have a tissue, thanks. They're not infectious, are they?"

"Not at all, no. Clean as a whistle. We can't have them infecting their handlers or the populace of any target region. You'll survive. Lucky they're on our side, don't you think?"

Cleary looked at him incredulously.

"We had the audio switched off because it can scare the living shit out of you when they bellow at each other. The noise they make in combat generates a flight reflex in most humans. In here, you usually find yourself scrambling towards the door even though your brain is telling you that it's all in a controlled environment. It's quite something." Jack laughed. It was the laugh of a proud parent, one who had just watched his son score the winning touchdown in a football game. Jack turned to his assistant and continued giving instructions.

"I think we might count that as a win for the 400. Can you write that up and get me a form to sign for the asset damage, please? And give me the results of the medical on the 400 as soon as you can. I want a scan of his upper arm ligaments, both arms."

"It'll be on your note pad in twenty minutes," the assistant said and went off to do what he was asked without any further clarification.

"The new modifications might slow them down a bit, aerobically I mean, but the added strength is needed to carry the new pulse weaponry." Jack was talking to himself rather than the detective as they started to walk back to the office area. "It's certainly a significant step up in strength."

"You know, I've always wondered why you guys didn't give these military Augments wings. You know, make 'em fly."

"Fancy yourself as a bit of a bio-designer, do you, Detective?"

"I have my moments. Surely being able to fly would give them an advantage in the field?"

"Well, actually, no. Firstly, there are too many issues when you transfer that amount of genetic material across species, which you would have to do to achieve the result that you are talking about, birdmen shall we say. There are reasons species develop the way they do along particular phylogenetic trees. There are consequences of such a gene transfer that militate against utility in a flying human." Cleary was nodding but he had no idea what Jack was talking about. "Besides, biological wings would have to be huge to carry the weight of an Augment in flight and they would just get in the way when it's on the ground, which is where these guys were designed to be. You ever seen a bird walk along the ground, you know, top heavy, clumsy? The skies are the domain of the robots, Detective, smart bombs. If we want to move the Augment from one theatre of engagement to another, we are better off using mechanical transport. The Augment could use individual flight inducers if needed but even that is not efficient, you saw how fast they moved. Horses for courses, my new friend."

"Well, I'll shut up now." They both laughed. "But feel free to use the idea if you wish." Cleary decided that his days as a bio-engineer were over.

"No, keep 'em coming, Detective. We can use all the input we can get."

"Call me Cleary."

"Sure. I'm sorry, Detective, you had some questions… I mean, Cleary. Let's go to my office."

"Jack's office was nearly as big as the caged area they had just visited. It was expensively decorated, with several different work areas within it, all open-plan. Jack ushered Cleary over to his desk, which was an old wooden partner's desk sitting in a corner of a room otherwise furnished in modern décor. The desk sat next to one of the large windows that looked back over the complex and to the city beyond. Jack took off his lab coat and hung it on a matching antique standalone coat rack, then sat down behind his desk.

"Please," Jack gestured to one of the leather chairs opposite him. Cleary obliged. "How's the investigation going?"

"I've got more rabbit holes than I've got rabbits," Cleary answered.

The buzzer rang on Jack's desk phone, indicating an incoming call.

"Who is it?" Jack asked without picking up the headset, and the female voice of the computer interface program answered, "It's your wife. Do you want to talk to her?"

"No," Jack answered without hesitation, "and hold my calls, please. I'm in a meeting."

"Trouble in paradise?"

"Something like that," Jack said frankly.

Cleary's mind went straight back to his favourite theory about murder cases — it was always the spouse.

"Is there a… third party?"

"Apparently, but I'm not sure what that has to do with you."

"Do you know the guy?" Cleary persisted without bothering to justify his inquiry.

"No."

"Do you know his name?"

"No."

Cleary made a mental note to follow that through with Francine.

"Do you think he had anything to do…?"

"No."

Cleary understood the sensitivity of the situation. His earlier bout with alcoholism had cost him a liver and a relationship, both of which he had since realised were important to him. The liver was easily replaced, but he now lived alone. He changed the subject back to less sensitive issues.

"So, what do you think happened that night? Have you had the chance to mull it over?"

"I've mulled, yes. But I've got squat. What about those protestors?"

"We've spoken to them all. They're mostly a bunch of religious types, which of course, by no means, rules them out given the history of religious types. Except this one guy, an ex-Marine, with a serious case of the shits about what you guys are doing up here, especially you."

"Well, there you go then, case closed."

Cleary did a double-take. Jack was being sarcastic, he was starting to feel drained by events, and by the prospect of an extended police inquiry. There was a bang on the door.

"You guys testing? I could feel the vibrations..." George burst through Jack's office door with the familiarity of a close friend, then stopped mid-sentence noticing Jack was not alone. "Oh! Sorry. You're that copper dude, right? I'll leave you two guys to it," and he turned to leave.

"No, no," Cleary said, "the dude wants to talk to you, too. Pull up a chair."

"I'm sure that I have given you all that I know, Detective," George said, yet complying with Cleary's request to sit.

"Sure, but it's always the second time you ask the question that counts. Let's start with an easy one. Why hasn't anybody pinched this technology yet?" Cleary asked, indicating with his hands palm up that either party could answer, then taking out his notebook.

"I could think of a million reasons," George jumped in, "and who says that they haven't pinched it?"

"Well, nobody we know of," Cleary clarified his earlier question.

"To start with, nobody knows how to solve the problem with CTs, culmination times, you see. We grow them quick so we don't have to wait thirty years to harvest them. You can't grow full body Augments without controlling CTs, we get it done in about a week per instig. You mess around with CTs, you usually turn the zygote into a tumour and it dies."

"Instig?"

"Instigation. You've also got a serious problem starting the growth. If you can't get it going in the right direction, the growth I mean, you end up with a tumour and it dies."

Surprisingly to Cleary, it was George Sanders who was giving the answers.

"You're the IT guy, right?"

"Sure, but that doesn't mean I'm stupid."

"OK. What else?"

"It's not just the CTs and the instigs, there's a bunch of stuff related to full replication. The cultures are unstable if you don't know what you're doing and don't have the right equipment to store and control them. And of course, there is the muscle maturity thing; their muscles are fully developed and in prime condition when we harvest them. We got that from looking at the gestation of baby quadrupeds, you know, horses and so on. You can't harvest them and not have them equipped with full strength muscles; they'd be useless. And don't get me started on the electronic interfaces, the electro-biogenetics. That's a real bitch. That's where the genius here comes in."

"I get it, it's complex. But what I meant was, why hasn't someone been able to pinch it yet?"

"Well, maybe they have. I don't know."

Cleary's ears pricked up.

"That's the second time you've said that, George. What do you mean 'maybe they have'?"

"I don't know," George replied hurriedly. "I don't know whether they have or they haven't."

"What are you talking about, George?" Jack jumped in. "Nobody's got this."

"Do you have firsthand knowledge, Mr. Sanders, that someone has stolen the technology?" Cleary's instincts kicked in.

"No, no, of course not. I'm just saying that they could have it, and we may not necessarily know that they do."

"Tell me again where you were the night of the bombing?"

Cleary remembered George's original answer; he was at the party when Jack left. He just wanted to see whether he could rattle it off again and perhaps rattle George, but it was Jack who answered.

"Come on, Cleary, George is a lifelong friend of mine. You can't think that he had anything to do with this."

"It's not my job to make assumptions, Jack, just get the facts." Cleary had lost the opportunity to get a knee-jerk reaction from George so he lost interest. "So what does the head of IT do around here?"

"All of the IT systems in this building are my responsibility. It requires a large amount of processing power to do what we do and that all needs to be kept running."

"Does that include the security aspects of the systems?"

"Yes, in conjunction with the Head of Security, whom I think you've already spoken to."

"So Jack, how would someone steal this technology assuming he or she could get past all the building security… In fact, would they actually need to be in the building?"

"Yes, not possible otherwise because he or she would need to get access to the systems from inside, then they would need to know a lot about what we do here, where things are and what they are looking for, it wouldn't be your average thief."

"You can't access these computers from outside the building. It's not physically possible," George chimes in again, more than a little patronizingly. "You can't get at the coms spine even from one of the other AIOGEN offices. We set it up that way. All the IP is here."

"Give me a list of what you would take if you got in."

"They would need a copy of the computer protocols that we use to control the inception process. If this gets too technical, just stop me, please."

"Not so far, George. So a copy of the software?"

"Yes, that's one thing. There are certain changes made to the organic zygote, the initial organic material that's being regenerated.

Changes are made to its genetic makeup that impart the desired characteristics, including no brain, and those changes that enable the regulation of the speed of growth. Once we have made those changes, we produce what is called *incept material*. We grow a fair bit of it and store it for use on the production line. All the military equipment is made from the same material, all the police from other incept material and the domestic models are of course different again."

"So you need some gunk and you got to know how to turn the gunk on, and I presume turn it off."

"This guy could get a job here," George says sarcastically. The remark generates a look from Cleary that made George deicide to sit quietly.

"Stealing the *gunk* would be very helpful to them, no doubt," Jack steps in, "but they would still need the growth protocols and as George says the electronic interface methodology. So that's four things: the software, a copy of the schematics for the growth chamber, a sample of the incept medium, and a sample of the subject organism both pre- and post-initiation, otherwise the software procedures would make no sense. That's five things, I guess. I'll stop counting now. You would also need to know how we make those genetic adjustments to the material and how to hook everything up."

"You can't tell how that's done just by looking at the finished product?"

"God, no." A bit of a chuckle came from Jack. "We have a screening process that makes it impossible to discern how the genetic adjustments were made after the fact, that is, after the organism has been grown. It's impossible to reverse engineer. It is part of our security measures, and it's foolproof. If you had the organism or a piece of the biological material after the process had been stopped or turned off, as you say, then there is no way to figure out how it was started in the first place. It just looks like organic tissue. You could map its genome, I guess, but that's not going to help you understand how that genome was created. One of the things we realised early on when developing this industry was that this type of organic complexity, combined with the very complexity of genetics itself, offered the industry a substantial advantage over the robotics industry. Functionality and aesthetics aside, with a robot, that is, equipment manufactured from non-organic material, there is always the possibility — no matter how complex the machine is — that the machine could be copied, reverse engineered. That's not possible with an Augment. The genetic possibilities of the end product are infinite."

"I've always wondered about that. Surely, we have lost Augments in the field? The enemy has taken them and tried to disassemble them or analyse them?"

"Yeah, but not whole military ones. We've lost bits of them from injured Augments, taken with what you just said in mind. Usually, the military models are very good at cleaning up after themselves, and no enemy combatant is going to try to beat a military Augment to the carcass of a dead one unless they had a death wish." Jack threw his head back and laughed out loud with pride of authorship. "There have been losses of material, but even then that material wouldn't do them any good, no matter how hard they tried to replicate it or how large the piece was that they had obtained. Even if they got the electronic brain — which has never happened. The electronic programming for the brain is complex, but not unfathomable. The linkages to the nervous system are impossible to replicate without having all of the IP, including the genetic makeup of the organic receptors that link to the electronics, you know, the brain stem to the electronic brain. Very, very hard. I know just how hard."

"You did it," Cleary says to Jack.

"Good luck to the next guy," George chimes in. "There's maybe one guy in the world that could help you there, and you're lookin' at him."

"But why do you need the electronic brain?"

"Surely, you know, Cleary," Jack continues, "remember the debates."

"I'm just a cop, man. Politics bore me."

"Society wouldn't accept an organism identical to a human, with a human brain. That would make them human. No can do. Any possibility of self-awareness and they'd shut us down. You can only provide that certainty with electronics, not organics."

"So they could copy the electronics of the brain… if they got their hands on one, right?"

"The IP is in the linkage. Besides, if you separate the electronic brain from its Augment body, the electronics automatically self-destruct, and the organism dies, or the other way round. So you're screwed, anyway. If they managed to pull an electronic brain out of a military Augment, they would just get a molten mess."

"But we sell domestic Augments overseas. Why can't they work off them?"

"Yeah, different animal, literally. And different brain with the same protective devices. You know the domestics are leased, not bought. AOIGEN never loses ownership. You can't reprogram either a military or a domestic Augment once it comes off the production line, and all Augments are manufactured by us here in the States. If you want a new model with new functionality, you have to buy a whole new one from us. Try and reprogram it, and… fizz."

"Well, good for you guys. Now how do I steal it? What about the smashes you guys do? How hard is that to replicate or steal? If they had your smash, wouldn't they effectively have you?"

"The procedure and the equipment for the download would be difficult to copy but not impossible. Much of the basic early work on copied brain content is in the public domain. What would be hard would be to get the download right — and by right, I mean perfect. And the upload has only been done once, and that is a whole other kettle of fish."

"Could someone steal a smash and read it?"

"The answer is no, but to what end? Firstly, it would be known to be missing, and secondly, it's not possible to read in the absence of the donor. Just not possible."

"How did they read yours then? You were dead."

"They didn't read it. They uploaded it into a genetically identical receptacle. Jesus, I'm talking about my own brain here. It is the genetic makeup, the constitution of the brain at a molecular level, that allows the smash to be retrieved, decoded if you like. You need the donor present to match up the storage protocols of the donor brain with the recorded synaptic shadows. Each brain is different, like fingerprints. The boys in the lab call that uniqueness the soul, but Socrates might disagree with them." Jack laughed, but Cleary didn't get it. "There is a particular nexus between a given human brain with a given genetic makeup and the information it contains. It's the combination of the two that gives rise to intentionality."

"Sounds like the Pope might have a problem with some of what you just said as well as that other guy you mentioned." Cleary was a non-practicing Catholic.

"The Pope disagrees with everything that happens around here."

"So it seems like a lot of trouble someone would have to go to if they wanted to take this technology. What if it was someone here at AIOGEN other than you, of course?"

"Detective, Cleary, I would go further and say that the *only* way it could be done is to have someone here at AIOGEN involved."

"I have a colleague over at the FBI who is insisting that this is all part of at least an attempt to take it. You should meet her, lovely gently little creature, you'd like her."

"If we are going to meet up with the FBI maybe our Head of Security should be in the room, and Head Council, as a courtesy I mean?"

"Maybe that's a good idea. I'll set it up," Cleary declared, standing up to leave. As he did so, he pointed at George. "And I haven't finished with you yet. Being a smartass makes me suspicious, if you get my drift."

George wore an incredulous look on his face and pursed his lips as if he were about to respond, but didn't.

"My guys are going to talk to Francine," Cleary turned back to Jack as he approached the door. "I hope that doesn't cause you any distress."

"Go for your life. Tell her I said hi."

"You know you should do something about that if you want to fix it. None of my business though, I guess."

"No, it isn't, but… thanks. I'm sure that's right. I'm just not sure yet whether I want to."

Cleary acknowledged this with a nod. "I'll call you with a time to meet the agent from hell. But don't mess with her. Either of you. She bites."

As he exited the room, Jack's assistant came in with the results from the medical examination of the 400.

"The ligaments connecting its right triceps brachii were completely torn off the bone… damn it," Jack said out loud, closing the file and throwing it on his desk with such force it fell off the other side. "The muscle mass and bone density are right for what we want, but the ligaments keep letting go."

"Better fix that, Jack," George said as he rose to leave. He picked up the notepad from the floor and placed it back on Jack's desk. "Before the boss finds out. He's keen to sell a batch of the new ones to the military."

"Thanks, George, that's good advice. Now fuck off."

The discussion with Cleary and his own inability to solve the persistent problems with the 400 had put Jack in a dark mood as he headed back to the club that evening. Had the Replant caused him to lose his acumen? A feeling of inadequacy was overtaking him. It ballooned into a sentiment of inadequacy about his entire life, encompassing everything, including his marriage. He had plunged himself back into his work, but it wasn't providing the validation it once did. Maybe he wasn't good at it anymore. Cleary's presence in his office that afternoon had drained him of all sociability. The conversation raised personal concerns about the danger he might still face. Cleary's insinuation about Francine's possible involvement in the bombing, and the surprising ambivalence of his feelings towards her, only fuelled the engulfing melancholy he now bore.

He decided to take a detour to Lincoln Park for a stroll along the river before returning to the club. Always the scientist, he wanted to examine his feelings and perhaps make a decision about Francine. He fetched a cigar from the glove box, lit it, and stepped out of the car.

As he walked, his introspection sent him further into a depressive state until, after a while, a numbness of emotion overcame him. He found himself muttering, "I don't give a shit," out loud repeatedly as each problem cascaded through his brain, dismissed with that derisive comment.

He stopped walking and looked back over the darkened park. The lights from the top half of the Empire State Building were striking against the horizon as he looked towards Jersey City and the Hudson, both hidden by the park's trees. The trees drew a black jagged border beneath the vibrant lights of Manhattan. The Empire State Building stood like a crystal obelisk resting on a ruffled black blanket, reminding him that life existed outside of his own and it was indifferent to his participation. For the first time in his life, he felt alone.

Within him, a desperate scream was building. Vigorously ashing his cigar and tsking under his breath, he gazed back towards the river, drawn to its dark, resolute flow. His dejection led him to unfamiliar and unwelcome thoughts. It made him turn abruptly towards his car. His pace quickened as though he was a man who had spotted an impending storm, a storm from which he urgently needed to find shelter.

As Jack approached the desk of the concierge at the club, he noticed the overly familiar couple seated in the adjacent waiting room. His mood lifted as he began without hesitation to walk towards them.

"Your father and mother are here to see you, Dr. Pierce. I had them wait in the lounge." The information provided by the clerk was superfluous. All parties had recognised each other and were walking with open arms towards their reunion.

"Sweetheart. How are you feeling? You look absolutely fantastic." His mother put a hand on each of Jack's cheeks, squeezing them together and rubbing them in small circles, causing his mouth to look like a puffer fish.

"Jack, my boy," his father said, putting one hand out for Jack to take, the other patting Jack's shoulder.

"Mum, Dad, what brings you all the way to New York City?"

"Well, you," they both said at the same time. "And it's not all that far," his mother added. "It's no trouble to come over to see you. I'm just sorry we couldn't do it earlier, that silly cruise thing. You know we couldn't get away. We heard you were doing well, though. Francine called us, but it took her a while to track us down. By the time she got hold of us, it was all resolved, thank God. What an incredible thing. Lucky you're with that big company. What's its name, dear?"

Jack didn't answer and instead turned to the clerk. "Are there any tables in the dining room, Mat? You guys haven't eaten yet, have you?"

"They'll still have your reservation, Dr. Pierce. I'm sure that there will be no trouble to add two more to your table," the clerk replied.

Jack's father, Benjamin Bradley Pierce, was a tall, slim man with a fine crop of white hair that made him look younger than his seventy-five years. He still had all his faculties about him, despite resisting any work done on brain cell regeneration. In fact, he had not taken anything from the substantial menu offered by the New Science. He still retained all his original organs. All that new stuff was "nonsense," he would tell anyone who cared to listen. Ben had the distinction of having worked fifty-three years with the same company, originally selling, and later managing the sale of, household electrical appliances. He started when he was just sixteen and retired, unusually young for the day, at seventy-two. There was a three-year absence from the company when he volunteered for the first Afghani war in 1990, but he was too late to see action and served out his enlistment at the Marine Corps Logistics Base in Barstow, California. This is where he met Judith, who worked in Barstow as a primary school teacher. The couple still lived in Barstow, near Judith's family, and had done so for their entire forty-five-year marriage.

The town of Barstow in California had grown substantially since they built the DesertXpress high-speed train back in 2039. After many false starts to that project, the State had finally added the necessary funding to a federal grant to make the train a reality. With the advent of the high-speed train, the west coast had become easily accessible from Barstow, and the town had steadily accumulated a number of commuters who worked in San Bernardino and even LA. The town boasted three well-regarded high schools, and the local Park University campus had grown to offer many agricultural and engineering courses.

Ben and Judith had acquired a two-and-a-half-acre lot just outside of town towards the desert. They built themselves a country hacienda in the Pueblo style, more typical of the Santa Fe area in New Mexico than of California. It was warm in the winter and cool in the summer and had a rustic appeal as it sat in its Mojave surroundings, it imbued a warmth that went beyond that of a normal home. Their hacienda formed part of what had become something of an artist's enclave that had grown up around the Pierce home. Some of them were fellow retirees, but the community had also attracted some native artisans. This was not in small part due to Judith's passion for oil painting and her gregarious and welcoming nature. It was fair to say that Judith was the mother hen of the group. It was her idea to open a shop in town that carried the product of their joint labours. They manned it on a rotational basis, which Judith worked out. The gallery was enjoying more than a little success, servicing the plentiful day-trippers that came out from the coast on the DesertXpress each weekend to sample the desert air and wander the many walking trails that winded their way through the Mojave National Reserve. They had recently acquired the shop next door and added a café for the pleasure of their patrons. Ben had discovered an interest and ability in firing pottery and enamels in the two ovens he had built for himself on their property. Together, he and Judith regularly found solace in a pitcher of margaritas at the end of a creative day, watching the sun go down over the creosote.

The New Science hadn't really found its way to Barstow. There were very few domestic Augments in service for the townspeople, and none in service in the town's restaurants and cafes, at least not as waiters or front-of-business personnel. The nearest police Augment was in San Bernardino. The townsfolk, and more particularly the people who belonged to the small artist commune where the Pierces lived, had no time for the newer ways. Instead, they sought the peace that welled up from the desert as an ample gift from the planet, which fed the soul and soothed the conflicted mind.

Ben had a gentleness in his eyes that would mask, for those unfamiliar with him, the bright intelligence that lay beneath. He could almost certainly have done more with his career but his insistence on staying in Barstow had limited his options. Judith loved it there and her family was there and for Ben, all that he loved was Judith. Judith was a formidable woman. She was conservative and strong willed but very gracious and kind to most people, the only notable exception being parking police of which there were still an unfortunate few in Barstow. She remained a doting mother to her only child, Jack. Jack often missed the presence of a sibling and sometimes felt the consequences of being an only child but reconciled himself to it knowing he had two parents who cared deeply for him and who ensured that all opportunities both academic and personal were made available to him as best as they could endeavour and afford to provide them.

Judith was ten years younger than Ben and remained a good-looking woman. Most said that Jack got his looks from her, most except for Francine. Judith had strong genes to match her strong will. Unlike Ben, she had succumbed to the call of the New Science and had the skin of a much younger woman to show for it after a skin cell regeneration procedure. This and her raven hair, which because of the skin procedure had no grey in it, made her a striking individual. It wasn't vanity, she would tell her family when explaining why she had it done, it was just the whimsical needs of a woman growing old seeking to allow herself some well-deserved self-indulgence. The procedure had served to heighten the apparent age difference between Ben and Judith, something about which Ben rarely complained but was always aware. He was comfortable with the original "ten or so years" difference in their ages when he had met and married her but it now looked as though it was closer to thirty years difference and that regularly caused him distress when they were in public. It was a problem that many older couples faced if they held opposing attitudes towards the New Science.

Now seated in the club's dining room Judith went to work on Jack regarding his recent experiences and why he never called to share them.

"Killed, in a car accident, my God. That is hard to reconcile for a God-fearing woman, Jack, regardless of how happy we are to still have you. It was a week before they could contact us, you know."

"It wasn't any accident, Mum. It was a bomb. I was only speaking to the coppers about it this afternoon." Jack had slipped easily into a very familiar feeling, a comforting feeling of sharing his day with his mother and father. It provided welcome, even necessary, relief from his mood of earlier that night.

"I understand, dear. 'Accident' is easier for me to say. Who would want to kill you, Jack, my darling Jack?" Judith reached into her bag for a tissue as she began to cry.

"The authorities seem to know as much about it as you do. I had the lead detective in my office this afternoon, and I believe they're still somewhat in the dark."

"They have no suspects, Jack?" Ben asked, taking over from Judith and consoling her by rubbing her forearm.

"There was one protester there that night with a military background, a Marine Special Services guy, I believe. But that doesn't necessarily lead to any conclusions, as you're well aware."

"What about those who might want to steal that technology at your work?"

"Dad, can we discuss something else? I've been dealing with nothing but this since I got out of the hospital. And please, not the 'are you feeling okay' question, either. I'm okay. My faculties are intact, as far as I can tell, and my memory is apparently a hundred percent. Can we skip all that, please? I don't mean to be rude; I'm just a bit depressed by it, that's all."

"Depressed, dear, but…" Judith was seeking more information than Jack was willing to provide, but Jack pre-empted her question.

"Francine and I have separated."

"Jack, sweetheart, are you okay?" Judith asked, but a look from Jack reminded her of his recent request. "Sorry, dear, is there anything we can do?"

"Son, I know a bit about depression," Ben interjected. "There are resources available, and it's okay to ask for them. Don't be one of those guys who's too tough to ask. Are you talking to someone?"

"Yes, the company has a counsellor. I'm scheduled to see him in a couple of days. I might try to move that up given my mood earlier tonight."

"That's the spirit. Churchill called it the 'black dog'; he suffered from depression. He said it always followed him around. That's why he drank so much, always had a glass of scotch on his desk. There are other ways to cope these days, other than booze, I mean. Don't let it overwhelm you, son."

"It started after the bombing. I don't recall feeling like this before, but my therapist says I'm at the right age for this sort of thing. I'm unsure whether the bombing had anything to do with it. The therapist doesn't think so, aside from the shock of it. But Francine and I splitting up hasn't helped, especially since she's been distant ever since the bombing. Apparently, we had some sort of fight the night of the gala, but I don't remember it."

"What are you going to do about Francine?"

"She's seeing someone else."

"Oh, dear God," Judith exclaimed, unable to contain her shock or her opinions about Francine. "How can she, I always thought…" But a look from Ben stopped her mid-sentence. "Would you like to come and stay with us for a while?" Judith asked after a moment of reflection, rather than criticising Francine for her untimely betrayal.

"That's a sterling idea," Ben added.

"I've got my work, Mom, and I'm unsure about what's happening with Francine. I feel a bit lost. All I ever wanted since I first met her was to be married to her, and now that feeling has suddenly disappeared. It's not the only emotion I'm struggling with. I'm having difficulty discerning what's transient. Maybe I was in love with the idea of her. She's a beautiful woman, and we built a beautiful life together. Perhaps it was the process, the building, not the loving or the living of it. It's hard for me to analyse my feelings right now."

"We're planning to stay in town for a week or so." That was news to Judith, but before she could contradict Ben, she realised his intentions. Staying in town with Jack in his current state of mind was the right thing to do. She remembered why she had loved Ben for so many years. "There are a couple of things I need to do while we're here," Ben continued, implying their plans to stay weren't solely due to Jack's situation. "So, we should meet up. Maybe we could go out to dinner. Can you make some time for us?" Ben was a thoughtful and considerate man.

"Of course, I can. My social calendar isn't exactly full…" Jack caught himself. "I mean… there's nothing I wouldn't rearrange for you guys." Jack signalled the waiter. "Shall we order dinner?"

"And maybe you can come and stay over Thanksgiving," Judith added. "It would be wonderful to have you home again. I know you've missed out the past couple of years because of Francine's family. That woman, her mother."

"Now, dear," Ben said, patting Judith's hand. "We'd love to have you, son. What do you say?"

"I'd like that, yes. Count me in."

Both Ben and Judith were pleased to hear Jack's acceptance, and they returned to studying their menus as the waiter approached.

The next morning, at the One Nine, Jacobs had come into Cleary's office.

"You remember how you asked me to drop by Mrs. Pierce's place on the way back from visiting Thomason's Marine buddy yesterday? You know, the one who didn't provide any useful information, by the way. You wanted me to inquire about her new boyfriend?"

"Sure." Cleary was half-listening.

"She's quite a character, that Francine. Reminds me of Marlene Dietrich," Jacobs continued.

"Who?"

"'I want to be alone,' you know, Mrs. Pierce actually said that when I was there. It floored me."

"What on earth are you going on about, Jacobs?"

"Marlene Dietrich, she's the persona of my home's AI assistant. You don't remember her? Movie star… no? Mrs. Pierce reminds me of her."

"Is there something here I need to know, or are you losing your grip on the job?"

"I know you're not a fan of coincidences, but I have one here that's a doozy. The boyfriend is also a Marine, still serving, and a good-looking guy at that. She showed me a photo of him she had in her purse, it seems serious. But here's the kicker: guess who his platoon sergeant was in basic training?"

"No way," Cleary jumped to his feet, immediately connecting the dots, "you're not going to tell me it was Thomason?"

"One and the same."

"Well, fuck me!"

"Pass."

"No, this is too simple. Thomason, who's the boyfriend of the wife? What's his name?"

"Nannis, Sergeant Daniel Broderick Nannis."

"So, the wife's boyfriend calls in a favour from an old Marine Special Forces buddy, who despises AIOGEN and considers Jack Pierce the devil, who Nannis thinks can't be connected back to him or Jack's wife, to eliminate the husband. This clears the way for wifey to become Mrs. Marlene Dietrich-Nannis. No, that's too easy. You don't need a detective to figure that out. Did you pull Nannis's file? Where is he?" Cleary skimmed through the file Jacobs handed him, searching for any history that might support his suspicions.

"He's currently stationed at Marine Corps Base Quantico in Virginia, but he's on extended leave and staying at the Lexington, just around the corner. Thomason's definitely angry and vengeful enough to help Nannis deal with Pierce if that's what was planned."

"Nobody says 'deal with' these days, Jacobs. We need to talk to this guy. Call the Lexington and ask if Nannis is there now and if not, when they expect him back. Special Agent 'I'll-kick-your-head-in-if-you-cross-me' would be irate if we're right. She'd be livid. Look, there's enough here to get a warrant for the phone records of all three of them, and a search warrant. Thomason doesn't have a cell, but pull the records from his home and that pit where he works in Union City. And take a photo of Thomason to the Lexington to see if anyone there can connect Nannis and Thomason. This case can't be this simple, can it?"

CHAPTER SEVEN

"You are a very cunning little boy, aren't you, Master Frederick, if that is your real name?"

A balding, bespectacled face stood at Frederick's bedroom door, uniformed, a tiny moustache, the heel of his boot making a sharp sound as he brought it down hard next to the other to punctuate his always important pronouncements.

"Herr Himmler, you startled me."

Himmler had entered the open door without knocking. He stood staring at the boy, saying nothing but smacking his gloves against his thigh.

"You think I don't know what you are doing."

"I am reading."

"Be smart with me boy and you will find yourself missing somewhere where no one will find you. I am not as gullible as the Führer and his friends."

"He will be pleased to hear it."

"Yes, of course," undeterred by the implied threat of being told on, "your little pantomime for Hitler was quite something, I am told. I have been making enquiries. There is no one to vouch for you, boy. I have unearthed an old photograph of the von Eichmann family. The boy in the picture hardly bears a resemblance to you. Do you want to tell me who you are?"

"How dare you insult my family." Frederick rose accusatively. "Get out."

"Or what? Your stocks with the Führer are not so high since your argument with him." Then said in an ironic whisper, "*You know,*" *the one about the Jews."* Returning to full voice, "Of course, he told me, you are a Jew lover. It got me wondering. The Führer's view of you will be even less when I tell him that you are an imposter as well. You wish to interfere with our plans in regard to the Jews? You are so puny you can hardly keep your britches up. Tell me what the future looks like now I have discovered you?"

Frederick was surprisingly calm, surprising to both him and Himmler given that of which he had just been accused. His hatred of Himmler and his resignation to his fate after his outburst with Hitler left him bereft of concern and now resigned to having been caught. He ceased to pretend.

"So you have not spoken to Herr Hitler?"

"Not yet. I wanted to meet you in person to be sure, gauge your reaction."

"And are you now sure?"

"You are guilty as hell."

"So you have come here alone to arrest me."

Frederick had strolled over to the door and was looking down the empty corridor. He closed the door and gestured for Himmler to sit. Himmler, unthreatened and curious, obliged, removing his hat and throwing his gloves into it, placing it on his lap.

"Your hatred of the Jews is irreconcilable with intelligent behaviour," Frederick began, "and your plan to eliminate them is barbaric and will destine this country to humiliation and destruction."

Frederick casually sat down in the chair opposite Himmler, staring straight into his weedy eyes as he crossed his legs, calmly placing his arms relaxed on the armrests of the chair, hands flopping over the end pointing towards the floor.

Himmler laughed.

"You have a set of balls on you, that is for sure."

Himmler reached into his uniform for a pack of cigarettes and lighter, expecting to be entertained further before he arrested the boy.

"Do you mind if I have one of those. It has been quite a long time. I don't suspect it will hurt now."

Himmler accommodated him, a last wish perhaps, puzzling over the boy's manner.

"You know you are much smaller than I imagined you to be, Herr Himmler, and fatter." Frederick lit his cigarette. "But just as ugly."

Frederick half stood to casually pass the lighter back to Himmler before falling back into his chair, slouching, relaxed, cigarette poised alongside his face, his elbow on the rest of the chair, smoke billowing, their eyes clenched in a wrestling match. He drew heavily on the cigarette again, looking for a reaction from Himmler to his insult. Himmler burst out laughing, thinking the boy an ant complaining about the boot that was about to step on him. Frederick continued enjoying his opportunity.

"Maybe your attitudes have been influenced by the ravings of Walther Darré or that racist vermin Alfred Rosenberg? Are you sexually aroused by those men?" Himmler stopped smiling. "That is an impressive uniform, Herr Reichsführer, but have you ever worn it in battle, have you had the courage to kill anyone up close, to face the danger personally or are you still just an… agronomist? How are the flowers in your garden?"

"You know too much for a little boy. Those fools who advise Hitler are too stupid to see that you cannot be who you say you are."

"You are right, of course. I have come here for the specific purpose of stopping you from killing the Jews." Frederick paused for effect. "Or kill you if you are too stupid to reconsider your opinions."

More laughter, coughing.

"I haven't yet decided what the best course of action is with the Jewish problem, but extermination sounds like as good an idea as any. Why do you think you can influence anybody's opinion on that matter, you little shit? Perhaps we should start with a spanking on your bare bottom."

"You would enjoy that?"

"You are full of good ideas. Who are you boy? An answer, NOW."

"My name is Franz Gothenburg. I am one hundred and thirty-five years old, assuming you don't count the last two twice and I look pretty damn good for my age."

"And demented it would appear."

"I have come here from the future. A future that has seen Germany destroyed, six million Jews killed by you and you yourself dead of a poison cowardly self-inflicted after you were arrested by the British."

"Ridiculous. Do you think me an idiot? I think we will start this extermination with you, Master Gothenburg, a Jew I assume. You have that smell about you."

"I am a Jew, and unlike you, human." Himmler threw his cigarette on the floor and sat up in his chair but before he could act further Frederick quickly added. "There is one thing I could show you to prove what I say."

Frederick stood, dropping his cigarette butt on the floor and extinguishing it with his shoe. He walked over and reached into his desk drawer. He turned to reveal that it was a pistol. He had stolen it from the guard station the day after his fight with Hitler, the beginnings of Plan B. Himmler lurched back into his chair and began to fondle with his leather holster.

"Pull that gun and I will shoot you." Frederick cocked the weapon to demonstrate that he understood the mechanism. Himmler paused, half-raising his hands. "There is one further thing I want to say before I let you go."

"And what would that be?"

"You are a dirty little gutless murdering cunt." Frederick picked up the cushion from his desk chair and stepping closer to Himmler, continued, "Perhaps we will start with you instead."

A muffled bang.

Himmler fell to the floor, blood streaming from his temple.

"Smell that, you prick."

Frederick was standing over him, watching the blood spurt, wanting to fire a second time, watching the life drain from Himmler's body. He was mesmerised imagining the parents that he had lost at Himmler's hand. He pulled himself back into reality and went quickly to the door, smoking gun in hand and opening it ajar, waiting to see if the noise had been detected. There was no one.

He went to Himmler prostrate on the floor now almost dead and opened his holster, removing his gun and placing it in his hand, hiding the gun he had just used. He searched through Himmler's coat for the family photograph he said he had found. He had indeed brought it with him presumably to show the boy, but Frederick's forthrightness had made any proof unnecessary. He destroyed the photograph. He opened Himmler's coat and unbuckled his belt, pulling down his trousers and underpants. He thought for a second that the scene better reflected the man but that was not his purpose. He tore up what was left of the cushion placing it in the garbage, picking up the fragments of it from the floor, using Himmler's gun now in Himmler's hand, he expended the weapon, firing out the open window this time so that the shot could be heard and went out into the hall and began to scream.

The nurse was the first to attend the boy having heard the second shot and the boy's screams. Viewing the wretched scene, she immediately called the police and Hitler was quickly told and was within moments on the scene. Frederick pretended to be deeply distressed and almost incoherent.

"Tell us, boy, settle yourself. What happened?" Hitler asked impatiently, distressed.

"He came to my study unexpectedly" Frederick sobbed. "We talked. He said he had seen me around and was impressed by me… and my good looks."

Hitler's eyes went skyward. He knelt on one knee and put his hand on the boy's shoulder. "Go on."

"He said he loved me." Hitler's head dropped. "I didn't know what to say." Frederick's explanation became hurried. "He pulled down his pants and sat down. He asked me to hold his penis. I said no… no and ran to the door. He pulled out his gun and beckoned me over. I began to scream. I told him I was going to tell you and I ran out screaming for help when I was in the hallway I heard the shot."

"Stop. Stop." Hitler stood. "You two get this body out of here," Hitler said to the two attending policemen. "Nurse, clean up this mess. You heard nothing of this, do you understand, none of you." Everyone in the room nodded. "Sergeant, you will be advised of what to put in your report, give me that notebook and get out."

Hitler summoned over his adjutant. "Get SS-Obergruppenführer Heydrich in my office… tonight." Hitler always preoccupied with his agenda. "He'll have to take over Heinrich's duties, at least for now."

"There is no shortage of arseholes around here," Frederick said under his breath.

"What?" Hitler asked tersely, angry with what had transpired.

"I said I want to go to nurse Helga's room."

"Of course. Go."

Sepp Dietrich walked through the door after letting the boy and the nurse pass, having heard Frederick's account from the hallway. Hitler looked at him despairingly, shaking his head. General Dietrich worked for Himmler but was once Hitler's personal bodyguard and remained a trusted friend.

"I had heard rumours," Dietrich said.

"I don't want to hear it. Leave the man in peace. Whatever he was, he has paid a price here tonight, and I will desperately miss his organisational skills. Of all the times for this to happen."

"I will ensure that this is attended to, you go."

"My friend. Come see me when you finish here."

"Why would he shoot himself?" Hitler asked Dietrich, now in Hitler's office an hour later, Heydrich waiting in the anteroom. "He seemed so motivated."

"He was a troubled man. I could never figure him out; he was always so stressed. Maybe he was infatuated with the boy, and the rejection was enough to push him over the top, or the fear of you finding out. He knew you trusted the boy and he knew your views on sexual perversion."

"He was that fragile?"

"His secret out, who knows what he would do? He's dead. It was his gun, by his hand. You can't think the boy had anything to do with it."

"Of course not. Heinrich was the only one armed in that room, and Frederick is… a feeble eight-year-old. Besides, how would a boy from a family such as his know anything about buggery to tell such a story?" Then Hitler said under his breath, talking only to himself, "it is sadly something that I knew too well as a child."

"You should get Joseph to write the press release."

"I already have. It was a heart attack. Any hint of violence would be unwelcome. He will have the police records reflect that fact."

"We will give him a state funeral, of course. We can't have any questions asked." After a pause. "So, you trust the boy?"

"Yes, he has a temper, but nothing Heinrich could not have handled even if they did fight. The boy is quite delicate physically, even for his age. I know from experience." Hitler recalled their fight with a half-smile, Frederick pounding on his chest with little or no effect. "His mind will be a great asset to us one day if he can become a little more open-minded and give up his obsession with the Jews."

"You care for him."

"Yes, I do, despite his inadequacies and misconceptions." Hitler felt the need to clarify that statement, adding quickly, "not in the way that Himmler did, that is a sickness."

"Of course, I didn't mean to…"

"Stop. I have no stomach for that conversation." There was an awkward pause. Hitler moved to the window. "Do you think Heydrich will fit the role? I thought of you, but I want you by my side, to come work for me again as my military advisor."

"Reinhard has the strength for it, that much is certain. They say he has an iron heart. The way things are headed, he will need it. He did a remarkable job as the head of the Sicherheitsdienst." Heydrich was the founding Head of the Intelligence Agency of the SS. "In many respects, he is a harder and more determined man than Heinrich… was."

"There is much to do. Heydrich it is, then." Hitler went over and put his hands on Dietrich's shoulders. "You always seem to be around when I need someone, my old friend."

"It will always be so, my Führer."

"Ask Martin to come in as you leave and to bring Heydrich with him."

Frederick was back in nurse Helga's room alone, panicking. The nurse was still in his room, cleaning. Should he escape and hide, he wondered? Sperenburg beckoned. His parents would be so happy to see him, but the terrible fate that awaits them had not been subverted. Perhaps they all could hide or flee, but would they believe him, at least sufficient for them to act, to leave, but what of the others, so many others. There was no way that the authorities were going to believe that Himmler killed himself; he was a machine. But Frederick recalled that he did in the end kill himself when faced with arrest by the British after the war. Frederick pondered whether that proclivity was obvious to Hitler. His mind was racing. He had no other alternative than to make it look like suicide. He could not dispose of the body; he couldn't even lift the fat bastard. He still had his own gun. He would ask to see Hitler urgently and finish it for whatever good that would do. He had already witnessed how easily Himmler was replaced by a man at least as evil. The SS was without its head for a matter of five minutes; no plans were disturbed, no destiny changed. From what he had read about Heydrich, by killing Himmler, he may even have made matters worse, if that were possible. "No, no, no," he said out loud, rubbing his head with both hands, pacing.

There was a gentle knock on his door; it opened, a head appeared.

"May I come in, Frederick?"

"Certainly, Herr Speer."

Frederick was quick to look behind Speer as he opened the door to see if anyone else had come with him, someone from the SS. He went over and gave Speer a hug around his waist. He needed as many friends as he could find.

"Are you alright?" Speer asked, unclasping the boy.

"Shaken."

"Of course. Himmler is a bad man. I think even Adolf feared him. I never liked the man and always wondered what was behind those spectacles. Now we know. You shouldn't worry. I am sure Adolf will see the truth of it."

"Do you really think so?" Frederick said trepidatiously, sitting back down on his nurse's bed and fearing that Hitler would in fact see the truth.

"I am certain of it."

"Is Herr Hitler alright. He was very angry" Frederick asked nervously.

"Sepp said he has settled down and was with Martin Bormann and Heydrich when he left him. He tells me that Heydrich is going to replace Himmler."

"A good choice given the job at hand."

"I don't approve of his methods and he is no friend of Martin's, but then again neither was Himmler. I am certain Martin will have something to say about that to the Führer."

"Herr Bormann is Head of the Chancellery, is he not, Hitler's departmental head and secretary? Does he have enough say to stop Herr Heydrich from becoming Head of the SS?"

"Martin is the Reich Leader of the NSDAP, secretary to Hess, and sometimes assists the Führer, but you are right, he's probably headed for bigger things," Frederick corrected himself, having mixed up the timeline of Martin Bormann's advancement amidst all the drama. "Adolf holds Martin in high regard, but in this case, he will not influence this decision. Not promoting Heydrich would be politically dangerous. The Führer is forever the pragmatist."

"I don't want to be alone, Herr Speer."

"I will arrange for a guard."

"No. No police. They frighten me."

"Fine, but you must get some rest. You must be in shock. You should keep warm. I will ask the nurse to come in when I leave."

"Can I come to work with you tomorrow?" Back to Plan B.

"Frederick…"

"You are building the New Reich Chancellery at the moment, aren't you? Will you let me be on site tomorrow with you? I want to see the progress, maybe do some drawings. It would be a distraction. I want to be an architect like you, Herr Speer."

Speer sensed the boy's desperation and felt flattered, as the boy intended. Frederick had no interest in being an architect, he was interested in the explosives that they would keep on site as the demolition of the old building was well underway. Guns he struggled with, but explosives were his stock in trade from his days manufacturing smart bombs for the American military.

"I will arrange it. I will have my assistant Fräulein Adler come and get you in the morning. I will tell the nurse our plans. Now try and get some sleep. Everything will be better tomorrow."

The next morning, Heydrich turned up at Frederick's door just as he and Fräulein Adler were leaving for the Chancellery building site.

"A word with you, boy. Will you excuse us a moment, Fräulein?"

"Of course, Herr Obergruppenführer," Fräulein Adler replied, with Heydrich still wearing his old uniform.

"It is Reichsführer now... but you were not to know. Wait in the hall."

"Congratulations, Herr Heydrich," Frederick chirped.

"Apparently, I have you to thank, boy," Heydrich said, aloof and arrogant. "Why was Heinrich here last night?"

"He came to introduce himself. I have told Herr Hitler what happened."

"Tell me."

"I have been told not to speak of it."

"Is that right... Wunderknabe? Is it possible that you are as smart as they say? I don't like things I don't understand; they make me nervous."

"You must be nervous all the time then, Herr Reichsführer." Frederick said, staring Heydrich in the eye. The secretary in the hall heard the comment and cringed in fright. Frederick felt a show of strength was appropriate, something Heydrich might understand.

"And a smartass to boot."

"Did you come here to bugger me as well, Reichsführer? Do you think it a perk of the job?" Heydrich's face went bright red, but not from embarrassment. He wasn't capable of that emotion. "If you want to talk to me further, we will do it in the presence of the Führer. It is to him that I have given an undertaking of secrecy."

Heydrich didn't respond, taken aback, still assessing the boy, caught between grabbing Frederick by the neck and stunned inaction. Frederick walked around him and out into the hall to collect Fräulein

Adler. Heydrich was left alone in Frederick's bedroom, puzzled and a little wounded. It crossed his mind to search it, but he felt the boy was too feeble, as the Führer had suggested, to get the better of a man like Heinrich.

In the car, Fräulein Adler began to counsel the boy.

"You should not speak to people like Herr Heydrich in such a manner. These people have powers to deal with you without recourse to the law."

"What law? They are the law. These people are arseholes and should be dealt with like the vermin that they are."

Frederick had picked his mark correctly. Fräulein Adler was one of the many Berliners who did not agree with the methods of the SS.

"Albert said you were quite the young man, but I had no idea," Fräulein Adler was glancing at Frederick with a look of admiration.

"There is far too much leeway given to the SS by the people of Berlin. You should stand up to them."

"Yea, sure. Anyone but you would have been in prison right about now." Frederick began to consider her point and wondered why indeed he had not been arrested. He had just shot Himmler and vilified his replacement to his face. "They have done so much to bring the country out of depression," Fräulein Adler continued. "They have offered us our dignity back and stood up to the foreigners who would enslave us with their peace treaty."

"Yes, but at what price to our freedoms, Fraulein," Frederick mumbled as he watched the pedestrians through the closed car window, still fascinated by their attire and lack of electronic paraphernalia. "What do they do with their day?" Frederick said out loud, referring to their lack of access to the internet and social media, a comment lost on Fräulein Adler.

"They probably work, thanks to Herr Hitler. There will be elections soon," she continued.

"If there are, they will be meaningless. You will need to go to the streets to make a change now."

"Yes, to meet the Sturmabteilung there. That would be most pleasant."

"A more desperate fate awaits you than the Brownshirts, my dear, if you fail to act now."

"*My dear*, excuse me, what are you, my father? Do you at least know that you are an eight-year-old?"

"I'm getting used to it."

"We don't all have your courage, Frederick."

"It is within us all, Fräulein, as I am just discovering." Frederick changed the subject. "You call your boss by his first name. Are you close?"

"Herr Speer is married."

"You didn't answer. You were going to add that *he is intelligent and sooooo good looking,* is that correct?"

"Are you going to give me a taste of your famous insight now, Frederick?" Then she added, laughing, "Yes… very handsome."

"I like your honesty Fräulein."

"Call me Yana."

"You too are very handsome, Yana."

"You need to be older to say that to a girl my age, Frederick."

"You have no idea. You can only be… what, eighteen?"

"Nineteen. Most of my friends are married."

"How wonderful for them," Frederick turned back to look out the window again, now relaxed and somewhat disinterested in the conversation, having come quietly to the conclusion that he had gotten away with killing Himmler. "You all must have had a large dose of Nazi indoctrination at school, yet you seem to dislike them."

"My father is a professor at Humboldt University. My education was broader than just school."

"Ah yes, one of the Nazis' favourite people, a professor." They both laughed. "They have quite a large botanical department at Humboldt, do they not?"

"Yes, I often go into their greenhouses when I visit my father. Do you also love botany?"

"I do. Would you take me sometime, Yana?"

"What about today? I actually need to see my father about a family matter. Herr Speer has given me the day off to entertain you. We could go there before we go to the Reich Chancellery."

"I think we are going to be good friends, Yana."

"I think so too, Frederick."

At the university, Yana was giving Frederick the penny tour of the greenhouses, having just visited her father, when they came upon a stand of castor bean plants.

"I was hoping we would see this species. Usually only found in North America. This is indeed a fine botanical department."

"The best in Europe. Does that plant particularly interest you, Frederick?" Yana asked.

"Yes, castor oil and so on. Do you think your father would allow me to have some of the beans?"

"I think they are studying the effects of fertilisation on yield and growth rates of all of these plant species in this room, so I am not sure. Let me check with the technical assistant."

Yana disappeared for a moment and returned with the research assistant responsible for the study.

"We harvested the beans yesterday," the assistant said. "We discard them once they are weighed and checked. How much do you want?"

"How much do you have?"

"About seventeen kilos."

"More than enough for what I have in mind. Can you give me four, no, five kilos in a carry bag, please?"

"Of course. What do you want to use them for?"

"A project with my tutor to determine the oil yield per bean. We were going to use rapeseed, but this is much more interesting."

"It is good to see a boy as young as you taking an interest in such matters."

"You have no idea how interested."

It was four months before Frederick would see Hitler again. It had been harrowing. He still thought that he might be arrested, despite Speer's reassurances to the contrary. He had killed Himmler but had witnessed an equally racist miscreant take his place, as he always thought would happen if he acted with violence. Nonetheless, he still had the gun that he had taken from the guardhouse. He couldn't believe that, with all his meticulous preparation prior to the BCD smash, he hadn't thought of becoming competent with firearms. At a close enough range, he consoled himself, it didn't seem to matter.

Frederick had been left to his own devices with his tutor and his nurse. He occasionally heard that Hitler was asking after him but didn't know his mood or intentions. The absence of his arrest was a good sign, Frederick thought or at least hoped. Even so, Frederick believed that he had missed his chance to persuade Hitler to an alternative path and that he had overplayed his hand. With rising domestic violence against German Jews, Frederick needed to act. He had managed to collect various items of interest to him, sometimes with Yana's help as with the castor beans, all pieces of the puzzle that went to make up his Plan B. Three detonators from the building site, various solvents, receptacles, and other items including a Bunsen burner, all by themselves, with the exception of the well-hidden detonators, innocuous and seemingly appropriate for a boy with an interest in science, all of which had been assembled without attracting attention. He felt it appropriate to lay low until matters surrounding Himmler's death disappeared behind more pressing national objectives, an aspiration which, given the times, quickly became a reality with current events now overshadowing Himmler's death.

One day, word came that Frederick and his nurse were going up to the Berghof, Hitler's mountain retreat near Berchtesgaden in Bavaria for a week's holiday. Hitler would be there, as well as the usual crew including Eva and her sister Gretl, some of Eva's friends such as Marianne Schönmann, Herta Schneider and her children, Hitler's now secretary Martin Bormann, the new head of the SS Reinhard Heydrich and support staff, and the most trusted of his senior personnel, including their wives and children. Albert Speer and Joseph Goebbels would be there, both of whom Frederick now knew well, and all of whom Hitler took up there to socialise in an environment controlled by him for the purpose of discussing public affairs in the clean mountain air. It was the week before Hitler's birthday on the 20th of April, and they would all pose for the annual photograph at Berghof a week early this year because of the planned festivities back in the city with a parade and other celebrations surrounding Hitler's fiftieth birthday in 1939. The day had been declared a national holiday.

When Frederick first arrived at Berghof, he was ignored by Hitler. He spent his time for the first couple of days willingly distracted in the company of Sepp Dietrich's daughter, who he knew only as Mädchen. She was ten years old and was beautiful with long flowing blonde hair that she wore without plates, instead letting it run straight down her back like a river of honey that shone in the sun as a beacon to a forlorn eight-year-old boy who had been lonely for most of the last eighty years. She was always immaculately groomed Frederick noticed and intelligent and inquisitive of nature. He was glad to have the diversion from matters too ugly to contemplate, matters that he was now planning in great detail, the violence that those actions required frightened him. For now, he finally had some company who had no predispositions about him other than a desire to be friends. In those two days, they had become quite the pair and it drew comment from the other guests at Berghof. They were saying what a cute couple they both made and how it would be a great match for Mädchen if she were to eventually marry a boy with Frederick's breeding. On the morning of the third day at Berghof, Frederick and Mädchen had gone out walking after breakfast on their own having taken one of the many trails that went away from the house through the woods within the nine-hundred-hectare secure compound that surrounded it. Frederick felt he needed to clear his head and return his focus to the miserable task at hand. They had stopped and were seated resting on a large rock after walking for quite a while both perched with a view of the valley beneath.

Frederick had spent most of his life alone, the last thirty years in almost complete isolation. Never having been married or having had children, he had not sustained a long-term relationship with any woman since an ill-fated courtship whilst he was in college. The open and playful conversations with Mädchen, even though the subject matter was primitive, were providing him with an unexpected release and he found himself enjoying them even more than he should, given the real age disparity between the two of them.

"It's beautiful," Mädchen said. "The valley, I mean."

"Yes. And so are you. Your skin is just amazing and your hair is a gift from heaven," Frederick said almost involuntarily.

"That is nice of you to say, Frederick. You are such the young gentleman. You shouldn't try to flirt with me, though, I am much older than you."

"You don't know the half of it or perhaps the tenth of it or whatever the math is."

"You say some silly things sometimes, Frederick. You are trying to flirt with me, I know it, aren't you, Frederick?" Mädchen said, seeking the answer needed by all girls of her age.

"What does a small girl like you know about flirting?"

"I am almost two years older than you and I know quite a lot, thank you very much, more than you do, I suspect."

"I don't think that you do." Frederick's tone was condescending, but she had piqued his interest. "What do you know?"

"I have kissed a boy." Frederick looked at her in disbelief and the disappointment was apparent on his face. She felt a little embarrassed by her bold admission. "Well, I didn't really want to but he ran up and kissed me and then ran away so I'm not sure whether that counts or whether he liked it or not. I didn't like it so much."

"It doesn't count," Frederick said, making a ruling on the matter, relieved it was inconsequential, the tension in his body releasing because the event was trivial. "But I can see why he would want to do such a thing."

"You are making me blush, Frederick. See, you are flirting with me. Do you want to kiss me?" Mädchen said as if to prove she was the older and more sophisticated of the pair.

"Very much… but we shouldn't. I am in fact much, much older than…"

"Than you seem? Yes. But who will know out here?"

Frederick stopped and thought. If he pursued his plans, plans on which he was now set, his arrest and execution were certain. Some self-indulgence was deserved, perhaps timely, and Mädchen was right, they were alone. He couldn't explain his real age without appearing demented, what harm could it do to indulge her? He shuffled his bottom along the rock to get a little closer, gently putting his hand on the top of her hand, which was resting on the rock supporting her as she sat. He leant over timidly and kissed her on the lips. It was a slow kiss. Her lips were soft.

"There, you have had one for real," Frederick said reassuringly, settling back into his original position, satisfied that he had provided the education that she needed.

"It was nice. Can I do it now?"

"You mean you didn't last time?"

"Silly."

She leant over and put her arms around his neck and kissed him again, this time a deep passionate kiss. It was a kiss that a girl of ten years of age had no business knowing about. Frederick fell off the rock onto the ground after she let him go.

"I see what you mean," Frederick said as he stood up dusting his hands against his pants.

"You obviously liked it, Frederick, you didn't run away. And besides, you seem… excited. Perhaps I should run away."

"What do you mean, **Mädchen?**"

Frederick looked down at the bulge in his pants and turned quickly around to face the other way, apologising for his indiscretion.

"It's alright, Frederick, it's quite natural. At least I know you really like me for sure."

"That is quite inappropriate of you to say, **Mädchen**, and rude. You are embarrassing me."

"My parents and I have been to Nature Camp. I know what a boy's thing looks like and what it's supposed to do. You see, I do know things, Frederick. That's because I'm older than you."

"Nature Camp? I didn't think they had those things in this day and age."

"What do you mean? You're not making sense again. It is a very popular pastime in Germany and I liked it."

"Does that mean that you…?"

"Nobody has any clothes on, Frederick, if that is what you are asking. Fraulein Braun goes to one with her sister. I think she even made a movie of it for Herr Hitler. He won't go with her because of his position in the government, but he quite likes to watch the movies she makes, or so I'm told. It is very German."

"That's not helping me, you know… thinking about you naked. It is making things worse." Frederick looked down again, still facing away from Mädchen. "My goodness, I am a healthy boy," he said to himself, not having had a full erection for many years, longer than he could remember, and this one was bigger than the ones he remembered. He never bothered to seek help for erectile dysfunction in New York because he felt it superfluous having nowhere to put it if he did fix it. He was morally opposed to prostitution even though he felt an unexplainable affiliation with the girls who were involved in the trade, perhaps from a previous life.

"Let me see it" Mädchen said. "If you do, I will show you mine." Frederick said nothing except muttering something to the contrary. "Come on, don't be scared. Scaredy cat, scaredy cat. I dare you. I double dare you, you chicken. My parents do it all the time. Pleaseeee?"

Childishness overtook him and he pulled down his pants and turned around to see Mädchen's mouth open wide in shock. "I've never seen one as stiff as that before. My, Frederick, it looks like it's going to snap off."

"Well, it's been a while, so yes, it just might explode." Frederick mumbled analytically, looking down at it. "You had better stay clear," he said, holding out his hand as if to protect her from it. "I don't think it's going back to normal anytime soon."

"Here, I will show you mine." Before Frederick could stop her, she pulled down here pants and took her dress completely off.

"Dear God in heaven," Frederick exclaimed, looking at Mädchen naked. "Mädchen. I can't breathe."

Mädchen stepped out of her panties and took a step towards him and he thrust out his hands again and started to pull up his pants with the other.

"No, no. This has gone too far already. You should stay right where you are."

"But Frederick, it is only natural." She continued to walk towards him and having reached him put her arms around his waist. Frederick had managed to get his short pants back up over the impediment and had turned his back on her again.

"I am going to regret this for the rest of my life, **Mädchen." He turned and kissed her on the forehead. "But put you**r dress back on, please, and we'll walk back. I am certain that you have no comprehension of where this could lead. I think that you are the most beautiful thing I have ever seen but we must go."

"Thank you, Frederick, but why…?"

"Mädchen, please!"

Mädchen complied reluctantly and dressed. After dressing, she went back over to him and took his hand. Frederick had tucked his shirt back in his pants and had collected himself. They began to walk back to the house. Not far up the track they encountered another couple from the Berghof walking toward them. Frederick was relieved that they had not come past a few minutes earlier and looked at Mädchen as if to infer that he had chosen the right course of action for them both.

"Don't look so smug, Frederick. They probably go to Nature Camp as well."

"What is it that your father does, Mädchen?"

"SS-ObergruppenFührer Dietrich."

"Sepp Dietrich? You are Sepp Dietrich's daughter?"

"Only his friends call him Sepp or your serene highness or someone like that." Mädchen giggled at her little joke, mocking her father's senior position in the Reich now holding a General's rank in the SS and back working directly for Hitler.

"How does he find working for Herr Heydrich?"

"Well, he works for the Führer now."

"I was never sure when I was going through my files who he actually worked for but I know he is very close to the Führer, a spy perhaps in Herr Himmler's camp. I suspect Herr Himmler didn't care for him looking over his shoulder, when he was alive, I mean, poor man, heart attack apparently." Frederick scoffed as he said *heart attack*. "Bullshit. He died of shame."

"What files, Frederick?"

"I like to study politics. Does your father like his new job?"

"Oh, I am sure he does. He is a very important man and he cares deeply for the Führer."

"That is certainly true, and a good man from what I could determine. I would like to meet him some time," Frederick said pensively, "ask him a few questions."

"I'll introduce you when we get back. He has heard of you, of course, from the night Herr Himmler had his heart attack. He was there that night."

"I thought that was him… in the hall."

"You have quite a reputation for a young boy, you and your politics. Are you really as smart as they say, Frederick? Do you truly see the future?"

"Smart enough to choose you as my friend and to hope you continue to be in my future."

Mädchen liked that answer very much.

Mädchen and Frederick strolled back into the Berghof hand in hand to find Frederick's nurse searching for him frantically. Hitler had summoned him. He was quickly ushered into Hitler's leather-lined drawing room where he and Speer were sitting in front of a huge open fire.

"Sit down, my boy," Hitler said. "I am sorry I have not had much time for you lately, but I have had a lot to contend with."

Frederick was relieved at the tone of his voice.

"I don't quite know what to make of you, Frederick. I was very angry with you — the fight we had, you striking me for what that was worth. You need to exercise more, boy, build yourself up a bit, and also learn some restraint. Your temper will get you into trouble. Then there was that incident with Himmler. You are a difficult person to understand. Herr Heydrich says you have been very rude to him as well, but that is perhaps easy to understand." Frederick thought of Heydrich as a tattle tale. "You have an intellect that is beyond your years, beyond that of many of my senior people. The fact that you would try to put Heydrich in his place does not surprise me. He is an arrogant prick, and I can just picture your response to him. I wish I was there."

Albert Speer threw his head back and laughed out loud, then had the reflex to look behind him to see if he could be overheard. "I wish I'd been there, too," he said, taking another sip of his coffee after wiping a tear of laughter from his eye.

"You have courage, boy, and you seem to have a clear vision of the future. Am I mad to even consider discussing my plans further with you?"

Frederick didn't answer.

"I have been speaking to my good friend Albert here, and it appears that he is your good friend as well. He tells me that we are fortunate to have such a boy in our ranks and that you will make a fine leader one day — a leader of men — and that your forward vision is an asset that we should embrace. Did you really tell Heydrich that he was a nervous idiot?" Hitler digressed, and both men laughed out loud again. "Please understand that the man is dangerous."

"He is a psychopath," Speer confirmed under his breath.

"I will be what you want me to be, my Führer, even an ignorant small boy if you desire it."

"I believe that you would attempt to do that, Frederick, for me, I think, but you could never be what you just claimed."

Hitler paused for a moment, and Frederick did not say another word, still unclear where Hitler was headed.

"I was with the Japanese ambassador last week with Ribbentrop. They had drafted a proposal for a pact between us, Italy, and Japan. He called it a Tripartite Agreement. When I heard his words, your exact words to me, Frederick, six months ago, I found myself reaching for my weapon. I was so angry, I intended to shoot that slanty-eyed-son-of-a-bitch where he sat and would have, except his chair was atop my favourite rug. Do you know why I wanted to shoot him, Frederick?"

There was no answer from Frederick, who began involuntarily to check what kind of rug was under his chair.

"I was angry because of you, Frederick," Hitler continued. "I was angry to think that you may be right about the destiny you painted for the Fatherland — a dark picture, and indeed a destiny for which I alone would be responsible."

Hitler stopped for a moment and thought further explanation of his mood was necessary.

"In March, we acquired the remainder of Slovakia, not because you had said so, but because the opportunity arose to do it, and I feel that the foreseeing of it was not a stretch for someone with your intelligence. Not so obvious was the Pact we formed with Italy, which Mussolini himself called the Pact of Steel — again, your exact words to me and Albert six months ago. The Japanese ambassador nearly got shot last week because of the frustration I feel inside me about you. I am conflicted by what you tell me, boy. Yet I hold a compulsion to believe you, that you have been right about many matters and therefore possibly right about the remainder. Do you still think it to be as you predicted, boy? Tell me truthfully; do not be scared of repercussions."

"I do. You have done nothing to change it, my Führer, and therefore it moves forward as I said it would, and as you make it to be."

Perhaps Himmler's absence had made a difference in Hitler's thinking. Perhaps Speer now had the greater sway. Hermann Göring was an idiot, Goebbels brilliant in his field but now on the outer because of his now well-known affair with the Czech actress. Hitler, forever the prude, had shunned him because of it. Hess was nothing more than a party mechanic, and Heydrich was the new boy in the inner circle, a killer. It was perhaps too early in his new role replacing Himmler for him to have any impact on Hitler's views. Maybe the balance had shifted, Frederick thought. At the very least, he might be in the clear regarding Himmler's murder. He felt relieved and welcomed another chance to move Hitler's thinking away from Hitler's perceived retribution against the Jews. This time, he resolved, he would be gentler.

"We are drawing up plans against Poland for September. What do you see for us in Poland?"

"Poland's cavalry will be crushed under your tanks and all of Europe will fear you because of it."

"That's it, yes."

"But now England and France will see you as unreliable after you break the Munich Agreement despite their tacit approval of your invasion of Czechoslovakia."

"Their approval was not tacit. It was clear for all to see nor was it an invasion, my boy. We restored order there and set the borders back to where they were under the Hapsburgs."

"Of course, my Führer. But your actions in Poland will weaken Chamberlain's hold on power to the point where he will not be able to negotiate with you any further."

"You are speaking as if it has already happened. I do not believe that they will declare war. I have publicly stated my aims clearly. I have no aspirations outside the reunification of Germany."

"And dealing with the Russians."

"You know too much, my boy, and should learn to keep your mouth shut."

"France and England will declare war, but America will stay out of it. Remember that Churchill sees a war with us as inevitable, even desirable; his political survival depends on it coming."

"I can't see why they would take such an approach despite Munich. The stakes are too high."

"Perhaps, but if they do, we must complain bitterly to the Americans through diplomatic channels and through their press and accuse France and England of having declared needless war. The American Ambassador to England, Joseph Kennedy, will support that view. King Edward will support your view. We should explain our reasons to him for the reinstatement of the Danzig corridor and say publicly that it is a matter of reconstituting the German-speaking parts of Europe driven apart as a consequence of Versailles, and that France and England have no right to intervene, let alone bring the continent back into conflict. You should be seen to make several overtures to both England and France for peace. Paint them as the aggressors."

"Sounds to me like you want Joseph's job, Frederick, and perhaps we should give it to you." Speer laughed. "You still feel the Americans are interested in what happens here?"

"The American public has no interest, but Roosevelt does. He shares his cousin Teddy's desire for great adventure. He seeks to be seen as a Rough Rider. He will back Churchill regardless of the domestic good of his people."

"Indeed. Him and Churchill must read the same comic books."

"We should open channels with the Americans in plain view of the rest of the world," Frederick continued. "Joseph Kennedy has aspirations toward the Presidency, and he is on record as saying that you have legitimate claims to reuniting Germany with East Prussia and Danzig, which cannot be united with Germany without re-obtaining the Polish Corridor. He will not want to go back on his words and he would relish the opportunity to establish a clear political point of difference between him and Roosevelt."

"So then what?" Speer asks.

"It depends perhaps on how quickly a deal could be reached with England and France, which is to say before Churchill takes over. The English will be divided on what to do, but Churchill will have no such confusion and his view will, in the end, win out despite the opposing view of the Labor Party. You cannot let matters fester without settlement after you engage with France, and a settlement will not come with Churchill in charge."

"If we do enter France?'

"It will take less than thirty days for you to achieve a complete victory. The Maginot Line will become a monument to the stupidity of fixed fortifications in a world where mobility is king. They will plan and execute the French campaign against you as if it was 1918, but you will use the weapons and the strategies of modern warfare. It will be a stunning victory that will leave France and its capital largely untouched because of the speed and ferocity of the German assault."

"Yes, that is exactly what I have been telling these idiots who work for me. You, boy, have put your finger on it. They are all living in the past, and I will drag them by their necks into the twentieth century."

"It would be so, my Führer."

"I like this conversation better than our last. But if England can then see what we are capable of in France, why won't they negotiate?

I have no interest in a war with the English if indeed they declare it. This is what I do not understand from you, boy. It would be patent stupidity; it would be immoral."

"Churchill will vow to fight on and will insist on nothing but the complete and unconditional surrender or destruction of Germany. His motives will be political and born of the schoolboy adventure novels he coveted as a child and indeed his hatred of all things German. He will want to be seen in sharp contrast to Chamberlain, to be offering a clear alternative to his leadership."

"That fat, pompous bastard. It is not his life with which he makes that bargain."

"It will, in the end, be twenty million lives on this continent alone that will be lost in that wager."

"You always seem so sure of your facts, Frederick. You are saying to me that all of Europe is plunged into a catastrophic war," Hitler continues, summarising, "a war that later brings in the Americans because of the actions of the Japanese in response to an American blockade. You say that the American blockade may have even been motivated by Roosevelt's desire to join the European war because we had allied ourselves with the Japanese. But nonetheless, the result is sixty million dead worldwide and that Europe, in the end, is left divided. Nothing achieved from the actions of the English. Churchill does not even succeed in freeing Poland or Czechoslovakia, his basic reasons for his war. They are in the end left under the iron boot of the Soviets. I do not understand why such a price would be paid to achieve... nothing, to achieve that worst of all outcomes."

"Because by the time that you act against the French, it will be May 1940, unless you bring forward your plans. Churchill will be Lord of the Admiralty, Chamberlain will be very ill, and Churchill will be one month away from taking over the government. Churchill's platform in coming to power will be bringing England onto a war footing to enforce the declaration of war made by Chamberlain when you enter Poland. It is my firm belief that Chamberlain felt he had to act in that way but had secret plans to negotiate a peace before it came to war."

"Why should I wait so long to act against them? I will enter Poland at the latest by September. You say that France and England declare war immediately. Why would I wait until May next year?"

"The reason is that you believe, quite understandably, that both France and England are not serious about a war that defies logic, even though they felt compelled to declare it. You believe that they will, in the end, negotiate, seeing your lack of interest in engaging with France. But Churchill will not see it that way."

"So I had better act decisively in the first instance and get it over with."

"You must be seen by the American public to be trying to settle it by negotiation first. Remember, the English will not allow any attempt to negotiate with them directly to become known to the Americans. You will even send Hess into Scotland, the second in command of the party, out of pure frustration with the English refusal to negotiate, but they will just arrest him and tell the world that he had gone mad."

"I will not send him. I will ask the Americans to sue for peace, and we will do it in full view of their press. I have no interest in ruling France or England or anyone else except the German-speaking peoples. I am only interested in uniting our people and relinquishing the yoke of the Treaty of Versailles. It is those damned communists that I want to wipe from the earth."

"Whatever it is, you must settle the matter with Britain prior to the Japanese attacking America. And we don't want any English government in exile operating out of Washington, so we must satisfy the Americans with any settlement that is made. The whole thing has to be put to bed and accepted by the Americans before the Pacific war is engaged, if indeed, after the English settlement, there is a Pacific war. And you must help the Americans with the Pacific war if it does occur and then later get their help with your fight with the Soviets. Above all this, you must let the Jews go. You cannot join this group of nations with that genocide on your hands. Acquire the British colonies, create the Jewish state, and let them go there. That is the key."

"Be careful what you say. We both have a temper. Why is that central?"

"Credibility. The Americans will not deal with a mass murderer."

"The Americans hate them as much as us, and you say they will deal with Stalin and treat him as a hero while he goes about slaughtering Jews. Which is it?"

"You will have to ask Churchill why that murderous communist is his friend, but this is the crux of it. Perhaps in his black and white world, Germany is the enemy, Russia was once an ally under the last Czar, even though Stalin has now turned that State into one large concentration camp, Churchill will still embrace him. I refuse to attempt to explain Churchill's actions; they are both inexplicable and abominable to me. But I can say with absolute certainty that if you mark this country with the stain of Jewish blood, we will never recover from it, and Churchill will be seen as a visionary."

"I hear you but I struggle to believe you. So, what… you would deport them?"

"I personally have nothing against them. I would leave them where they are. But if you must act, then yes, deport them. You will have the Middle Eastern colonies of the French and the English. That is the long-lost Jewish homeland. What better thing to do than to send them home. Cut out the bits from those old colonies that we want and give the rest to the Jews. They will love you for it, or at least the Jews will love you, more importantly, the Americans will love you. The English have ruled over these Middle-Eastern people unwanted since the Turks, and they are hated there. Alternatively, leave them here as part of a greater expanded Germany and enjoy the contribution they would make to our nationhood."

"The English and French colonies are an abomination," Speer comments. "All those who have suffered under their yoke would see you as a hero, my Führer. The Irish and the Scots, and the Indians as well, if you choose to disassemble the entire English Empire. The boy is right."

"If you wish to deny the Jews the right to be a citizen of Germany, then so be it. But do not mistreat them, or it will mean the destruction of any chance we have of a relationship with the rest of the world. And in doing the right thing by the Jews, you would put the spotlight on what Stalin is doing in Russia, rather than allowing him to hide behind Churchill."

"You seem so certain. The Americans do not love the Jews."

"The Americans always want to be seen to be doing the right thing, regardless of their internal politics and racist beliefs. If they engaged in a European war at great cost – twenty million lives lost, half a million of them American, Poland not liberated, most of Germany reduced to rubble – do you not think that they would need to justify why they engaged in such a war? They would seek to justify that misery by pointing to your genocide of the Jews; they cannot justify it otherwise. Their reasons given for their involvement in the first place are nonsense: to save Poland, which will not be saved, and to stop a dictator from taking over Europe, yet they hand it to Stalin on a plate. The death and misery brought upon the citizenry of Europe at their and their allies' hands will need to be explained. It cannot in the end be justified by the liberation of Poland – what do Americans care about Poland, and they don't achieve that end in any case. Can they blame Churchill or Roosevelt? Never. What better than to blame you and the genocide of the Jews at your hands, asserting that you wanted to take over the world? That will be why they fought the war. Without that rationale, any reasonable person will look at the death and destruction in Europe in World War Two and ask, 'Why?' Was it all for the glorification of Stalin, Churchill's friend? If they do not discover the underlying evil of Jewish genocide in Germany, all will ask what has been achieved by such a war. They will blame Churchill and Roosevelt for unnecessarily prosecuting a war that achieved nothing, a war that put the Soviets in charge of half of Europe. And for me, the saddest thing of all is that the war will allow Stalin to perpetrate and hide the genocide within an expanded Soviet empire, the West apparently satisfied that they had stamped out Jewish persecution in Germany."

"Exhausted, more to the point. They would not go after Russia, their ally, after so much destruction," Speer added.

"But how do they know what our internal policies are towards the Jews? How can they use them to justify going to war with us?" Hitler asked.

"They don't know until after the war is over. Then all of Germany's secrets are laid bare, at least in the Western half of a divided Germany. It will be justification after the fact because they have no other way to justify it."

"Even as you speak of it, I become ill."

"Then you know it must be so, regardless of how you or the Americans feel about the Jews as a people. You should begin now by announcing that you wish the Jews to be treated respectfully. Announce that you will provide a better solution to the existing problem, a solution which retains German and Jewish dignity. But stop the violence and the mistreatment and restore Jewish rights to property and civil utilities. Do it today. Lead your people to the higher ground, my Führer, and do it in front of the Americans and the rest of the world."

"I can see that lifting international regard for Germany, for what that is worth, but it will matter naught to Churchill."

"So be it."

"I will consider it further. And Frederick, I know you mean well, I know you care about these people, but these are difficult matters and it goes to the core of promises the Party made to the peoples of Germany and to my own personal beliefs. I appreciate your persistence but you must tread carefully, please, especially with Herr Heydrich. Despite what you think, he is no fool. It would be wrong to make him your enemy. And… I forgive you for your outburst at our last meeting and for striking me. I know you have Germany in your heart and these visions of yours must trouble you as much as they do me."

"My Führer."

"Let me think it through." Hitler paused then rose, indicating the discussion was at an end. "And my boy, I approve of your new friend. She has a fine family. Sepp Dietrich is a fine soldier and a dear friend. Go… I have much to discuss with Herr Speer."

Frederick found Mädchen waiting for him as he left Hitler's study. The contrast between the discussion with Hitler and Mädchen's childish anticipation of further games was cleansing; it hit him like a bucket of cold water. He was happy to be washed clean of his encounter with Hitler and genuinely relieved that he had been heard and not arrested. He still had no real concept of what Hitler's true feelings were towards him. It was impossible for him to tell. Frederick's background would not allow him to believe that this man could do anything but evil. But for now, Frederick resolved to wait a little longer and see what transpired before pursuing any other plan. There was still time.

At Mädchen's command, they ran out to the courtyard to find something new with which to play. From inquisition to banality, Frederick thought as he chased Mädchen out of the house, watching her dress flap up. He had found his Alice, and they were off in search of a rabbit hole.

CHAPTER EIGHT

Jamison had been sent to Yemen to follow up on information provided in the Marsolet papers. FBI Section Chief Samuels was spreading out the files for a presentation resulting from that trip in a security briefing room at the Pentagon when the Undersecretary of Defence Intelligence, Jane Buckminster with her assistant entered the room along with the Deputy White House Chief of Staff, Jim Patterson. Patterson had come alone.

"I wasn't expecting you, Mr Patterson. I was expecting to brief Ms Buckminster."

"The President has a particular interest in what you guys were doing in Yemen the other day. He wasn't overly impressed with the shooting and he asked me to sit in at this meeting."

"That's fine, I guess, take a seat." Samuels was nervous about direct White House involvement. His boss knowing Patterson was in the meeting would want to attend himself or send additional representatives. "I think I should let the Executive Assistant Director know that you're here, Mr Patterson."

"Sure, sure, just get on with it. You can cover your arse later," Jim Patterson responded bluntly. "What were you guys doing in Yemen? Why were you shooting up that cafe? We have had hell to pay over that little display of macho bullshit."

"The agent was acting in defence of our contact, Professor Salam, who had information important to national security. Indeed, he was also acting to protect me and a fellow agent. Good god, man, we were attacked by machine gun-wielding terrorists on motorbikes."

"You were there? In Sana'a?"

"Under one of the tables at the café, yes. It was a close call. We only responded when they opened fire on us." Samuels never made any pretences about his competence in the field. His superiors thought his self-deprecation was an endearing trait given what his superior intellect brought to strategy formulation.

"You had an Augment with you. Why wasn't it used? It would have been a lot cleaner."

"Agent Jeffries felt that there wasn't time to initiate the Augment to contain the threat, so he returned fire. I concur that he needed to act to protect lives, Mr. Patterson, it was a judgment call."

"Who am I to question a judgment call made in the field under fire? Call me Jim, please, otherwise I'll start to think you're talking to someone important." Jim Patterson's modesty was false. He was one of the rising stars of the new Anderson administration. He was smart and efficient, and above all, he had the happy knack of being able to cut to the core of any subject. "Do you know why they were shooting at you?"

"I think we hit a nerve hooking up with the Professor. The Augment was used to arrest the second shooter who had fled the scene." The Augment had captured the second shooter alive; the first of the assassins had been shot dead.

"Were the shooters Iranians?"

"Yes, they were known to be connected to Iranian Intelligence. Contracted assassins." Samuels felt that it was always important to be definite about his answers to superiors.

"Why did they want this contact of yours, Professor…?"

"Salam. Well, that's what I'm here to show you." Turning to his assistant, Samuels instructed, "put that first display up, will you? To answer your question specifically, Professor Salam had information connecting some of his colleagues to the development by Iran of an Augment program."

"Shit," Patterson exclaimed, rubbing his forehead, "not this again."

"We believe that his information is sound. You can see here a photograph of a region outside Tehran where there is," the assistant changed the slide, "this warehouse to which we have tracked live biological material."

"Have they developed that material? I didn't think they had that capability."

"Stolen material. Here is a copy of the bill of lading," a new slide was placed up on the wall-sized electronic screen showing the bill of lading obtained from the old merchant in Sana'a, tracked down by Agent Jamison who had attended the meeting there with the professor because of her intimate knowledge of the case. She had found the merchant through examination of the paperwork given to her by Marsolet in Paris, which referred to a relationship between the merchant and Fahd. "This paperwork was used to make a shipment from this… warehouse in Sana'a." The assistant placed a photo of the old Sana'a warehouse up alongside the other slides already exhibited. Samuels arranged the images on the screen with his hand in an order that represented the flow of the material one to the other, thereby giving the whole graphic the appearance that it represented more certainty than it actually contained. "That sale was organised by this man, Yasser Fahd, a Yemeni national who has known ties to arms trading."

"Where is Fahd now?" Ms. Buckminster asked.

"We don't know. We have asked our friends over at the Agency whether they have any information on him, but we have received nothing back yet. The FBI has very little on him, Madam Undersecretary, except that he has shown up in New York in routine surveillance of the Iranian embassy. We have him meeting with their trade attaché, Imran Kalmati, who moonlights as the Iranian Head of Intelligence for North America. Do we have a slide of that? Kalmati has been ingratiating himself with the senior staff at AIOGEN for some time now." The assistant put up the photo of Fahd and Kalmati meeting with Zimmermann. "This other guy is a New York local, a jeweller named Zimmermann, currently in custody, whom we know had been trying to recruit Jack Pierce at AIOGEN before he was killed."

"You've got yourself quite a pot boiler here, Section Chief," Ms. Buckminster said, turning to her assistant and said, "get me the

Director on the phone, will you? Do we know where this laboratory is in Iran?"

"We have good reason to believe that it is in Tehran, not far from this warehouse in Sadr, but we don't have anything definite."

"What do…" Ms. Buckminster is interrupted by her assistant handing her the phone.

"Mr. Director, Jane Buckminster… yes, well thank you. We have a situation. I'm going to need your help. We are going to need some resources from you… yes, that's right. I'm here with Section Chief Samuels from the FBI and Deputy White House Chief of Staff Jim Patterson. Mr. Samuels is about to tell us what he needs from the CIA to track down an arms dealer who's got his hands on some Augment technology. Just a minute. I'll put you on speaker."

"Jim, hi," the voice on the phone said. "Chief Samuels, are we onto something?"

"Yes, sir," Samuels answered. "We have tracked down what we believe to be a technology theft. We have identified a particular person but not a specific location. We are certain that the deal is about to be completed and a new lab commissioned on the outskirts of Tehran tasked with developing augments. We have clean information on a movement of high-level personnel to Tehran, friends of our informant Professor Salam, they probably will staff the laboratory. The nature of these people could only mean that the lab is for Augment technology. The person we're looking at is a low life called Yasser Fahd, a known arms trafficker. We have the location of a shipment he made to his holding warehouse in Sadr, stolen biological material critical to the development of Augments, but we don't know its final destination as yet. We haven't made a move on it because we want to see where it leads us."

"Your information good, Section Chief?" the Director asked.

"Other than the lab location and the location of Fahd, it is solid, yes sir."

"What do you need?"

"We need some eyes, both in the air and on the ground. We believe there is going to be some movement soon at that warehouse where the material is held and that our arms dealing friend is going to show up in Tehran looking to get paid. We want to get a look at him and the shipment when they move it. We believe it will lead us to the lab."

"How did they get their hands on this technology?"

"We have one of our best agents trying to answer that question as we speak, sir. Special Agent Jamison. But I think the most important thing right now is to find the lab and verify what they actually have in there."

"Are we all agreed then?" Ms Buckminster said, looking for consensus from the meeting. "Let me be specific: Section Chief Samuels here is going to send to you, Mr. Director, what he has on the Yemeni situation along with a specific set of contacts for his agents on the case in Yemen. You, Mr. Director, are going to put whatever assets you need in play to find this lab and this Fahd character, and to find out what they've got. Is that okay with everybody?"

"That's a done deal, Jane. Send the material on my secure line, Section Chief. I'll be in touch." The Director hung up.

"Is that alright with you, Jim?" Ms Buckminster asked.

"Sure, sure that's fine. Give me a timeline."

"Seventy-two hours," Samuels estimated.

"We should meet again on Friday, then," Ms Buckminster confirmed.

"I'll set something up at the White House. I'll let you know where," Patterson said. "And maybe you should bring your boss with you next time, Samuels, or he'll start to feel you're trying to steal his thunder."

Section Chief Samuels smiled a nervous smile, privately agreeing with Patterson's assessment.

Back at the 19th Precinct that same morning, Cleary and Jacobs had begun reviewing their position in the Pierce murder investigation with Lieutenant Burgess. The lieutenant wasn't happy with their progress.

"So you've got a solid motive and opportunity with Sergeant Dan, the wife's boyfriend, but no evidence. You've got a separate motive and a conspiracy with the boyfriend and Thomason, the crazy protester with the demolition expertise, but no linkages or evidence. And you've got this Zimmerman character that potentially was tied up with some technology theft who has admitted lining up some of the AIOGEN people for his Middle Eastern contact and who therefore has access to the necessary expertise to do the bombing but you have no evidence linking him or this Kalmati guy to the crime. And we have a spouse apparently far too cute to hurt anybody, so she's not a suspect. Did I get all that about right?"

"That's about the size of it, yeah," Cleary confirmed meekly.

"I can't believe you haven't been able to shake anything loose on the boyfriend. Man, that fits…"

"…Like a glove, yeah," Cleary finished the Lieutenant's sentence for him. "We shook that tree pretty hard, too. We have executed a search warrant on him, Thomason, and the wife. Jacobs here has gone through their phone records and bank records with a fine-toothed comb. We've been to all three premises with photo arrays of the parties, and nobody, and I mean nobody, has seen anyone in the wrong spot at the wrong time. We can't link any of them to the explosives. We have got a grand total of squat."

"What about the forensics on the vehicle?"

"Nothing. No fingerprints. There is a shitload of DNA, but it all belongs to Pierce. The bomb was a real work of art, top-drawer, absolutely the latest shit out there."

"What does that tell you?"

"The perp is no amateur. Thomason could have access to that kind of explosive. We're told he was pretty good at blowing shit up when he was in the military. But so are the Iranians, even though the bomb is US military-grade."

"Fuck it. I want you to re-interview all three of them, and I want you to push, okay?" The lieutenant's frustration was on full display. "These FBI dickheads, they always play it so close to their chest. They had no right to hang onto those tapes or that Zimmerman file for so long. I've asked the captain to ensure we get a copy of their tapes of Kalmati's discussions with the AIOGEN people. If you don't get anything out of your three friends, then we have to change tack on this and assume it's got something to do with an IP theft. I want you to stay ahead of the FBI, is that clear? If you can't get anything concrete on the boyfriend or Thomason today, then I want you to move on. Start with those tapes."

"Yes, sir."

The lieutenant left the room, and Cleary and Jacobs looked at each other, feeling comprehensively chastened.

"Call logistics and tell them I want those tapes up here as soon as they arrive. And send a black and white over to pick up the boyfriend and Mrs. Pierce. Make it two different units, will ya? I don't want them talking to each other on the way over. We'll get them in separate rooms and see if we can punch a hole in their stories."

"What about Thomason?" Jacobs asked, remembering Thomason's promise to go hard at anyone trying to arrest him.

"I know, I know. This could get ugly real quick and for no good reason. But you heard the lieutenant; we need to shit or get off the pot. Send the Tactical Response Unit over to where he works. Tell them that the guy is dangerous but that we don't want him hurt, or anybody else for that matter. Tell them to take an Augment with them."

Ninety minutes later, Cleary had all three of his suspects in three different interview rooms. Thomason wasn't happy but was solidly restrained. Mrs. Pierce was in tears and her boyfriend was pacing up and down, unrestrained, in Interview Room 1203, seriously agitated. Cleary decided he'd work his way up to Thomason and entered the interview room in which Francine Pierce was seated, crying. Jacobs stayed outside and watched through the glass.

"Mrs. Pierce, this interview is being taped. I want to know more about your relationship with Daniel Nannis. How long have you known Sergeant Nannis?"

Francine collected herself and answered, "About five months now."

"You're in love with him?"

"…Yes."

"Plan to leave your husband to be with him?"

"I hadn't decided… but yes, I think so."

"Nannis ever beat you, or threaten you?"

"God, no. He is the gentlest man I've ever met."

"I suppose that's why he joined the Marines."

"He respects his country."

"It would have been easier for you both if Jack wasn't around, is that right?"

"No, I told Jack about Dan."

"You told him this time around, but you hadn't told him prior to the bombing, is that right?" Cleary had been talking to Francine's friend, Julia.

"Yes, but that doesn't mean I wasn't going to tell him."

"You lied to Jack about your relationship and now you are lying to me. You told Dan about your predicament and your distress. He promised to sort it out with Jack, is that right?"

"No, no. I needed to confront Jack myself."

"He did sort it out for you, and he told you he had killed Jack so he could be with you, and you agreed to keep it quiet. But as it turned out, Jack wasn't dead enough."

"No, no, Dan would never do anything like that."

"You know Nannis has a special friend, a demolitions expert, someone who hates AIOGEN and the people who work there, particularly your husband."

"I didn't know that, no."

Cleary lowered his voice a little. "You know, I would understand it if you accidentally got Dan all fired up about this and you inadvertently pushed him in a direction you never wanted him to go. We could make your part in this go away if you were frank with us about what you know."

"There's nothing to be frank about. Dan would never do anything wrong."

Cleary looked over to the glass behind which he knew Jacobs was watching. He stood up and left the room. Once outside, he said to Jacobs, "I think I believe her. If Nannis did this, I don't think she knew about it. Let's see what lover boy has got to say."

"Sergeant Nannis, you should know that this interview is being taped."

"Why am I here? I saw Francine go into the other room. Why is she here?"

"I have questions, you have answers, that's the way this works. And you better think carefully before you give me any of those answers. You're only going to get one go at this. Yes, we have been talking to Francine, and she has been most forthcoming. Now sit down and think carefully." Nannis obliged. "You're in love with Mrs. Pierce?"

"Yes."

"You want to be with her, marry her. Is that right?"

Nannis thought carefully, as Cleary had suggested. "Yes."

"But Jack Pierce was in the way. You could see that she was upset with having to deal with Jack, couldn't you?"

"I can see where you're going with this, and no, I had nothing to do with the bombing."

"Let's not get ahead of ourselves here. Francine has told us all about it. It would be better for you if you did the same."

"There's nothing to tell. I had nothing to do with the bombing."

"We've also got your good mate, Sergeant Thomason, in custody. He's a particularly angry man. Threatened the police officers sent to talk to him about this. It didn't take much for you to get him fired up about Pierce, did it?"

"I've never spoken to Thomason about Pierce. Do I need to get some help here? My unit has legal support staff."

"You can if you wish, but it wouldn't look that good. And do you want your unit mixed up in this?"

"I guess not, no."

"Do you want a lawyer assigned to you?"

"No, I haven't done anything."

"So, keeping in mind that we've spoken to Francine and to Thomason, do you want to tell us what happened? It would look a lot better if you tell us your side of the story. Maybe Thomason got the wrong idea."

"I've never spoken to Thomason about this."

"That can't be right. You know we've been through your phone records."

"I haven't called him about it either."

"But we know you've called him."

"We went out for a beer a couple of months ago."

"I'm going to offer Thomason a deal if he fingers you for this. Do you want to beat him to the punch, or do you want to take your chances?"

"I haven't done anything."

"I'm going to get up and walk to the door. Once that door closes, then any deal for you is off the table." Cleary got up and walked to the door and opened it. He looked back at Nannis, but he said nothing.

"That's none for two," Cleary said to Jacobs when he got outside the meeting room. "Get a fire extinguisher ready, will you, in case this next one explodes."

"Mr. Thomason, I should tell you…"

"Get fucked."

"Now that's not nice. You're going to make me feel that you've got something to hide, sergeant."

"I don't give a fuck what you feel. Let me loose, and I'll explain it to you… personally."

"Well that's not going to happen. Is that what you tried to do to AIOGEN Corporation, *explain* it to them by blowing up one of their key executives?"

"No, but if you had come to arrest me yourself then I would have explained it to you. Those fucking Augments."

"It collared you pretty easy, didn't it? A lot of whimpering but it collected you no problem at all. You're all talk, Thomason."

"It snuck up on me."

"Yea that's it. More like you blinked and it had you. You're an angry man, sergeant, angry about what they are doing over there at AIOGEN."

"That's right. Angrier now that freak laid its hands on me."

"An angry man who knows how to get things done, got the skills to make things happen, knows how to make sure that people listen."

"I told you I had nothing to do with that bombing."

"Protesting didn't work, did it? You needed to make a bigger show of it. Then you get this call from an old Marine buddy of yours who's got a problem he wants your help with and some money changes hands to help solve it, access to some marine munitions, right. He shows you where Pierce parks his car and *boom!* Problem solved, point made." There was no answer from Thomason. "Your mate Dan is in the next room and he's been quite happy to talk to us about you. How does that make you feel? Do you want to *explain* how you feel to him?" There was no answer. "He's willing to take a deal from us, if we offered him one. He's in there thinking about it right now."

"Look, shithead, if you had something you wouldn't be talkin', you'd be doin'. So you can shovel all that bullshit out of here."

"I assure you, sergeant, that this is a very serious matter. We think you and your mate conspired to kill Jack Pierce. We think you got your hands on some of the good stuff and blew the shit out of his car, with him in it."

"Denied," Thomason said with a dismissive direct tone.

"You killed Pierce to make your point to AIOGEN and your buddy funded it."

"Denied."

"You've got an opportunity here to make it easy on yourself."

"Look, I've got work to do. You've got a bomber to catch. So why don't we cut to the chase. Are you arresting me? Do I need to get a lawyer here? I've got nothing left to say to you."

"I'll let you know." Cleary stood up, disgusted, and threw the chair back behind him in frustration. "Don't go anywhere. Ah, that's right, you can't. I'll be back in a minute."

"That's none for three," Cleary said to Jacobs when he got outside.

"We've got him for resisting arrest if you want."

"Yeah, the problem is we weren't arresting him, and that could get embarrassing. I know, I know, we could still make that stick. I think we're back to square one, my friend." Cleary paused and thought carefully, rubbing his head. "Fuck it. Let 'em go. All three of them. Where's those fucking tapes from the FBI?"

Later that day, Cleary and Jacobs had received the surveillance tapes that the FBI had made of Kalmati talking to the senior staff at AIOGEN and they were reviewing them to see what they might yield. They had been at it for several hours.

"This is the best part about this job," Jacobs said sarcastically. "There's nothing useful on these tapes."

Cleary ignored him. "That's Jack Pierce, right. Here, I mean," pointing to a frame that he had paused on one of the tapes. "Talking to Kalmati."

"Yeah, he must have known Kalmati. But they all did. Kalmati was promising to set up some customers for AIOGEN or something." Jacobs set the tape to play again and listened with one half of the headphone set pressed against his ear. "What they are saying sounds pretty innocuous. Time of day, yada yada."

"That's right, but we have Pierce talking to Zimmermann, too. Remember those phone records we pulled right at the start? We don't have tapes of the phone conversations between Pierce and Zimmermann, but we know that there were a couple of phone calls exchanged between them, right?"

"Yeah, but…" then Jacobs twigged to what Cleary was on about. "Yeah, that's right. So Pierce was mixed up in this somehow, and it got out of control?"

"Wouldn't be the first time. Arms trafficking is a nasty business, full of nasty people."

"Okay, I'll bite," Jacobs said. "Where to from here?"

"There's nothing else on these damn tapes that helps us. That's all we got. I think we need to talk to Pierce again."

"But he doesn't have anything he can tell us."

"A suspicious person might think that that is a little convenient. Maybe he messed up that last smash deliberately and then blew himself up."

"Really? Maybe."

"What was the name of that security guy over there at AIOGEN?"

"You're the one that met him. Hang on a sec." Jacobs looked up the file. "Dick Chambers."

"Yeah, that's right. Give Dick a call in the morning and set up a meeting. I want to get more background on Pierce. And see if you can get a warrant for Pierce's bank account, use the Official Secrets Act, there should be enough there given his contact with Zimmermann. And go back over his phone records tomorrow and see what else you can find, looking at him as the perp, not the vic. The call pattern might mean something else if we look at it from the point of view that Pierce is involved."

"Do you think he would really blow himself up? Come on."

"It would be a hell of a way to throw us off the scent. But I don't think he'd have the skills to set a device like that. If he was involved, I would say it would have been one of his mates that did the job on him, maybe to shut him up. Pierce may not even remember who it was or why they did it. He may actually think he's innocent. How's that for an alibi?"

"All but perfect."

"If we can prove he was involved and we can find out who he was dealing with, that will lead us to who set the bomb. And we catch a technology trafficker into the bargain."

"Good deal."

Cleary wasn't absolutely sure that the boyfriend's part in this was a dead end. Both men were satisfied that they had a new direction in the case, and Cleary, in particular, was keen to see them beat the FBI to the perpetrator and to any arms trafficker that might be involved. He visualized the look on Jamison's face if it turned out to be Pierce. That would just be too sweet.

CHAPTER NINE

Frederick had befriended Yana Adler, Albert Speer's personal assistant, and they had once again stolen a day together, ostensibly to undertake an architectural tour of the city. It was August 1939. Frederick was now nine. Hitler was due to invade Poland on the first of the following month according to the old timeline. Frederick hadn't heard anything of substance from Hitler since their discussion in the study at Berghof. Frederick had been reluctant to push the matter but was beginning to feel that the absence of discussion about the Jews was a sign that nothing was going to change. Since Hitler's speech in January of that year, violence against German Jews was on the rise. Frederick had become glad that he had taken steps against Himmler.

Frederick and Yana had taken a break from their tour and were having lunch in a café with a view of the Brandenburg Gate, which Frederick had just photographed. He had decided to seek Yana's view on the Jewish issue and it was not for the sake of making conversation.

"So what do you make of the treatment of our Jewish citizens?"

"It is obscene." Frederick's relief was palpable but he had guessed that would be her view. "I have friends. Life has become very tough for them."

"I share your opinion and worry about where this is all leading."

"To their deportation, everyone assumes. They have been expelled from the schools, forbidden to own businesses, someone said they will be required to wear a uniform soon."

"Deported to where?"

"I don't know, out of Germany? East, I think. Someone said they were looking at Mauritius."

"Someone said. Aren't you being naïve?"

"About what?"

"Their fate."

"What do you mean, *their fate*?" Yana said mockingly, not appreciating being called naïve by a nine-year-old.

"I fear that you may know exactly what I mean but let's go round the Maypole anyway. You know that I am very close to matters in the government. I hear things, bad things. Can I speak frankly?"

"Of course, we are friends."

"Confidentially?"

"Of course," Yana said, putting her folded arms onto the table, ducking her head, and looking around her, thinking it was going to be gossip.

"They will be killed, all of them," Frederick said in a whisper.

There was a pause as Yana sat up straight and looked deeply at Frederick to see if he was being playful. He was not. She didn't know how to react.

"Exterminated," Frederick continued, stone-faced. "They are building the camps and making the plans as we sit here." Frederick was exaggerating for effect, knowing that what he just said would eventually be true but those actions had not yet been put in place or indeed yet envisaged.

"Frederick, you shouldn't say such a thing. We are Germans, not barbarians."

"Germans led by barbarians. Hitler spoke of it in January. You choose to ignore the Führer's speeches?"

"It was just hyperbole. He was exaggerating to make his point, thinking later he will present a more palatable policy. He was speaking of Jewish financiers possibly causing a war."

"You hear what you want to hear like everybody else in this damn city. Nobody ever does anything. The world is a dangerous place to live not because of the people who are evil but because of the people who don't do anything about it." Frederick smacked the table.

"Very clever," Yana said tersely.

"It's not my words, it was said by a Jew, a very smart one."

"So what do you want me to do about it, vote?" Yana was now feeling offended as if she was being accused of standing by and letting bad things happen.

"I know you are special, Yana," Frederick had sensed her mood. "I would never think you would not act if you had to." Yana was placated. "But I am telling you that I have a vote that can't be ignored. I just need some help to cast it."

"Go on."

"There is a meeting at 56–58 Am Großen Wannsee next weekend. It is about thirty minutes from here by car. It is the first of several meetings chaired by your friend and mine, Herr Heydrich. It is about this very subject. They were not supposed to have started these meetings until 1942, but I know now that they start this Saturday. Heydrich must have brought the matter forward. Perhaps it was his agenda that was driving things behind the scenes all along and now with Himmler out of the way, he is free to progress them faster. I have always said that if you poke around with this stuff, you get potentially worse outcomes than the ones that went before. A complete systemic change is the best answer."

"1942? What are you talking about, Frederick?"

"Forget it. Can you drive me to Wannsee next Saturday? The Führer is tied up with the Russian delegation signing the mutual non-aggression pact, I assume, plans for Poland and so on, we are to have a war apparently. My nurse will be at her mother's. Will you drive me?"

"You say too much about Herr Hitler's plans, Frederick."

"Yes, so I've been told. Look, the lives of millions of Jews are at stake here, Yana. Are you one of those good people who do nothing? In or out?"

"What can you do to change these peoples' minds, anyway?"

"Trust me, I am bringing with me the proof that there is a just God."

"Do I want to know what it is? Don't answer that. Where shall I meet you?"

"So there are Berliners who would act if they knew what was happening. You are the proof of it."

Heydrich, now in charge at the SS, had thought it important to bring forward the planning for a comprehensive *Jewish solution,* as Frederick had feared his interference had made things worse. Heydrich had assembled many of the people who would have eventually attended the conference in January 1942. Heydrich had made an assessment of the number of Jews in Europe, approximately eleven million, half of whom would be in German territories once the reunification of Germany was complete. In his view, something needed to be done about those that will be under German control. The attendees as well as the convener, Heydrich included Adolf Eichmann, the head of the Gestapo, Dr. Roland Freisler, State Secretary of the Party, Richard Walther Darré, Head of the SS Race Settlement Department appointed by Heydrich, Friedrich Wilhelm Kritzinger, Permanent State Secretary, Dr. Rudolf Lange, now Eichmann's second in charge at the Gestapo, Dr. Georg Leibbrandt, Martin Luther, Heinrich Müller, and Dr. Wilhelm Stuckart with no note takers and assistants in attendance given the nature of the discussion. Frederick had seen the list of attendees now being adept at sneaking into Hitler's office.

For Frederick, it was too good an opportunity to miss especially now he knew that Heydrich was driving things forward faster than before. He thought he would never have to deal with this group, he had hoped that by persuasion it would not have come to this, but Hitler clearly was reluctant to interfere with Heydrich or Himmler before him. So here they were again, all of the key players who had developed the most diabolical plan in history, all of them thirty minutes away by car. Whilst anti-Semitism was rampant, it was made worse by Hitler's insane ranting about Germany's economic condition being the fault of the Jews but it was this group of people who had taken that rage and translated it into deadly action. Without them, Frederick wondered whether another such group would consider the same response. Of all those who deserved to be punished for the horror about to be inflicted on German Jews, it was this group.

Frederick and Yana arrived early that Saturday morning outside the Wannsee villa. Frederick had been busy in his makeshift lab; he had felt right at home. He had taken the present that he had received from Humboldt University and crushed the beans down into castor oil, leaving a sediment after the oils removal that was rich in lectins, a particularly nasty class of carbohydrate-binding proteins. The weaponisation of ricin was something about which Frederick knew a great deal from the days his company serviced the American weapons industry but it was knowledge that the Nazis did not yet possess nor did he intend for them to have it. He intended instead for them to try it. Atomised and inhaled, it would present if delivered in the correct quantity as a respiratory ailment, perhaps infection, eventually resulting in heart or organ failure. A nasty way to die but suitable in the circumstances, he thought. If he had properly calculated the dose, it would take days for the infected men to die and forty-eight hours before any symptoms appeared, reinforcing the view that it was some kind of disease brought to the meeting by one of its participants or at least that is what Frederick hoped.

Frederick had created a welcome letter for each of the meeting's members, congratulations from the motherland along with good wishes for the job ahead. He was careful not to have the letter signed by Hitler in the event that it was later uncovered, but the letters looked official. He delivered them to the guard station at Wannsee saying that he was under instructions to place them in the room personally. The security detachment's captain recognised the boy and had the guard assist him with the delivery. For their assistance and as a memorial of the event he gave one of the unmarked envelopes to each of the captain and the guard with instructions not to open them until after the conference, his intent being to eliminate any record of him being there. The captain had been instructed by Frederick not to log the delivery so as not to spoil the surprise.

Frederick had been very careful to avoid contaminating the outer envelope, each note being personally addressed to the attendees and sealed with the Chancellery's stamp, so he was comfortable to have him and the guard place them at the meeting table by unprotected hand. The resulting dust when opened would be barely visible given how Frederick had prepared the material. It was a risk that Heydrich or one of the other meeting officials might take the opportunity to thank the Führer from whom, they would have all assumed, the letter had come even though it was not signed but Frederick believed the attendees and sadly the captain and his charge wouldn't get the opportunity to speak of it. The letters would just appear to have been part of Heydrich's proceedings and with no means by which to detect the insidious protein, each letter would remain in the cherished possession of each of the participant's families… post-mortem.

He completed his delivery and went back to the car with Yana waiting. Frederick was careful not to involve her in the delivery in case things went horribly wrong. He had willingly climbed out on a limb by shooting Himmler but did not want anyone out there next to him.

"What did you give them?"

"A dose of the flu," he chuckled, pleased with himself.

"What?"

"It was a personal plea that I believe will carry quite an impact."

"You think you can talk these people out of doing what Nazis do?"

"I don't think that they will want to do anything once they open those letters. Let's go get some breakfast. I'm feeling as if I deserve a treat."

Within twenty-two days of the conference at Wannsee, all participants, the captain and the security guard included, were dead. A medical enquiry had been convened to identify the cause but no results were yet available nor apparently were likely. It remained a puzzle but suspicion had turned to the Soviets who had a large delegation in town to sign the non-aggression pact with Hitler the week of the Wannsee Conference. Could it be that they had developed weapons that defied detection? Hitler had asked the then obscure but highly intelligent SS-Hauptsturmführer, Josef Rudolf Mengele, to undertake a military enquiry into whether such weapons were possible. A doctor and anthropologist, he was considered uniquely qualified for the task. When Frederick heard of Mengele's involvement, he began to wonder how he could demonstrate the process to him personally. Perhaps in uncovering the reason for the deaths he too could fall victim to it without revealing the cause.

Yana had put two and two together and had come up with Frederick. She had sought him out at his rooms and confronted him after reading a newspaper article of the deaths. They were in his study, standing, arguing.

"It was you, you killed them. How could you involve me in this?"

"Settle yourself. You are not involved. And keep your voice down before you implicate us both."

"You deny it then?"

"Of course."

"Frederick how… why… you are just a little boy. You only talked about what these people might do but you executed them as if they had already done it."

"They had done it… in another life."

"What? Are you mad?"

"Yana, tell me how exactly I could do such a thing. It was a coincidence, I wrote them a letter, how can a letter kill people. I do not like those men but how could I be involved. They died of some illness spread amongst themselves. I do not have it; how could I be to blame for it. The SS do not know what happened so how could I?"

"I guess that has to be true. But don't expect too many car rides for you in the near future."

"I know you're upset, we all are. We can't let this affect our friendship. In a couple of years, I'm going to ask you to be my girlfriend."

Yana laughed. "Make that ten tears and I would probably say yes if I weren't married by then. You are an interesting boy, Frederick. Most boys I know these days only want to talk about Nazi things. The school system has done a real good job on them."

"Let's go get a coffee and catch up on the gossip. I sure could use a break from this place; the tension here is palpable."

"Sure, but no car ride, you're grounded."

They both laughed.

Frederick lay awake that night, scheming. He couldn't believe that he had gotten all of them. His thoughts continuously circled back to Mengele. Dare he test his luck again? Another senior Nazi death, albeit not that senior at this moment — an unknown captain. But it was too risky, surely. This man was responsible for so much misery in the years after the camps were built. Frederick had to do something. Mengele had escaped Germany after the war, fleeing to South America and living as Wolfgang Gerhard to the end of his natural life, never being brought to justice. Now was Frederick's chance for retribution for at least what this man was capable of, if not what he had already done in this timeline. Frederick thought he would ask to see him, to ask of his methods perhaps on the Wannsee case, but then face-to-face, do what? Frederick had a reputation for being very bright — perhaps Mengele would welcome his input. But if so, where would Frederick lead him? No one but Yana knew of his presence at Wannsee, so it was not as if his visits might be connected to the deaths.

In the morning, he convinced his tutor that a trip back to the university for a chemistry tutorial would be in order. Frederick was already learning at a very advanced level — or so his tutor saw it — and felt such a trip appropriate for his student. In the three weeks that followed, this became something of a regular event. Frederick had managed to charm most of the chemistry faculty's senior staff, including one Professor Gersten, with whom he now swapped stories and ideas. Frederick had become the tutor, and the professor his student. The stories weren't of great importance, with Frederick being careful not to disturb the natural evolution of knowledge on any subject — particularly careful given that this was Nazi Germany. Nonetheless, the professor had come to welcome Frederick's regular visits.

He had obtained at those moments when left alone, various compounds that he felt may be of use to him in the coming months. Among them were several forms of sodium amalgams, iodomethanes, and other methyl halides. The quantities were small, and the thefts went unnoticed, but Frederick had built up quite the laboratory at home, which was neither particularly noticeable nor unexplainable — all of it, of course, had to do with his studies.

He had made the relevant approaches through Martin Bormann to see if he could have a meeting with Mengele to assist him, were it possible to do so, and to ask of Mengele's methodology in regard to the cause of death at Wannsee. Regardless of his prime intent, Frederick was keen to know where Mengele was up to with his investigation. Hitler was made aware of Frederick's suggestions and endorsed a meeting, and Frederick found himself in Mengele's office this Saturday afternoon, having been dropped there by one of the assistants at the Chancellery. Mengele had created his own laboratory in the room attached to his office and was busy studying a variety of tissue samples from the dead Wannsee Conference participants when Frederick arrived as scheduled.

"Dr. Mengele, a pleasure to finally meet you. You are a hard man to catch."

"Wonder boy. Martin speaks highly of you. Please, come in."

"You're the second person to call me that — the other, perhaps, being part of those samples in your test tube there. Did you know Herr Heydrich?"

"I never had the pleasure but I admired him."

"As did we all. A loss to the Reich. How are we progressing?"

"The cause escapes me so far. There is no evidence of pathogens or poisons, at least any that I can detect."

"You mean no evidence other than the fact that they are all dead."

"Yes… of course."

"A bacteria?"

"No. It looks as though the cells themselves have been compromised."

"By what?"

"Nothing that I can identify."

"How was it delivered?"

"The lungs are the entry point. The lungs were attacked, and it spread to the other organs. It must have been airborne. I have reduced some of the affected cells and am running tests to identify any substances that don't belong. Take a look at this."

Mengele beckoned Frederick over to his microscope.

"It looks like a protein," Frederick observed after studying it for a moment.

"My view exactly. You are the smart boy. But a protein from what?"

"The whole cell is made up of proteins in various forms. It's hard to tell whether this one belongs or does not belong. I may be smart, but I'm not clairvoyant. Something they ate?"

"They breathed it in, not ate it."

"And smelt it before they ate it."

"I'll check the menus from the conference again."

"I have something here that may colour your sample to give us a better look. I've been chatting with my friend, the professor, and he's given me some liquid litmus to bring to our discussion."

Frederick excitedly went to his carry bag and brought out a small vial of clear liquid. As he opened it, he bumped into Mengele, spilling it on his gloved hand.

"I'm terribly sorry, Doctor."

"No harm. But I think that you're right. Various dyes may assist. In fact, I'll set up a test now. I'll report back to Martin that your visit was most helpful. If you'll excuse me, I feel I must undertake the new testing immediately."

Frederick knew that the testing would be too unsophisticated to yield a result. Any dyes available to Mengele would not point to the ricin — a substance about which Mengele knew nothing and would not recognise its chemical signature with a mere optical microscope. Frederick, in preparing for his visit to Mengele's office, had combined the sodium amalgam he had stolen with one of his methyl halides, forming dimethylmercury. He added this to the water he had just spilt on Mengele's glove. The liquid was clear, and the potency of the substance was unaffected by its mixture with the water. The glove would not save Mengele from his inevitable death — the material would find its way through even any rubber or latex glove, let alone the cotton gloves worn by Mengele. It would take a couple of months, the timing would distance his death from the others, and neither Frederick's visit nor the spilt water would be remembered. Mengele would have already dismissed the accident, given that his hand was protected and the water apparently innocuous. There would be no symptoms until near the end, and again, the cause would be undetectable, perhaps natural causes, or an affliction acquired from who knows which part of Mengele's work. But Mengele's fate was sealed. There was no cure — the poisoning was now inescapable, and the death unpleasant.

Frederick wondered why he had chosen a weapon that, by its very application, brought him into close proximity with Mengele. Why not the ricin? Perhaps another death by apparently the same cause would be too much and would cause new resources to be applied to the problem. Frederick knew Mengele was headed nowhere, but he also knew within himself that it was the release he felt in killing Himmler that drew him close to Mengele. The knot in his stomach, the one he had carried since the death of his parents a century before, had loosened the moment he had seen Himmler on the floor with blood gushing from his temple. The release wasn't as immediate with Mengele but was just as real.

CSI and forensics were neither a science nor common practice in 1939. Crimes were investigated and criminals found based on what was seen or heard, not what lay in the fabric of the offense or the environment in which it was perpetrated. Frederick knew that close examination by the homicide division of NYPD in 2060 would find the crumbs that would lead them to him, but in this day and age, he believed that he could sleep easy.

Three months later, in January 1940, Hitler had finally confirmed Karl Hanke as the Head of the SS, replacing Heydrich who was killed at Wannsee. Hitler's hesitancy was due to there being no obvious replacement and because of Hanke's recent run-in with Goebbels over Goebbels's affair with Lida Baarova. This affair, which Frederick had referred to at his first meeting with Goebbels, had, by independent means, now become public. Hanke had taken

Goebbels's wife Magna's side, Magna having her own predispositions towards the rising Nazi general. Both affairs were ended by decree from the Führer, sending Goebbels into a self-destructive spin and his career into decline, while Hanke's relationship with Magda gave Hitler pause when considering Hanke's promotion.

Hanke was not a self-starter, Frederick believed, and would only do as instructed by Hitler, independently representing no threat to the Jews despite being nicknamed the "Hangman of Breslau" in another timeline. He had proved capable of ruthlessness but acted only on instruction and, unlike Himmler and Heydrich, was unlikely to form his own view, Frederick believed, on what should be done with the Jewish citizenry. As such, he was not on Frederick's mind as someone that needed his attention. Besides, three SS Heads dying one after the other would have been too great a coincidence to ignore.

Frederick did, however, have a new list. Flush with success at Wannsee, Frederick was already looking further afield to Nazis whom he did think were consequential to the persecution of the Jews. He had come to believe that weeding out the cancer was having a beneficial effect on his negotiations with Hitler. The removal of certain influences had already proved to be most useful. Many of the individuals of interest to Frederick by 1940 had not yet come to prominence nor had they committed the horrifying acts that later made them despised by humanity. He had nonetheless identified where each of them currently were and was drawing his plans to have them join Himmler, Heydrich, Mengele, and their associates from Wannsee in the Nazi cemetery.

Ernst Kaltenbrunner was not amongst the attendees at Wannsee, as Frederick had hoped. Frederick was surprised and relieved that Hitler didn't think enough of him to have him replace Heydrich as Head of the SS. If it had been so, Frederick believed that there would be little difference in the outcomes directed by Himmler, Heydrich, or Kaltenbrunner. Having replaced Heydrich as chief of security in the Reich when Heydrich rose to be second in charge at the SS, Kaltenbrunner rose to head of Interpol in 1943. With that authority, he became one of the key perpetrators in the Holocaust, being personally responsible for over one hundred thousand deaths, and eventually being the highest-ranking SS officer to be hanged at Nuremberg. Frederick thought that he might bring that sentence forward to keep him from his future crimes and away from the top job at the SS and Hitler's ear.

Ilse Koch, the "Bitch of Buchenwald," had used the Buchenwald camp to exercise her own particular brand of depravity and she had made Frederick's list along with her husband, Standartenführer Karl Otto Koch, the murderous Commandant of Buchenwald. The Nazis had caught up with Otto themselves in 1945 because he was not just murdering racial or political prisoners, he was choosing his victims from a broader menu of German citizens, but his wife escaped prosecution until eventually being imprisoned for other crimes and hanging herself in her cell in 1967.

Frederick also listed Paul Blobel who was responsible for the Babi Yar massacre in Kiev in 1941 where over sixty thousand prisoners were murdered. He was brought to justice by the Americans in 1951. He added Josef Kramer to his list who was the Commandant of the Bergen-Belsen concentration camp, the "Beast of Belsen." Him and Irma Grese terrorised Auschwitz and Belsen until the end of the war when the English arrested and eventually hanged him.

Franz Stangl was the commandant of the Sobibor and Treblinka camps and was promoted directly by Himmler to be superintendent of the T-4 Euthanasia Program at the Euthanasia Institute at Schloss Hartheim, where he murdered mentally and physically disabled people, referring to them and his later racial prisoners as "cargo." He escaped to Brazil after the war. He was arrested in 1967 and was tried for the murder of nine hundred thousand people but died of natural causes in prison in 1971. Friedrich Jeckeln made the list. He led one of the largest collections of Einsatzgruppen, or task forces, and was personally responsible for ordering the deaths of over one hundred thousand Jews and other "lesser" peoples in the occupied Soviet Union. Jeckeln was also responsible for developing new ways to kill large groups of people, the "Jeckeln System." The Russians caught up with him and hanged him in 1946, not because of his crimes, but simply because he was a Nazi. The Russians, even by 1946, were already bringing their own brand of barbarism to Eastern Europe.

Dr. Oskar Dirlewanger led the infamous SS Dirlewanger Brigade. He was disbarred as a doctor after raping two thirteen-year-old girls in Germany in the 1930s but had his position reinstated after his bravery in the Spanish Civil War. As part of the SS, he and his soldiers raped and murdered women and children in the war with the Soviet Union, amongst other things, poisoning female prisoners to watch them die in agony as entertainment for his men. He eventually died as a result of torture in the custody of the Polish in 1945.

And first amongst equals on Frederick's list was Odilo Globocnik, an Austrian Nazi and senior SS officer who was, possibly after Himmler and Heydrich, the man most responsible for the murder of millions during the Holocaust. Globocnik was directly responsible for the murder of over five hundred thousand Jews in the Warsaw and Bialystok Ghettos and later ran the Lublin labor camps. Frederick believed that Globocnik was the originator of the industrialised murder concept eventually used by the Nazis in the camps. At a two-hour meeting with Himmler on 13 October 1941 in the original timeline, Globocnik received verbal approval to start construction work on the Belzec extermination camp the first of many such camps. He died by his own had in May 1945.

It was quite a list, but Frederick had, through various surreptitious means, found the current address of each of these sociopaths. Frederick didn't know what to do with Goebbels, Goering, or, for that matter, Hitler himself. He believed Goering to be a fatuous idiot and he did not necessarily see Goebbels as evil, just merely a misguided criminal and now a very miserable and ineffective one. In any event, he believed that totally destabilising the government by killing them all now might lead to higher levels of radicalism and disorder, a dangerous prospect given the current levels of violence being perpetrated against the Jews. So, the destiny of Goebbels and Goering would have to be determined at a later time if indeed he was going to have any say in it at all. Frederick had not yet given up on using Hitler to change direction on current policies towards the Jews. Besides, given Frederick's recent activities and hopefully the effectiveness of this morning's mail out, Hitler would have few on whom to rely if he didn't eventually see reason, assuming he survived the rejection of Frederick's views.

Frederick now faced a moral dilemma. Did the people on his list, and indeed the attendees at Wannsee, deserve to die because of their actions in another timeline? He recalled with disdain the left-wing wokeism with which American university students were indoctrinated in the first third of the twenty-first century and the hugely negative impact that had on societal attitudes and political outcomes when all it turned out to be was one academic trying to assert moral superiority over the other using trivial word games. Nearly two generations, he estimated, were lost to valuable social and scientific free thought by that brainwashing. He felt himself fortunate to have gone through the American tertiary education system when free thinking and free speech were deified. He believed wholeheartedly that he never would have developed his scientific breakthroughs or indeed his huge business if his tutors would have constrained his mind rather than pursued his abilities for unconstrained thought. Were these Nazis driven by social circumstances or educational indoctrination? Was it military orders that made them do evil things or were they intrinsically evil within their nature? Was it the war that drove them or the devils inside them? Frederick had no way to resolve those concerns; all that he knew were the deeds they perpetrated once they found themselves in the circumstances that allowed their demonic behaviour to manifest. Did anyone, regardless of circumstance, have the right to give rise to such suffering?

Frederick had been cooking again and had prepared an official-looking letter addressed as highly confidential to each of the people on his list. The letter contained nothing but general administrative information and was unsigned so as to not generate enquiry after reading. It was likely to be discarded after it was read because of its banality, but the recipients would not know that the letter was of no value from its official and important-looking exterior. This time it contained Abrin, which he had also distilled from the castor oil beans. Abrin, like ricin, is a ribosome-inhibiting protein but about thirty-two times more potent than ricin. The symptoms would manifest differently than at the Wannsee. He sent only one copy to the Kotchs, to Lise, hoping she would show it to her husband, thinking two letters would not be opened at the same time; the second perhaps being shown to authorities as suspicious and of the two, it was Lise that he wanted to be sure of reaching. The outbreak of a strange flu in these people would likely go unconnected; the recipients themselves being geographically disparate and death from untreatable viral or bacterial infections were commonplace in the 1930s. There was, at this moment, no operational or organisational connection between any of the recipients. It may, if noticed, be seen as part of the same disease found at Wannsee and that in itself could be a good thing, but as with forensics, there was no central authority for disease control that would routinely investigate and connect the deaths.

Frederick was returning from his trip to the post office when he got word that Hitler wanted to see him. The invasion of Poland on the first of September 1939 had brought the declaration of war from England and France that Frederick had predicted but that Hitler believed would not occur. Hitler had spent most of the last three months attempting to extract non-aggression pacts from England and France without success. He realised that matters were progressing just as Frederick had foreseen and he wanted an update from the boy. In Hitler's office in the Chancellery, the two were alone.

"The English won't talk to me."

"No?"

"Nor the French."

"Is that right?"

"You are being smug. Do you have anything helpful to add?"

"It is as I said. Churchill will be in charge soon, May, maybe June, and then you will have no chance to talk with the English. Chamberlain is dying of bowel cancer so you have a matter of months before you will be talking to a fat, drunk brick wall in England."

"I have no idea how you know these things, Frederick. Sometimes you scare me."

"I have a gift."

"Apparently. I have no interest in a fight with the English."

"They are not about whom you need to worry. Roosevelt is emotionally connected to them. He would join with the English if he had a good enough reason that he could sell to his electorate."

"I have not signed and won't sign any pact with the Japanese, that much I have decided subsequent to our discussions, nor will I declare war on the Americans if they engage the Japanese. Roosevelt will have to find another excuse if he is to enter this war. This world domination talk about me, a hypocritical accusation coming from the British, a country upon whose Empire the sun never sets. They are the imperialists. Remind me again who is ruling India and the Middle East?"

"That is not the accepted mantra among Britain's allies. You forget the British write the history books. They are not ruling; they are guiding the lesser peoples of the world."

"Ask the Indians or the Chinese who is the world aggressor, or the Canadians or indeed the Americans; they have already fought one war against those who would guide the world. Roosevelt is a sycophant to the British. George Washington would be ashamed."

"Maybe you will get the chance to put that in the new textbooks, but Churchill, Roosevelt, and Stalin would record the events to come differently."

"So, what is the strategy then to achieve a better outcome for us?"

"You use military aggression as a solution to all your problems; what do you expect them to think of you now?"

"Let them talk to the Wehrmacht then."

"You see, it is your fault."

"Can you please get back to my original question?"

"They fear you, so the appeasers are withdrawing and the warmongers are taking charge. You have made it so by invading Poland. Twenty million people's lives depend on your next move."

"I am aware of the stakes. Force seems to be the only answer, the only thing they understand."

"Or your withdrawal from Poland."

"And what, leave it to the Russians? Their fate is sealed, boy. The Russians would have it in a blink, and we would lose Danzig and East Prussia along with them. I will not let that happen."

"Withdraw and seek English and French help to extract the Soviets from Poland."

Hitler laughed out loud.

"That's it, me in a war allied with the French and the English. You forget we are at war with them right now at their insistence. They have declared it, although no one would know it from all that they are doing about it."

"If you attack the French now, you will have that done within a month. But you must do the same to the English. Establish a base in Southern England and then seek terms. If you destroy London as Herr Goering wants you to do, then they will harden against you."

"Look who's the little aggressor now."

"It has merit compared to a five-year conflagration in Europe that takes twenty million lives and destroys Germany."

"What do you know of Goering's plans?"

"Only that he is a fat, pompous idiot who has an inflated opinion of his abilities, and he will be telling you that he and his mighty Luftwaffe can win the war for you without ground forces. I am telling you he cannot; it cannot be won from the air."

"You should watch your temper, Frederick. Hermann is a friend of mine, but I fear you may be right about needing to invade to neutralise the threat."

"A lightning attack in England before Churchill is Prime Minister, and then offer them terms that would see your complete withdrawal and a return to normality in exchange for peace… and their Middle Eastern territories. Such a proposition would succeed."

"Your beloved Jews again."

"And oil resources beyond Germany's needs for the next century. The English know nothing of the oil beneath that sand, nor are they interested in the region other than ridding it of Turks. Their current interests lie only in the canal as their passage to India. You can offer them unencumbered use of the Suez, allow them to keep their navy as insurance."

"And you know of this oil, how? Don't answer that, the same way you know everything else, I presume."

Hitler appeared to be considering it, pacing, so Frederick continued, embellishing.

"You would trap the English expeditionary forces when you invade France. Capture them and strike England immediately, use their return as a negotiating chip. It could be over in a matter of weeks."

"Then woo the Americans, that is your plan. And if the English fight on?"

"They may, but without the Americans, England will not succeed against you, and if you have openly placated the US by publishing your peace plan for England and France, then they will have little option but to deal with you. You should have the Americans offer them the peace, perhaps through Kennedy. A complete withdrawal from England and France, how could they refuse? The Americans would make them accept. Roosevelt would have his English victory without shedding one American life. You said it yourself; you have no interest in ruling them."

"How long before we can pursue the Soviets?"

"That will be up to the Americans."

"Why?"

"Because we must act in concert with them or risk our fledgling alliance."

"You seem to have thought it through. And your Jews?"

"We would then have a place to send them, the English Middle Eastern Territories, for whatever that miserable country is worth. You agree then?"

"We will try it your way first. Going down that path does not compromise my other options. And I will take your advice on Goering's plans and an early strike against the French; I know they are unprepared and have no stomach for another war. The English campaign can't be completed from the air, I agree, and while any other race would respond to the pressure we could put them under with our U-boats and bombers, the English are a stubborn lot."

Frederick left his meeting satisfied but unconvinced. He too would keep his options open.

In the six months that followed, Hitler had taken France in a matter of four weeks as he had in the other timeline, but had done it three months sooner and had established his bases in the south and southeast of England immediately after the French surrender. The air and naval battles were devastating, but this time Hitler followed through with a land-based assault. The Wehrmacht had taken the airfields at Biggin Hill, North Weald to the northeast of London, and Rochford to the east, as well as the new radar station at Debden. The British air assault had been crippled by those losses, and London lay unprotected by air support. The Germans had London surrounded on three sides and were bringing up massive reinforcements. A large British force was assembled northwest of the German lines to undertake what increasingly looked like being the decisive battle of Britain. London lay between the two armies. Hitler had called for a ceasefire and had by July of 1940 asked for the Americans to broker a peace. They had made personal and secret contact with Joseph Kennedy to implore him to undertake the task.

Frederick was deeply distressed both by the loss of life and by the thought that he had been responsible for directing Hitler's attention toward Britain although London was as yet largely undamaged. Roosevelt was prevented from helping militarily by the virtual unanimous opinion in America that they should not enter another European war, a sentiment confirmed by the well-publicised, and generally well-regarded, peace plan offered by the Germans. Frederick placed his hope in the peace talks and in a quick end to the violence. He placated himself remembering the massive loss of British lives during the Blitz and later in the five-year war that raged on the continent. But all that would be worth nothing if Kennedy could not broker the peace now. There were positive signs from the English government in that Churchill had not survived a vote of No Confidence on the floor of the parliament and the Labor government, known to favour reconciliation with the Germans, had taken power under their leader Earl Attlee, now considered a reformist not an appeaser.

He also consoled himself with the success of his mail out. All targets had been eliminated but there had been collateral damage. In the Kotch household, he had in the end managed to get both Lise and Otto but also the housemaid and the family dog Ludwig. Globocnik's wife, Grete Michner, and their two children had also been killed. There had been other unintended victims but no one had yet connected the deaths. Frederick had withdrawn into himself deeply concerned about the killings and the current war raging in England. What if he had gotten his plans horribly wrong?

CHAPTER TEN

Jack was sitting in his office looking out the window, drifting in and out of a negative frame of mind. Jamison, Cleary, the Head of AOGEN Security Dick Chambers and Jack had met that morning to discuss progress, Cleary met privately with Chambers after the meeting to get more background on Jack. Jack flipped the business card Agent Jamison had given him that morning around in his fingers. Jamison believed that business cards, although uncommon in this day and age, were more tactile than electronically swopped tags, it was more personal as Jack was just discovering. He began to rub his head as he muttered to himself out loud, "This is a mistake."

Jack went back to his desk and picked up his phone and dialled her cell.

"Hello?"

"Hi. It's Jack Pierce. We met this morning, you know, in the interview with the NYPD."

"I know who you are, Jack Pierce. Do you have something for me?"

"Well, no… well, maybe. What are you doing for dinner tonight?" Jack immediately thought that was too blunt. "I'm a bit sick of eating at the club and I thought… no, that's not what I want to say. I mean, I'm pretty good at getting short-notice reservations at restaurants. You're from out of town… is there somewhere you'd like to try?" Jack was exasperated by his incapability to be lucid.

"It sounds like you're out of practice, Jack. But sure, why not?" Jamison was bored, too, and maybe she could glean something of use in her case. Jack was pleasantly surprised. "I've been wanting to try that place on Houston near Mercer, what's it called, the new Italian place?"

"Giovanni's, I've seen it. I hear it's pretty good. Should I pick you up around eight?"

"Can we make it seven, and I'll meet you there? It can't be a late one, all the travel you know."

"See you at seven."

Jack was happy with that result despite his lack of charm. He vowed to do better next time. Consistent with his current frame of mind, it occurred to him that her acceptance might have been predicated on business, not pleasure.

Later that night after dinner, Jack and Jamison were standing on the curb outside the brownstone walk-up in Chelsea owned by Jamison's sister Christine, where Jamison was staying. It had been a good dinner; they had found common ground philosophically about the social changes happening around them, and while Jamison had come seeking information as Jack had feared, she had also found something else. The cupcakes they had purchased from the small bakery in the Village, with coffee after dinner, seemed to be the perfect end to the evening. Jack had asked the cab driver to wait. They had stopped shaking and were now just holding each other's hand.

"That was nice, Jack... very nice."

"I enjoyed it, too."

"I'd ask you up but we both have work in the morning." Jamison had taken her cue from the waiting cab.

"I would like to. I'll take a rain check if that's okay. There's been a lot happening."

"No problem. Just so there is no mistake, this ended up as pleasure, not business, right?"

"Glad you cleared that up; it was personal, yes."

She leaned over and placed her cheek against his, kissing him gently on the earlobe, her breath on his ear a welcome reminder of intimacy. She began to walk towards the house, but Jack didn't let go of her hand. His grip caused her to stop and turn back towards him. She looked straight into his eyes, expecting to be kissed.

"Yeah, that kind of personal." He paused for a moment, for the first time seeing the striking purple colour of Jamison's eyes. "A man could lose himself in those eyes. He might never find his way home."

"Maybe that's just what you need, Jack, to find your way home."

"Are you asking me to leave?"

"No. I think I'm asking you to stay."

Jack smiled, nervously, still watching her lips.

He wasn't ready.

With that hesitation, she let his hand go and turned to walk towards the stoop. Jack watched her walk away, and as the distance between them expanded, he felt a desire to follow her, like the tide would follow the moon. He stayed moored to the pavement, unable or unwilling to act, washed from side to side by the beat of his heart.

She opened the door when she got to the top of the stairs, glancing back to see him still watching her. She felt for the first time the fledgling bond between them and the just-promised prospects of what lay ahead.

Jack had got into work early the next morning, having extracted a new lease on life from his date with Jamison. He went back to working on the particularly curly problem related to the genetic changes needed to perfect an alteration in bone density in the stronger TPS400 Augments. The ligaments were tearing away at the bone, particularly the hamstring and the linkages on the triceps and bicep muscles in the new models, and the genetics needed to be adjusted further to compensate for the extra muscle load. He was engrossed in his gene mapping software when George Sanders walked into his office, unannounced as usual.

"I'm busy, George."

"Your mate from NYPD has just arrived back in the building. He's talking to Chambers again."

"So what?" Jack hadn't stopped manually rotating the gene matrix that he had up on his holographic screen. He was literally surrounded by the problem. He had his cause-and-effect map up as well, and as he rotated the holographic figures, he could differentiate the outcomes further down the sequence. Jack was marking the name and function for each pairing with an electronic cursor as he delimited the ones he thought were functionally OK.

"Maybe he's not so convinced that the boyfriend did it after all. Why else would he be pursuing matters here?"

"I would actually be relieved if the boyfriend didn't do it, George." The question caused Jack to lose his train of thought and he stopped, closing the map, and turned to talk to George. "The thought of Francine being involved with a guy capable of doing something like that makes me ill."

"You haven't given up on the old girl then?"

"What is it, George? I really want to get through this today."

"Jack, I've been thinking…"

"Did you hurt yourself?"

"The FBI girl seemed to be convinced that a technology theft has taken place. And if that is correct, logic would have it that someone here was involved, someone senior."

"You're making giant strides, George. You should talk to the copper about getting a job."

"That means we know him… well. Can you think of who it would be?"

Jack leaned back in his chair. He hadn't quite thought of it in those terms. "You're assuming she's right."

"Do you remember anything, before the bombing, I mean? Something running up to that time that caused you any suspicion."

"No, nothing."

"I was just thinking the same thing. I don't remember anything either. I'll go round and pump Chambers later in the day and tell you what transpired with the cop." George always liked to stay ahead of all the gossip, Jack thought. He got up to leave but then turned back to Jack and said, "Do you think you found something out in those seven weeks, Jack, the one's you're missing, something that someone didn't want you to know?"

"Jesus, George, not until you just mentioned it. Look, why don't you take your conspiracy theories somewhere else? I've got work to do."

Jack didn't like the feeling that one of his colleagues might be involved in such a matter. Worse still, he had found out about it and was killed for it. For some reason, the thought of such betrayal led him back to Jamison's motives. Perhaps she may be more interested in pursuing her case than in pursuing him despite the kiss on the earlobe. That thought caused him to shudder. "Jesus. Fuck that," he said out loud. He went to staring out the window again, thinking that might be the reason they had hit it off, she was scamming him. His self-confidence was still shot to pieces. It occurred to him that despite the short time he had known her, he may have already made an emotional investment. It would not be a good outcome for him if he had misjudged Jamison's intentions. He was just considering calling her when the phone rang. Jamison was not in the habit of waiting for a male friend to call after a date if she was interested in him.

"I was just thinking about you," Jack said sheepishly.

"Yea, that's nice, I hope."

"George Sanders was in here suggesting you were only after me because you wanted to better your case or career."

"You told him about us?"

"No, not in any detail." George knew nothing but was a handy scapegoat.

"Did you tell him to go fuck himself?"

Jack laughed. "No, not really. Besides, I was extrapolating his position."

"Is that mathematics talk for you are fucked in the head, Jack? That's not a good sign. Maybe we should rethink this? I don't have the time to waste on poor emotional investments."

"I was just thinking the same thing. Bear with me, please. I am a little fragile. It would be nice if you made allowances, for a while at least."

"That's one of the things I like about you, Jack. I have too much testosterone floating around this office. You seem to be very much in touch with your feelings and are not afraid to admit it when you're behaving like a dick."

"Are you saying I'm effeminate?"

"Have dinner with me tonight and we'll discuss who's interested in doing what to whom."

"Don't you think you're rushing me a bit? I feel pressured. Two nights in a row."

"Now you are being a big girl."

"I'll pick you up. About eight?"

"Sure, see you then."

Cleary knocked on Jack's door just as Jack hung up the phone from Jamison. Cleary opened it and walked in.

"You got some time for me, Jack?"

"I am a bit pressed but, sure, come on in."

"I'm preoccupied with this Kalmati thing. Just been talking to Chambers. What do you know about the guy?"

"Not a lot. I met him a couple of times running up to the bombing, apparently, including shaking his hand at the function that night. I can only remember meeting him once before then. George was showing him around."

"How did George get to know him?"

"George knows everybody. He's a member of every club going around. He makes it his business to know people. He figures it's one of the things he brings to his job here."

"But he's IT, right?"

"Yea, but the company does value executives making it their business to bring potential clients in the door, and George has always been good at that. It's one of the reasons that he has gone as far as he has."

"Yea, that's what Chambers said. Is George an ambitious guy?"

"Sure, we all are."

"Frustrated in his ambition?"

"No, I wouldn't say that. He's done pretty well."

"What about you, Jack? Doing alright for yourself?"

"Talkin' to Chambers about me too?" There was no response from Cleary, so Jack answered his question instead. "Doing better lately, thanks."

"Why's that?"

"I've met someone."

"Good for you. Serious?"

"Too early to say."

"Mrs. Pierce know?"

"Too early to tell her… or you, for that matter now that I think about it."

"Understood. Can you remember anything about what was happening around here before the bombing that you would regard as suspicious?"

"Funny, George just asked me that question."

Cleary made a mental note. "George an amateur detective?"

"He's a professional gossip."

"Maybe I should talk to him, then. But you didn't answer my question."

"I had a think about it when George asked me, but no. There is one unusual thing that no one has picked up on yet. There has only been one smash done in this place that was unusable since it became standard operating procedure for everyone to put one on file monthly, and that was mine, the one immediately prior to the bombing. That process is meant to be foolproof. If you don't like coincidences, then there's a good one to get paranoid about."

"Have they found out why?"

"They're still working on it. They have checked every smash from before that day and since; they are all okay."

"Do you think you found out about something in that period and it was corrupted to destroy the evidence and then they wiped the slate clean with you, too?"

"You and George are certainly on the same page. Maybe, but that doesn't sit too well with me."

"Sure, why would it? Did Francine talk to you about soldier boy before the bombing?"

"If she did, it was in that period that is missing. We were fighting the night of the function, apparently. She didn't come to the gala, and she always goes to those things, she is built to go to those things. There must have been a good reason for her not to go, and that would qualify, I guess. You don't think he's involved in the bombing anymore, the boyfriend, I mean?"

"Can't get any proof. It fits, but we can't connect him to it, no. Why did you think we've given up on him?"

"You're here, sniffing around."

"Ah yes, I forget you guys are pretty smart. Well, he's still a suspect. We're just being thorough. You look disappointed."

"Well, if he's dangerous, shouldn't you let Francine know?"

"We'll keep her in the loop. And you, of course." Cleary got up to leave. "Just one last thing, Jack. Have you given any thought to what you were talking to Zimmermann about before the bombing?"

"I've got nothing. He's a jeweller, isn't he? Maybe I was looking to patch things up with Francine. I don't know."

"I'm going to be around for most of the day. Chambers is getting me permission to look at some of the personnel files. Call me if you think of anything. Maybe go through your purchase records and see if you bought anything or ordered anything from Zimmermann."

Cleary left with Jack still wondering about his contact with Zimmermann. He started to go through his phone to see if he could find a receipt or a note that would give him some clue about why he was talking to Zimmermann. Just then, the buzzer rang; it was Frank Dugan wanting to see Jack in his office. "This place is a madhouse this morning," Jack said to himself out loud as he got up to make his way up to Frank's office. Frank had an office at the plant as well as in town.

The availability of the new pulse weapons was weighing on Frank Dugan's mind because the new 400s had been designed specifically to carry them. Frank was under a great deal of pressure from his biggest customer to release the first batch of 400s so they could deploy the new weaponry. Apparently, there was a mission in the works at the Pentagon, and they wanted to use the new Augments. While the intergalactic travel proposed by the Star Trek generation seemed nowhere on the horizon in 2065, the same wasn't true in regard to pulse weaponry. Not the little hand-held devices used by Captain Kirk and Spock but larger, rifle-type devices were already in use within the US military. These weapons had their substantial energy requirement serviced by a backpack storage module, and the whole unit was very heavy and cumbersome but extremely effective.

The basic technology had been around prior to the advent of the military Augments, but it was the Augments, with their size and strength, that made the devices more viable for field use. This had brought a surge of development in that technology, which had taken the device design to new levels. That development had not reduced their size or weight — in fact, the new ones were slightly heavier — but the new devices had more than triple the energy output and significantly enhanced endurance and range. One of the benefits delivered to the field combatant by this new generation of pulse weaponry was the variability of the energy output. It could, like the sidearm carried by Captain Kirk, be turned down to a point where the pulse delivered by the weapon would only shock and subsequently disable a human target, rendering them unconscious as opposed to killing them. "Set your phasers to stun," Kirk used to say, and now they could. The shock delivered penetrated all contemporary armour, and on that setting, it was extremely effective in lowering the enemy combatant body count, assuming that the recipient of the blast had no prior heart or nervous system impairments. The new weapon could be turned up to energy levels where the pulse could level a building or destroy an enemy armed vehicle, or if brought to bear on a human, completely obliterate the target.

Frank had summoned Jack up to his office to get an update on the 400.

"Jack, sit down. How are you feeling?"

"Just fine, Frank, thanks."

"I'm getting pressure on these TPS400s from the Pentagon. They want to deploy them for a mission coming up. How are we doing down there?"

"Better if I didn't keep getting interrupted," Jack said. "I have a problem with the connective tissue dynamics. But I'm close. Maybe one or two more instigs." Jack was referring to the whole-body regeneration process, which took nearly a week. "Instigs" was lab slang for body growth instigations.

"One or two?"

"I think so. No more than four, to be precise. It can only be one of two more possible genetic combinations, which gives me four possible iterations, all of which I've worked through on my simulator. I can run them together if you like. It would increase the cost."

"Run them all together; it will save us time."

"Done. I'll set them this afternoon."

"That detective's been snooping around, has he? I thought he'd wrapped it up."

"Apparently not. He's back to thinking it was something to do with a technology theft. That means we've got a serious problem if he's right, Frank. It means one of our key people is moonlighting."

"To say the least. It puts a shudder up my spine. The thought of working with some crud who'd sell you out. How sure is he?"

"Don't know, didn't say."

"He's down there going through the personnel files as we speak."

"Those files have got some pretty sensitive stuff in them, Frank. Are you sure that's a good idea? You could stop him, you know."

"Yes. But if we have got a problem, I would prefer to know about it. Sadly, there's something else I haven't let NYPD know yet."

"What is it, Frank? You seem worried."

"I had Dick Chalmers do an inventory and yield analysis on the biogenetic precursor material that we have in stock. With all this talk of theft, I thought I'd do some investigating of my own. The inventory counts don't reconcile, and worse still, it didn't show up on the QC reports. I don't understand how those reports could be wrong, but we're short on that material. He's been over it several times. The amount we've grown and the amount we've used don't add back to what we have. There's what look like two cases, about eighty kilos, missing."

"Jesus, Frank. With that amount of material, you could make a lot of problems go away if you were trying to reverse engineer what we do here. How the hell did that happen?"

"Chalmers is working on it. It must have happened just before the bombing. We conducted a full stock take at the end of the September quarter for the published accounts, and everything reconciled. I have to inform them, Jack. I planned to let the Detective know this afternoon, once he's finished with personnel."

"Cleary would relish that, getting one up on the FBI. Just make sure he informs Helen Jamison over at the FBI, or better yet, tell her yourself. Cleary's got a competitive streak with her."

"Perhaps it's best if I let the Director of Media Relations handle it in writing, to both agencies. You're right; we shouldn't be seen as favouring one or the other. Good call, Jack."

"When are you planning to do that? Just in case I run into one of them?"

"I'll handle it now." Frank turned to his office phone and asked his PA to summon the Director of Media Relations to his office. "Listen, Jack. Please keep me updated on the TPS400. I have some anxious customers. One week, no more, OK? I want to get a full squad into production."

"Absolutely. Send me a copy of the communication with NYPD and the FBI so I know what I can divulge to these guys."

Frank agreed, and Jack headed back to the lab to set up the instigs. He was pleased with the outcome of the discussion. By setting four instigs in motion, the pressure was off him to figure out which one gave him the best outcome. Now, all he had to do was grow them and see.

Jamison had returned to the New York office of the FBI, looking forward to her date with Jack that evening. Her junior colleague, Briers, was with her when Section Chief Samuels appeared at their door.

"We've got the early satellite telemetry on the Sadr warehouse," Samuels said. "Nothing suspicious so far and no sign of your friend Fahd. We've got a CIA asset on the ground undercover, monitoring the comings and goings. I want you to take a look at this." Jamison and Briers moved over to examine the wall monitor as Samuels inserted his notepad into the secure desk computer portal, displaying the 3D images he wanted them to see.

"Look here. It's a photo taken through the door of a warehouse at a site that the CIA identified as suspicious near the warehouse where Fahd allegedly stored the biological material. It has to be Iranian military personnel inside; you can see at least four uniformed men.

Now, why do you think they're hanging around inside a warehouse in Sadr?"

"Do we have an aerial shot?" Jamison asks.

"Sure, here."

"It's a large compound," Jamison observes as the aerial view appears. "There could easily be something in there or beneath it. It's well located for what we're discussing, and it fits the professor's description."

Just then, Samuels's assistant walks in with the latest batch of intel from the CIA. The photos have been printed out. They all start sifting through them. Briers picks one out. "Isn't this…" he goes back to his whiteboard to compare photos, "isn't this Yasser Fahd? He's standing next to that truck driver."

"I can't see it; it's too small. Ask the lab to do a comparison," Samuels responds, and Briers gets on the communicator.

"He could be right, boss. That might be our guy," Jamison says, scrutinising the photo closely. "How did they single out this warehouse?"

"They won't tell me. It came to their attention due to its proximity to what they call a high level of type sensitive activity."

"If it is him, then we've likely found our location."

"The probability that it's him in that photo is ninety-two percent," Briers reports after hanging up.

"You've got sharp eyes, Brier. Good job," Samuels praises. "Jamison, can you confirm twenty-four-hour surveillance with the CIA, please? If we're right and that's Fahd, then that shipment should be moving soon, and that will be our final ID on the lab."

"We just got this from AIOGEN," Jamison says, picking up a communication on her notepad from the Director of Media Relations. "Apparently, they've reviewed their inventory records again and now claim they're missing two cases — around eighty kilos — of their genetic precursor material, whatever that is."

"It's the initial material that is the precursor to all full body growth instigations they perform for humanoid body type duplication over at AIOGEN," Briers offers. "What? I like to read."

"I'm not much of a warehouseman," Jamison says, "but the material in Sana'a was labelled biological material, and the bill of lading mentions one hundred and twenty kilos in two cases, not eighty. Briers, call our contact at AIOGEN, maybe Jack Pierce, and ask him how much they put in each case and how much each case weighs." Briers immediately gets on the phone. "They have to specify the correct weight on these shipping bills, or it would cause a delay when they try to load them onto the ship. So the one-twenty-kilo total weight on the bill of lading is likely correct."

"So what are you suggesting? If these cases weigh about twenty kilos each, then it's highly probable that the shipment from that old warehouse in Sana'a, which you and Jeffries visited, is AIOGEN's missing… stuff?"

"Precursor material, yes, sir." Jamison had to read it again from the email from AIOGEN.

"Twenty kilos each," Briers announces after thanking the person on the phone and hanging up. "QED."

Jamison and Samuels look at him, puzzled.

"It's what you write at the end of a mathematical equation when you've solved it, QED," Briers, the walking encyclopedia, explained. "It's an abbreviation of the Latin phrase *quod erat demonstrandum*, which means 'what was to be demonstrated,' implying that you just demonstrated it."

"Briers, you really need to get a life," Samuels says, turning his attention back to the photos and the paperwork assembled on the desk to assess whether he has enough to draw a firm conclusion. "QED indeed," he repeats to himself quietly.

"All we need now is for those cases to be delivered to the warehouse that the CIA has staked out, and I think we have enough to initiate the recovery operation." Samuels packs up the material and heads to his office to write that very recommendation, hoping the CIA will close the loop on the investigation.

Jack was early to pick Jamison up that night. She was working on her third outfit upstairs in her bedroom.

"Ask him to wait just a minute, please," she yelled down the stairs to her sister.

Jack and most of the neighbourhood heard it so there was no need for Christine to relay the message. Instead, Christine winced in response to Jamison yelling and then gave Jack a half a smile as if to apologise for Jamison's boisterousness.

"So Jack, I've heard a lot about you. And read a lot about you. You're something of a celebrity. Can I offer you a drink, we might be here for a while?"

"Love one, thanks. Scotch if you've got it. Celebrity isn't all it's cracked up to be. All you've got to do is get yourself blown up in a car park and you're a star."

"Well, being blown up is a lot more than some of these so-called celebrities have got going for them, that's for sure." Christine went over to her highboy to fix Jack a drink. "Although that's probably what some of them need. Neat?"

"Sure."

"She likes you, you know," Christine said, handing Jack the drink and turning back to fix herself one. "She'll be up there all night trying stuff on unless I put my foot down. I hope you're not hungry."

"It's my pleasure to wait, Christine, and thank you for saying."

"I haven't seen her get this excited since we were teenagers. She's so much into her job, you know. It takes up so much of her time. I have never thought that was healthy for her. Especially, given..."

"I don't think I can criticise her for that. I've been a bit the same, I'm afraid."

"I'm glad to see her get an outlet. You haven't got a cab waiting, have you? Cheers."

"I brought a town car and a driver. Makes it easier, especially when there's a bit of rain about."

Jamison made her way down the stairs. "See, I said just a minute," she said a little breathless.

"You look absolutely stunning," Jack said, genuinely taken aback.

"He's a keeper, Helen," Christine said.

"Is this one of your dresses, Christine, it's beautiful?" Jack asked.

"I shopped," Jamison said before Christine could answer. "We'd better go, eh?"

"It was a delight to meet you, Christine," Jack said, finishing his drink and handing Christine the glass. "We won't be late, given it's a work night."

"Have a good time."

"Don't wait up," Jamison said to Christine with a wry smile.

After dinner, Jack and Jamison were walking through the village. The weather had cleared, but the streets were still wet with rain. The town car was a polite distance behind.

"Don't you just love it when it's like this, Jack? The smell and it looks so clean."

"Getting a bit brisk, though. Christmas is in the air." Jack put his arms around her, wrapping half his coat over her shoulders. They began to stumble in a four-legged walk.

"I love Christmas time, but the change of season is the best. You just get tired of the weather being too hot or too cold then along comes spring or autumn," Jamison said.

"Yes, I agree, that promise of change, the warm sun and a cool breeze. It heightens the senses, doesn't it?"

"Are you coming back to my place?" Jamison asked. There was an uneasy silence. They stopped walking for a moment and looked to each other for guidance.

"Can I say no? I'm kind of stuck, you know, the switches are off, the defences are up, and there doesn't seem to be much I can do about it except wait. It's not that…"

Jamison put her fingers on his lips. "Please don't explain, I respect what you are saying." That decided, they started again to stroll. "There is something that you should know. It's personal."

"So was that kiss on the ear." They stopped walking again. "Spill it."

"I think this might be going somewhere, Jack. I feel the need to run up a red flag."

"This is a terrible time to tell me you're married."

"You should talk. I want you to know that I can't promise anything long term. I have a genetic disorder, Huntington's."

"And you think I might have caught it when you kissed me?"

"No, stupid, it's a…"

"A trinucleotide repeat disorder, on the inside of the forebrain, subcortical, the striatum. It's a bitch to treat. They can't get at it with cell regeneration treatment without significant risk to the forebrain and they can't replace it without basically… well, killing you. Even if they do treat it with targeted cell regeneration treatment, the cells tend to go back to their nasty old habits and keep producing that fucked-up protein that it's named after."

"Of course, you'd know that."

"It's not contagious."

"I know. But it is fatal."

"Eventually. We all die eventually, I should know, been there, done that. You're telling me this because?"

"Because of the look you had in your eyes the other night."

"That look wasn't rational. But it's still there somewhere."

"So you don't mind?"

"Get over yourself. The science is moving so quickly. I'll decide how long this relationship lasts, thank you, not some fucked-up disease."

Jamison forced them to start walking again with a dismissive look. "So, you think you're the boss?"

"What are you doing for Thanksgiving?" Jack asked, ignoring her question.

"Well, I was going to be at Christine's. Her in-laws are such a pain, though. What have you got in mind?" Jamison said, snuggling into Jack's arm and holding it with both hands, putting on the cutest expression she could muster, pulling him in close to her.

"Where are your parents?"

"They've both passed," she said dismissively. Jack noticed the don't-ask-me-about-it tone. One of them had to have been from Huntington's, Jack assumed.

"No other siblings?"

"Just the one sister. We're very close."

"I suppose it's a bit of an ask to take you away at Thanksgiving."

Jamison laughed. "She'd probably come, too, if you ask her. Come on, what have you got in mind?"

"My parents have asked me over to Barstow. Frank usually goes to his mother's in San Francisco for that weekend. I was thinking we could hop a ride on the company jet and get him to drop us off on his way, there's an airstrip just outside town, and maybe pick us up on his way back on the Sunday. Want to come?"

"I would love to, thank you."

"Great."

"Jack, where's Barstow?"

Jack laughed. "It will be a surprise then."

CHAPTER ELEVEN

The year was 1948. Frederick was standing in full uniform in the anteroom of the Oval Office in Washington waiting to see President Truman. Frederick had come to Washington to honour the Eighth Anniversary on August third of the European Armistice and the subsequent formation two years later of the European Union on the same date in August of 1942. There was to be a military parade at eleven that morning which was straight after his visit with the President, the parade being why Frederick had worn his uniform. The uniform was that of a Kapitanleutnant in the Kriegsmarine, the equivalent of a Captain in the American Navy. Frederick had done a year of national service in the Navy at seventeen, military service being required by all German youths, but the rank was an honorary one bestowed on him by the Führer who always preferred to see him in uniform ever since that first meeting in his office with Albert Speer. The uniforms of the ruling class in Germany were different than all other uniforms, a very specific shade of purple, vibrant and deeply rich, set off by black lapels and cuffs and gold insignia on the chest pocket with a red swastika on a white armband. The swastika had never become the symbol of evil that it would have become without Frederick. That colour of purple was restricted for use only by the elite in the German Government and armed forces, General or Admiral, but Frederick was royalty now, being the adopted son of Hitler and his expected heir. The colour could not be used anywhere else even to colour walls or cars and, of course, not for clothes, it was illegal. Frederick cast an imposing figure as he stood waiting for Truman.

The world order had changed in the years surrounding the conflict with the English, as it had become known. Hitler, having taken Frederick's advice, focused on settling matters with England after the successful invasion of France before taking any further steps against Russia - a task that he regarded as still outstanding. By then, Germany had completely withdrawn from France, now requiring no coastal bulwark to secure its position against England. Democracy with certain constraints had returned to both England and France and no occupying forces remained in either country. Hitler regarded action against the Soviets as pressing unfinished business but at Frederick's insistence he would act only in concert with the Americans which was expected in order to redress the Russian invasion of Poland and the Baltic States. Given the success of events in Europe and the avoidance of any broader conflict with the Americans, Frederick's tactical advice was now considered irreproachable. Frederick had been right about everything. He had accurately anticipated every move by the English, the Russians and Japan as well as astutely reading and assisting in the manipulation of public opinion in America. Hitler, always superstitious, now regarded Frederick as a gift from Heaven sent to assist him in liberating his people from the imperialistic yolk imposed on them by the allies after the Great War.

During the conflict with England, Hitler had carefully kept the American public informed about his intentions and had successfully portrayed Churchill as a warmonger holding out against a full European peace. The war in France was over in a matter of four weeks in 1940, a fact Frederick had predicted, which gave Hitler the motivation to press on with the rest of Frederick's agenda. The Soviets had signed up to an armistice even before Hitler had entered Poland and the new French Government had signed a treaty in 1940 as part of the arrangements that ended war with the Germans and the German occupation in that same year. The English had found themselves alone against what the Germans had described in the American press as a total European settlement. From their newly acquired bases in Southern England post the cessation of hostilities in France, Germany had threatened a push north unless a settlement could be found. In the end Joseph Kennedy was able to find that agreement. The British would retain the core of their surface naval fleet and a rudimentary army but no air force and in return obtain a full German withdrawal. The English would withdraw from the Middle East leaving it to German rule with the exception that the Suez would remain under British administration as a sweetener to negotiations. The English were asked to reconsider the abdication of Edward given his predispositions and apparent enlightened attitude towards the Germans, a request to which the English acceded.

The 1940 plan for a European Union was welcomed by an American public deeply weary of the incessant and bloody wrangling on that continent. Over the last two thousand years the drawing of country borders had been the subject of hundreds of wars with millions of lives lost as a consequence. The American public could no longer see the sense of it and were more than happy to see it come to its logical end with unification. Hitler was now viewed by Europeans and Americans alike as the man with the strength to have made it happen.

Germany had captured the retreating European Expeditionary Forces at Dunkirk in 1939 when hostilities had been joined with France three months sooner than in the previous timeline. All four hundred and twenty thousand men of those British Expeditionary Forces had been caught, killed or imprisoned, including one Colonel Bernard Law Montgomery who would have led the English back into Europe with American support under Eisenhower in an alternate version of events. That capture had shaken the confidence of the English populous and along with the German landings in Southern England had pushed the Labor government into negotiations. In March 1940, Germany had invaded southern England after the Luftwaffe had successfully and systematically eliminated all of the English air defences, including their new radar towers - a task they had failed to fully complete in Frederick's alternative timeline. Germany had reached terms with the English within three months of establishing their bases in Southern England. Germany had surrounded London on three sides but had not entered the city nor had they yet started to bomb it. Without air power and with the channel controlled by the Germans and no help from the Americans in sight, the English position was untenable. Edward was re-inaugurated as King with Wallace as his Queen. Churchill had retired to Blenheim Palace and gone back to his painting and drinking in peace. True to his word, Hitler left the English to their own devices insisting only that they became part of the European Union. All foreign affairs powers were ceded to the yet-to-be-formed European Parliament but at the moment they remained with the Nazi Government. With an end to war with the English in August of 1940 and no war with the Soviets yet engaged, Germany was left able to invest heavily in the development of their military equipment. Advances in jet and rocket propulsion had by late 1948 been fully realised and Germany had beaten the Americans to the development of the atomic bomb.

Frederick had quite deliberately stayed out of weapons development in Germany. He was cautious not to give the Germans too great an edge post the settlement of matters with England. The Americans had not been confronted with the urgency to develop nuclear weapons given that they did not face a war with Japan and had been kept out of the war between England and Germany in Europe. So, in Frederick's new timeline, the bombings at Hiroshima and Nagasaki never occurred and most European cities remained untouched including London, Berlin and Dresden. By 1948, however, America had the bomb once the imperative to match Germany in arms development had become clear, even though they did not have the intercontinental ballistic delivery platforms possessed by the Germans. Once again it was Oppenheimer who spearheaded the development of nuclear weapons for the Americans but he was in this timeline left without the guilt of being the first to both develop and use atomic weapons. The Soviets had not yet entered the nuclear arms race mainly because they failed to get access to German scientific personnel as they had done when they successfully invaded Germany in the other timeline. But both Germany and the USA were fearful that the Soviets would soon develop such weapons, and a high-level meeting had been called to discuss the matter, attendance at which was Frederick's main reason for coming to Washington.

Frederick was privately happy with the outcome in England. He had, in his previous life, blamed the English for dragging their feet regarding the formation of a self-determined Jewish State in Palestine, which was at the time part of the English Empire. It had been the Jewish domestic bombings that had placed pressure on the English to provide provincial independence. The terrorist bombings of English administrative buildings and hotels were a part of Jewish history that Frederick was happy to see erased. He felt that the bombings were beneath them as a people and had demeaned the otherwise desirable outcome of the formation of Israel. Nonetheless, those bombings in the previous timeline had seen the English dump the former colony in 1949 and leave it to the residents to sort out what was left.

After the end of military hostilities in England, it was apparent to Roosevelt that further inflammation of matters with Japan would be counterproductive to any developing relationship with the then-proposed European Union, so Roosevelt had put aside his desire to enter the European conflict on behalf of England or contain Japanese territorial ambitions in the Pacific and went back to embracing pacifism until he died in office in April of 1945. Truman had succeeded him and was up for re-election in November 1948, facing the highly favoured Governor of New York, Thomas E. Dewey.

In this environment, Hitler was able to have Ribbentrop negotiate Japan's position in Asia, and with the new East German Arabian oil fields scheduled to come online in 1944, Japan was happy to accept Germany's assurances that they would have secure access to oil in the future. In that Tripartite Agreement between Germany, the USA, and Japan, the Japanese were allowed to keep their territorial holdings on the Korean peninsula, which they had held since 1592, and to hold onto their Chinese acquisitions in Manchuria as a buffer, Ribbentrop argued, against Chinese communism. Beyond those concessions, Japan was to look no further in Asia for territorial gain. They had been secretly promised, however, the better part of the resource-rich eastern Siberian peninsula north of Manchuria to the Arctic Ocean and then East to the Bering Sea, provided they were to assist Germany in their eventual conflict with Russia. It was the Soviets, Hitler had planned, that would face war on two fronts and not Germany. More importantly, Germany would have the assistance of the American industrial machine, if not American military personnel, in that conflict if the meeting scheduled for the next day went the way the Germans expected. Ribbentrop had proposed that if matters in Asia were properly managed, then the two great powers of the region, China and Japan, would act to balance each other's military aspirations, and juxtaposed, they would not present a threat to peace in the wider international community. Just as he felt Japan could keep the Chinese communists in check, he also felt that China would keep Japanese expansionism under control.

The Jewish predicament, as Frederick referred to it, had also been resolved to Frederick's liking. Predicament was a better word, Frederick thought, than problem. The new Jewish independent state of Israel had been created after the Germans had broken up the French and English colonial holdings in the Middle East, India, and Asia. After strong and relentless diplomatic pressure, Ireland, Scotland, and Wales were granted independence and their own membership of the European Union. Hitler applied the same logic to breaking up Great Britain as the British had applied to breaking up the Habsburg Empire after the Great War. In Asia, Hong Kong was retained as a German protectorate both as an adjunct to European trade with Asia and to keep China and Taiwan separated, both of which had been recognised as independent nations by the European Union. Chiang Kai-shek, having been successfully routed by Mao to Taiwan earlier in this timeline because the war with Japan was stopped by the Germans, with the mainland Chinese northern border being drawn at Manchuria and both Chiang and Mao acquiescing, not wanting to involve Germany in the resolution of their own conflict. The remainder of French and English Asia was allowed to form their own governments, including Vietnam. Hitler had no interest in replacing the French colonialists in Vietnam and viewed that country to be of no strategic or economic value and felt it would never become of any importance in the future. In so doing, the Vietnam War of Independence became an internal matter which was quickly resolved without western involvement, but with Chinese assistance, in favour of the communists and all believed that war to be of no consequence in the greater scheme of international affairs. The so-called Domino Effect was of no concern to Hitler or Ribbentrop because they were fully confident that they could hold up any unwanted communist expansion in the region if needed and that there was no reason to make an expensive and bloody example of Vietnam.

Hitler had become the toast of the post-colonial world, with many countries viewing him as their liberator. In 1945, he once again became *Time Magazine*'s "Man of the Year." After the Tripartite Pact was signed, there were no Asian conflicts on the horizon except for the tensions between China and Taiwan, then known as the Republic of China, and the ongoing rivalry between China and Japan, particularly regarding Japanese Manchuria. With all these developments brokered by the Germans, the Asian region had slipped into a period of peace.

As per Frederick's design, the new state of Israel was nearly three times the size of the country that Churchill and Truman had provided for it in the other timeline. Its new capital was Jerusalem. Frederick believed it needed to be larger to accommodate the bigger population inherited from the European and Middle Eastern expulsions. However, he also thought that the Middle Eastern borders as they were created in his previous life were overly complex and bred too much conflict. The Independent State of Palestine remained as it was in the past, but Israel extended much further north and east and included part of the yet to be discovered middle-eastern oil fields. Israel was bordered to the east by the German East Indies, its protector, which included the former Arabian oil fields, now German-owned. The Jewish state was made to feel confident of its security within the region and it began its own deportation program, whereby all Palestinian nationals were deported to the new Independent State of Palestine. The Israelis argued that they needed more living space for their immigration program. As a result, the

Palestinian State's population swelled to nearly six million, largely made up of displaced people living in refugee camps.

To the north of Israel, the countries designated by the British in Frederick's previous life — Lebanon, Jordan, Syria, and Afghanistan — were combined into one country under Jordanian control. This new country was what remained after the formation of the German East Indies, Israel, Palestine, Iran, Egypt and Saudi Arabia. The Jordanians were left to decide who got what within its borders. This outcome largely mirrored the views held by the ancient Ottoman Empire which ruled most of the Middle East for six hundred years. The Jewish deportation from Europe was completed in an orderly fashion. At Frederick's insistence, Hitler put a stop to the internal violence against the Jews after settling with England and became outwardly satisfied with their expulsion.

In Truman's first term, he was able to fund universal health cover for all Americans and undertake the building of numerous public works that advanced productivity and stimulated economic growth within the country because the costs of a Pacific and European war had both been avoided. This was referred to as the Real Deal by the American press, in contrast to Roosevelt's New Deal. Truman privately credited much of the success in avoiding a worldwide catastrophic conflagration to Frederick, who was waiting to see him in his anteroom. He had seen Frederick's influence with the Führer during the war and witnessed his single-minded pursuit of peace at a rally at Heidelberg University in the summer of 1941, giving the German public their first glimpse of the intellect of the young Von Eichmann.

"Doctor Von Eichmann, a delight to finally meet you in person," the President said, personally coming into the anteroom to usher Frederick into his office. "Or is it Captain Von Eichmann?" Frederick had gained a doctorate from Heidelburg University at sixteen, the youngest person to do so.

"Frederick, please, Mr. President. The honour is entirely mine, I assure you."

"Your accent is American. How did you manage that?" the President said as they strolled together into the Oval Office. The

President gestured for Frederick to take a seat on one of the two couches that faced each other in front of the President's desk. The couches were separated by an antique wooden coffee table with ornate inlays, a pitcher of water placed on a lace doily, and several glasses.

"I study linguistics, Mr. President." It was of course because Frederick had spent most of the last one hundred and twenty years in the USA.

"It appears to me that you study a lot, Frederick. I will have to put our military chiefs in touch with your tailor." Both men laughed.

"You are too kind. They are very… bright," Frederick replied with genuine modesty.

"I have to congratulate you on that Jewish thing, Frederick. I understand that much of the political push behind that move came from you. Truly a stroke of genius. Your views on anti-Semitism are well known and timely."

"Thank you, sir. We must, however, remain vigilant. They are doing just fine as a young nation, I hear. I am going to visit them next month to progress relations. A Jew still cannot be a German citizen, something that we must work towards as the mindset of the nation changes."

"Indeed. We have work to do here at home as well."

"I have been asked to convey the Führer's personal regards to you and his best wishes, Mr. President, to your family."

"Please give him mine in return."

"I will, thank you. And on this day in particular, we as a nation wish to convey our thanks to you for the part you played in securing a final agreement with the English."

"There was some foot-dragging around here, I can tell you. President Roosevelt was very much against it, that's for sure. But the English position was untenable. It was just going to be a waste of more young lives to persist with it."

"I wish to assure you personally that we didn't want any part of a war with the English. We, that is to say, my Führer, viewed the English as much the same as the German peoples; light-skinned, well-educated, and stubborn." Both men laughed at the description.

"The elections went well there in '44. They are due again, aren't they?"

"Yes, in December, I think. They are getting used to the new order. After all, there haven't been many changes to get used to."

"You guys were smart to get well out of it and smart to put a believer like Edward back on the throne. Us Americans feel like we have a real foothold in the palace with Mrs. Simpson as his Queen."

"Is that so, Mr. President? I hadn't seen it that way. But of course, Edward has helped with the transition enormously. His brother King George was the puppet of Churchill and their imperialist military, despite having a very high regard for Chamberlain's policies privately. He had no voice of his own."

"You are being unkind."

"I didn't mean to refer to his speech impediment."

"Understood. But I do wish we had the luxury of not having a military budget."

"Well, the English contribute significantly, and they still have something of their own military and their beloved navy, but all of the EU countries do fund the Defence Forces of the European Union."

"Of course. But I've seen what we think are the numbers, and the English are getting off lightly."

"Perhaps. There are synergies in having one primary force. In any case, we are well set to progress matters with the Soviets, something else I wish to talk to you about."

"Yes, in our meeting tomorrow."

"I'm also here to invite you to the Führer's birthday on April 20th next year, his sixtieth. It's going to be quite a show. You would be our guest of honour."

"We had some pre-warning about that invitation through the regular channels. I think they have cleared my schedule for it. Just let me check. We are assuming, of course, I get re-elected."

"Need you even suggest otherwise, sir? But the invitation stands regardless."

The President got up and went over to his desk and pressed his communications device. He asked his Chief of Staff, John Steelman, to come in and bring the Assistant in charge of European Affairs with him.

"I would love to go, of course," Truman said, standing at his desk after having communicated his instructions over the intercom. "Let's see what the boss has to say."

It was only a moment before Steelman appeared at the door. He and Frederick exchanged pleasantries, and then a very familiar face followed Steelman into the Oval Office.

"Mädchen?" Frederick said. "Is it you?" Both Frederick and Mädchen went to each other and embraced. "I knew that you had taken an overseas post but my goodness, you have done very well for yourself."

"You two know each other?" the President asked.

"Well, I'm only the assistant to the Assistant. You know the exchange thing we have going with the Americans. I am a liaison officer, really a translator. My boss was away from his desk so I came instead. You look wonderful, Frederick. Should I salute you or what?"

"Silly question, I guess," the President answered his own question, mumbling, then continued more loudly. "I'm glad that we have such influential and well-connected people on our staff," giving Steelman a look that indicated that he didn't necessarily think that having someone so close to the upper echelons of the German Government on his staff was a good idea, even given his own enthusiasm for the exchange program.

"Yes, Mr President, I'm sorry. Childhood acquaintances. Mädchen and I used to see a lot of each other." Both Frederick and Mädchen laughed out loud at Frederick's unintended reference to certain private events of years past.

"So am I clear for the German trip in April, Miss…?" the President said, trying to get back to business.

"Oh. Dietrich, Mr President. Yes, Sir. We have also teed up a visit to France and England post their elections," Mädchen replied.

"Good. Then, Frederick, I think we have a date. We'll let the relevant people work out the details."

"Excellent news. The Führer will be pleased."

"Now if you will excuse me, I would like to go over my speech for the commemoration. I will see you tomorrow, Frederick. And Miss Dietrich, I think we, and the Chief of Staff here, need to have a little refresher course with you regarding confidentiality," the President said, smiling and ushering Frederick out of his office.

Mädchen and Frederick met up later that night. Frederick had waited for her in the anteroom at the White House, and they had arranged to have dinner. It was at a small French bistro in Georgetown that Mädchen had picked out. They had just been seated at their table.

"I can't take my eyes off you, Mädchen. You are as beautiful now as you were then."

"I see you dumped the uniform," Mädchen said playfully.

"Yes, it was pretentious, wasn't it?"

"It had me going, that's for sure. I wanted to jump on you right there."

"You always were a little forward. I don't think the President would have thought much of you jumping on me."

"I might have to ask you to put it back on later."

"Who said we were going anywhere later?"

"Well, we can't go now… I'm hungry."

"It will have to be later, then," Frederick said laughing and tossing his menu down before leaning across the table and taking her hand. "How have you been? You look absolutely wonderful. That long blonde hair of yours nearly killed me the first time I saw it."

"You seemed to have survived. Ruling the world, are we?"

"A little bit, yes." More laughter.

"And your new family? My goodness, Frederick, congratulations, the Führer no less."

"Yes, 'Daddy's' just fine," Frederick said flippantly, picking the menu back up. "And Eva is frantically trying to get pregnant."

"No. You don't call him 'daddy,' do you?" Mädchen said, leaning forward with intrigue all over her face.

"I wouldn't have the guts. Did you see a killed-in-action medal on my uniform today? I don't think so."

"What do you call him?"

"He prefers 'Mein Vater' when we are alone." There was a moment of silence while Mädchen looked at Frederick as they both absorbed the intimacy that the phrase imparted, the closeness of the relationship that now existed between Hitler and Frederick, once Franz. Frederick's gut twisted as the realisation of that hit him, thinking of his own father. He looked, perhaps for the first time, at the totality of the new reality he had created.

"Are you here for the Foreign Affairs meeting tomorrow?" Mädchen said, changing the subject.

"What?" Frederick was distracted by his thoughts. "Yes, yes. That is primarily why I came. The Führer is keen to sort something out about the Soviets before they get hold of the bomb. Ribbentrop and your father are coming in for it. The Führer has been very patient with the Americans. Enough said."

"Indeed. I have already had one lecture today about confidentiality. I am looking forward to seeing Mein Vater tomorrow night though. I would ask you to come but I should tell him first before I invite you and he is in the air now, I think."

"I can't in any case. I am flying out after the meeting unless there is something pressing that arises from it. The Führer was insistent that I give him a firsthand report immediately. He has been waiting for progress on this matter for so long."

"So, it's just tonight then," Mädchen said with a mischievous grin. "I am going to have the clams. You should try them."

"Done." Frederick discarded the menu, called over the waiter and, in perfect French, gave him both their orders and ordered a bottle of Champagne.

"I see you've been working on your French."

"I have access to some people, yes," Frederick said, pushing his chair back a little and crossing his legs, pounding a cigarette on his leg then offering it to Mädchen.

"Would they be French people?" Mädchen asked as Frederick lit her cigarette, then his own.

"More like French restaurateurs. Paris is a beautiful city, Mädchen, and I was so pleased that it remained untouched. And fortunately, the English saw the light before London was hit."

"You must show me around Paris sometime."

"Sure. How about this weekend?"

"Of course, you're joking."

"I assure you that I'm not joking, I am German. I will send a plane if you say yes. One of those new jet transports from Fokker. We can cross the Atlantic in seven hours, eight at most. I have thought about you almost daily since I saw you last, Mädchen. And why wouldn't I? You left quite an impression on this innocent little German boy."

"You have never been innocent, Frederick, and not so little if I remember correctly."

"How inappropriate of you to say, my dear. You started all that 'show me your stuff' business if I recall correctly."

"Indeed, and it is my plan tonight to finish it if you're game this time."

"That is the best plan I have had the opportunity to review in a long time."

"Send a plane, you say? Frederick, you have been ruling the world without me."

"It has its privileges, but time is limited, and there is much to do."

"It seems strange that someone so young and so accomplished would talk in that way, Frederick. You have done more than most people would do in any lifetime."

"But not two lifetimes perhaps," Frederick said with disguised irony. "These have been difficult times, critical times with so many lives at stake, there was no time to daydream. But events should now unfold in a way that is better than before."

"Before what, Frederick?"

"Before… now, Mädchen. We could have had a world war. We could have lost so many lives, so much could have been destroyed. But those lives have been saved. There was no world war or Korean war, and there will not be a Vietnamese war, and there was no Holocaust. It is better than before is what I mean."

"Some of the things you say, Frederick, I don't understand. What is a Holocaust?"

"Exactly, my dear. I rest my case. You should never know of such a thing, and you will never know of it." Frederick held up his glass of champagne and said, "Let's drink to that, please. I will explain it another day. Here's to no Holocaust."

They touched glasses and held each other's gaze while they did, as was the polite German custom, but the look spoke of things other than good manners.

Frederick arrived on time for his meeting at the White House the next morning despite a very late night with Mädchen. The President attended personally given the importance of matters under discussion, along with his Secretary of State, George Marshall, his long-term Chief of Staff and close friend John Steelman, the Attorney General Tom Clark who would speak to any matters of international law, and the Secretary of Defence James Forrestal all with their key support staff who would sit against the wall and not at the main table. The Vice President, Joseph Kennedy, was on a goodwill tour of Europe and to date was not in the loop on the Russian proposal.

For the Germans, it was Frederick, Ulrich von Ribbentrop, the German Foreign Minister, and General Josep "Sepp" Dietrich, Mädchen's father and close confidant and military advisor to Hitler representing the Führer directly on military matters, along with their relevant assistants and note takers.

"I think this is your meeting, Herr Ribbentrop, so perhaps you can lead us off," the President said sternly, keen to get to the heart of the matter.

"Very well, Mr President." Ribbentrop stood. "I am here to convey Germany's interest in immediately pursuing matters against the Soviets."

"By matters I assume you mean a war?" Steelman said, blunt as always.

"Yes, you are correct, Mr Steelman, but allow me to make the case for the urgent action that we believe is necessary, with your indulgence, Mr President." A nod from both men was enough for Ribbentrop to continue. "Much of this you would have already seen in various correspondences but allow me to summarise the matter for this meeting. We see the Soviets as a threat to our national security and to the peace and wellbeing of the citizens of the hard-won European Union. Whilst they have signed a nonaggression pact with Germany, they remain armed to the teeth, with large armed forces assembled at the German border and the actions of their leaders have proven in recent years to be aggressive, ruthless and entirely without regard for human life and personal freedoms. Their actions in Poland with the execution of Polish prisoners of war in May of 1940 in the Katyn Forest massacre was a mass murder that cannot be allowed to go without recognition or deliverance. It was directly authorised by Stalin and it is a clear indication of his methods and his intentions toward the Soviet-occupied states. We estimate the number of people murdered in that massacre alone, including the entire senior ranks of the Polish military, to be 21,768, the details of which have been documented and that paperwork is available for your review. Further his forcible removal, recently documented, of grain and crops in 1933 from the Ukrainian people, grain that was eventually exported to this country, caused over seven million of those people to die of starvation and all because he needed your greenback to finance his military expansion. His bloody invasion of Norway in 1939 caused over one hundred and fifty thousand deaths in the local populace and twice that many of Soviets combatants. Mr Churchill felt that it was appropriate to undertake a war against Germany in response to our legitimate reunification efforts through Poland to East Prussia but left the major crimes and territorial acquisition inflicted by the Soviets at that very same time both unmentioned and unredeemed. Churchill's reasoning on that matter and his desire to protract the war with Germany whilst calling Stalin his ally is beyond my modest intellect to comprehend or explain to this meeting. We have word of further atrocities against the Jewish citizens of the Baltic States and the Ukraine and western Russia. Some say as many as ten percent of the Russian peoples have been killed by him in political, racial or religious purges. Gentlemen, I would ask you for a moment to pause and comprehend what I just said: ten percent of the populations under Stalin's control have been massacred since his rise to power. Most alarming of all is the fact that the Soviets are well progressed in the development of nuclear weaponry, and if obtained, Stalin's record would suggest that he will not hesitate to use these weapons of mass destruction. We firmly believe that any further delay in acting against him risks a future massive loss of life on the continent in a nuclear conflagration the like of which this world has never seen."

Ribbentrop retakes his seat.

"It is a grim picture indeed that you so eloquently paint, Mr Foreign Minister," George Marshall said. "The extremes of that totalitarian regime are well known to us on this side of the Atlantic. But what is your proposed solution?"

"There can be no solution without force, Mr Marshall. If nothing else, the intransigence of Stalin's friend and ally Mr Churchill and our eventual need to invade England has proven that reality to all at this table. We believe Stalin would be prepared to sacrifice every man under arms in Russia to prolong his hold on power and would not act on a simple invitation to step down regardless of what threats that invitation may tender."

"A war is a difficult and costly task to execute," the President added. "Especially an invasion."

"We have a plan, Mr President."

With that, Sepp Dietrich took the podium and outlined using graphs and diagrams a two-fronted war whereby Japanese forces would attack from the East and a German assault would come from the West. Action would commence with a comprehensive air strike on all Soviet bases in sparsely populated areas using their newly developed tactical nuclear weapons.

"Within seventy-two hours from the commencement of hostilities the Soviets will be deaf, dumb and blind." Ribbentrop resumed the dialogue from his seat. "They will be denied any opportunity to respond with any of their air or naval assets. Those assets will all be largely eliminated by the end of the first week of engagement, another lesson our English friends have taught us. Their command and control will be completely eliminated within the first seventy-two hours. The German panzers using the new Tiger tanks and under the cover of complete air superiority will thereafter be in Moscow within a week. It is our intention at that stage to offer them a proposal. Release their leaders for trial, those that have not already been captured or killed, and lay down their arms and submit to the introduction of a new constitution. We are tracking Stalin's movements daily, he and his henchmen will be an early target using our new stealth V3 conventionally armed rockets. The new constitution would offer them capitalism and democracy and, subsequent to proper elections, membership of the EU. We have members of an interim Russian government, all Russian nationals themselves currently exiled in Germany, ready to be installed upon the arrival of our forces in Moscow. We shall widely announce that they have taken power. The remainder of their armed forces would at that point be implored to lay down arms and submit to the authority of the new government."

"You've obviously thought this through."

"We are Germans."

"Nuclear weapons?" Truman said. "What about the danger to the citizenry?"

It was all Frederick could do not to laugh out loud at the irony given that it was Truman asking that question, a man who had devastated Hiroshima and Nagasaki with just such weapons in another timeline. "The nuclear targets will be carefully selected with your concern in mind, Mr President. Besides, they are essential to the shock and awe of the campaign, the fear they will place in the mind of the remainder of the military and politburo."

"You can do all of that, in that time frame, General Dietrich?" the Secretary of Defence James Forrestal asked, looking directly for Sepp Dietrich's opinion.

"Yes," was Dietrich's simple and forceful response.

"And what role do you see the US playing?" the President asked with some anxiety.

"We need your public support for this police action against the Soviets and, if necessary, any diplomatic access that may be required to negotiate the terms of their surrender. We would also like you to make a special effort to defuse any anxiety with the Chinese given the involvement of Japan and the fact that the two countries, Russia and China, share a similar communist doctrine."

"Similar but by no means the same," Tom Clark clarified.

"*Police action*, that's a new term for it," the President commented. "I like it, though."

"Our personnel would not be directly involved?" Clark continued.

"No. We see your continued neutrality in European affairs as sacrosanct." Frederick entered the conversation.

"A wise move," the President confirmed, relieved at what was being asked of him and the US. "I'm not sure I could sell any other position to my electorate. But a role as a peace broker, I am entirely happy with that."

"Mr. President," Frederick continued, "people are losing their lives as we speak here today. The oppression of Stalin is manifold. The Jewish citizens along with any semblance of political opposition are systematically being rounded up and shot. We must act or lose our souls to ambivalence and indecision."

"A compelling argument, but what of your own territorial ambitions to the east?" Marshall added.

"Ah! Lebensraum," Ribbentrop responded. "I see you have read the Führer's manifesto. This is a term often misunderstood. It referred to the reunification of the German-speaking peoples of Middle Europe. We do not see living space as a key political policy any more since we have already undone all of the injustices of the Treaty at Versailles. We would seek to free the Baltic States and the Ukraine and give them each independent membership of the EU, we see that as both strategically wise and a popular outcome within those communities. We would be looking for a small adjustment in our border with the Soviets, a movement to the East, including the recovery of the remainder of Poland which they occupy and its re-inclusion into Greater Germany. This would give us a permanent border with Russia, no longer Soviet Russia, and the movement east of the German border closer to Moscow should assist us if there is any further trouble down the track. The Japanese would claim Siberia."

"I think we can live with all of that," the President said on board with the Plan given the zero-risk position that the USA would need to take. "Besides my refusal to commit troops to it, which is the way I shall frame it, will reinforce my credentials as a pacifist. And if you are successful as you say you will be, at least if you get it bedded down before November, I would have gazumped that accursed McCarthy. There can't be a *red under every bed* if we have gotten rid of the bastards." Everyone in the room laughed. "There might be a third term in this for me."

"Then we have a deal, gentlemen?" Ribbentrop pressed the meeting for a formal commitment.

"We will have to discuss it further," Steelman was quick to say. "But it would appear that we may have a deal, yes."

CHAPTER TWELVE

The BIE Meeting

Frank Dugan, Su-Ming Lee, and Jack Pierce sat down in front of the full Policy Committee of the BIE in their hearing rooms on Madison and 39th Street. The room was set up somewhat like a Senate Committee hearing room. However, this BIE had greater legal standing and executive rights than a Senate Committee and had to date exhibited much greater agility in responding to the needs arising from social change driven by emerging technologies. The grand wooden bench where the Committee sat and the courtroom-like internals of the venue added to the gravity pursuant to the power that resided here. A series of portraits ran around the room, painted specifically for this place, of all the key innovators and scientists of the modern world who seemingly, by their presence, provided the necessary supervision of the processes conducted within these four walls.

The AIOGEN team sat at one long table on a level below that of the Committee's bench. Their assistants were seated behind them, and all faced the board members sitting in front of them, ten in total, with the Chairperson holding a casting vote. The meeting was being videotaped and electronically transcribed, and it was a closed meeting with no one from the general public or the press attending. The Committee Clerk brought the meeting to order with a stamp of his gavel, and Frank Dugan read a small opening statement into the record based on the papers submitted to the BIE prior to the hearing.

Mr Chairman and Distinguished Members, if it pleases the Committee:

AIOGEN would submit for the Committee's consideration the following propositions.

It is the intention in these submissions that each proposition be considered severally and that if any of these submissions meets with the disapproval of the Committee then the others, each in their turn, should be considered separately upon their merits.

The Committee is referred to the supporting papers to these submissions that include the background of the research, a study of the social impact of each protocol if legalised, clinical notes and a psychological and physiological analysis all with the appropriate statistics and projections. The proposed fee structure for each of these procedures, if they were commercialised, can be found in Annexure C24.

We submit for the Committee's consideration the following:

Proposition A.1   *That the Committee allow the commercial availability of a procedure which draws down and electronic stores a human person's brain content, referred to in these papers as a BCD, and allows the subsequent reload of such brain content into a fully reconstituted age-specific biological replica genetically identical to that donor human being, such a procedure is referred to in these papers as a Replant, for the sole purpose of saving that human being's life in the event of a disaster or in anticipation of the imminent death of that individual. We have subtitled this proposal, "The Pierce Proposition," in honour of the first recipient of this procedure for which the Committee's prior approval is most gratefully recognised.*

Proposition A.2   *That during any of the procedures noted in the preceding proposition that a vetting for genetic diseases be allowed and appropriate correction in genetic code be legalised for the purpose of executing the re-growth protocol in A.1 above in such a way as to eliminate the genetics exposures that have been identified. Such analysis and adjustments would take place prior to the full body re-growth of the individual the effects of which therefore being present in their fully reconstituted body. We propose that this vetting be governed by the same laws applying at any*

215

given time to the Pre-Vet Zygote Program as currently legislated in the United States of America.

Proposition A.3 *That the procedure noted in A.1 be extended to encompass those individuals suffering from a significant biological impairment who cannot be adequately treated using currently available medical procedures. Various definitions of such impairments can be found in the attached schedules for the Committee's consideration and each such definition varies in breadth so as to provide the Committee with options as to how far it would wish to go in allowing the availability of this procedure in non-life-threatening circumstances. In general, however, we refer here to the possible inclusion of such afflictions as loss of a limb or limbs or the use of one's limbs, burns, irreparable loss of site or hearing, the onset of regressive old age, and the inclusion of degenerative and debilitating diseases of any kind regardless of the prognosis as to life expectancy. This process could also represent the ultimate answer to those suffering from gender dysphoria in that they could comprehensively and completely change their gender without intrusive surgery.*

Proposition A.4 *That the procedure noted above be extended to include individuals wishing to enhance their life enjoyment by reducing their chronological age.*

Proposition A.5 *That during any of the procedures noted in the preceding propositions that variations may be offered to the patient in regard to the expression of the genes they already possess during the full body re-growth. The type and nature of such adjustments could be codified by this Committee and examples of such codifications have been provided. As can be seen from the attached schedules these regulations could be extended to include the cosmetic enhancement of the re-grown body other than that pertaining to age as specified in A.4 which we wish the Committee to consider as a separate proposition to A.5.*

That ends my statement to the Committee.

Then, as is the protocol for such meetings with the BIE Committee, the floor was opened for unstructured discussion and the prior review of the documentation attached to the submission was assumed. It was the Chairman of the Committee that leads off.

"My God, Frank, are you aware of the ramifications of all this?" Frank and the Chairman had known and dealt with each other for many years. The Chairman had a distinguished career in industry, had a doctorate in Biology from MIT and had held a senior post in the previous government's economic advisory department. All of the members of the Committee were distinguished in their relevant fields. The Committee included a cross-section of interests including those possessing theological training.

"One of the ramifications is sitting right next to me, Mr Chairman. It's all in the papers, but to answer your question specifically, yes, I am aware and I for one can't wait to get my hands on it. I would ask the Committee members to consider what this means for their own personal position given that many of us here are getting on in life and whilst they are considering this matter that they take into account the ramifications for their families if this were to be made generally available."

"Save the sales pitch, Frank. We can do our own analysis. Let's just stick to the facts, shall we?"

"We're seeking approval on the Pierce Proposition as a minimum outcome here, Mr. Chairman. To do otherwise would be akin to the Vatican executing Galileo, whose portrait, I note with appreciation, adorns these very walls."

"It hasn't been our practice to execute people in the past, Frank, but I could make an exception in your case if you keep pushing the way you are. What about it, Dr. Pierce, what have you got to say about all this?"

"Hard for me to argue otherwise, Mr. Chairman. If you're asking what effect it has had on me, I can say little because I have nothing with which to compare it pre-procedure. But I can say I feel fine, and that my friends and colleagues see no difference in me now compared to then, which is all confirmed by the array of clinical tests done by AIOGEN, the results of which are attached to the submission. The psychological effects, at least on me, were limited to momentary disorientation and a bout of depression, with no psychosis or mental health defect being apparent. I think someone who had signed up for this procedure beforehand would be much better prepared psychologically to cope with it, better than I was in any case. If it's of any comfort to the Committee, AIOGEN screened out my genetic disorders and all of that also turned out fine and is very comforting to me personally."

"Yes," the Chairman said, "I had been made aware of that subsequent to your procedure, Dr. Pierce, but given the time frames that we had after the bombing, I accept that it was done in good faith. Let the record show that Dr. Pierce's screening during his full body re-growth is approved by the committee, post event. There's not much we can do about it now anyway. But there will be no further leeway taken, Mr. Dugan, prior to this Committee's full consideration of these matters. We approved Dr. Pierce's regeneration at the time because of his pre-eminence in a field considered essential to the national security of this country, but nobody said anything about fiddling with his genome. Consider yourself rebuked, Mr. Dugan."

"Understood, Mr. Chairman, with my apologies but the confusion and haste surrounding Jack's Replant is precisely why we are here. May I then add, moving the discussion forward, that if you're going to approve the Pierce Proposition then surely Proposition A.2 follows logically, especially given that we already screen fertilised embryos in the same way. How could you refuse the benefit of that screening to a Replant if you approve of it for a newborn?"

"The answer, Mr. Dugan, is that in screening a Replant, you are manipulating the genome not selecting the preferred zygote from various available embryos," one of the other members of the Committee responds with a degree of forcefulness. "And there is quite a difference in the two, philosophically speaking. Dr. Lee, can you please tell me a bit more about how you modify gene expression in the Replant?"

"As I understand it, sir, you and three of the other members of this Committee have had training in epigenetics, so I apologise in advance if I oversimplify matters for the benefit of the other Committee members. I won't bore you with the full details here, but as you would know, we are not talking about altering the human genome or the specific genetic makeup of the individual. We are not taking away genes or adding genes from another species or another human. In fact, each human already carries a vast suite of genes, many of which are dormant genes that go back millennia and are no longer expressed as the embryo develops. We also have genes that inadequately express themselves, or their expression is impaired in some way because of a biological disorder from which the individual suffers, such as Huntington's disease, for example. The expression of dormant or impaired genes, potentially in combination with the action of other genes that are already activated, can change the biological outcomes for the re-grown body in many different and sometimes very substantial ways. I disagree with your prior conclusion that this screening lacks similarity to the Pre-Vet Program, sir. This Committee has enacted a law requiring zygotes to be screened for genetic disorders prior to implantation, and in so doing, we have eliminated a large number of genetic diseases and predispositions. To deny the same opportunity to the general populace who were born before Pre-Vet became law would be, in my opinion, reprehensible. There are at least two ways to look at this. Do we become proactive in changing the gene expression of a human during the Replant procedure, which is what we are proposing, and in so doing, substantially modify the biological outcome of the re-growth in a way that is determined by the patient, given that they would, of course, be constrained by the laws that you determine here? You might categorise this as the cosmetic option. In this area, I agree with your view that this would indeed be new and additional to what is currently legislated in Pre-Vet zygote screening. But if one is simply switching off a gene in a Replant that will in the future cause, or is already causing, a patient with health problems, then I believe that not to modify it, to turn it off so to speak, would be medical malpractice. If I may add, I think Proposition A.2 stands as sound social and therapeutic policy, and that the Committee should see it as a natural extension of existing Pre-Vet policy. Of course, in the same way as Pre-Vet, you can limit the application to genetic disorders, which is why we linked the proposition to the Pre-Vet legislation. If the Committee decides that in future Pre-Vet can be used for cosmetic reasons, then so should the Replant procedure be made available to the patient for cosmetic enhancements. I feel the same about Proposition A.4, the resetting of the biological age. How could you leave someone to suffer from an existing debilitating impairment such as senility when a procedure is at hand to fix it? Propositions A.4 and A.5 are, however, a step in a new direction, a step toward, in my opinion, at long last, taking control of our own destiny as a species."

"But A.4 brings with it the possibility of immortality," one of the religious members of the Committee asserts. "The fact that we were rushed into a discussion regarding Dr. Pierce's predicament should not disqualify us from a more considered judgment here."

"Yes," one of the other conservatively minded members agrees, "if we step over this line now, it changes forever, and may I emphasize the word forever, what we are as a species."

"Only if you include old age as an impairment that would warrant a Replant," Lee responds. "You could restrain it and lock it into being age-specific, if you wish. That is to say, you must be the same age post-procedure that you were pre-procedure. It is only A.4 that steps outside this and sends us towards immortality."

"But even there," Frank adds with some urgency, "you, this Committee, are still in control. Don't necessarily look at A.4 as either immortality or no immortality. You could limit the human lifespan and still use this procedure to reset your chronological age. That is to say, you could rule, for example, that you get 150 years, and after that, you do not have access to further Replant procedures. But realise that you could spend those 150 years in a twenty-one-year-old's body, retaining the education and the experience that you have accumulated over your life on the planet. Youth would no longer be wasted on the young and reckless. Consider the beneficial economic consequences regarding the availability of trained but also physically vibrant and strong personnel. And may I add from my own perspective that having advanced to this point, not to avail ourselves of it, would be inexplicable to the general populace. You could limit the number of Replants that a person can legally receive if you wanted, but I personally can't see why you would. That is, you could have only one, for example, which resets your age, and make any other Replant subject to the criteria you determine when defining medical necessity. The Committee can pick and choose from this menu and get any outcome they want."

"Thank you, Frank, for telling us what we can and can't do. What we decide here is not determined by opinion polls. This is a non-political, non-partisan, independent body, Frank. Opinion polls are for politicians. Besides, you are omitting the small fact that it will not be available to all, only those with the appropriate bank balance. Therein lies a whole other set of considerations. If you feel that wealth divides this community now, consider what this would add to the expanse of that division. All the wealthy people will be running around in twenty-one-year-old bodies, as you rightly say, driving Ferraris and thumbing their noses at the poor souls with walking canes and droopy skin."

"Very vivid, Mr. Chairman, but you are asserting that wealth does not already, in many circumstances, have medical and life quality implications," Frank added. "Besides, there is always the prospect of insurance or benevolence."

"How sure are you of your outcomes, Dr. Lee, post this genetic manipulation?" the Chairman asked.

"I refer you to the submission, sir, for the full answer. All the clinical data is there. But the short answer is that we have all the necessary precision at our fingertips. We have it, it works and there is no turning back. To be specific: we have control of this procedure and the outcomes from it can be identified with one hundred percent certainty. The genie, Mr Chairman, is out of the bottle."

CHAPTER THIRTEEN

It was coming up to Christmas 1952 and Frederick had again come to Washington to meet with President Truman. It was early December and Truman had just been re-elected in what was technically his third term. He was now sixty-eight years old. Joseph Kennedy had stepped down as his running mate to enable him to mount his own campaign for the Presidency in 1956.

The war with the Soviets had been more protracted than the German's had predicted but their plans had substantially been fulfilled by the November elections in 1948, sufficient at least for Truman to properly claim during the campaign that it was all under control, which by the middle of 1949 it proved to be. Truman had asserted in that campaign that he had once again averted a European catastrophe by supporting and assisting the Germans in their *police action* against the Soviets and had, in conjunction with the Germans, removed the last threat to a lasting peace on that continent and in the process had made the world a safer place for all Americans.

Neither he nor the American people would in fact ever know the true extent of what had been averted with the Soviet Union being brought into the fold of the EU before they acquired nuclear weapons. Nonetheless, Truman's argument that America had avoided a great tragedy seemed self-evident to most, especially with the possibility of nuclear war threatening. It was an assertion that the electorate gratefully accepted given that Europe was finally fully unified and conflict between the EU states now appeared to be restricted to heated debate within its various committees. Growing democracy within the EU member states, including Germany, also provided comfort to the American people. Truman had successfully removed the Reds from underneath all American beds and Senator Joseph McCarthy was delegated to a footnote in the history of the American Senate and his kangaroo court hunting out communist subversives in American society had never taken hold.

So Truman and Kennedy had handsomely won his first elected term in 1948, and in 1952, Truman had faced down the Republican candidate from Ohio, Senator Robert Taft, and vice-presidential candidate Richard Nixon in what was a closer encounter due mainly to Truman's advancing years. It was, Truman had decided, going to be his last term.

General Eisenhower was just another military man who never became the war hero of a disastrous European war and, therefore, was never considered as a political leader, nor did he consider himself a candidate for the election in 1952, an election that he had won in the alternate timeline. Joseph Kennedy, then Truman's Vice President, had intentions of standing in Truman's stead at the election in 1956, even though he was only four years younger than Truman and would be sixty-eight himself at the next election. Joe Kennedy Jr. had lost his life in an aircraft accident earlier in the year, a strangely similar fate to that which befell him in the other timeline but this time, it was as a test pilot for the United States Air Force. Jack Kennedy, also, as per the alternate timeline, was already embedded in the House of Representatives with a clear eye on the 1960 presidential election or 1964 should his father win in 1956 and seek a second term. He was considering whether he would run with his father in '56 should Joe Sr. obtain the democratic nomination, as seemed likely, but he would probably be considered too young for the vice-presidency, and the electorate might react poorly to the perceived nepotism.

A new government and constitution had been installed in Russia. They had, in 1951, gone through their first set of elections, a little later than had been planned as a longer period of autocratic rule was required to bring matters firmly under control in that country. Stalin and a number of his politburo associates had been brought to trial for war crimes against Poland and the Ukraine and atrocities against its Jewish peoples, and some, including Stalin himself, had by 1952 been executed for those crimes. In the alternate timeline, Stalin had died of a cerebral haemorrhage in 1953 after enjoying a life of privilege and power. Russia had taken their position within the European Union and, like all of its members, did not now have much of a military but instead were protected by the considerable might of the Joint Forces of the European Union which were still under the direct control of the German Führer.

The territorial breakup after the Russian conflict was just as Ribbentrop had described it at the meeting with Truman in 1948. Greater Germany now consisted of its pre-1938 boundaries plus what was then Austria, the Sudetenland, including parts of Slovakia, and it had absorbed Poland, Hungary, and Prussia. Greater Germany had also absorbed the southern part of Belarus to give it a common border with the new Russia. The other Baltic States were returned to their pre-war borders and granted entry into the EU. France and Italy had remained as they were pre-war. The remainder of Europe consisted of independent states, all part of the European Union, which spread all the way to Greece and the Black Sea in the East, and Northeast to the border with Japanese Siberia, and West to Spain, Portugal, and England. Germany held the German East Indies as a protectorate in the Middle East which contained the majority of the world's known oil reserves and the Suez Canal was part of that Protectorate but administered by the British. Mussolini had been deposed by the Italian people in 1943 with assistance from the German Secret Police, the Gestapo. He had been tried and convicted of crimes against the citizenry and had been executed in that same year. There had been four national elections there in the period from 1945 to 1952, but matters were settling down into a stable political routine in that country. The Italian defence forces had also been largely absorbed into the European Military as a condition of Italy's entry into the EU.

The European Union was quickly becoming the economic powerhouse of the world, outstripping the United States in total GDP output in 1951. Within its boundaries, it was a free trade zone, and moves were afoot to unify the currency under the Deutschmark, which proudly carried Hitler's likeness on all of its notes and coins. The EU had recently tightened import restrictions for goods coming in from outside the Union, and it was this development that had brought about this meeting between Truman and his now long-term friend, Frederick Von Eichmann.

Hitler as yet had no formal plans to retire, even though by 1952 he was sixty-three. Hitler had suffered many health issues related to his gut and bouts of addiction to narcotics brought about by treatments prescribed to him by Theodor Morell, his personal physician. But since Frederick had uncovered the foul-smelling Morell's quackery, Hitler's health had steadily improved after obtaining appropriate medical care. Nonetheless, he had begun to turn over many of his public appearances to Frederick, who had become, with his young family, hugely popular with the German people. Frederick had married Mädchen after a whirlwind relationship in March of 1948, with Mädchen being pregnant with their first child, Franz, who was conceived the night of their meeting in Washington, the unexpected but joyous outcome of their unexpected and joyous reunion. Mädchen was expecting again. Franz had just turned four. Hitler and Eva never conceived a child of their own, and Frederick had been nominated as Hitler's future replacement, but with no firm date set for that transfer of power. With the finalisation of the Russian matter, Hitler had achieved all that he had set out to do in 1933 and was taking less and less part in the day-to-day running of the country. The German Bundestag was again reacquiring many of the powers that had been ceded to the Führer. Regular popular elections for the Bundestag were a feature of the German political topography, with a thriving democracy growing within it. The general press had become mostly uncensored, given the lack of any threat to the hugely popular Nazi Government. The European Parliament had acquired much of the foreign policy powers of its member states, including Germany. These new arrangements suited Hitler, given that he was never prone to overexertion. Some would even accuse him of laziness if one could make that accusation without being overheard.

It was the plan of both Hitler and Frederick to return full domestic governance to the Bundestag and its elected Chancellor, with Hitler's post dropping back to that of President, not Führer, holding powers somewhere between that of the English monarch and an American President. It was planned that the German Presidency would become hereditary and not an elected post, and that the control of the military would eventually be handed over to the new European Parliament. The European Parliament consisted of representatives appointed by the governments of all the member states, with the number of representatives being appointed by each state being proportional to that state's population, plus ten permanent members nominated by the German Bundestag, making eighty-seven office holders in total by 1952. Unlike America, not just anyone could become a member of the European Parliaments despite the fact that they were elected posts. It required years of study with the accomplishment of high grades in nominated courses, plus various political apprenticeships, including at least five years at management level in industry, before one could run for election. It had not yet been decided whether the Chancellor of the European Parliament, its executive head, would be elected by its members or by direct election from the European peoples. For the moment, the Chancellor was appointed directly by Hitler. It had been agreed in principle that this post could only be held by a German.

Truman and Frederick were genuinely delighted to see each other again and, after pleasantries, they sat down on the couches in the Oval Office for their meeting. The only other parties present were Truman's long-term Chief of Staff, John Steelman, and Frederick's private secretary. The meeting was to be an informal affair and intended to get matters dealt with quickly and efficiently.

"So a reduction to zero on the tariffs on goods coming from the United States to the EU is acceptable to you, Frederick?" Truman said, and they both laughed.

"Only if we could, Mr. President. I can see you have finely tuned your negotiating skills."

"I have no time for negotiating these days, Frederick. Life is too short, my friend. What can we do amongst ourselves about this terrible matter of being locked out of your European markets?"

"We can do little here, Mr. President, except perhaps identify a general direction for our two trade policies to take. But allow me to reassure you that it is not our intention to lock you out of anything. The EU is abundant with Committees, all of which aggressively guard their allotted power base. What we can and should do here is set the broad parameters of a strategy, and I can promise you little else from this meeting. Matters will need to be worked through at the appropriate levels."

"Ah, yes. German administration, it is indeed a beautiful thing. Gone are the days when two people, two friends, can sit down and decide the destiny of nations."

"Perhaps a good thing, Mr. President."

"Perhaps. But I am catching hell from my constituents about your tariff barriers, access that we need to your lucrative markets on the continent."

"With economic growth the way it is within the EU, we need your goods. Jokes aside, do you really favour a zero-tariff regime? Is that indeed possible?"

"No, not for a long time yet, I fear. But reciprocity may be a worthwhile target, along with reductions in specific areas."

"What areas?"

"Agriculture."

"Can't do it, not with the way you subsidise your farmers."

"And you don't?"

"I think what we should recommend is a duplication, a mirror, reciprocity as you call it. Your tariffs and our tariffs would substantially be locked together, with the lower comparative rate being adopted in each trade category. That will bring about pressure on our side and yours for market access to both America and Europe. Perhaps we should also recommend a one percentage point drop across the board on both sides to be effective immediately and perhaps a similar percentage each year until a nominal figure is reached, say no higher than five percent. Let us see if we can get it past our relevant authorities."

"Done. Let's start there. You see, two friends can agree and get things done without vacillation."

"Congratulations on your re-election, Mr. President. I hear there is talk of a constitutional change that would limit a president to two elected terms."

"Yes, but I think I can sink it. It would leave a second term president with nowhere to go and not enough authority to organise a sack race at a picnic. All the Republicans had to do is come up with a decent candidate to get me out of here."

"Mr. Taft is a fine man, and there is talk he will run again in '56. He and that Nixon fellow almost had you last month."

"Yes, it was close. I don't like Nixon, though, I don't trust him. But regardless, I think it should always be up to the people to decide and it should not be based on some arbitrary rule. What about Germany? When will you have an elected President?"

"Never, I believe. But we are moving toward the Presidency as a Head of State rather than as an executive head of government. Much the same as an olden day monarch with certain veto powers."

"But the Führer is still head of the military."

"And probably will be for the remainder of his tenure. But once he retires, the control of the military will fall to the European Parliament."

"Yes, a United States of Europe, that is quite an accomplishment for you. When do you think the Führer will step down?"

"That, Mr. President, is entirely up to the Führer to decide and no one else. But there is no pressure from any quarter. Hitler remains extremely popular."

"I'll bet he does given what he has achieved over there with your assistance. There would be no hurry to move him along, especially if he is quietly fading into the background."

"He is removing himself from the day-to-day running of the executive and he has always seen that as a necessary process. The 1930s were hard times for us all and the situation needed a firm hand at the helm. But times have changed and we are once again blessed with economic prosperity in large quantity."

Frederick hesitated for a minute but thought that it was time to press the President on a personal matter.

"I have one thing I must ask of you, Mr. President, indeed it is a favour."

"Ask it. I can only say no."

"The parents of a particularly important political ally in Israel, I would rather not say who, want to come to the United States. They will be financially independent and will in fact have capital to start a business here if they wish and to buy a residence. They will initially be provided with a job in the German consulate in New York and we are happy to confirm that in writing to your immigration people. Life in Israel is improving but things are still very difficult. Time is of the essence and I wish to ask you to facilitate their papers?"

"I have never been one to cut across administrative channels but I think given the importance of our relationship we can do something, can't we, John?" the President looked to Steelman.

"I'll arrange it, Mr. President. Just give me their details, Doctor, and I will attend to it."

"I appreciate your assistance and your discretion. I will pass it on. It will be most useful, thank you. I leave for New York by the end of the week and it would be greatly appreciated if the papers could be made available prior to my departure."

Frederick had never forgotten his real parents. He had personally ensured from a distance that they were comfortably transported out of Germany and then properly set up in Israel during the implementation of the European Deportation Scheme. He had made a job available to his father at the German embassy in Israel. He had always ensured that no one, including his parents, ever knew what assistance was being provided by him. He had purchased once again the three-story walk-up on 10th Street in New York that he once owned as Franz and that he had used as his laboratory. This time, however, he bought it in the name of his father. He planned to pass it off as a gift from an anonymous Jewish donor assisting his father because of some kind deed done to the donor by his father but not divulged. He hoped that his father would leave the source of this patronage unexamined. He longed to see them again and planned to do so this trip to New York under the guise of an administrative inquiry about the Deportation Scheme. He had put in place the transfer of his father to the German Consul's offices in New York. He would wait in New York once he had acquired and sent the relevant papers and instructions to the Israeli embassy. He planned to receive his parents personally at his old premises.

Almost three weeks passed before Frederick found himself waiting on 10th Street outside his old home for the car that he had dispatched to the airport to pick up his parents. His parents had put their household goods onto a ship but had flown over at the "urgent request of the German Consul in New York" who apparently required assistance from Franz Senior immediately. When the car pulled up, Frederick was transfixed. All these years, all this effort that he had made to ensure that they were spared the horror that awaited them in the camps in an alternative life. So many thoughts ran through his head. He had succeeded, he had done it, they were alive and unharmed, displaced but alive.

"Mr. and Mrs. Gothenburg, I am pleased to meet you," Frederick said as his father and mother got out of the car somewhat unsure as to why it had brought them to this spot in New York City. "I am Frederick Von Eichmann. I have been sent here by the Department of Internal Affairs to review your transfer."

"We know exactly who you are, Herr Doctor." Both parents hesitated and began what looked like a bow and a curtsey.

"No, no. Don't be silly. There is no need for any formality. I simply wish to understand whether all has gone well for you so that I can report back. I was here in New York in any case on business and I suggested to the Resettlement Department that it may be interesting for me to review your case." No department was interested in what Frederick was doing that day, but no department could refuse his request to do anything that he wished.

"Here are your keys," Frederick said, trying to contain his emotions. "Please come with me."

The Gothenburgs silently followed Frederick up the stoop to the front door of the brownstone. Frederick took the keys from his father's still outstretched hand that held them transfixed and opened the door, and they walked into the entry foyer.

"What, is this?" Franz Senior managed to get out a question.

"It is your new home, Mr. Gothenburg." Frederick, in order to hide his true emotions, had adopted a formal, matter-of-fact demeanour whereby he seemed to simply be performing a duty. He held himself back from hugging both of them and conveying his affection and joy, all of which would have been impossible to explain and dangerous to reveal.

"It is the present of a very wealthy Jewish American who has singled you out for his patronage. He has met you at some point in his life and you had done him some favour, apparently very important to him at the time. Now he is returning your kindness in a way that only very wealthy people can. His only request is that you take it and not seek further explanation or contact."

"I don't understand. This is ours?"

"Here are the deeds of the property and once again your keys, and here are your personal papers. You are free to work in the USA and to apply for citizenship, and this benefit is independent of whether you continue to work for the German Consul. You can read all of that in there. Your citizenship here is guaranteed. You are free to do as you please. We have arranged for the delivery of your things to this place, but in the meantime, there are a few pieces of essential furniture that have been provided as part of the bequest so that you may make yourselves comfortable in the interim."

They had strolled through to the kitchen at the back of the property as Frederick was explaining what was happening. There was a breakfast table and chairs.

"Please sit down here and I will answer your questions and if you don't mind, I have a few of my own."

"I can't begin to tell you how grateful we are to you and who did you say it was that gave us this wonderful place?" Franz Senior asked disbelievingly.

"I did not say who it was nor can I. It is to remain confidential at the donor's request. He has asked that you do not pursue the matter but instead enjoy your new life here."

"Why us?"

"Serendipity."

"This is our house?"

"In your name, yes, see here," Frederick pointed to the header page of the deeds for the property. "May I ask whether you have any children?"

"We did have a boy, but he was lost to us." Mrs. Gothenburg took her husband's hand as tears appeared in her eyes. "We don't know what happened. He just did not return one Sunday evening. There may have been an accident or something worse. We never found out."

"When was that?"

"1936. If I may say, you remind me of him. He would be about your age." Frederick had to get up and walk toward the window so as not to show the expression on his face. "My apologies if I have offended you, Doctor Von Eichmann."

"There is no offence, Frau Gothenburg," Frederick said without turning away from the window. After a silence in order to collect himself, Frederick continued. "Did the deportation go well for you, did you retain all of your possessions?"

"We did. And I managed to get work immediately on arrival in Jerusalem. We have been very fortunate, someone has been looking out for us, I think."

"It is Franz," Mrs. Gothenburg added, overcome with emotion.

"We thought things were going to get much worse in Germany, and we were pleased to see a civilised resolution to it."

"If you call deportation from your ancestral home civilised." Frederick managed to contain himself sufficiently enough to turn around. "Then you were pleased to get the transfer here?"

"It was another godsend. We wanted to contribute in Israel as best as we could, but life there is very hard."

"But improving? I am scheduled to go there again next month."

"Yes, improving, and your visits and interest in Israel are highly regarded. I believe we have you to thank for giving us our homeland back."

"Not at all. It was the doing of the Führer himself, I assure you. You are happy then with your move here?"

"Yes, thank you, very happy. And this gift… we could never have imagined it. Gretchen has always wanted to come to America…"

"Ah! yes, there is a little girl, Gretchen, my…" Frederick almost said sister. He had discovered when arranging the paperwork for their transfer to New York that his parents had conceived another child in Israel. "…My… paperwork says there is a living child."

"Yes. She was born in Israel, an unexpected blessing. We thought we were too old to have another child. She is finishing this semester in school and will join us in two weeks. Everything was such a rush. She is staying with friends."

"She is six now, is that correct?" Frederick was again facing the window so as not to give away anything in his facial expressions.

"Yes, and very precocious, like her brother."

"I am sure that she is wonderful."

"That is very nice of you to say, Doctor Von Eichmann. Would you like to meet her? She is a great admirer of you and your family."

Frederick turned back hurriedly and with an excited expression forgetting his disguise said, "I would… yes, very much." The shocked look on his parents' face caused him to jolt back to reality. "But I cannot stay in New York any longer. I have neglected my duties in Berlin for too long. Perhaps next time."

"That would be our honour, Herr Doctor."

"I would be happy to check in on you from time to time if that is permissible? My little project, you understand."

"Most certainly," the father replied incredulously.

"It is so, then. I will bid you goodbye."

The Gothenburgs were left holding each other's hand and wondering what had fallen into their laps.

Frederick and Mädchen had been out to see a show that evening in New York, and young Franz was asleep in the bedroom of their hotel suite at the Plaza. They had ordered a late supper, and it had been set for them on the balcony as they enjoyed the view and discussed the day. They were still dressed in tuxedo and evening dress.

"You have been distant tonight, Frederick."

"Have I? Perhaps a little pensive, my dear."

"About anything in particular?"

"I met up with a Jewish couple in the Village today. I thought I would like to get some firsthand information about how they had been treated during Deportation. They were working for us in Israel and have come to work here at the German Consulate."

"How fortunate for them."

"Indeed."

"And what did you discover that has made you so introspective?"

"We live very fortunate lives, my dear, you and I and Franz. I wonder if I have done enough for them."

"For this Jewish couple?"

"For the Jewish people more generally."

"My goodness, Frederick. Can you be serious? You placed your position in the Reich at great risk to push this Jewish issue. You have most certainly done more than you needed to do for those people."

"Those people, Mädchen, really?"

"Yes. What do you mean?"

Frederick got up and threw his napkin onto the table. "What if it was our family, Mädchen, that had been sent from pillar to post because of some unholy prejudice? What if the people I met today were your parents?"

"Frederick, darling, matters were getting out of hand in Germany fifteen years ago. Violence against the lesser peoples was on the rise. You almost single-handedly brought it back from the brink, from what could have been awful consequences for them, for us all. You saved these people, Frederick, and Germany. You shouldn't be punishing yourself for not doing enough."

"I love you dearly, Mädchen, but when you talk about one person being lesser or greater than the other, you make me want to cry in despair. Don't you see that we are all essentially the same? People call me the brightest mind in the Reich but am I any smarter than Einstein, or Tesla or these Americans Edison or Julian. I think not. I feel ashamed to put myself in the same sentence with those fellows, a Jew, an Italian, a Dutch Canadian American, and a black man. All of whom I have met and would regard myself privileged to have done so. All very much smarter than I, that much I can assure you."

"That's all very high-minded of you…"

"Please stop there. I cannot hear anymore poison from those beautiful lips of yours." Frederick rubbed his head in frustration and turned again to look out at the darkened park. After a pause, he continued. "There is something I need to tell you, my dear."

"Tell me? I know I frustrate you sometimes but tonight you seem so distant. I don't understand."

"What if I told you that I was a Jew, that your son is a Jew? That the Third Reich will have as its next leader a Jew."

"I am sure that you are trying to illustrate some point, but you forget sometimes that I struggle to keep up with your reasoning."

Frederick went over to her, pulled up his chair, and sat, taking her by the hand intending to tell her everything. But as he looked deeply into her trusting and loving eyes, he said nothing. He had at one glance lost the courage to pursue the conversation any further and instead said that he needed some air and was going for a walk in the park.

He left Mädchen wondering what mistake she had made and what standard in the eyes of her husband she had failed to meet.

CHAPTER FOURTEEN

The Raid of the Secret Augment Lab:
1730 Hours, 2nd December 2065 Washington time
0200 hours 3rd December 2065 Tehran time

The President and his advisors had assembled in the Situation Room at the White House. The recovery operation for the stolen intellectual property had been approved and the new TPS400 Augments had been acquired to undertake it. The identification and probable shipment of incept material being the final trigger that generated urgent action from the White House. The President with his Chief of Staff Hubert McMahon, Deputy Chief of Staff Jim Patterson, the Director of the CIA Fredrick Bennett, the Head of the FBI Daniel O'Brien, now taking a direct interest in the case, and his Assistant Director Eric Riefenstahl who had been dealing with the case for the FBI up to the point of the last meeting, the Chairman of the Joint Chiefs General Harold Brennan and the General in charge of the Middle Eastern Theatre and directly in charge of this operation General Christine Baxter were all attending. The group, eight in all, had a direct hook up with Colonel Griffiths and his team at Kaneohe Bay in Hawaii. Colonel Griffiths was the mission commander and he was up on the big screen briefing the group. From the Situation Room the group could see Colonel Griffiths' twelve-man team sitting at their consoles in front of him with their communications head gear on.

"Did the squad get away on time, Colonel?" the President asked Griffiths.

"Yes, sir. They left here forty-six minutes ago. I'm going to have the J470 standoff in the Gulf of Oman in order to assimilate final telemetry, sir. They are just coming up to that rally point now. We have a second J470 with them which will remain at the rally point and will only be used if needed. We expect to set the squad down 0230 local time as per plan, sir."

The J470 were the new pilotless stealth troop carriers.

"This is a very civilised hour to conduct the operation General Baxter, my compliments," Fred Bennett said, it being only half past five in the afternoon in Washington.

"I'm sure the Iranians wouldn't share your view, Director." General Baxter replied, to the amusement of some.

"Harry, why do you need all those men there with Colonel Griffiths at Kaneohe?" Hubert McMahon asked the Chairman. "Aren't these Augments autonomous?"

"We've doubled up, Mac. Normally, we would only have one sergeant at the base per squad of twelve Augments on the ground at any given op site. But we thought, given the delicacy of this operation, we would put a man on each Augment as a precaution. So, each of those guys has direct one-on-one communication with his Augment. He sees what the Augment sees and talks directly with it and the other squad members as it makes its way through the op."

"We'll get a direct feed from each Augment up here, Harry?" the President asked.

"Yes, sir." General Baxter replied directly to the President. "You can see on the screen straight ahead of you the way Colonel Griffiths is set up. We also have exactly the same display that he is seeing on the screens to your left, sir. So, you can see him and his team directly in front of you in the task room, and you can see the Colonel's console array on the screens to your left. He's got each operative numbered, and he has a direct line of sight to each of his team members at the base from where he is sitting. He will make direct voice commands to those operatives using the allocated numbers as and when he sees fit, and the operative will interpret those commands and convey them to the Augment under that operative's control after considering the situation in which the operative finds his Augment. The human operatives you see sitting there will, for all intents and purposes, be in the action. They will get all the sights, sounds, and even smells from the operations site fed into their headgear. Their headsets are fully three-dimensional, including an insert which has a view of the task room so they don't lose sight of the command environment. I can tell you those headsets take some getting used to; they are quite something, Mr. President. On the Colonel's screens, coinciding with each operative number, he will get the direct visual feed from each Augment as it goes about its assigned task. He's got twelve partitioned screens on his display, one for each Augment, with its number in the top left-hand corner of each screen partition. You can see the numbers there as we look at the Colonel's task room on the big screen. The person sitting to his left and just in front of him is his console operator. The Colonel's eyes won't leave the screens during the operation, so he needs someone to press the buttons. And the two operators directly to his right hand are the Flight Officers for the two J470s. They will be flying each craft; the one closest to him is the Flight Officer flying the J470 that is carrying the team."

"That was most comprehensive, General, thank you. So, the Augments can't do this autonomously?"

"Yes sir, they could, including flying the craft. The Augments already have the operations plan in their heads, so if we lose them, they will carry on regardless. We are taking a belts and braces approach here, sir, one that we normally wouldn't bother to do."

"Are we going to lose them, General?"

"Absolutely not, sir. I'm just saying that we would normally drop the Augments in and let them go about their tasks. And they will do just that if, for some unknown reason, we lose communications."

"God forbid. What are the other five screen segments for, the ones we have showing over here to my right as screens lettered A through E, four of them currently being blacked out?"

"There is one from the J470 carrying the team, screen A, which is the one that is live. That is a direct feed off the forward view cameras from the aircraft. B through E are the feed from each of the four I3200 drone observer pods that the Colonel will deploy above the site during the operation. They are currently dormant, sitting in the launch bay of the craft; that is why there is no feed yet on those screens. They are carried by the J470 to the op zone and they will be deployed from that craft just prior to the set down. They will be reacquired when the J470 extracts the squad."

"So the pods just give him a view from various points above the site?"

"Yes, sir and the approaches to the op site. It assists his tactical intel and provides another level of security. He can move the pods round at will, they hover, and are radar obscured. But they are not just there to provide intel, they are armed to the teeth and employ naked eye masking capability, they can't be seen."

"Armed?"

"Yes, sir. Each pod has pulse weaponry on board."

"So when you say masking capability you mean that they're invisible?" The President pushes.

"They are obscured, sir. The J470 has the same capability. Very hard to see with the naked eye, especially at night, but they are completely invisible to conventional radar. You can see them with the naked eye if they move and you know what to look for, like the swirl of a rifle bullet in flight, it looks like a blur running across your field of view. But if they are still you wouldn't notice them hovering."

"Why don't you equip the Augments with this camouflage?"

"Because they are always on the move. That is one of their great tactical strengths, they move so quickly. Besides they carry a substantial weapons and equipment load already, no room for the camouflage gear even with these new TPS400s."

"You guys have got this down to a fine art," Jim Patterson comments.

"We hope so, Mr. Patterson. However, there is always the unexpected, especially now that you have made that comment," General Baxter replies.

"What, are you superstitious, General?"

"Absolutely, sir. Every soldier is superstitious, Mr. Patterson." There was a nervous chuckle that went around the room.

"Jesus, who's got the popcorn?" Patterson replies.

"Now, now, Jim. This is not for your amusement," his boss, Hubert McMahon, lightly chastises him.

"Superstition aside, Mac, my money's on our guys. Phasers on stun. Let's go!" Patterson replied.

Local time 0230:01 Set Down:

It was a warm night with no breeze in the streets of the mainly industrial suburb of Sadr in Tehran early that Thursday morning. The street was empty of traffic and people. Suddenly, a strong whirlwind blew up, but there was no noise to betray its source; the only sound came from the dust and rubbish being blown around the street. The J470 hovered about six feet off the road as it opened its cargo bay doors two blocks from the target warehouse. The silhouette of the blackened cargo bay could be clearly seen, highlighted against the street lights, as it hung there suspended, seemingly with nothing to buttress it - a hole in space. The i3200s had been deployed and were hovering about thirty feet above the street, moving towards the op site watchfully and silently. The twelve TPS400 Augments alighted from the craft and were gone in a moment as they took off down the street toward the op site. Just as quickly and as unexpectedly, the hole in space closed and the J470 was gone in a blur of wind and bent light. It took up a position about one thousand feet above the op site, completely still and unseen in the night sky, to wait for extraction and to assist with the telemetry from the operation.

"Let me see straight down from the J470," the Colonel was heard to say to his assistant, who adjusted the view from the forward camera of the J470 to the camera installed on the underside of the craft. "And move the third i3200 about five hundred metres east of where it is now and put the second drone over the road halfway to the army base, please. Not all the way there - we don't want to scare the chickens." Except for the Colonel's voice, the task room at Kaneohe and the Situation Room at the White House were silent.

0230:15 Arrival on Site:

The twelve Augments arrived on site, and at the same time, they broke through the fence as if it didn't even exist and fanned out into the yard, moving at high speed towards the warehouse. Three Augments disappeared down the small laneway next to the warehouse to obtain entry from the rear of the building and provide surveillance from that side of the building. There were three Iranian guards next to the northern corner of the building, seated under a light having a smoke and joking loudly as the squad arrived. One of the guards noticed a noise as the Augments breached the fence and he stood up, telling the other two to shut up. Before he could even focus his eyes into the night toward the direction of the sound, each of the three men was struck in the chest by a bright, glowing green pulse about four inches long and about one inch wide. Each guard was rendered immediately unconscious by the jolt of energy the pulse imparted as it struck and penetrated their bodies. It left a burn mark on their uniforms about six inches in diameter.

Augment 12 drew back without instruction but as per plan steeping away from the large roller door of the warehouse. Each squad member, knowing what it was about to do, stood clear. The Augment changed the settings on his pulse rifle to red and it let go four blasts that stuck each corner of the roller door. Bright red and much larger than the pulses used to disable the guards the pulses struck the roller door in its four corners with a large bang and blew large holes out of the sheet metal in the places that it struck and the roller door crumpling came crashing to the ground.

"Knock, knock," Griffiths said out loud.

Augments 3 and 4 picked up the three guards and carried them about two hundred metres up the hard stand outside the front of the warehouse and placed them face up on the concrete lying side by side in a row and then immediately returned to the squad.

0230:29 Entry:

The warehouse door having been breached all but one of the Augments at the front of the warehouse stormed into it just as the three Augments who had gone to the back of the warehouse blasted their way through the back wall. Two of the three Augments at the back entered, arriving into the same large open space of the warehouse darkened except for three small lights showing the entry to the chamber which lay beneath and a light shining through the window of the guard's office in the eastern corner of the building.

"Let me see it, 6," came the command from Griffiths.

With that, Augment 6 pulled three large incendiary devices from its backpack and threw each of them to the roof where they stuck and ignited. The interior of the large warehouse was suddenly lit up like a football stadium. Just as the light filled the darkened warehouse, the guard who was stationed in the corner office of the warehouse opened fire on the squad with his automatic rifle, and three more Iranian Army guards came running out of the office to join the exchange of fire. All four were left lying on the floor near the office doorway as they were simultaneously hit by numerous green pulses fired at them from various members of the Augment squad.

"That's it, baby, take that green shit, man," one of the Augment operators yelled from his console.

"Shut up, 6. Eye on the ball," Griffiths rebuked the operator.

The warehouse looked largely empty except for a few crates sitting on racking and five pallets of material lying on the ground not far from the entry to what they presumed was the lab below.

"6, get a look in those crates." A groan came from the console operator of number 6 Augment as he complied and undertook what he thought was a mundane task. "7 and 8, pull those pallets apart and see what we got," Griffiths barked. "11, get the door that leads to the chamber underneath."

Just then, one of the i3200s opened up in the yard. A small squad of six security guards had come out of an unseen barracks at the far end of the yard about five hundred and fifty yards to the east of the warehouse, having heard the roller door being brought down. The security guards were running towards the warehouse fully armed, and the i3200 had seen them. It had descended without instruction to about fifteen feet off the ground so that the light from its pulse gun couldn't be detected from a distance, and it had opened up on the security squad, immobilising all six guards. It was re-ascending to its monitoring position when Griffiths directed his attention back to the yard and barked, "4 and 5, get out there and clean out that barracks. How the fuck did we NOT know that was there!"

"That can't be it, those six guards, thirteen in total?" Patterson said in a whisper at the back of the Situation Room. Nobody answered. All were gripped by the action on the screen that was unfolding quickly in front of them. They had each pushed back into their seats, overcome by the ferocity and speed at which the operation was moving.

Operative 11 switched his pulse rifle to red and fired one pulse at the large and substantial steel door blocking entry to the chamber beneath. The door exploded upon being struck with the pulse and flew twenty feet into the air, landing with a clang next to Operative 11, which didn't flinch, having accurately tracked the flight of the door. "Fuck me, did you see that?" the operator exclaimed. "These new pulse rifles are great. Hey, Jimbo, go get that door, will ya? I want to do that again!"

"Shut up, 11, and get down there," came the command.

The all-clear came from the barracks at the eastern end of the compound.

"5, stay where you are, 4, get back into the warehouse and help clear the lab," Griffith directed.

"6 and 8, give me a report on that material on the pallets and on the racking and search the remainder of the ground floor of the warehouse. The rest of you, get down there." Griffith was the only one speaking. All seemed to know exactly what they were doing and were doing it very quickly.

0231:30 The Lab

Six Augments ran down the stairs leading to the lab. It was four flights, and they got to the bottom in about the same amount of time as they would have if they had jumped down, which they had mostly done from landing to landing. They didn't take the lift for fear of getting delayed in it or triggering an alarm back at the Iranian army's main security monitoring station about five kilometres away.

Nonetheless, Griffiths assumed that the duty officer back at the Iranian monitoring base had caught on that something was afoot and had raised the alert. He wasn't concerned by that prospect because the base was still five minutes away by truck. He figured he still had a good eight, maybe ten minutes on site if he needed it before reinforcements arrived. He could see no movement from the base in the visual feed from the drone that he had placed halfway to the army base. Nor could he see any other movement from the other three drones in the vicinity of the warehouse that would indicate the presence of further security personnel. Griffiths allowed himself to be reassured by the fact that it probably wouldn't matter even if the reinforcements arrived from the army base.

As they entered the lab, there was a sigh of relief from CIA Director Frederick Bennett and his colleague at the FBI, Daniel O'Brien, as the lab came into view from the headset of the first Augment through the door. The lab did exist. They had gotten it right. There was even more relief as the two AIOGEN instig material boxes came into plain view and could be seen sitting on a stainless-steel examination bench in the corner of the lab. The boxes were still powered up. The President turned back to his intelligence men and said quietly, "Good job," and returned to watching the events unfold in front of them, now with a smile on his face.

The Augments found fourteen laboratory staff working in the lab that night on that level. There appeared to be one further level below still to be examined, and three of the Augments went directly to the connecting staircase to examine what and who was down there. There were three military personnel in an office attached to level one of the lab, one of whom could be seen on the phone through the window of the office, presumably raising the alarm. The two Augments first in the room sprayed it with stun pulses, and within seconds all lab personnel were immobilised and lying on the ground. One of the military personnel from the office had brought his automatic weapon to bear and had opened fire at the Augments just as a green pulse hit him in the chest and he fell to the floor. The guard on the phone got a pulse fired through the window that struck him in the middle of his back. The third, who had come out of the office with his hands in the air, got a pulse in the chest without further discussion of the matter.

Three of the Augments immediately began ferrying the laboratory staff and the immobilised guards to the yard on the surface as the three Augments that went below reappeared on level one of the lab, confirming that there were no further personnel or material of interest in the facility below. On the surface, the Augments were placing the unconscious personnel in one line alongside the first thirteen guards who were lying at a safe distance from the lab, which they shortly intended to incinerate.

The other three Augments began to aggregate all of the electronic equipment and place the equipment on top of three cargo nets that had been spread out flat on the floor of the lab, with a view to using the nets to assist the Augments in transporting the equipment to the surface. One of the Augments carried the AIOGEN boxes separately to the surface to ensure that they didn't disturb the material inside. The entire lab was emptied within three minutes.

"6 and 4, give me another look around the lab. 8, set the charges on both levels of the lab," Griffiths commanded.

Griffiths had one further glance at all the feeds from each of the i3200s to see if there were any further local threats before giving the command, "Flight, give me the J470 on the deck, please."

0235:55 The Extraction

On the surface, the Augments had all the staff and military personnel lying on the concrete in one line side by side, and all of the electronic equipment wrapped up in cargo nets sitting in the middle of the yard with the AIOGEN boxes sitting next to the nets. The J470 descended, opened its cargo doors, and the Augments began to load the equipment and the boxes. Two Augments were still below, doing a final search of the lab with another setting the incendiary charges.

"7, give me a look at their faces," Griffiths turned to his assistant and said, "Run those through the database and find out if any of these guys are coming with us, please." With that, the assistant was grabbing the images of the faces that the Augment was uploading as it walked along the line of personnel lying on the ground, looking particularly for those scientists that had the expertise to make use of the stolen IP. "2, I want you back over with the rest. You too, 5." Griffiths called up the Augments which were on lookout at the back of the warehouse and the one he had left watching the eastern barracks. "3, check to see if anybody is seriously hurt." With that, the last three Augments from the lab made their way out of the warehouse and started to help with the loading.

"Everybody's breathing, no obvious contusions, sir," 3 responded.

The assistant had gotten the results back from the face recognition database check. Griffiths had her give the directions to the Augments directly to avoid any transposition error from him. She had found four scientists from those identified on the list given to Jamison by Professor Salam in Yemen.

"Give me the 14th, 16th, 18th, and 19th in that line starting from this end where you're standing, 7," she directed with clarity and authority, and the Augments began to pick up those designated by Griffiths' assistant and put them onto the transport. In the meantime, the other Augments had completed loading the equipment taken from the lab.

"Everybody in the transport," Griffiths commanded. "2, give me a headcount and an all clear, please."

Augment 2 went around the craft systematically and accounted for each Augment, the AIOGEN boxes, the four lab members, and the three nets full of computer equipment. "Present and accounted for, sir," came the reply only seconds later as the Augment sat and buckled up with the rest of the squad.

"Get 'em out of there, Flight."

0236:48 Liftoff

All equipment, personnel, and Augments were on board and the J470 began to ascend. Griffiths gave the order, "Light it up, 8," at which time Augment 8 pressed the detonator for the charges they had placed in the lab. There were several explosions, and within seconds the whole warehouse was seen to be in a ball of flames. All four i3200s were reacquired without incident on ascent.

"Anything on the radar?" Griffiths asked his console operative, who gave him a negative response.

"Bring it home, Flight. That's a wrap," Griffiths said, getting up out of his command seat to go over to his men and congratulate them on a good operation. Most of the operatives were already unbuckled and doing some congratulating of their own.

"What was the op time you called in the meeting with the President a week ago?" General Brennan turned around from where he was sitting and asked General Baxter.

"6:45, sir," she replied.

"Missed it, Baxter, you're slipping. I read it as seven minutes even." General Brennan turned back to the communications screen and said, "Good job, Colonel," Brennan had to raise his voice to be heard in the rowdy Task Room, "give your people a well-done for me, will you, and let me know when the J470 is back at base, please."

"There's no chance they can catch that J470?" Patterson asked.

"Catch it?" Brennan said, "They can't even see it."

"Outstanding," the President said, slapping the arms of the chair and rising to his feet. "And that, my friends, is how you do that. I tell you what! Given the time of day, would anybody care to join me for a drink in the residence? I assume it will be at least a couple of hours before I get a phone call from the Iranian embassy."

CHAPTER FIFTEEN

It was the European summer of 1963, and in August, the Von Eichmann family had made their annual trek south to the French Riviera for a holiday along with a significant proportion of the German population. The country basically closed down in August to allow the affluent German community to holiday at their chosen destinations, mostly in the south of France, Italy, and Sardinia. Hitler had, as usual, gone up to Berghof, his mountain retreat near Berchtesgaden, preferring the mountain air of the Bavarian Alps to the sand and sea, happier to revisit the history and memories that he and Eva had accumulated there. Frederick and Mädchen would join them in about three weeks, but for now, Frederick and his family had headed south to Nice where they owned a holiday home on the beach near Saint-Jean-Cap-Ferrat. The home was on sizable acreage, and the family kept a conspicuously large motor yacht moored at the end of the long pier that they had specially constructed for their private use, which stretched out into the bay. For anyone else, there would have been planning restrictions preventing the construction of such a jetty, given the beauty of the coastline, but such rules did not apply to the Von Eichmanns. They enjoyed all the benefits allowed to a man of Frederick's position and wealth, and he felt no need to deny himself or his family access to such luxuries.

This year, the Gothenburgs had joined Frederick and his family there, at Frederick's expense, with their daughter Gretchen, now eighteen and just about to enter college at Harvard University. Frederick had nurtured the relationship with the Gothenburgs.

Mädchen and his son Franz, now sixteen, and his daughter Gretel, now twelve, had become accepting of the close ties that had evolved over the years between the two families. It had not been an easy proposition for Frederick to assimilate his biological parents, never identified, into the family circle given the predispositions of the day. But at the family compound in Nice, away from the glare of the Berlin media, they found themselves in a comfortable setting within which they could all enjoy a summer break.

Frederick had become quite the entrepreneur and was very wealthy, independent of his adopted family and regardless of the privileges provided to him by his position in the Reich. He had selectively and discreetly used his knowledge of markets and trends from his previous timeline to ensure an aggregation of wealth unseen outside the Americas of the early 1900s. He was considered the wealthiest man in Europe, and it was widely seen as a wealth that he had obtained via prudent and expeditious endeavour rather than one obtained surreptitiously and corruptly by using his position in the government. The fact that he had not abused his authority to make his fortune, or indeed in the execution of any of his formal public duties, had made him even more highly regarded by the German people, and indeed by Hitler, who saw himself reflected in Frederick. Frederick had always been munificent, but his philanthropy was less altruistic, designed more to placate his conscience given the unfair advantage he enjoyed compared to other investors. But he had never denied himself or his family anything.

Frederick had found himself torn over the years as to where or even whether he should use his knowledge of events to intervene in the progression of world affairs. He had never stepped in to expedite the development of new scientific developments, always being uncertain as to whether his intervention in such matters would cause unseen complications that would send world history off in directions unpredicted and unwelcome. He had never lent his mind to the development of weapons of war, a matter that he saw as sacrosanct in the hierarchy of disciplines that he had judiciously assembled around himself to help him navigate his circumstances without going insane.

Social trends and the people that surrounded them, including political leaders, scientists, and writers all seemed to make their way into public view at around the same time as they did in the previous timeline. Frederick was constantly reminded how robust the unfolding of events remained despite his interventions in Germany in the thirties and forties. People he remembered in the old timeline still found their way to prominence in this one and to his constant surprise, events and trends reappeared on schedule and as per his expectations. He was particularly glad that financial events tended to repeat themselves as per his recollection because that allowed him to profit from their reoccurrence.

He had never told Mädchen or his family about the true reason that he had fostered the relationship with the Gothenburgs or about his own true origins. He had on occasion, like that time on the balcony of the Plaza in New York, come close to revealing his real identity but had on all such occasions concluded that the truth was too bizarre to believe and the telling of it would only cause him and his family pain and risk the undoing of that which he had so diligently sought to construct. There were times when he felt the need to seek council but he had always denied himself of it. The uncertain consequences for him, his family and more broadly for mankind had always prevented him from divulging his origins to anyone. He had even considered meddling in personal matters of the heart. Now with his wealth and stature, he thought of paying a visit to his college girlfriend in the other timeline whom he had come to love deeply when he first went to Harvard and who had dropped him for a protestant boy from a wealthy family just as they all graduated. It was an event that scarred him early in life and left him less capable of forming permanent bonds with any woman after her. He often fixated over the great seduction and then abandonment of her as retribution for what she had done to him in a past life. He had even gone as far as to enquire about her attendance at the university in this timeline and found that she was indeed there, even staying in the same dorm as she did before. But it was, in the end, always left as a pleasant fiction because he was never able to reconcile its undertaking with his love and commitment to

Mädchen. Mädchen indeed compensated him fully, he rationalised, for many such objectionable matters in his earlier life.

There was, however, an event approaching that he was finding most difficult to ignore. It was only three months away, if it reoccurred on schedule, and he would have to act now if he was going to act at all. It was precisely this matter that was on his mind this day that found him on his terrace overlooking the Mediterranean Sea admiring his motor yacht, salt air in his face, as Mädchen came out with a tray of tea and biscuits, bringing him back to the pleasant reality and the circumstances that he had so assiduously created.

"Such a beautiful day."

"Yes, my dear, but it pales in comparison to your beauty," Frederick responded, smoking his cigar, awakening from his considerations ever ready to count his blessings.

"You always have something nice to say to me, Frederick. Have I told you lately how lucky you make me feel? I am so glad we bought this property," Mädchen said, pausing to take in the view, standing next to him, hands on her hips, making that assessment. "It's a little piece of heaven, isn't it?"

"Ahh! Tea," Frederick said, noticing the contents of the tray that Mädchen had placed on the table behind him. "We have, in fact, been able to learn a thing or two from the English after all."

"Yes, dear."

"Where are the children?"

"On the beach, I think."

As they spoke, Franz and Gretchen came through the open French doors of the balcony to confirm their whereabouts and inform the parents, the good children that they were, of their next escapade. They were hand in hand in bathing clothes, having just come up from the private beach tanned after several days in the sun, healthy, each with a towel wrapped around their waists. She was in a bikini, the latest fashion, looking very much the grown woman, and he was so obviously aware of her womanhood.

"We're just going to have a dip in the pool, to get the sand and salt away. What time is lunch, Mutter?" Franz asked.

"Where are the two youngsters?" Mädchen replied.

"They are in the library with Mr. Gothenburg, playing Scrabble."

"Lunch will be in an hour. Make sure you get dressed before you come to the table, please," Mädchen said.

Frederick was alarmed and distressed as the two adolescents rushed off to the pool. Mädchen could see the concern on his face.

"You're just noticing that now," she said. "They've been at it ever since we got here."

"That can't be," Frederick responded, "I mean, that it can't be!"

"What's wrong? You're the one that's been going on and on about overcoming social limits. Are you saying they can't be involved because she's a Jew? You surprise me, Frederick."

Frederick extinguished his cigar and made his way over to the balcony railing and yelled down to the lawn where the two teenagers who were crossing it hurriedly were headed towards the pool.

"Can I see you two please for a moment in my study? I'll come down."

Mädchen grabbed Frederick by the arm as he made his way past her towards the French doors of the balcony. "Don't say anything to them you will regret, Frederick. You need to practice what you preach."

Frederick pulled his arm away from her hand and, without answering, left to go downstairs. Mädchen followed him.

"What is it, Dad?" Franz said as he came into the study with Gretchen trailing behind, Mädchen already there and about to plead with Frederick to say nothing. The elder Gothenburg came in to see what the fuss was about.

"I don't want you two to be seeing each other, not in that way."

"Dad?"

"You can't become serious about Gretchen. Is that clear?"

"What, why? Is it because she is a Jew?" Franz and Gretchen looked horrified.

"I am not going to give you my reason. I am telling you, and I want you to respect my wishes."

"Dad. I can't do that." Franz reached around to take Gretchen's hand. "We are in love with each other."

"Rubbish. You are only sixteen, and she's not much older. What do you know about such things?"

"You were married at eighteen. I know as much as you did then."

"Don't be smart with me, boy. You know nothing about me. I might have been eighteen, but… I knew a hell of a lot more than you do now."

"Dad?"

Gretchen left crying, and Franz followed her, casting a disgusted look back at his father.

"I never thought you capable of it, Frederick," Mr Gothenburg said. "How…" he stopped what he was about to say. "We should get our things," and he turned to leave not saying anything further, remembering how much he owed Frederick and that he had no right to question his motives.

"Wait," Frederick said.

Mr Gothenburg turned back to face Frederick and looked into his eyes.

"I can't be angry with you, Frederick, with all that you have done. But we are not welcome here, it is clear."

"Mädchen, can you see to the children, please. Mr Gothenburg, Franz, can I talk to you for a moment? Please, sit. I have a story for you that will be difficult for you to hear and difficult for me to tell. Mädchen, can you close the door behind you… please, dear." Mädchen left thinking she would like to hear it as well.

Frederick and his father sat down with Frederick having the full intention to tell him the truth behind his outburst. He began with great difficulty.

"There is something you need to know about me, that you and your wife both need to know about me." Frederick paused and collected his thoughts. He started to form the words that Gretchen was his sister and that she could not be bonded sexually to his son. But they were not the words that came out of his mouth. "I am not anti-Semitic. You must know that by now." He paused again finding his proposed disclosures very difficult to articulate. "But you were there, in Germany, in the thirties and you know how far we have come from then to now and how close we as a nation came to a precipice, an outcome much uglier than deportation."

"I do, Frederick. And I know that you are the person that drew us back from that calamity."

"There remains much to do. There is much public education still to undertake. I cannot risk, we cannot risk any mistake."

Frederick had already introduced many changes to the public services and police departments, procedures aimed at ensuring that over time racism would be weeded out but the old prejudices still remained.

"I will be taking over the Presidency in less than two years. I need the support of the people to achieve the remainder of what is left to be done. I would risk losing that support if my son was to marry into a Jewish family. I am sorry to say it and I hope with all my heart that it won't be so forever. But it is so now."

Frederick had backed away once again from disclosing the reality of his situation. As much as Frederick didn't like to admit it, the changing of public opinion in Europe had been slow. The absence of the horror of the Holocaust, an event that demonstrated so clearly the inhumanity of racist beliefs and the misery generated by fundamentalism, had made his task much harder than he at first thought it would be. In a strange way, the absence of the consequences of racism had nurtured their endurance. He had attempted to vilify Stalin because of his treatment of the Jews but it didn't seem to have the same impact on public opinion as had the disgust and horror that the Holocaust generated. For some reason, Stalin was simply thought of as a communist dictator whose genocide seemed motivated by issues broader than just racism. Frederick didn't understand why it was viewed any differently than that which Hitler had once perpetrated. He remained committed to re-educating the European public in regard to the futility and fundamental evilness of racist beliefs.

"I can see what you are trying to achieve, Frederick, and what indeed you have already achieved. It is not proper for me to criticise your motives. Can I ask you to consider that it may be just what our society needs, to have such a union in a family as prominent as your own. But perhaps you are right and I will not go against you. Nonetheless, I think we should leave to avoid any further complications."

Frederick's heart was broken and he could not even stand to argue as his father left the room. He knew that if he told him the truth and was believed it would mend a hole in his father's heart that had tortured him ever since their son disappeared in 1936. But could he ever be believed and if he was what did he risk in achieving the acceptance of that truth. He felt so very alone.

Just three months later, it was approaching midday on November 22nd, 1963 in Dallas, Texas.

A member of the highly secretive Geheime Staatspolizei, the German Secret State Police, the GSP but once called the Gestapo had hidden himself on the sixth floor of the Texas School Book Depository building on the North West corner of Elm and North Houston Streets. The GSP also had operatives in the Dal-Tex building across the road and two snipers in the railroad interlocker tower overlooking the car park and the picket fence just north of the grassy knoll that lay alongside Elm Street. The agents had temporarily anesthetised Lee Bowers who was operating the rail switches in the tower on that day.

The operative on the sixth floor of the book depository lay in wait for a person that they had been tracking for the last three months, a person that they had previously identified as Lee Harvey Oswald. They knew Oswald was in the building, but it wasn't Oswald who opened a window facing Elm Street and set himself up with a 6.5 Italian Mannlicher Carcano rifle, propping it up on a set of boxes intending to use the weapon to fire out the window. The GPS agent on the sixth floor with him put two bullets into the chest of the gunman using a silenced Lugar45 Long Frame and walked over to the window and put one further bullet into the gunman's brain. The agent crouched down and looked out the window to ensure that no one had seen what had just transpired and then signalled his colleagues by radio on the seventh and fifth floors that they were free to leave the building now that the gunman had been killed. The agent took photos of the dead assailant and then left the building and as he left, peered inquisitively at Oswald sitting in the tearoom having a cup of coffee, seemingly oblivious to what was happening on the sixth floor.

About thirty minutes later, the snipers in the railway tower saw two men get out of a pickup truck and come up to the picket fence of the car park. They took weapons out of a duffle bag and set themselves against the picket fence above the grassy knoll just as the President's car turned into Elm Street. Both men were killed instantly by a single shot to the back of the head from the silenced Karabiner 98k rifles being used by each of the two Gestapo snipers in the railway tower. Both snipers packed up their equipment and left after ensuring that Mr Bowers was sleeping peacefully. There was no one suspicious to be seen in the Dal-Tex building as the GSP agents vacated their positions there immediately after they were told that the snipers had hit their marks.

Frederick was waiting in the White House anteroom to see President Kennedy the next morning at 11:00 a.m. Frederick had insisted that the previously arranged meeting go ahead even given the frightening events of the day before, and he had enough clout in Washington not to be refused. He had asked that only Jack and Bobby be at the meeting. Frederick had brought with him the Head of the GSP and a large briefcase carrying photos, films, surveillance wire taps, and explanatory documents that related to the attempted assassination of the day before.

Jack Kennedy had been elected in 1960 as per the old timeline, although his road to the White House had taken somewhat of a different path this time around. His father failed to gain party endorsement for a crack at the Presidency in 1956 with Truman not seeking another term. Joseph lost the Democratic nomination to Carey Estes Kefauver with Jack Kennedy chosen to be his running mate ahead of Albert Gore Sr. to the surprise of most at the Conference. The election was subsequently won, thanks mostly to the vigorous campaigning by Truman on Kefauver's behalf, with Kefauver becoming the 34th President of the United States. In 1960, however, Kefauver did not seek a second term due to his health; a heavy smoker and drinker, he subsequently died of a heart attack in 1963. Kennedy was elected in a landslide as the Democratic candidate for the 1960 election with his father, then seventy-two years old, happily taking a back seat and throwing his now considerable political weight behind his number two son.

Jack Kennedy beat Richard Nixon by a considerable margin, unlike the close call in another life with Kennedy having the White House experience this time around and Nixon having no national profile because he never was Vice President for eight years to Dwight David "Ike" Eisenhower who was at the time, and remained by 1960, a retired general. With no White House experience and having been trounced by Jack Kennedy in 1960, it was unlikely, Frederick noted with some satisfaction, that Nixon would ever be President.

"They were going to kill you," Frederick began dramatically, now in the Oval Office.

"You know something about what happened yesterday?" the President said, walking over to Frederick, his comments amplified by his distress at yesterday's events.

"We have had them under surveillance for nearly three months."

"Wait, wait," Bobby interrupted. "You knew these guys were going to take a pot shot at my brother?"

"Allow me to play a recorded conversation for you; perhaps it will give you some context."

The Head of the GSP, Hans Gruber, pressed the play button on a recorder that he had brought with him.

"You have something on your mind, Jim?"

The unmistakable voice of Lyndon Johnson pervaded the room. Jim Henderson was a senior operative at the CIA.

"You need to do something about your Boston buddies. They have become a substantial threat to this country," Henderson responded.

"You think."

"We have devised a solution."

"So why are you sitting there talking to me."

"We need your help to organise a trip for our friends to Dallas. We have resources there that we can use."

"Why Dallas?"

"Long story."

"I have a feeling I don't want to hear it."

"You've been making noises lately about foreign policy changes that you would implement if it was all up to you."

"Sure, we're chasen' the wrong rabbits and usen' the wrong dogs to do it."

"You know we have munitions left that we built for the European war that didn't happen that goes back to Roosevelt's time. We need to destroy them or dump them on some third world country so that our contributors in the military manufacturing industry can make some money. We are capitalists in this country not communists."

"So, a Dallas trip it is, then."

"I have no idea what you are talking about."

"Yes, you do."

After a long silence on the tape.

"I'm sick of having these Ivy League frat boys embarrass me. So, when?"

"It's up to you. Make sure you go along so you can give us the itinerary."

"We could all probably use a campaign trip to the South, I guess."

"That's the idea. Let me know."

The tape was stopped.

"Are you saying that a trip was organised for the purpose of assassinating my brother?" Bobby asked.

"But Lyndon was there, in the car ahead," Jack adds.

"Hiding under the seat if you check the TV footage," Frederick clarified. "He organised the trip, right?"

"Yes, Lyndon organised it. How the hell did you get that tape?"

"That's a silly question," Frederick explained. "We heard rumblings of an attempt on your life, we worked backwards from what we knew of activity in Texas."

"Worked backwards?"

"Why do it if you don't get what you want if you succeed."

"The CIA was involved," Bobby asked incredulously.

"You Americans are so naïve. The CIA and FBI control your press and the public mood better than Goebbels's ever did ours. They permeate your life. They believe they have the right to make decisions like this for and on behalf of a stupid uninformed nation, just ask them."

"We have a free press."

Frederick laughed out loud.

"Your press relies on information acquired through government leaks. They believe those leaks without question, and in part, they have to believe them or risk losing their sources for lack of cooperation. The CIA leaks what they want to leak. The press is not the guardians of your democracy, and without an independent free press, democracy doesn't work; you'd be better off with a system like ours."

"So you've known about this so-called plot for some time?"

"We hadn't alerted you to it because we were not sure until the very end who was pulling the strings. By letting you know, we would have risked them flying the coop. We didn't know whether or not there was someone in this very office that was involved."

"Let me get this right. It was your people who shot those guys yesterday?" the President said.

"Yes," Frederick responded.

"How the fuck do we know that it wasn't you doing all the shooting and cleaning up after you left?" Bobby continued.

"Settle down, Bobby," Jack intervened, "let's hear what they have to say."

"Well, you were not shot, may I point out. The three men shot were all heavily armed and lying in wait for your cavalcade. Don't you think it's a little suspicious that they were there? You would have been dead on a slab if we hadn't been there to take care of you."

The President was momentarily caught between his emotions, gratitude and alarm, and didn't know what to think. "So what do you think happened?"

"They were all ex-CIA operatives, except Oswald in the book depository, who was to be the patsy. I assume you will find their identities in your CIA personnel files if you haven't already. Lee Harvey Oswald, who has a pro-Castro background, was duped into being in the book depository. He was going to be your assassin."

"CIA acting under whose instructions?"

"You heard the tape."

"And your guys were there to meet them, is that what you're saying?"

"Yes, we were there, and lucky for you that we were. The assassins knew Oswald, through their contacts at the CIA, and had decided to use him for this operation because of his delusions. The plan was to have him take the blame, knowing that the American people would want an immediate resolution of the matter."

"I'm flabbergasted. Johnson?"

"We waited until the last minute to get the best answer we could to that very question. They tried to do it through the mob. The mobster that they tried to involve thought he had an implicit deal with your father when they assisted him with your election in 1960 in Chicago, a deal that they think was breached, by you. Instead of going easy on them, Bobby has been kicking their ass all over town."

"We know nothing about any deal with any mobster and our father," Bobby replied.

"This group had arranged for Oswald to be assassinated upon his arrest. They intended to anonymously finger Oswald to the local police straight after the shooting, tell them where he was hiding, and have him take the blame. Then once he was arrested, they planned to kill him to shut him up. The guy who was going to shoot Oswald was a local bar owner with links to the mafia, Jack Ruby."

"It *was* Jack Ruby? They had intended to use him to further diffuse attention away from themselves and towards the mafia?"

"They felt that Ruby killing Oswald would bring an end to any investigation. But with their plan foiled, they had no further use for Ruby and it was he that was the loose end. They hit him last night at his bar."

"So everyone who can confirm your story is dead."

"We had little time to consider it but I am surprised by your comment. You Americans usually see violence as a solution to any given problem."

"This from the adopted son of Adolf Hitler."

"The fact is that the assassination attempt was afoot and having waited as long as we did, we had to kill the shooters to ensure your safety. The phone tapes and documents that are in this briefcase will answer all your questions. Do with it what you will. We thought that you may want to keep this under your hat and claim that the shootings yesterday were a foiled assassination attempt, perhaps foiled by the upper echelons of your Secret Service. The truth is they were asleep at the wheel yesterday. But I can tell you this for sure: you getting these guys so quickly and decisively will give your enemies cause to reconsider trying again. They won't know how you knew about the attack and the decisiveness and cold bloodedness of yesterday's action will leave them thinking that maybe they shouldn't fuck with you or Bobby at all."

"I can see why they might think that. I'm thinking that about you."

"You have nothing to fear from me. I am your friend. That said, you need to do something about Johnson, for as long as he is VP he may try again. But may I suggest in any case that you stop driving around with your head sticking out of the car."

"So, you have given us all the results of your investigation?"

"Yes. Whether you chose to continue the investigation is up to you."

"How did you come across the plot?" Bobby asked again.

"I can't tell you anything further about how we hooked into this matter. Just put it down to German efficiency."

"I know Truman always thought a lot of you, Frederick. I can now see why. We seem to owe you a debt."

"In that case, allow me to claim it now. You have a fine mind, Mr President, as does your brother. You are not governed by the influences that infest this capital. You have great instincts for the truth in things political and are amongst the very few politicians who have ever shown the inclination and the courage to do what is right whatever the consequences. I am going to ask you to use this second chance, if I may call it that, to follow your heart. Make the difference for the American people that you always promised and that they always thought you capable of making."

"Of course."

"Then with your indulgence, gentlemen, we can call this matter at an end… and Mr President, may I strongly suggest you clean house with your security arrangements. Surely, there are better people available than those on show yesterday. Thank you for meeting with us."

Frederick and the Head of the GSP were ushered out and Bobby and Jack remained to put their heads together on what had transpired.

"What do you make of that?" the President said to his Attorney General as the Oval Office door closed behind Frederick.

"It scares the living shit out of me, that's what I make of it, and I'm not talking about what happened yesterday. I wouldn't trust these guys as far as I could throw them."

"They are senior members of a totalitarian state. Herr Doctor is set to take over there in '65."

"He doesn't think a lot of our State either, apparently, but it wouldn't surprise me if they staged all of this themselves to bring influence to bear on us."

"There's not much we can get from the so-called conspirators, they are all dead."

"Killed by the CIA or the GSP?"

"How the shit would they find out about something like that in the first place. It must be all bullshit. They must have put it together themselves. They shoot up a few guys, leave a trail of dead bodies and then dump a case full of dummied up wire tapes on my desk and think I'll fall all over him," the President said. "I always thought this guy's relationship with Truman was a bit dodgy, maybe he tried the same bullshit with Harry."

"The question is what we do about it. We can't have them coming in here and shooting the place up, killing American citizens."

"Condescending bastard. They are certainly dangerous, that much we know. I think they are telling us that they can reach in here any time they like and knock us off. He's right about one thing and that is our guys were asleep at the wheel yesterday. Get McBride over here and we'll see what the CIA has to say about this."

"The Germans are not our friends, Mr. President," was McBride's opening statement as he sat down with Bobby and President Kennedy later that afternoon. "They possess sufficient nuclear firepower to blow us off the map several times over. We have fallen behind them in the development of nuclear and military resources and in rocketry. We believe they will make an attempt next month to put a man in orbit. I assure you, Mr. President, that we had better catch up fast."

"Truman thought an awful lot of this Von Eichmann guy," the President said.

"He felt that Von Eichmann had something to do with avoiding a full-scale European war and he credited him with keeping the US out of it. There are people that say that we should have brought it on with the Germans then and got it over and done with. Now we have a German totalitarian state to deal with, a massive economic and military Goliath that has the largest nuclear armoury in the world," McBride asserted. "To bring on a fight with them now would be suicide."

"And Truman thought that the solution the Doctor came up with for the European Jews was a good resolution of a difficult situation," Bobby added.

"If you call having every last mother's son of them deported a good solution. They were more German than Jewish," Jack replied. "What can be worse than that, getting tossed out of your own homeland? I'm not sure many Jews would thank him for it."

"If I may quote popular opinion, Mr. President, fuck the Jews. We should arrest Eichmann before he leaves the country."

"That was possibly the stupidest thing I have ever heard you say, Mr. Director," Bobby asserted.

"More to the point, John, what the fuck happened yesterday?" Jack asked pointedly, moving away from any discussion of Eichmann's arrest.

"We have no idea. There was nothing on our radar."

"Well, there fucking well ought to have been," Bobby stood and pointed his finger at McBride. "My brother was left hanging out on the line yesterday. You are paid to know about these things and you've got nothing on your radar." The President gestured for Bobby to sit back down and he obliged but continued. "What the fuck are you guys doing over there, reading comic books all day?

There were at least five gunmen in that street and you say you have nothing. Well, fuck me!"

"If you want my resignation, Mr. President…"

Jack interrupted him, "John, no… we want answers, not scapegoats. We had the Head of the GSP in here this morning telling us that we had a conspiracy of ex-CIA operatives trying to assassinate me. He says he has a case full of proof, that case sitting right there. It contains proof of their ring leader – the Vice President."

"You had the Gestapo in here. They were involved. Well, there's your answer. CIA… ridiculous. Lyndon is as loyal to you as any VP in history. You can't believe a word those bastards in the Gestapo say."

"There can only be two possibilities," the President continued calmly despite McBride's interjection. "One is that Von Eichmann was right and if so, all you guys over at the CIA should be sent packing. Or the Germans organised it themselves as a show of strength in an attempt to intimidate me."

"Well, I think you have all the answers you need. A CIA conspiracy or German muscle men? Do you really need to think hard about that?" Jack looked at Bobby, not so convinced it was an easy choice. "If they were there, then we need to act, Mr. President. They can't be taking pot shots at our Head of State and expect to walk away from it."

"Do what, John?" Bobby asked. "Shoot back?"

"Maybe. I would need to work up some options."

"Look, that's a good idea. Why don't you do that and take that briefcase with you? I want to know whether there is any reliable information in those files. And find out whether any of those dead bodies yesterday ever worked for or with the CIA. John, give it to your top guy and tell him to keep his mouth shut until we decide what we are going to do." McBride got up to leave, but the President continued. "And John, we need to talk some more about what happened yesterday and why you guys knew nothing about it. My office, tomorrow morning at 7:00 a.m. I want some answers… please."

The meeting reconvened the next morning at 7:00 a.m. sharp. Bobby and Jack had brought their Chief of Staff and longtime friend Kenneth O'Donnell into their confidence, and he was in attendance as McBride and his Head of Forensics sat for the meeting in the Oval Office. No one else attended, and the President had assumed that no one else had been told.

"What do you have for us, John?" the President began, seated in his rocking chair between those assembled.

"Everything in the suitcase is fake, everything," McBride asserted. "It was all dummied up to dupe you and Bobby into thinking they had saved you from an internal conspiracy to have you killed."

"You're certain?"

"And none of those guys yesterday ever worked with the CIA. The Oswald guy had been under surveillance at some point for pro-Castro activity, and he had tried to defect to Russia, but they had nothing concrete on him. Ruby was up to his neck with the mob, and in debt to them, who knows or cares why he was killed, but I think it's obvious."

"That's it?" Bobby responds. "You had no line on any of these guys?"

"None. And look, here is an example of the German's handiwork." McBride pulled out an enlarged photograph and put it in front of the President. "It supposed to be this Oswald guy standing there with the gun he was going to use to shoot you. Any fool can see that the shadows don't line up. All this stuff has similar telltale signs of forgery."

"So let me get this right," Ken O'Donnell chimes in, "these Germans come out here and put on the most elaborate circus you could ever wish to see, shoot up the place, kill people, and risk a serious international incident for what? To curry favour with the boys here? Bullshit. Von Eichmann has already got more muscle in this town than he will ever need."

"You would prefer to believe it was a domestic conspiracy, Mr. O'Donnell?" was McBride's response.

"You don't need to be a genius to know that a shitload of your guys, present and past, were pissed off with us because we held off the air support in that Bay of Pigshit disaster that you walked us into," O'Donnell pressed, "and a shitload of mobsters were unhappy with Jack about getting nothing in return for what they saw as their support in Chicago, except of course for a very effective anti-organised crime offensive from Bobby here. And LBJ's ego and ambitions, my God, they are as big as the state he comes from."

"You should be careful about the accusations you make, Mr. O'Donnell."

"You threatening me, sir?" O'Donnell was on the edge of his seat about to stand, pointing at McBride. "I can tell you this: I don't like you, sir, or the people you work with. You scare the living shit out of me, a hell of a lot more than these fucking Germans do, that's for sure."

"Let's keep it on point, shall we?" the President intervened. "Sit back down, Ken." The President waited until O'Donnell had settled back in his seat. "So, your conclusion, John, is that this was a ruse?"

"Yes, sir." McBride was looking back and forth between the President and O'Donnell, not sure whether to further refute O'Donnell's allegations.

"That the Germans themselves were solely responsible for it? They wheeled in some of their own operatives and then shot them in front of national television," the President pushed.

"Yea… that's it, sir."

"Now, wait a minute…" O'Donnell started up again.

"Just hold off for a moment, will you, Ken?" The President had put his hand out as if to stop O'Donnell from getting up without taking his gaze from McBride as he tried to get a fix on the reliability of the information he was being fed. "And your proposed course of action, John?"

"We need to hit 'em back. Otherwise, we look like a bunch of scared rabbits, to put it in the parlance that your friend here might understand."

"Like what?"

"Like for like. Keep it proportional. We make an attempt on his life just to show that he is vulnerable if he wants to try that shit with us. He's in Israel next week. We have some good contacts there and there are any number of disaffected locals we can call on. There are a number of groups around that area that don't like the way the Germans implanted the Jewish State there to solve a German domestic problem."

"How long would you need to set that up, John?"

"Well, the best part of a week."

"John, thanks, we'll let you know."

"Yes, sir." McBride and his associate got up to leave.

"John, we'll let you know, is that clear?" the President repeated. "Until then, do nothing."

"Yes, sir." And the two men left.

"Jesus, Jack," O'Donnell was straight into the face of the President as the door closed behind McBride.

"Just hold on a minute, Ken. Let's walk this through."

"I wish I had looked through the bag that von Eichmann left," Bobby said.

"Well, it's too late now. Those guys at the CIA have got it or what's left of it. God only knows what they've done to that stuff," O'Donnell asserted.

"If they've done anything to it," the President replied. "You're assuming that the Director is lying to his President. That's a pretty big jump, Ken. Look, gentlemen, work with me here. If the Germans had obtained information about an assassination attempt and acted in good faith, as they assert, then two things would need to be true. One is they have very good information sources, perhaps too good to be believably possible. And second, they had very good motives…"

"…Perhaps too good to be believably possible." Bobby finished the President's sentence for him.

"I believe it," O'Donnell said. "It makes perfect sense to me. You say their motives are too good to be true, but what could they hope to gain that would in any way equal the risk of acting in this way? On the other hand, some of those CIA guys, ex-CIA or otherwise, they are utterly mad, and I don't need to tell you what the Mob is capable of. Look what the CIA did to us as soon as you walked into office. Welcome to the Cuban revolution, baby, here's a shit-burger for you to eat."

"Kefauver authorised that operation, not me."

"Yeah, they fed him the same nonsense they're feeding us right now," O'Donnell insisted. "Look, Jack, fire all of them. Shut them down and do it today. And send a thank you card to this Eichmann guy. Consider if what he says is true."

"Ken, thank you. Could you please leave Bobby and me alone now? We appreciate your input." Ken looked back at the President, wanting to push his point of view further. "Please, we appreciate your help with this."

On the morning of December 19th, 1963, one week after the foiled assassination attempt on President Kennedy in Dealey Plaza, Frederick and Mädchen travelled to Jerusalem, the new city of religious enlightenment, for their semi-compulsory twice-yearly visit. Frederick brought news of what he believed was renewed American political support for the Israeli State, wrested from the hands of the nearly assassinated President. Several official meetings had been lined up for Frederick to discuss matters, including economic development and national security. Frederick was a trusted advisor to the State of Israel, a trust partly borne of necessity. Nonetheless, his input into such matters, peripheral or otherwise, was seemingly well-regarded across all facets of Israeli politics.

What he hadn't told his biological father in Nice was still weighing on his mind. He had accepted his father's promise to understand and not interfere, but it still gnawed at his heart. The relief his father would have shown had he told him the truth, assuming he would have believed it, was playing over and over in his head like a movie. He was obsessing to the point of potentially unbalancing his mind. He was anxious about how much further he could bear it before telling his family. What damage the revelation would do to his work in Germany and to what he had achieved for the Jews, he did not know. The potential impact of the knowledge of his true past on his relationship with Mädchen was excruciatingly uncertain. He decided in the car on his way to his next meetings that he would have to tell her that night.

The meeting he was headed to was with Ben-Gurion, at his home. The note-takers were unexpectedly asked to leave the room and Ben-Gurion leaned forward in his chair as if to share a secret with Frederick. The old sage of Israeli politics was indeed an imposing figure and Frederick was a bit starstruck as he found himself alone with one of his lifelong heroes.

"I understand that you intervened in the assassination attempt last week in Dallas."

"How… why would you say that?"

"Our own intelligence organisation and that of the CIA talk regularly. I don't think you made many friends at the CIA last week."

"I don't think that this is a matter…"

"I assure you that it is just such a matter, young Frederick. You need to hear me. You have been a good friend to us. You need to put aside your cloak and dagger and we must speak freely. Do you understand me?"

"Yes, sir."

"Good. Then hear this. Questions have been asked of our people by the CIA as to your schedule and as to your whereabouts on various days during this trip. That can only mean one of two things: they are concerned about the adequacy of the security being afforded you here or that they intend to use that information to breach that security."

"Was that information provided?"

"A version of it, yes. But I think some mistakes were made and a previously discarded schedule might have been provided to them instead."

"What the hell are they on about?"

Ben-Gurion laughed.

"You can't waltz with the devil my friend and not get burned. You can't just walk into the White House and tell the President of the United States that he is surrounded by CIA thugs who are conspiring against him and expect him or them to thank you for it. I suspect the CIA has painted you as the threat and themselves as the saviour."

"You have very good sources, Mr Ben-Gurion. Did they mention that we saved the President's life?"

"That may well be true… a very peculiar story. You must tell me about your own sources of information. Finding out about that assassination attempt and who was planning it was either the most brilliant piece of espionage the world has ever seen or the clumsiest story ever proffered to cover up your own attempt on the President's life. I am sure you know which one of those explanations the CIA has chosen to offer their President. The Kennedy boys have shown that they are not slow to reach for the gun. You must be careful."

"I appreciate your candour. I guess this is what you get if you meddle."

"Meddling in another country's internal affairs is often prone to yield a different result than the one intended."

"I hope that is not true in all cases, Mr Ben-Gurion. I think the Germany of the mid-thirties needed some meddling."

"Perhaps. And perhaps the right person arose to do it."

"That seemed to work out OK."

"It's not over yet. Many prejudices remain and Hitler is now at the head of the largest army ever assembled in the history of the world, one with a nuclear capacity."

"Meaning?"

"A tiger cannot change his strips and the lamb cannot cease to be its prey simply by wishing it were not so. There are those amongst us who would have their way regardless of how much meddling you do. It is in their nature to impose their will on others."

"I have often wondered to what extent one should push events in any particular direction, assuming, of course, one has the option."

"Life has a peculiar way of righting itself, whether you think you may have pushed it off course or not. We cannot play God, dear boy; that is up to Him alone."

"I deeply fear that you are right."

Frederick and Ben-Gurion spent most of the afternoon exchanging reminiscences and philosophies. It was a good day, Frederick thought, as he left Ben-Gurion's home. His bodyguard showed him to his car and, after securing Frederick inside, got into the security vehicle designated to follow him to the hotel. When Frederick's driver turned the ignition key, the car was engulfed in an explosion.

Frederick had been evacuated to Berlin from Jerusalem via military hospital transport. He was in a perilous condition. Mädchen and the children accompanied him on the flight. Sepp Dietrich arrived at the hospital later that afternoon, there to console Mädchen and receive instructions from the Führer, who had been at the hospital since Frederick's arrival. Upon seeing him, Hitler took Dietrich firmly by the arm and, with urgency, walked him into the next room. Dismissing the nurse working there, he summoned the Head of the GSP, General Edelman, who had been waiting in the hallway at Hitler's instruction. Hitler wore his uniform to the hospital that night, as he perceived the Fatherland was under attack once again.

"What is the situation?" Hitler asked his longtime friend and key military advisor.

"A group calling itself the Palestinian Liberation Army has claimed responsibility for the bombing. It is led by a man named Yasser Arafat," Dietrich confirmed after consulting his notepad and then continuing. "They claim that the lands occupied by Israel were stolen from them illegally and they are seeking the return of the original Palestinian territories and the liberation of the Palestinian people."

"How could a group of ignorant sheep herders plan and execute such an act?" Hitler asked with indignation. "How could this happen in Israel? Were they complicit? Frederick has done so much for them; how could they not have protected him?" Hitler ceased his rationalising. "Those damned Jews," he muttered under his breath.

"We have our people in the region looking for this Arafat," General Dietrich continued. "General Edelman here was with Frederick in Washington."

Edelman picked up the briefing.

"My people suggest that this group received assistance from the American CIA, which has been in close contact with Mossad, the Israeli secret police, my Führer. The attack was precise — too sophisticated for the Palestinians to act alone — and information about Frederick's whereabouts was only known at the highest levels." Hitler stood silently, nodding and staring through Edelman. "I was in Washington last week and Frederick and I acted on a domestic American matter. I warned Frederick that they might interpret our intervention poorly."

Hitler took two steps towards Edelman, coming face-to-face with him.

"Intervention? What are you doing meddling in American domestic affairs?" Hitler's calm demeanour hid his underlying frustration; his gaze darkened.

"It was at Frederick's insistence, my Führer."

"What do you know about the involvement of the Americans or the Israelis in this bombing?"

"The Americans have close ties with the Israeli secret police. I am saying that whoever did this, this Arafat, he must have had some help."

"You can return to your duties, General Edelman, immediately. If you obtain any further information, please let me know."

Edelman saluted and left.

"Here's what I want you to do…" Hitler said calmly, watching Edelman get into the elevator before closing the door, him and Dietrich now alone. Though outwardly calm, his demeanour was resolute. "Have Edelman arrested. I don't want to hear anything further about that man, ever. Do you understand me? Replace him with one of your people, someone you trust. That incompetent fool. He should have been in that car instead of Frederick."

"Yes, Mein Führer."

"I want you to seal off the Palestinian and Israeli borders to ensure that no one including this Arafat can leave, assuming that Arafat is still in the region. I want you to do that by tonight, do you understand? Not a rat gets in or out of there."

"Yes, Mein Führer."

"Then I want you to proceed to liberate every man, woman, and child in this miserable Palestinian country as requested by this Arafat."

"Mein Führer?"

"Liberate them from this planet."

"I don't understand, Mein Führer."

"Flatten it," Hitler said, agitated and with gritted teeth he added for clarity, "turn that miserable country into rubble. They have declared war on us and I will give them their war," Hitler yelled, now venting. "This Arafat, if he survives, can carry the responsibility for it on his conscience. But he must not survive it, do you hear me? If he makes it out of there, I want him found, I want him made to wish that he had died with his countrymen."

"But there are six million of them, Mein Führer."

Hitler turned to Dietrich red-faced.

"Wipe them from the face of the earth, do you hear me? They shall have their liberation and it will be at my hand. Is that clear enough for you, General? Have the military spokesman read a declaration of war to the press as soon as the borders are sealed. Make that your very next task."

"Yes, Mein Führer. What units shall I deploy to the Middle East?"

Hitler walked over to Dietrich slowly and grabbed him by the lapel of his uniform and pulled him close so that the two men were chest to chest.

"Use everyone!"

With that, Hitler released Dietrich, collected himself again and straightened the front of his own uniform pulling down firmly on the bottom of his jacket.

"When the Panzers and the bombers are finished in Palestine, have them aggregate on the western border of Israel and bring up the divisions stationed in German East Indies. Have them hold there on the eastern border for further orders from me. I will want some answers from our Jewish friends as to why the security provided for Frederick's visit was insufficient. I can tell you this with absolute certainty, my old friend, that if Frederick dies, their answers had best be extremely compelling. Perhaps Frederick was right after all in aggregating these people in one place. It will make them easier to deal with as a single group. If the assassination of Archduke Franz Ferdinand was sufficient cause to start the Great War, then Frederick's attempted assassination, the heir to the German leadership will be sufficient justification to start a war with Israel. A war that leads to the destruction of that entire race. Frederick was right, eliminating them in death camps in Germany would have been a stain on our history, but eliminating them in a legitimate war is an entirely different proposition. I wonder if this is what he always intended. He had foresight beyond my ability to understand it."

"A brilliant and patriotic German, Mein Führer."

"Frederick represents everything that is good about Germany, his intelligence, his breeding. He is the epitome of the Aryan line. He is my son."

"Mein Führer."

"Bring the military onto full alert and assemble my military heads for a meeting tonight. I want the entire European Defence Forces brought up to full alert by morning. By the time we finish in the Middle East, I will want to have some answers from Frederick's new American friends as well. See if your new man at the GSP can link them to this, make it his top priority. The American CIA is clumsy, they would have left their fingerprints all over this. The Americans will no doubt respond to our actions in Israel in any case. Perhaps they will now have the war with Germany that Roosevelt so desperately coveted."

Hitler went back into Frederick's room and to his bedside, leaving General Dietrich to implement the instructions that he had given him.

As Hitler placed his hand on Frederick's forehead, there was a groan from the bed and Frederick's heart monitor went flat.

Everything went black.

To die, to sleep--
No more--and by a sleep to say we end
The heartache, and the thousand natural shocks
That flesh is heir to. 'Tis a consummation
Devoutly to be wished. To die, to sleep--
To sleep--perchance to dream: ay, there's the rub...

"For in that sleep of death what dreams may come?" Jack said in a whisper lying in bed with one arm resting on his forehead as he stared out the window, no blinds, just watching the clouds, Jamison's head lying on his other arm, her back to him.

"You're quoting Shakespeare now," Jamison said half asleep rolling over, yawning as she put her hand on Jack's chest and began to scratch the hairy part. "How hard did Cleary hit you?"

"Sorry, I didn't realise I said that out loud."

"What did he say to you in your office?" There was no answer; Jamison yawned again. "You're not getting all melancholy on me again, are you?"

"Is this all a dream, Jamison? Am I actually dead or in a coma somewhere and this is not real?"

"I hope not."

Jack sat up retrieving his arm that was now completely lacking any circulation and got out of bed. He walked over to the chair and put on his shorts.

"Jesus, baby, what am I going to do about this?" Jack sat back down on one of the two kitchen chairs that they had brought upstairs to the bedroom as interim furniture for Jack's new townhouse. He put his head in his hands and began to rub furiously, attempting to bring enough blood to his brain to make it function. He stopped rubbing and looked over to Jamison. "What if Cleary's right about me?"

Jamison sat up and put her pillow and Jack's pillow behind her back and fell back against them, covering her naked body with the quilt.

"Problems always seem worse than they really are in the morning. We'll work through it," she said. "Cleary's gone off half-cocked, as usual."

"Has he? I don't remember anything from around the time he's talking about. And you know something that is really weird?"

"What would that be?" Jamison said, knowing that it was going to be a self-serving explanation regarding something that was actually totally irrelevant to his current predicament. For a scientist, he could be pretty obtuse sometimes.

"If I did commit a crime in my previous body, a body that is now dead, and all the memories of me doing it are dead with that body, and the intention to do it was formed in that body not in my current body then am I still guilty of the crime now… in this body?"

"Jesus, Jack, that's pretty deep for six o'clock in the morning. I'm going to need at least one cup of coffee before I ask you to say that again." Jamison got up and began to walk to the bathroom.

Jack followed her. "In fact, the way I see it is that in my case the body that did it is dead. So, I am innocent, right?"

"Do you mind?" Jamison said, putting a hand on Jack's chest, pushing him back out of the bathroom so she could use the toilet. "Jack," she said through the closed door. "You didn't do anything wrong, in this body or any other body."

"Easy for you to say, Special Agent." Jack turned and walked over to the window to contemplate the matter further.

"Yes, it is easy for me to say," Jamison said, busting back through the bathroom door, her task completed and putting on her robe. "And it should be easy for you, too. You are not capable of getting involved in some IP theft and blowing yourself up in a car to avoid suspicion, you are a good person. Besides blowing yourself up would have been a hell of a risk given that Replants had never been done or approved before. Stop trying to forgive yourself for something you didn't do. We need to figure out who did this and we need to do it fast. Cleary probably thinks it is *case closed…* again. So have your shower and get dressed and let's make a plan."

Jack walked over to Jamison and put his arms around her and said dramatically, "Thanks for sticking with me, baby. I think I'd be in a ditch somewhere licking my wounds if it wasn't for you."

"Stop licking and start washing. I'll go make some coffee."

In the kitchen after her first coffee, Jamison was very much awake and was thinking deeply, problem solving, replete with the intense frown on her forehead that always for her accompanied that task.

"Tell me again what Cleary said to you when he came to the office and told you that he thought you were involved in this?" she said as she sat back down at the kitchen table opposite Jack, bringing with her a second cup of coffee.

"I love it when you get like this. I've seen you do it before. I'm glad you're on my side."

"Tell me, shithead, or I'll arrest you myself. You're making my head spin with all this *unbearable lightness of bullshit!*"

"Yes, madam. Cleary said that he had found a transaction in, or from, an overseas account in my name that pointed to me as the seller of the stolen intellectual property. He asked if I had anything to say about that."

"And did you?"

"I told him that I knew nothing about it. I don't have any overseas accounts. But, of course, that could be true and I could have still done something in those seven weeks before the bombing that I don't remember. He then essentially accused me of dealing with the Iranians."

"Jack, people don't just wake up one morning and decide to become a crook. You are either born one due to some sociopathic mental disorder or you become one over a long period of time because of your socio-economic circumstances."

"But I was under pressure with Francine, or so I've been told. What's to say that those circumstances didn't drive me to it? Or maybe this Kalmati guy threatened me."

"You seemed to have dealt well with the breakup with Francine this time around. My sitting here after sleeping with you being a case in point. Did you need the money?"

"Not at all. I am financially secure and will still be even after Francine has had her way with me in the divorce."

"Did some gangster chase you for a gambling debt?"

"I've never gambled in my life."

"Are you inclined to respond positively to threats from, say, Iranians?"

"Absolutely not."

"Then shut up and work with me on this, will you? What it really means is that someone is or was trying to set you up, and Cleary has stumbled onto the paper trail that they laid down, like the good cop that he is. What did he say he was going to do next?"

"He said that they had court orders in progress overseas to find out the full details of the overseas entity and the transactions. If they yield what he thinks they will, he'll be back to get me. He told me not to leave town."

"That sounds like Cleary alright. He's always putting the noose over some poor bastard's neck to see how hard they wriggle. But he must be onto something. You're sure you don't have any overseas accounts?"

"None that I know of, but…"

Before Jack could finish, Jamison interjected, "If you say that you can't remember one more time, I'll punch you. OK?"

Jamison sat there for a while sipping her coffee and thinking about their next step, not allowing Jack to say anything further while she did so.

Jamison had collected Agent Briers from the FBI office in New York later that morning, and they had both headed down to the forensics lab where the material and the computer equipment recovered from the Iranian raid were being held. The lab was run by an old field associate of Jamison's, so they had no problem getting access to the recovered equipment. Jack had come with them; Jamison having explained his presence to the security personnel by posing him as a technical expert obtained to assist in the evaluation of the captured software. They were all standing in front of the benches where the equipment had been set up and powered up in an attempt to glean any information from them that might have assisted the Iranians in the theft. The FBI hadn't yet made much progress in obtaining usable information from the recovered computers.

"This is all black magic to me," Jamison said. "What button do I press?"

"Don't touch it," the Forensics Officer and Briers said in unison.

The supervising Forensics Officer handed Jamison a pair of rubber gloves with a disapproving stare. "In fact, you all should put a pair of these on," she said, giving a pair to Briers and Jack.

"Look, Briers, bring that small yellow device that's on the other table over there and connect it into the port on that side of the console. Take that connector out of there," Jack pulled out one of the connectors and handed it to Briers, "and put it in the back of there, same-sized hole. And turn that on." Jack said, looking over to the FBI Forensics Officer for her approval. "Is it OK if he does that?"

She nodded her approval sceptically, and Jack stepped forward to initiate the machine but stopped. Jack looked to the Forensics Officer and said, "you should do this." She agreed, stepping over ready to receive instructions from Jack.

"There is a security sub-protocol built into this software," Jack began. "It's supposed to log all those who gain access to the main security procedures menu. You can only download the software via access from that menu. You can't erase that log... or you're not supposed to be able to. I'm guessing that whoever stole this software didn't care about deleting anything anyway because they thought it would be in the hands of the Iranians, not in an FBI lab with us fiddling with it." Jack smiled nervously, looking around, thinking what he had just said was amusing but got nothing but blank stares in response.

"Sure thing. How do I gain access?" the Forensics Officer asked, unimpressed so far with Jack's ramblings.

"You need to bring up the main menu using this keyboard; you can't do it by voice. Hold this down and press that."

"Damn, look at that. We have lift-off," she said as the menu appeared.

"You're actually not supposed to be able to do that without signing on," Jack noted. "As I suspected, all of the security protocols have been disabled. Go to the machine log."

"Alright," the Forensics Officer said.

"Press Control L and select 'yes'," Jack instructed. "Okay, that's the log. Go to the date around the time that we think this equipment was stolen from the lab." The Forensics Officer complied.

The log was intact, just as Jack thought it would be. They all stood there, reading as the log displayed on the screen. The Forensics Officer began scrolling through it.

"Damn it, Sanders!" Jamison exclaimed first. "Stop there, look, George Sanders. I never liked that guy. He was the last one to log in. He must have disabled the security protocols. Who better to do it than the Head of IT?"

"George!" Jack interjected. "No, it can't be. Check it again."

"It is. See, the last function run under his sign-on was to switch off the security protocols," Briers stated, with the Forensics Officer confirming with a nod. "That's our guy."

"Can you download that log and send it to my boss and over to a detective at the One Nine named Cleary?" Jamison asked, visibly excited.

"I'll need to get clearance," the Forensics Officer said.

"Do you have Sanders's address, Jack?"

"Sure."

"Briers, stay here and ensure that this information gets to the relevant people, especially Cleary, ASAP. Tell Cleary I'll text him George's address and that we're headed there now. You and I, Jack, are going to pay Mr. Sanders a visit."

Jack and Jamison approached the front door of George's apartment.

"He's in there; I can hear him moving about," Jamison whispered.

"I don't hear anything."

"Trust me, he's in there. How's that new gym working out for you, big guy?"

Jack rolled his eyes and put his shoulder to the door. On his second attempt, the doorjamb cracked and they pushed their way into the apartment. George was in the living room, standing next to the dining table and hurriedly stuffing travel papers into a duffle bag. Hearing Jack and Jamison burst in, he reached into the bag and pulled out a handgun.

"Stay right where you are, both of you. The dynamic duo, I presume," George said with a hint of arrogance.

"George," Jack began, holding out his hand and subconsciously making himself a smaller target. "You don't want to shoot anybody."

"I don't plan to, old buddy. Unless I have to, that is. I'm not sure about you, Special Agent. Step forward and keep your hands where

I can see them. Both of you. Been examining some second-hand computer equipment, have we? I didn't think it would take you long to download those logs. I should've erased them."

"George," Jamison interjected calmly, "you've been very naughty."

"Very clever, Agent. Now shut up and move back against that wall. There's some duct tape in the kitchen, Jack, top drawer on the right. Why don't you go fetch it? By the time they find you, I'll be halfway to… wherever it is that I'm going, and I'll have more money than I know what to do with when I get there."

"No problem, George, I'm getting it. Just don't do anything you'll regret, alright?" Jack backed into the kitchen and began to rummage through one of the drawers as directed. "Just tell me why. I thought we were friends. You killed me."

"Do you know how stupid that sounds Jack? What are you, *Casper the Ghost?* Besides it wasn't me, it was that fucking Gothenburg, the ruthless bastard." Both Jamison and Jack looked puzzled. "I sold him that missing BCD that fucking White just found out about. I thought I may as well go all in and get two payoffs whilst I was dealing with the Iranians."

"Franz Gothenburg?"

"The one and only. The mad doctor, yes. He had some project he needed it for in Germany or something. But he thought he had to try it out, to see if it worked. He thought they would use it on you if you were killed. With his background in smart bombs the mechanics were easy enough for him. I didn't know anything about it but I took the opportunity to corrupt your last smash after he blew you up. You were sniffing around some security breach before the bombing so I grabbed the chance to get rid of those seven weeks from your memory. I have to admit it was fun watching a smarty pants like you flail around like an ignorant schoolboy."

"What about the incept material and the software?" Jamison interceded.

"Don't play dumb with me, Agent. I know you've figured this all out. Why would you be here otherwise? I sold it to Kalmati.

Zimmermann set it up. So *I'm leaving on a jet plane*. Confessions over, tape her hands, Jack."

"Just a minute, Jack," Jamison interjected. "George, I've always thought you talk too much. That's usually a bad sign."

"A sign of what, super girl?"

"Batgirl, please, it's sexier. It's actually quite hard to shoot someone, George, very hard. Your chatter tells me that you're nervous."

"Don't provoke me, Batgirl… and put your bag on the floor, kick it away," George demanded, suddenly realising she would be armed.

"Here's what we're going to do. We're going to have one of those old-fashioned duels, you and I."

"Put your bag on the floor."

Ignoring his instructions, Jamison continued, her voice icy.

"Jack will be my second and… well, I guess you don't get one."

"Helen, no," Jack pleaded.

"I'm going to count to three, George," she paused for effect. "If you're still holding that gun when I get to three, I'm going to reach into my bag, take out my weapon, and shoot you in the face. Understand? On three. Seconds out. Jack, would you step back a bit, please?"

Jack found himself involuntarily backing away, terrorised by the prospect of a firefight.

"I'll shoot you where you stand, Agent."

"Here's your chance. One…" George's face reddened, and his hand started shaking.

"SHUT UP! I will shoot!"

"Two…"

"Damn it!" George threw the gun onto the table. "I'm no gangster, stop counting!" He covered his face with his hands. "Jesus… You scared the hell out of me."

"Take three steps back, George, put your hands behind your head, and kneel on the floor," Jamison commanded, her voice booming. "DO IT NOW." Startled, George complied. Jamison threw her bag onto the couch, walked over to the table, and picked up George's gun.

"You need to cock these things, you idiot." She cocked the gun with an audible click and pointed it at George's head. George groaned. Just then, Cleary and Jacobs burst through the door, guns drawn.

"Relax, Cleary. We've got the guy already."

"Sure," Cleary said, holstering his weapon. "Jacobs, cuff him."

Jamison moved to the table and started rifling through George's carry bag. George was now standing, crying, cuffed.

"She's not a good woman, Jack. I don't think you should be with her. She threatened to shoot me in the face. At least Francine had manners."

"Shut up, George," Jamison retorted, continuing to go through the bag. "Mention her name again, and I will shoot you."

"You see, she's a thug, Jack. You heartless woman."

"I wasn't going to shoot you, George. I don't need a gun to handle a worm like you," Jamison said without looking at George, still rummaging through the bag. She pulled out travel papers and what must have been fifty thousand dollars in small-denominated US currency, threw the money on the table, and began examining the plane tickets. "Mexico and then the Caymans? Mind if we tag along, George? And new identity documents. Looks like we got to this guy just in time, Cleary."

George groaned again.

"Helen, my God," Jack said, walking towards her. "You were bluffing? Remind me never to play cards with you."

"He wasn't going to shoot me. Shooters don't blab, Jack, they shoot. I guess that's *case closed*, eh, Cleary?"

"Yes, but we got the collar, so make sure you put that in your report," Cleary said with a half-smile. "Nice work, Agent. Jim, could you take him down to the squad car?"

"And I got it all on tape," Jamison confirmed proudly, pulling out her phone. She had switched it to record mode when they entered the apartment. "There's another guy you need to arrest, some mad scientist. It's on the tape."

"Thanks," Cleary said, taking the device and transferring the confession to his notebook. "That will make two collars for me and none for you, but who's counting?"

"Just you and me, baby," Jamison quipped, coming over to Jack and pinching his cheek. "The dynamic duo."

"Well, thanks for the equal billing, but…"

"Hold this for me, will you? I have to go pee," Jamison interrupted, handing the gun to Jack. "All this excitement." She then disappeared down the hallway.

"No, no… I have the same problem with guns that George has," Jack protested, holding the gun with two fingers and passing it to Cleary.

"I guess I owe you an apology, Jack," Cleary admitted.

"No need, Cleary. I was ready to arrest myself this morning."

"Nice of you to say, but it looks to me like Jamison might end up with at least one collar. I think you're done for, buddy."

"Yeah, twenty-five to life for sure," Jack concurred.

CHAPTER SIXTEEN

Jack arrived at the visitor's room at Rikers Island prison in June of 2066, following the trial and conviction of Dr. Franz Gothenburg for the first-degree murder of Jack Pierce. It was deemed to be first-degree murder because the bombing was perpetrated as part of a major felony: the theft of national secrets. Once Cleary knew where to look, it wasn't difficult to trace the bomb fragments back to one of Gothenburg's companies. That, along with George's testimony and various bank and phone records, had sealed Gothenburg's fate. Cleary had ultimately wrapped the matter up quickly and cleanly. For him, it was *case closed.*

On this day, Gothenburg had requested to see Jack. Jack thought perhaps Gothenburg wanted to explain, or maybe apologise. The visitor's room was cold and austere, like a scene from an old crime movie. Time seemed to have left this place behind. Jack sat down at the assigned cubicle and looked through the glass at a small lime-green bench with an empty steel-framed chair behind it. It wasn't long before a guard ushered in Gothenburg, dressed in the mandatory bright orange jumpsuit. Gothenburg sat down, pulling up his chair with a scrape along the concrete floor that Jack couldn't hear due to the sound-proofing. Gothenburg, expressionless, looked through the glass at Jack. He pointed to the communication device at the side of the cubicle, and both men picked up the handsets.

"So… Jack, thank you for coming."

"That's Dr. Pierce," Jack responded, formal and indignant.

"You couldn't resist coming out to see me. I thought that would be the case."

"Yeah, but I'm not happy about it. Can we get on with this, please?"

"Sure. I wanted to… apologise to you in person." Jack found himself almost involuntarily standing to leave, a realisation washing over him that he wasn't really interested in facilitating Gothenburg's contrition. However, Gothenburg continued hurriedly.

"No, no, please sit. That's not all I have for you. I think you might find my reasoning interesting. And I have a puzzle for you, one that a scientist as bright as yourself might enjoy solving."

Jack brushed off the flattery like an unwanted bird dropping.

"Did they tell you about the equipment that I had developed?"

"Time displacement. Dangerous stuff to be dicking around with, Dr. Gothenburg."

"Ah! Apparently, they have told you quite a bit more than that, about my little project in Germany. I want you to understand, mine has not been an ordinary life, Dr. Pierce. At eleven years of age, I had the misfortune of seeing my loving parents dragged off to a Nazi camp and killed. Do you think… can you possibly imagine how you would react if it were your parents?"

The question made Jack settle back into his chair, ready to listen. He didn't respond; he didn't know how to, but he empathised as best he could with the anguish this experience would have caused.

"I can tell you a little about how it feels, but you will never truly know it, thank God. It has affected my entire life."

"I'm sure that it would," Jack said quietly, with genuine sympathy.

"I had to do something about it. Do you understand that? I had to. What is the good of having a brain, what purpose does it serve if not to enable me to correct a horrible wrong, a wrong that, if possible, must be undone? How could I ever have peace of mind knowing that it was possible but not doing anything about it?"

"But why kill me to get it?" Jack asked.

"Those words seem harsh given that it is you, alive and sitting there, asking that very question when it is I who am going to die. I didn't kill you to get it. I had it when I set the bomb. I needed to know if it worked. I needed to be sure. The task I had set for young Franz was far too important for him to fail, for me to fail.

Don't you see? When I set the bomb, I knew that they wouldn't let you die. Instead, they would push the Replant procedure through the BIE. They wouldn't have done that for anyone else but you, the famous Dr. Pierce. Your mind was essential to the company's wellbeing, to the country. The fact that you are here proves that I was right."

"So you found out that the upload worked on me just fine, so you sent it back to yourself." Jack was trying to move things along quickly. But then it struck him how ingenious the development of the time translation device was, as was the plan Gothenburg had devised to go with it. "I have to admit, that was a pretty smart idea and a pretty nifty piece of gear," Jack said, as one scientist would congratulate another. "The BCU would only work on you because you and your six-year-old counterpart would have a genetically identical brain. It would be like time travel but using your own genome as the time tunnel."

"Yes. That is exactly correct. But now we are sitting here discussing it, and my parents are still dead in a Nazi concentration camp, Dr. Pierce."

"You mean to say that it didn't work." A blush of realisation came over Jack's face. "You mean you want me to sit here and help you figure out why it didn't work? Well, that's just great." Jack got up disgusted, pushing the chair back behind him. "You kill me and then want my help to analyse your plan. You can shove that right up your arse, you murderous bastard." Jack slammed down the phone.

Gothenburg stood and leaned against the glass in despair, watching Jack walk over to the exit and summon the guard. He tried to cry out to Jack but he couldn't be heard. Everything he had worked for his whole life had failed, and he didn't understand it. He slumped back down onto the chair. He couldn't figure out, with all of his massive intellect, why he had failed.

By the time Jack had come back to the cubicle, Gothenburg had his face buried in his hands and was crying. He looked up hearing Jack knock on the glass with the headpiece of the phone, and he jumped to his feet, grabbed at the phone, fumbling it in his haste to get a proper grasp.

"Thank you, Dr. Pierce. Thank you. I am so sorry for what I did to you. I am truly sorry. But I must know what happened. I must know. And you are the only one I know who's smart enough to help me. Please, help me."

Jack sat down again, resigned to assist if he could.

"There's no way to know for sure. I read your paper some years ago on the creation of the timeline. You're a pretty smart guy for a convict. Your logic was sound. You figure it out."

Gothenburg ignored Jack's invitation to work it out for himself and instead sought to engage Jack in a discussion about what might have been the cause of the failure.

"The device went back. I am certain of it. I am certain that I received it in my hiding place at six years of age. I am certain that I moved it, that the boy moved it. But from that point, I have no idea what happened."

"If you did in fact receive it as a boy, then who is to say whether it worked or didn't work?"

"Yes, yes, of course. But why wouldn't it have worked? It worked on you. I have no recollection of receiving such a box at six years of age. If I received it and discarded it because it didn't work, I would remember, surely."

"Perhaps you are right. The fact that you don't remember it means it must have worked." Jack stopped momentarily. "And that, of course, is the clue"

"I'm sorry?"

"You see it can't be partially successful. No. Not at all." Jack repeated what he was saying as he pieced it together in his own head.

"See what? What do you mean?"

"It is your own logic, Doctor. The two timelines, the new and the old, may exist for a moment, however long a moment, like two sprouts on the same vine. But in the end, there can only be one timeline, one vine. We as a planet do not have multiple pasts, just check the history books. There can be only one past in this universe and I agree with the proposition in your paper that there is as we sit here no future."

"Yes, we know of only one past, but who is to say that it is the original. So what stopped this sprout, as you call it, from becoming the vine, the actual timeline?"

"The existing timeline has to persist if there was no replacement timeline intact. The exact point at which the box appeared is the nexus, right? The point of origin of the new line you sought to create."

"The point at which things would change, the crossroads."

"Yes. It must have created a new possible timeline, but then it didn't take hold, so the old timeline remained in place right from that same nexus point. No part of that new timeline could exist once it had begun but failed to take hold. Every part of it was obliterated, including your memory of the box arriving because, in this timeline it didn't arrive. Time went on from that nexus just as it had before. Surely, you see it. I thought after reading your paper that a timeline, once laid down, would be robust and that it would be difficult to dislodge because of all the factors in any new timeline that would need to line up to change it. To change the primary timeline, that is to change it into the one that becomes the real timeline, into the main vine to continue the analogy, you would have to close the loop perfectly in the new timeline."

"Close the loop?"

"Yes. Young Franz in Nazi Germany would have to, at some point in that timeline, send himself the box, the BCU device, for that version of events to become real. You sending him the box in this timeline wouldn't do it. Not at all, no, of course not. For this timeline to be replaced by the new one, then someone in the new reality would have had to have sent him the box and developed the technology for both the BCD and BCU equipment and your time-translation equipment. Otherwise, the box never existed in that timeline and therefore the new timeline could not exist. You have no idea how the BCD and BCU technology works and who says I would have developed it in your brave new order. Don't you see it? What started that version of events, the nexus, would not have been created; the box is the seminal event and you receiving the box at six would never happen in the new version. You needed to close the loop in the new timeline. Did you make plans for him to develop all the technology needed and send himself the box?"

"Close the loop," Gothenburg said, processing what Jack was saying to him.

"I'll take that as a no. So regardless of whether you progressed at six years of age one minute on your assigned duty or a hundred years, that timeline gets erased, doesn't happen, if you never developed the technology and sent it back to the boy in the new timeline. I suspect it would erase itself as soon as it became certain that the box would never be sent back, perhaps as soon as Franz died without developing it and sending it or having made arrangements to send the box back, that timeline would disappear."

"Close the loop. Of course. I can't believe I didn't see it."

"And who's to say that in your new timeline, the boy's timeline, the BCD and BCU were ever developed. You can't keep the box you sent back; that technology doesn't exist in the new timeline."

"I instructed him to destroy it."

"No matter. No doubt you could recreate the technology to send the same box back to yourself, it is your technology, but you have no idea how to develop the technology it contained. There it is, then. You would have had to come to see me and get another one, in that timeline. But what if in your new timeline I never developed the BCD and BCU device. A million things could have happened to me in your new timeline to stop me from developing it. Who's to say that in your new timeline I wasn't a teacher or a cook? You know, ripples in a pool and all that. That is why I am saying to you that once the timeline is laid down, it would, I think, be pretty hard to change because you would have to ensure that so many things lined up again in the new timeline before any change in that new direction would stick. If a person changes the timeline and in that new reality that person's parents never meet, unlike what happens in the movies where everything is suddenly changed, in fact nothing would change because that person was never conceived in the new timeline and therefore the change perpetrated by that person in the new timeline wasn't possible because the person that initiated the change was never born. Nothing changes. The existing timeline persists."

"Of course, you're right. I might have made some progress in altering events in Nazi Germany, potentially achieving what I set out to do. But unless I acknowledged at some point that I needed to close the loop by sending myself the box again, I would fail to establish this as today's reality."

"It's unlikely the boy ever comprehended it in his new life. You didn't understand it here until today, despite knowing there was an issue. There would be no indication in the boy's life that anything was amiss. Things would simply proceed in the new direction, I presume. Unaware of any further action required to solidify the new timeline, he would have passed away believing he'd accomplished his objective."

"Yes, as that boy, I would have needed both the foresight to do it and the equipment, including your BCD and my translation device, to accomplish it. Naturally, that's correct. Perhaps I lived to a ripe old age, satisfied with all my achievements. However, if I never sent myself the box again, the entire timeline would collapse. This conclusion must be accurate since we're here now. But then, where is the BCU device I sent to young Franz? Where is it now if the new timeline collapsed?"

"Probably..." Before Jack could complete his sentence, Gothenburg finished it for him.

"Right where I left it, in Sperenburg. At the old mill."

"Unless someone in this timeline moved it, that's where it would have ended up, exactly at the moment the new timeline failed. If it wasn't there when you left, someone else has it. Is it secure? I'll send someone to Sperenburg to retrieve it."

"Yes, only I could have opened it. It'll be there somewhere. What about the box in my lab? It stayed where it was."

"They told me that story. It wasn't there when you opened the wall because you hadn't sent it yet. But once you did, it materialised rather than reappeared, both events occurring in this current timeline. If it caused no disturbance in the timeline, then your little box did nothing to effect change."

Gothenburg realised that Jack must be right. "Well then, QED."

"Indeed. Now, all you need is another chance to try it all again."

"Yes," Gothenburg said with a wry smile.

"Just leave me out of it next time, OK?"

"I don't know. You've done pretty well for yourself. I heard the BIE approved all of Frank's plans to legalise Replants and the BCU, including full-body regrowth for cosmetic purposes. That's got to be worth a few billion dollars a year, hasn't it, for you and your shareholders? We are all immortals now."

"Not all of us, doctor."

"Ah, yes. Of course."

"And don't forget you're a shareholder, too." Jack stood up but added with some melancholy, "You know, you're not going to get that second chance, Doc, or a chance to spend any of that money."

"Apparently not, no." Gothenburg had resolved his problem, but he felt devastated.

"For what it's worth, Doctor, I forgive you for what you did to me. But I wouldn't want you tampering with the timeline again. I'm pretty content with this one."

"And so it came to pass, yes, yes. Your forgiveness means a lot to me, Dr. Pierce. Thank you for granting it and for assisting me with my little science quiz. My head was about to explode."

Jack departed, feeling significantly better about events than when he arrived, yet deeply troubled about his newfound colleague's predicament.

In the years that followed, the BIE approved Dr Gothenburg's time translation device for use in scientific studies of the Earth's geological history and for the examination of historical events that were deemed to warrant the risk. They sent back automated probes that reviewed Earth's history programming the probe so that once its task was complete, it would implant itself on the moon's surface always in the same place for later retrieval in the current time. In using the moon as the hiding place for the probes as time passed to the present day, the risk was avoided of them ever being uncovered on Earth earlier than they were designed to be and, as a result, causing a disturbance in the timeline. The mining companies on the moon were always happy to retrieve a probe and return it to Earth, for a fee.

In the three years to 2069 since its approval, the time translation probes had managed to solve many mysteries regarding the development of the species and various historical intrigues that had puzzled mankind for millennia, like the building of the pyramids, the fate of the dinosaurs, the death of Christ and whether Lee Harvey Oswald had acted alone – there were as it was finally disclosed three shooters that day as Frederick had discovered. Scientists grew to love these experiments because of their immediacy. The device would be available for collection on the lunar surface immediately after they were sent back to their predetermined positions in time. It was thought that it was indeed time translation probes that sometimes were the cause of UFO sightings in Earth's past and it was now known that the star that hung over the stable in Bethlehem on that fateful night was just such an observational satellite.

Franz Gothenburg was executed for the murder of Jack Pierce on March 15, 2066. He made no attempt to appeal his death sentence. A group, which included Jack Pierce, funded a legal fight to overturn the sentence. However, since Gothenburg wouldn't participate, the effort was futile. Although it didn't help Dr. Gothenburg, his execution stirred such a furore that by June of the following year, the death penalty was abolished from the statute books for murderers whose victims were revived using Replant technology. Dr. Gothenburg received full recognition for the development of his time translation technology, and a life-sized statue of him was erected in the park at the end of 10th Street where his lab was located. The statue was funded by AIOGEN.

By 2070, the US had managed to protect the secrets of biogenetic engineering that led to the development of the Augments. There hadn't been another comprehensive attempt to steal the technology. Many believed this was because potential thieves had resigned themselves to the fact that retaining the technology would be difficult, even if they succeeded in stealing it. In the US military, Jack's TPS400s remained the soldier of choice, but at AIOGEN, Replants had become the single largest source of revenue.

In 2066, the BIE introduced a new statute whereby felons were denied access to regrown body parts and full body replacements.

Continuing the genome of a felon was considered socially undesirable, even though they fully understood the genealogy of psychopathic behaviour and knew how to correct it during any regrowth procedure. Traditional medical techniques could still be used on convicted felons, except those provided by the New Science. Six months later, these amendments restricting access to Replant technology were extended to include those who had committed suicide. This, combined with the accessibility to medically supervised euthanasia, ensured that a dignified end could be found by those for whom eternity was unappealing. George Sanders, convicted for the AIOGEN technology theft, died in prison in 2071 due to liver failure induced by a heroin addiction he developed in jail. A suitable liver donor couldn't be found, making him the first known felon to succumb to these changes in the New Law.

By 2067, telemetry had begun to return from the Alpha Centauri probe launched in early 2058. By 2068, the probe was focusing its attention on a terrestrial-sized planet orbiting Alpha Centauri B at a distance of about 160 million kilometres from its nearest sun. Early indications suggested the existence of primitive life, sparking momentum for a manned journey. With all that had transpired on Earth, and man's life expectancy now virtually limitless thanks to Jack Pierce and AIOGEN, the trip became not only plausible but also desirable. Now, mankind needed to determine what to do with eternity. It was proposed that the spaceships would include on-board Replant capability, ensuring that any colony established on the New World would be self-sustaining no matter how long it took for another ship to arrive. There was no need to put crew members in stasis during the trip to preserve their now unlimited life expectancy; they just needed a self-sustaining ecosystem within which to live, several thousand interesting books, and productive tasks to employ their time. Hydrogen collected from open space would provide an unending supply of energy. It was suggested that the participants would focus on the betterment of their minds, with their self-sustaining environment eliminating the need to pursue material gain. The ancient concept of monastic enlightenment was about to reach unprecedented heights, literally, and the aspirations for a higher moral plane seemed destined to be realised.

That was not to understate the danger of the journey. If the ship was destroyed, perhaps by an asteroid, there was nothing that could be done to save the occupants. Nonetheless, there was talk of an expedition to the inner reaches of the galaxy, not Mao Zedong's six-thousand-mile Long March but man's six-thousand-lightyear star trek was the way the papers were describing it. Such a trip would get humans almost a quarter of the way from Earth to the centre of the Milky Way using current propulsion technology and potentially bring the ship into contact with close to half a billion planets along its journey, a sufficient number to answer once and for all the question as to whom or what was out there. The remarkable thing, the media went on to propose, was that if the explorers ever did return to Earth, their families and friends may still be here to welcome them back, assuming that they had the money for the Replants. So there was no need for the explorers to sacrifice those relationships. It was thought, however, the returning journeymen would have some catching up to do. If mankind ever did conceive of a way to build ships that manipulated time-space, then such ships could be sent to retrieve or assist the intrepid explorers if indeed they wanted to be retrieved or assisted.

Jack Pierce married Helen Jamison in a July ceremony in New York City in 2066. They had two beautiful children, a boy and a girl, both of whom were fully vetted for genetic diseases, most notably screening out all trace of Jamison's Huntington's disorder. Apart from that vetting and a deliberate choice of the sex, one boy and one girl, their children's genetic makeup was decided by chance. Jack became the President of AIOGEN after his return from his honeymoon in August 2066 when Frank Duggan left the presidency to pursue a political career. As one of his first duties as president, Jack amended the personnel benefits scheme at AIOGEN to include Replants free of charge to all employees with over five years of service and that benefit was extended to the direct family of all of its directors and senior managers holding a similar period of service.

Jack's parents were both convinced to undertake a Replant the following year and by 2067 both had the same biological age of thirty-four years and the often well-meaning but sometimes hurtful age-related tussling between them was brought to a close and plans were now afoot to give Jack a sibling. Equally importantly and no small factor in deciding to have the procedure, the grandparents would be around to contribute to the upbringing of Jack and Jamison's children. In 2067, Jack and Helen followed suit, trading up for a pair of twenty-one-year-old Replants so as to conserve at least some semblance of appropriate age difference between them and Jack's parents. It was said to be a show of support for the company product but it was of course because of Jamison's Huntington's. With Jamison's Replant, her Huntington's was screened out just at a time when it was beginning to manifest itself. The disease would never bother her or her family again.

Jack found his second Replant far more agreeable than the first and the outcome physically far more advantageous, with Jack having decided to make a couple of cosmetic tweaks of his own, with Jamison's approval. Jack and Jamison never had any difficulty keeping up with their sometimes exuberant and always precocious offspring.

And so it was that despite the occasional ride in Ben's truck, the Pierce family lived happily, forever after.

Unbeknownst to the authorities and AIOGEN back in Franz Gothenburg's old lab on 10th Street only two days after Jack Pierce's visit to Rikers, Franz was beavering away at his Nazi period research. Having learnt of George's betrayal of him to the police, he had uploaded his most recent smash into a twenty-one-year-old replicant of himself prior to his arrest. He had bought the replicant with the two BCD devices and the single upload device from George, a package deal. George had been kind enough not to mention the replicant nor the additional machinery to the police. Franz Junior was slightly taller, much better looking, and as strong as an ox, but other than that he was all Franz Gothenburg, including his one hundred and thirty-six-year-old mind. The replicant had hidden during Franz's arrest. Franz had been prepared for the police and he had moved the vast majority of his huge wealth through various circuitous routes into the name of Franz Junior, his replicant, for whom he had purchased a new identity, Dr Frederick Von Eichmann. Frederick was about to leave the old brownstone lab for good but was collecting the remainder of what he thought he might need for his new project.

Frederick had gone to visit Franz in jail after his visit from Jack Pierce. He now knew what the two scientists had concluded as to the cause of his original failure in Germany. As he packed up to leave for Sperenburg, he mused, "Now, let's try that again, shall we?"

www.ingramcontent.com/pod-product-compliance
Lightning Source LLC
Chambersburg PA
CBHW040518170726
48295CB00012B/251